Sentimental Journey

The Tempus Vector

By D.M. Cipres

Special Editor |K. Fulton|

Cover designed and illustrated by |April Estoch|

This book is dedicated to my incredible family! Mom and Dad who taught me to reach for the stars, and dream great dreams. My amazing children who encouraged me, and reminded me daily that I could do it. You are my ever-constant inspiration! My wonderful sister and dearest friend who loves me no matter what. Although we have always lived so far apart, you have always been present in my heart, cheering me on. I love you Dar! To my man in the blue suit, thank you for just being you. Your mere presence spurred me to the finish line.

Echoes of unsettling clamor that have been present for far too long, robbers of peace, blinded understanding that makes you feel as though your future is nothing more than an echo of your past. To those of you who have been abandoned, left behind, or in a seemingly hopeless plight bent with scars that have rendered hairline crevices or maybe even broken pieces scattered far and wide, listen carefully. This I know! Tomorrow will come, and with it, light and hope. Could it be that something deeper than you could ever imagine is waiting? A calling far greater than yourself? Read on fellow sojourner! This account, based on the truth of tenacious overcomers is for you. They moved forward in faith, knowing that nothing is impossible with God.

Table of Contents

1. Journey to Bar Rousse 6

2. Adina Chronicles 32

3. Journey Chronicles 55

4. The Wedding 88

5. A New Life 105

6. Friedlich Chronicle 119

7. Schuh Coffee – Malachi Chronicle 152

8. Sentimental Journey 178

9. Sweet Wil 200

10. Adina's Legacy 216

11. Catwalk Masquerade 235

12. The Tempus Vector 275

13. Leaving 312

14. Final Verdict 327

15. The Black Box 335

16. Devil's Knuckles 343

17. The Blessing 371

18. Ascent of the Monarch 384

19. Enigma Revelation 406

20. The Passage 452

"*Do not spend your time mourning what you have lost or do not have, rather pursue with all wisdom the journey that is before you.*"

|Malachi Coffee|

Chapter 1

Journey to Bar Rousse

People die every day leaving a trail of memories, inheritances, and sentimental heirlooms for those left behind to hold onto for comfort and to cherish for a lifetime. But something was coming that would prove to be far more than mere physical trinkets or things made by human hands; a legacy stirred by a calling. Like the others before me, I was about to discover my name clearly branded and unable to be erased from this binding task that would not only spill over into my own life, but require complete abandonment of myself into the all-consuming waters of the Tempus Vector. I suppose that I shouldn't be surprised at the chaotic and unwonted developments beginning early this morning, as my everyday life events, until the past few years, have proven to be anything but typical or effortless. Little did I know that this day would mark an unimaginable dawn that would transform my now comfortable and routine life into an unexpected and risky venture.

After racing through the airport, finally reaching my departure gate, I was relieved to hear the announcement that my eight o'clock morning flight to Bar Rousse, Maine had been delayed. The boarding agent confirmed that the postponement had something to do with a malfunction in the hydraulic brake system of the massive 747 airbus destined to carry hundreds of souls to the other side of the country. As far as I was concerned, the delay would allow a bit more time for me to catch my breath after such a hectic morning. Contrary to the other passengers, I was more than happy to wait for the repairs to be completed. Turmoil and agitation, rising up from anxious travelers, filled gate 12 as the original departure time arrived and then passed. But to me it seemed as though I had already lived an entire day. My whirlwind of events began when I received the early morning call from my Uncle Wil that his sister, my Aunt Adina, had passed away in her sleep during the night. The mournful anguish echoing over the phone was heartbreaking. I only hoped that in reality this was a cruel joke of a dream gone foul, and I would soon awake to find that this distressing news was false and my Adina was still alive. Her passing was twofold in my mind; on one hand, I was utterly consumed by grief, yet on the other hand, I found comfort in knowing that she died in her sleep, which I know suited her just fine. It was always the way she hoped to go. For her, a slow death filled with prolonged suffering was highly objectionable. She couldn't stand the thought of spending her last days in a care facility, causing anyone to fuss over her. This alone was her greatest fear.

In an attempt to make my early morning flight, all of my attention was focused on the vast preparations that needed to be accomplished in order to leave. I hadn't yet abandoned myself to the idea of properly grieving, and I dreaded the moment that I would finally submit. Although I tended to guard my emotions, even tuck them away neatly in an undisturbed corner of my heart, this situation was far different. It was personal. There was no curve or hidden niche in my heart that hadn't been touched by Adina. All of the happy memories and unconditional love that I had ever experienced in my life were due solely to her, and her absence would forever leave me heartbroken. I wasn't sure how I would ever survive knowing that she was gone. She had always been the one that brought balance to my life. Aunt Adina was my true home. If ever I was struggling, or when a problem seemed too big, she would know exactly what to say, and have the perfect words of wisdom that would remind me that everything would be alright. "Beni, take one day at a time," she would say. "The quickest way to rob today of its joy, is to worry about tomorrow." Her words were not profound or complicated, but they were always exactly what I needed to hear. It seemed the harder that I tried not to think of her, the more I fell short of that task. I knew that the only way to get through the here and now, was to try and think of *anything* but her.

While in the mix of the terminal, I was reminded of a nonsensical personal issue that I've always struggled with. For some strange reason, each time that I'm in a crowd of people, I feel as though someone in the throng is staring at me, or as if eyes are peering at me from an unknown source. I began noticing this gazing phenomenon when I was just a little girl. Of course, it's a different situation entirely when I'm in my classroom lecturing at the university. While in front of my students, I feel completely at ease with all eyes on me. Yet, within a crowd of strangers, it's a very different experience. This discernment is never eerie or scary, but strangely comforting, almost as if someone is watching over me. Although I'm aware of it, I generally just dismiss the feeling as a simple insecurity that is completely unwarranted. Nevertheless, this time it was different, as I actually came face to face with the individual whose eyes I felt.

Directly to my right, candidly staring at me, was an elderly man wearing a dapper-looking suit and bow tie, complete with a black fedora hat. His blue eyes smiled, as he tipped his hat and nodded toward me as a gesture of "greetings, and how-do-you-do." His face filled with creases reading like a script of a life well lived, and hands covered with the stains of difficulty and bitter times held tightly to a small worn leather carry-on. This time, the overpowering sense of being on display was not just my imagination. At first, I had no intention of stopping and having a conversation with this stranger, but for some reason I felt overwhelmingly drawn to him. Yet at the same time, I felt rather fearful. Reluctantly, I said hello, and in return he said hello back as he continued smiling at me.

Not knowing exactly what to say next, I returned a timid smile, telling him to have a great flight, and that I would see him on board.

"You as well," he responded with an indisputable German accent.

Almost rushing to get away from him, and trying to find one empty seat anywhere that wasn't next to him, he said one last thing that left me feeling perplexed.

"My dear Beni, you are feeling alone in this place full of people, I can tell, but you are not alone, my dear. You will never be alone."

I stopped in my tracks, wondering how he knew my name, but then continued walking forward without responding. I found it highly difficult to dismiss the discourse between the dapper Mr. "Fedora" and myself as mistaken identity on his part. He obviously had me confused with someone else - someone else named Beni, hmm? As odd as this all seemed, I chuckled to myself and wondered why he couldn't have been a tall good-looking man trying to have a conversation with me, rather than a cute little gray-haired man bringing to my attention my insecurity of feeling alone.

"So typical," I thought as I finally found a seat at the very end of the row. It seemed to always be the mothers, fathers, and grandparents who appreciated my maturity and accomplishments while their handsome sons and grandsons never seemed interested. My friend, Rae, always told me that they were just intimidated by my air of confidence. Little did they know, I was really rather shy, and my confidence was merely just a facade.

Nevertheless, I just couldn't stop wondering about the old gentleman. How did he know my name? And even more strange, how did he know that I felt alone? In my mind, there had to be an answer to every question, so I came to the conclusion that he was nearby as I was going through security and saw my name on my boarding pass perhaps, or even my driver's license. Although the entire encounter was a mystery, I had to admit that the instant I spoke with him, that uneasy perception that eyes were on me ceased.

Distractions were coming from every direction of the crowded terminal, mainly from impatient travelers who shared the same general complaint about the flight delay, but also from those irritated by missed connections and fussy children who were now running amok. One person in particular, a large man dressed in a navy blue suit, stood out among the others, voicing his complaints so that everyone could hear. He went on and on about how he was going to miss his afternoon meeting, and that his opportunity for a successful business deal would certainly be lost. He continued asking in a most irritating tone how the airline was going to make this right and make him whole. It was comical, to say the least, to see a grown man acting that way. It wasn't until the supervisor at the counter offered to upgrade his seat to first class that he finally sat down calmly, but then began boasting of his triumph to the travelers around him, which in turn caused an influx of travelers demanding the same benefit. Even though Gate 12 was a disorderly mess, I welcomed the distraction, if just for a few minutes. As both the waiting and chaos continued, my mind turned once again to Adina, my dearest relative and best friend. I just couldn't believe that she was gone. The thought of walking into her house without her being in it was upsetting. Her home was empty, and so was I.

I remember meeting Adina for the first time when I was five years old. My mother had just passed away, after a two-year battle with cancer, and even though my aunt was unwelcome in our house, she still came. That was just her way. My father, Rich Crawford, Adina's youngest brother (fifteen years her junior) was completely distraught over my mother's death. She had been his whole life. When Adina came for the funeral, I remember how horribly he treated her. He hurled bitter and crushing words at her like a sharp spear, using regurgitated resentment as a platform to embarrass and humiliate, leaving both Adina and the room full of guests speechless.

13

It was an incredible gesture of kindness that she stayed after such inappropriate behavior, but she did. From that moment on, she considered her time there a mission of mercy, lingering unnoticed in the shadows of the room, and serving as the hands and feet for menial tasks that needed be done. Mainly, her attentions were spent on me. As the other adults in the room passed me by, acting as if I wasn't even there, Adina came and sat next to me, and pulled from her bag a wrapped gift and handed it to me. As she did, she asked me a question that literally changed my life.

"Would you like to take a journey with your Aunt Adina?"

I nodded yes.

"Well then, open it up!"

As I tore off the paper, I was initially disappointed to see that it was a book, a rather thick one with no pictures except the one on the cover of four girls smiling and embracing one another. Slowly, I sounded out the words on the front covering.

"L i t t l e Wo - W o m e n?"

"Very good, Beni. This story is about four sisters, and *you* are going to love it!"

For hours, I sat in Adina's lap as she introduced me to the March sisters. She was right. Through that one novel, she not only took me on my first journey, but just as she had promised, to a place far away from that room full of strangers.

I later discovered that my father had never forgiven her for leaving Texas and marrying Carson when he was so young. Adina was the glue that held the Crawford kids together, and when she left, everything fell apart. Because father was so young at the time, he struggled the most of all the siblings. He spent his life fighting the demons of abandonment, and blaming Adina, as she was the only one who ever showed him love, and the only real parent he ever had. By the time she discovered that he had been all but deserted, he had already been placed in foster care and then adopted by a family in California. When she tried to get him back, the state wouldn't allow it.

Both of her sisters married before they were sixteen years old. The older one, Velma, married a man who was slightly twisted in his religious beliefs, but was also of the abusive sort. Adina's younger sister, Joanne, married a man who was seventeen years her senior. He was a demanding perfectionist who would never allow even a hair to be out of place, or a spot of dirt to be in his presence. He soon squashed her playful joy and enthusiasm for life, making her to take on the role of a servant rather than a wife. By the time she was thirty she had the appearance of an old haggard woman. For years Adina pled with her sisters to walk away from these unhealthy relationships and come and live with her, but they were both too afraid to leave, and never did. Adina never stopped grieving over the fact that she left them. She somehow felt that perhaps she could have prevented their harmful choices which were clearly prompted by their cruel circumstances. Yet at the same time, *leaving* Texas and marrying Carson was the best thing she ever did. She attempted throughout her entire life to make amends with her two sisters and Rich, my father, to no avail. On the other hand, Uncle Wil, her other brother, came to Bar Rousse at a young age to live with Adina, and they remained the best of friends over the years. Realizing that it was their parents who let them all down, he was the only one of her siblings who didn't blame her for leaving. My father remained bitter towards her, and the world in general, to be exact. He poured every bit of himself into his work until he was completely empty, and then sadly died a few years ago, leaving me forever. It was determined that he had a massive heart attack, but I believe that he died from another heart condition, one of brokenness and bitterness that finally ate away anything good inside of him.

In retrospect, I'm sure that Adina wanted to walk out of our house the very instant my father began his brutal discharge of words, but her replies to him, however difficult, were those of love which made him even more angry. She knew the only way to turn away his wrath was with kindness, which could not have been easy. She still loved her brother deeply, but I honestly believe that she put up with his nonsense for my sake. She and I had an immediate connection, and on my behalf, she refused to leave, thus beginning our lifelong journey together.

During the period following my mother's death, nannies took the place of my parents. They were both older when I was born, so without my mother, my father had no idea what to do with me, and it suited him better to simply stay away as much as possible. Adina continued to ask him if I could at least come and stay the

17

summers with her. Finally moving past the Crawford stubbornness and unyielding hesitation, he gave in to my aunt's invitation. From that point forward, every June when school let out I would fly by myself to Bar Rousse, Maine accompanied by whatever flight attendant happened to be on duty that day. It was actually quite a remarkable thing for one so young to travel solo the way I did. At the time I didn't think much about it; it was my "normal." But my life was anything but normal, and I now realize that most concerned and loving parents would never have allowed their six year old child to fly alone so often the way that I did.

What had just begun as mere summers with Adina, turned into *all* of my school breaks and holidays as well. Being with her in Bar Rousse was more of a home for me than the one with my father in southern California. During those younger years, I would be so distressed at the thought of leaving one so sad. By staying, I foolishly believed that I could make everything better. But as it turned out, I was wrong. Because of his completely shattered and unending sorrow over my mother, the only thing that allowed him to get up in the morning and function like a somewhat normal human being, was to invest all of his attention into his

18

professional life. This would allow him to escape into a place that he could control by means of power and money, removing all of the painful scraps of love and relationships.

When I would ask Adina why my father didn't want to spend time with me, she'd tell me that when he looked at me, he saw my mother and his heart would ache. "Nobody enjoys feeling pain in their heart, Beni. Because he was never able to resign himself to the loss of your mother, and embrace the blessing that stood right before him, the ache in his heart turned to darkness." She would show me pictures of my mother and tell me that because I looked so much like her, with my blue eyes and dark brown hair, that it was just too much of a reminder for him to bear.

Frankly, I always felt that I resembled Adina more than my mother, that was my hope anyway, as she was quite stunning. I not only wanted to look like her, but I wanted to be just like her. Whatever she would do, I would also do. I remember each night before bed, I would join in her beauty regime; she and I would sit in front of the large mirror above her dressing table, and lather our faces with exotic concoctions and beauty creams. Even as she got older, she was a true beauty. But her beauty on the outside was only a fraction of her inner beauty.

At the age of nine, my father sent me to live at a boarding school in upper state New York where I would receive a first-rate education with the added benefit of rubbing elbows with well-bred girls from the finest families across the country. In addition, I would be tutored in the elite skills of social etiquette, along with the lost arts of blue-blooded sophistication. Because he was gone so much of the time, he was convinced that this would be a better alternative than nannies, and that boarding school would help me to become a balanced and well-rounded individual. Once again, Adina invited me to come and live with her, but he declined the invitation and insisted that it was, and would always be, out of the question. For the most part, being away at a "highly reputed" institute was a positive experience, but I missed my father. Even though my relationship with him was strained, it was all I knew. Over the next nine years that I attended the very prestigious Yardley Academy, it was only my Aunt Adina who faithfully visited and was present for all of my important school events and ceremonies that occurred during that time. If not for her, I would have been alone, yearning for the fellowship of loved ones while watching the other Yardley students embark upon joyful reunions with their families. She would visit me often, and we would usually take the train into New York City, always choosing the simplicity of a picnic lunch in Central Park over dining in an expensive restaurant. The day wouldn't have been complete without stopping at Tony's Italian Custard Stand in an effort to humor our taste buds with a scoop of the finest gelato in the city. This was one of our favorite traditions to be sure! Without fail, Adina would choose chocolate and my choice would be vanilla. Afterwards, we would usually enjoy shopping for the rest of the day. We mainly searched out unusual boutiques where we would unearth rare and exotic treasures, mostly consisting of unique shoes, handbags, and jewelry.

As I began to get older, my summer breaks and New York shopping sprees with Adina were focused more on finding unique fabrics that would be the foundation for a new wardrobe for the school year. In *our* world this took the place of "school clothes shopping"… handmade rather than store-bought. Yardley Academy hosted countless promenades throughout the year, therefore, my wardrobes would include gowns for events such as winter formals and proms, and of course, a white gown for the highly celebrated May Day event. Because of Adina's skill as a seamstress, everything that I modeled was custom and exquisite. Numerous Yardley socialites departed from these events in a horrified state, because their so-called custom gown's counterpart was standing on the other side of the room, something that I never had to worry about. I always knew when walking into the ballroom that my gown, or whatever apparel I may have been wearing, was a "one of a kind." Over the years, my schoolmates would inevitably implore Adina to sew for them as well. Most of them were from wealthy families and were willing to pay any price for an original, but she would continually decline their requests for her services. Even though uniforms were required for everyday attire at Yardley, it was always special to have a custom-made wardrobe for the times that I was permitted to wear "conventional" clothes. Clothing could not be purchased anywhere that compared with her design and quality. It was a well-known and accepted fact that Adina's command as a seamstress would put Coco Chanel to shame. As a signature stamp of her work, every garment that she created was embellished with a small red embroidered rose on the back of the neckline which became the traditional hallmark of her apparel. I was never one of the most popular girls at Yardley, but because of Adina, certainly the best dressed.

From the moment that Adina arrived in Bar Rousse, she spent a good deal of time sewing clothes and overcoats for those in need. She was exceedingly aware of how it felt to be poor, and couldn't stand to see anyone in want. For this reason, she never went anywhere without her measuring tape, pencil, and pad of paper just in case she needed to take a few measurements. If she would happen to come upon a little girl or boy who looked as though they needed some new clothes, she would whip out her measuring tape and within moments, have all the dimensions necessary to create a new and perfect-fitting wardrobe She had a way of making each child feel special rather than needy. "My, how lovely (or handsome) you are….I bet you'd look perfect in pink (or blue), or stripes." Within a few weeks, normally before school began, these children would find a box of brand new clothes, along with a coat for the winter and a new pair of shoes, sitting on their porch. She never told anyone that the clothes were from her, but after a while when a child would be approached and measured by Adina, they would light up like a Christmas tree knowing that very soon a carton filled with original designs would show up on their porch. Practically every time I visited, I would spot a little girl wearing a beautiful dress with an embroidered red rose on the back of the neckline. I knew the truth about Adina, and the reality was that she had genuine love and concern for people.

Memories of her flooded my mind, and my throat began to tighten as grief set in. I had to hold it together though. If I started crying now, I feared that I would never stop. This feeling of pain brought to life the old adage of "the sting of death." I never really thought too much about what that meant until now. The sting, the pain that is left behind to those of us who remain, hurts and is unbearable. I felt an insatiable ache inside of me, an excruciating pain that would only subside with time. Death had most certainly been a part of my life before now, but this was different. I was so young when my mother died, and my father and I hadn't had a relationship for years when he passed away. But Adina was mother, father, and friend to me.

Trying to choke back tears that were welling up in my throat, I let out a deep breath and closed my eyes tightly. I was determined to get my mind on something else. I propped my leather carry-on suitcase and garment bag against the waiting chair, and reviewed in my mind, one by one, each article that I had packed so quickly this morning, hoping that I hadn't forgotten anything important. I brought enough clothes for only a few days - a week at the most. After all, there was nothing left in Bar Rousse anymore, nothing worth staying for anyway. My overstuffed garment bag held not only my favorite black suit and white chiffon blouse, but a winter coat as normal October weather was quite chilly. My black suit was of course an original. Adina had made it special for me to wear to my first job interview at the university. I couldn't seem to escape her memory, as everything I looked at, even the clothes that I had packed, reminded me of her. There were measures of her and her labors everywhere. I remember how excited she was to send me this sleek-fitted suit which turned out to be one of my favorites. She styled it with high-waisted pants, and a fitted blazer with oversized lapels. The fabric she used was smooth like butter, and upon completion, it had a glove-like fit; I always called it my lucky suit. Whenever I would wear it, good things seemed to happen. Maybe it's because she knew my size so well, or maybe it was simply that she had a passion for perfection that shone in everything she made.

I was suddenly alerted as I heard my name being called by the airline attendant at the front desk.

"Passenger Benidette Crawford, please come to the departure desk. Passenger Benidette Crawford, please come to the departure desk."

Picking up my bags, and making my way up to the origin of the broadcast, I wondered, out of all of the people in the room, why I would be the one getting summoned. While on my way up, I was curious to see if Mr. Fedora was still looking in my direction, but when I glanced over to where the old gentleman had been sitting, he was gone. Thoroughly scoping out the room, I found no trace of him or his hat among those in the crowd, which struck me as peculiar.

"Hello, yes, I'm Beni Crawford. You just called for me?"

"Yes, Miss Crawford, I wanted to let you know that your original coach ticket has been upgraded to first class. First class is now boarding, so please go on in and make yourself comfortable."

With a perplexed expression on my face, I exclaimed that I didn't really understand how this could have happened, and that someone must have made a mistake. She informed me that she had received an updated passenger list in which I had been moved from coach to first class.

"Someone must like you," she stated, and then told me to go ahead and find my seat. "Row One, Seat A. I hope you enjoy your flight with East Coastways!"

I headed toward my seat thinking that perhaps this was Adina's final work of generosity and kindness to me, or, maybe it was the mysterious "Mr. Fedora." I wasn't sure how I got upgraded, but it was truly ironic because any time I would fly out to see Adina, she would always make sure that I was in first class so that I'd get the best possible care.

The flight attendant collected my carry-on bags, and put them into storage. She told me her name was Heather, and that she would be my personal attendant for the duration of the flight. I felt as though I was a child again traveling by myself with my own personal handmaid. I made my way to my very over-sized and comfortable seat, preparing myself for the six-hour flight to the east coast.

Heather was kind and attentive, and must have noticed that I looked a bit disheveled and stressed. "Would you like some champagne?"

Normally I would not be drinking champagne at 9:30 in the morning, but after the day that I'd had thus far, champagne sounded like a brilliant idea.

Although I'd made arrangements for another professor to teach my class, I feared that he would not pour into them the same way that I do. If Adina were here sitting by me, she would tell me not to worry. "Beni, this is a situation that you can't do a thing about. Don't stress over the things you can't change!" I began thinking about her life, and what a remarkable person she was. She was what I would call an overcomer. Even though she came from a home of complete poverty, I never once heard her complain, or use it as an excuse to ever give up.

Once the flight achieved proper altitude, I made my way through the body of the plane, curious about the mysterious older gentleman from my gate. Perhaps I would even stop by to chat with him. Row after row, I looked both left and right, but he was nowhere to be found. It was a curious concern, as the general public was not allowed to walk freely through airports these days. If

28

he had no intention of boarding this flight, why was he sitting at my departing gate with bag in hand? My entire interaction with him was quite peculiar, and I couldn't help but wonder where he had gone. I even asked Heather if she had noticed a man of his description, but she had no recollection of such a person.

Reclining back into the comfort of my upgraded lounge, should have lulled me into a peaceful sleep, but for some unknown reason, I was beyond restless; every muscle in my body was tense. Maybe over-tiredness or bottled up grief was making me edgy. But whatever is was, I couldn't seem to shake the blanket of anxiety that was now looming above. Without warning, my anxiety turned into tormenting fear, almost as if I was being haunted by something that next generated a lather of sweat. Could it have been the brief yet strange encounter with the disappearing man? Maybe. But there was something else, something more bothersome eating away at me. Adina! Through this intense emotion, I seemed to sense both her presence and loss all at the same time. Thoughts of her didn't just fill my mind, but they were consuming me, and overflowing everywhere. Even worse, these brooding notions robbed my peace and stifled my breathing. My distressing crisis surly made me appear mental to the other passengers on the air bus. But to my surprise, they seemed blinded to my plight, focused only on their own state of settling in for the long journey ahead. They were oblivious to the passenger in their midst, who was struggling to stay within her skin. I wanted nothing more than to turn around and go back home, but the time had come to stand face to face with the truths about Adina. A detour leading into an unknown byway stood between my life that had been moving in a direction of my choosing, into a lane carved out by my aunt; I felt it in my bones, everything was about to change. From reflections to recollections, my thoughts bounced in all directions, like fleas on a dog. Maybe the origin of my peril was generated by the unspoken understanding of bridled truths. I knew without a doubt that if Adina's life were chronicled, it would one filled with many difficulties, sorrows, and clouded facts. But with those life barricades, she also experienced love that took her to the highest plateaus and into the deepest valleys. She didn't speak too often about events that she couldn't change, but believed her way of dealing, to be a more effective path to healing rather than conjuring up demons that were better left tightly corked. Even though we came from different times, and different worlds, we

30

were similar in so many ways. She was raised in a barren poverty like I had never known, other than my deficiency of love and affection. We both knew the brokenness of abandonment, and the scars of harsh words roused by liquid spirits. Through it all, she conquered overwhelming obstacles that would have destroyed most. She was strong and good, closing the door on bitterness, that if allowed, could have ravished every last morsel of her being. While she would allow me to rant and rave, crying thousands of tears over my estranged father, she remained tight-lipped in regards to her past. I knew bits and pieces, but even those brass tacks were hazy at best. I began to recollect what I knew to be true about Adina. She deserved to be remembered, her story begged to be told.

Chapter 2

Adina Chronicles

Adina Rae Crawford was born in Belen, Texas in 1923. She was the oldest of five siblings, two brothers and two sisters, and because of the self-centeredness of her parents, Ray and Molly Crawford, who regularly went away for long periods of time, she became the regular caregiver. Her parents' interests were centered around and within the circle of extended weekends of drinking and overindulging with classes of people far above their own. Ray and Molly stayed home only long enough to have more children, and then would leave them in Adina's care. Life became even more difficult for Adina at the age of ten when prohibition ended, and drinking and carousing became an easier way of life for her mother and father. When he wasn't on a spree of overindulgence, Ray would spend weeks on the road, driving cattle and beef to the west, and returning back eastward with oranges and grapefruit. He was a heavy drinker who would spend his days driving for Central Trucking Co. prior to spending his nights in a drunken stupor. Molly insisted on joining Ray regularly on his

32

travels, or so she said. By the time she had her last baby, Rich, Adina and her other siblings were unsure that Ray was even the real father. Rich's jet black hair, brown eyes, and olive complexion were unlike the rest of them. Many times, Molly would disappear, leaving the very young Adina alone to take care of her brothers and sisters. Although she was unsure of exactly where her mother was, she had no intention of verifying her whereabouts with her father. Molly was very selfish, and should have never had children in the first place, being that she couldn't stand staying home with them. She treated Adina the worst, as she was jealous of her youthful beauty, and became bitter with her own aging self. Molly was so preoccupied with her looks and the declining attention from men, that any time she and Adina would go anywhere together, she would instruct her daughter *not* to call her "mother", but to refer to her as her aunt, or on days that she was feeling especially youthful, "sister." After several episodes of bailing Ray out of jail for drunk and disorderly conduct, Molly decided that it would be in the best interest of all that she accompany him on his trips, so to keep him out of trouble. Even though most nights with Ray would end up in some sort of an uproar of violence, Molly chose this

33

life on the road as a more appealing alternative than staying home with her children.

Because they were gone for such long periods of time, Adina became both mother and father to her brothers and sisters. When they would leave, they gave no thought to the care of their children, and how they would live or even buy food. The Crawford children were on their own. At the age of 16, Adina not only managed the daily needs of her brothers and sisters, but also, made sure that they attended school each and every day.

Jobs didn't come easy in Belin, but Adina was able to secure a position as a ticket girl at the Maverick Movie House, and she worked as many hours as Gerald Maverick, the proprietor, would give her. Making twenty-five cents an hour wasn't bad, considering the havoc that the Great Depression had unleashed on this community. Even through the worst times of the Depression, the movie house stayed busy as people wanted to forget about their problems and be entertained by the dramatic swagger of Humphrey Bogart and Cary Grant. They were willing to spend money they didn't have for those few hours of entertainment that would capture their imaginations, and whisk them away to *Casablanca* or the

City of *Oz*. Laughter, tears, and a good scare was the best medicine for this depression-riddled community. On especially profitable nights when the theater was full, Mr. Maverick would give Adina an extra dollar or two, knowing her situation at home and wanting to help.

Like most young girls, Adina longed to spend her money on herself, new dresses and shoes, maybe even an occasional bottle of perfume from the five-and-dime. Instead, she used every bit of her hard-earned money to buy food and supplies for her younger siblings. As they prepared for school each day, she made certain that they were washed and their clothes were clean. Their clothing may not have been the fanciest of garments, but they were sure to be cleaned and pressed. Her sisters, Velma and Joanne, and brother, Wil, would walk to school every day, each carrying a metal bucket with a lunch that consisted of a leftover biscuit and piece of sausage from breakfast. Adina dropped out of school so that she could stay home and take care of Rich, who was only one year old at the time.

Out of all of the Crawford kids, Velma was the most embarrassed to be poor. She hated her metal bucket lunch, and wholeheartedly yearned for, even dreamed at night about, having a real sandwich made on white sliced bread like some of the rich and more privileged girls. Every day at noon, Velma sneaked around to the back of the schoolhouse and ate her lard and flour biscuit, and sausage patty alone so that no one would see her shameful display of poverty in a metal can. Brushing any crumbs of evidence from her mouth, she would covertly join the other girls, hoping not to be noticed. When they asked about her lunch, she would make them believe that maintaining her figure, that would someday land her in Hollywood, was far more important than eating a silly lunch.

Each day when the kids got home from school, Adina headed off to work selling tickets at the movie house. In addition to her regular job, she would take in sewing, mending mainly. A few times a week, she went to the market and bought small amounts of flour and bits of meat, just enough to get them through a few days. While at the market she always inquired as to whether there were any empty flour sacks for sale, which she used for fabric. Knowing that she would ask, the store owner regularly put aside any empty bags that he had, and kindly never made her pay for them. When her sisters would see her walk through the door with the dusty sacks, they knew that lovely dresses were soon to come, and waited with anticipation to see what new design Adina would come up with. Inevitably, they were always thrilled with the finished product. The flowered patterns were used for dresses, and the solid or striped bags for collared shirts for her brothers. With any leftover scraps, she would make hand towels and dishrags. Out of necessity, she became an excellent seamstress with the assistance of an old Singer pedal sewing machine that once belonged to her grandmother. Along with her tool of trade and a small wooden sewing box filled with scissors, three spools of thread, straight pins, and her grandmother's measuring tape, Adina was able to recycle flour sacks, old fabric and garments that no one else wanted, into beautiful clothing items. Very few people ever knew how poor they really were because of the magic that she could achieve with fabric, thread, and that old Singer.

One Christmas, Ray and Molly decided to drive to southern Texas and spend the holiday by the ocean. After a long shift at the movie house that Christmas Eve, Adina knew that any joy that would enter the Crawford home would need to be by her hand. On the way home, she stopped by Ed's Christmas Tree Farm and purchased a very small tree. Her next stop was the town market where she had two slices of ham wrapped up for Christmas dinner. Finally, she went to the five-and-dime, and bought each of her siblings a small but meaningful gift to leave from Santa. For their stockings, she bought them each a peppermint stick, an orange, and a few walnuts. For Velma and Joanne, Adina chose hair ribbons that would perfectly match dresses she had been sewing, along with a set of Jacks that they had been dying to receive for months. For Rich, a small wooden car, and for Wil, Adina chose something that she knew he would love - a slingshot and a set of glass marbles complete with a shooter and leather carrying bag.

When she arrived home, there sitting on the front porch were four long and utterly disappointed faces waiting to accost her with their hopeless notions regarding Christmas. When they saw that Adina was dragging a tree behind her and holding bags of surprises, they were so excited that they all jumped up and cheered for their sister, the savior of the holiday. As they went inside, Wil propped the tree in the corner of the room, and Velma and Joanne began cutting out stars from an old map book, using only the most colorful pages. They strategically placed the stars within the branches of the tree, and then Adina added a few tapered candles, which made the small tree light up the room with flickering fire that sparkled on the walls. They all sat around the lovely little tree and sang *Silent Night* as Wil played his version on his harmonica. There were no cookies to leave out for Santa, so Adina made some pie dough from flour and lard. Each of the children cut out a circle using an old can, and sprinkled sugar and cinnamon on top.

The smell of holiday spices baking in the oven filled the room with the warm aroma of the festivities yet to come. After placing a small plate of cookies on the kitchen table, and hanging socks on the fireplace that were hankering to be filled by Santa, the young ones went to bed, and Adina went to work. After finishing touches were completed on the flour sack dresses, she began thoughtfully wrapping each one, admiring her achievement of making something so beautiful out of articles that most would dispose of. The first dress was baby blue with white flowers and the other white with pink flowers. To add body to the cotton frocks, she attached two layers of tulle under the skirts and sleeves, knowing that the puffiness would make her sisters feel more grown up. As a final touch, she carefully laid the matching ribbons on top of the dresses, right before she wrapped them. Once she finished preparing all of the gifts, she placed them under the tree.

Even though it was dark and cold, she went outside into her small garden and gathered some green beans and new potatoes to serve with the ham for Christmas dinner. With the leftover pie crust, and the last can of applesauce, Adina prepared a pie that she would bake fresh, first thing in the morning. Exhausted from the long day, she headed off to bed, but before she did, she filled each of the stockings. Dropping in the orange, peppermint stick, and a few walnuts, she laughed as the toes of each stocking touched the floor from the weight of the juicy oranges. Being the last one to bed never allowed for a good night's sleep considering she had to share a small mattress with her two sisters. Instead of disturbing them, she curled up with an afghan on the worn couch, and fell into a dead sleep.

That Christmas was simple and sparse, but filled with joy which was so rarely had at the Crawford house. Even in their older age, each of Adina's brothers and sisters remembered this particular Christmas as the happiest of their childhood. Adina had many talents, but she definitely had a way of making something beautiful out of nothing. The kids knew that the reason this Christmas was so joyful, aside from what Adina did to make it so, was the fact that their mama and daddy were not there and none of them would have to deal with a difficult woman and a drunk and violent man, if only for a day.

One Saturday night a few months later, Adina heard from some of the locals in town, that there was going to be a highway dance beginning at nine that evening. Since her folks were home for once, and her shift at work would end in plenty of time to get there, she decided to live a little and go. Apparently highway dances were the newest and best, considered by all to be the "Clam Bake" of all dances, but she had never actually gone to one. Most people today would think it absurd to dance on the highway, but when Adina would tell this story, she would always start by saying that this event was truly a fascinating part of history, one that most people have never heard of. Due to the ugly remnants of the Great Depression and continued rationing, many people could not afford to drive their cars. If they did drive their vehicles, it was solely used out of necessity, in order to get to work and then back home. Since there were few to no cars on the road, each Saturday night, a

41

portion of the highway would be closed down and blocked off for a "shincracker", otherwise known as a dance party. Every week various wannabe bands would come and fill the quiet night with the sounds of Count Basie and Benny Goodman. Those who were able drive to this event, parked their cars all around the spinning and jittering of the promenade, and lit up the asphalt dance floor with their headlights. On this particular night at the highway dance, a tall and handsome, brown-haired Marine named Tom Morgan, who had just been transferred from Twenty-nine Palms, California showed up to the event. He was a poster Marine who knew that he was good looking, and as if that wasn't enough, he also possessed a smooth and charming disposition. As he walked past the long line of girls who were praying that he would ask them to dance, they swooned as if Cary Grant himself was walking by. If his bodily charm didn't knock them over, the powerful fragrance trail of Palmolive Aftershave that he left behind, certainly would. He had gold rings on both hands, and it was obvious by his overall perfection, that he spent many hours grooming himself.

When he saw Adina standing on the other side of the highway, he disregarded the brood of desperates, and with a surplus of confidence walked over, grabbed her hand and said, "What's cookin sugar, are you rationed?"

He could tell by her reaction of indifference that she had no idea what he was talking about.

"What I mean sugar, is, you here with anybody?"

Adina generally did not attend such events and was feeling completely out of place, even to the point of leaving, and going home. But when this confident and remarkably handsome man made a beeline in her direction, she decided to stay a bit longer.

"No, I'm not here with anyone. As a matter of fact, I was just about to go home."

"Home? What's eatin' you, beautiful? The night's just begun! We've both got our stompers on, let's go!"

Tom was a man who knew what he wanted when he saw it, and Adina was definitely what he wanted. He couldn't take his eyes off of her; she was as beautiful in her lilac-colored dress as he was handsome in his uniform. They danced until that last car drove away. By that time he had swept her completely off of her feet with his sappy words and baby browns, and then insisted on taking her home. She initially rejected the gesture, but after he refused to step out of her path until she agreed, she finally said yes. Down deep inside she knew that he was far from the kind of man that she wanted, but Adina had begun feeling fixed in this stifling abyss as months and years passed, and knew that someone like Tom could be her way out.

Even before they arrived at her house, Tom had resolved in his mind that Adina's beauty would go well with his own, and he had no intention of letting her go.

"Adina baby, I know we just met, but I can't let a jewel like you go. Let's get hitched.....tonight!"

"Tonight? That's kind of sudden, don't you think? My father is already asleep. Why don't you come back tomorrow and ask him?"

Adina was taken with Tom as well, and quite frankly, would have been entirely comfortable looking at his beautiful face forever. At the same time though, she was wise enough to know that a complete stranger waking her father in the middle of the night to ask a question of such magnitude was not only foolish, but dangerous as well.

Seeing as Tom was both arrogant and prideful, and not used to hearing the word "no", he opted to make the rather idiotic move right then and there.

"I'll ask him right now!"

Even though she told him that it was *way* too late, and then again warned him that her mother and father were sleeping, Tom didn't care. He insisted on asking at that very moment. They walked into her house, continuing straight back into Molly and Ray's bedroom.

Tom stood in the doorway, cleared his throat, and knocked lightly on the wall.

"Excuse me sir, my name is Tom Morgan, and I would like to marry your daughter, Adina."

Ray shot straight up in bed and shouted, "I don't know who in hell you think you are, but you better get out of this house, you son of a bitch, before I kill you!" He went on to call him a few other select names, and then told Tom that his daughter would never marry a jarhead.

As Adina would reflect on this horribly awkward situation later in her life, she would shake her head, still feeling humiliated as she told the story. Why in the world she would have ever allowed him to barge into her house, and ask her father a question like that in the middle of the night, she would never quite understand. The whole episode was a complete train wreck.

In a rage, Ray jumped up and abruptly flew to the bedroom closet, furiously rifling through clothes and shoes, searching for his shotgun. Molly told Adina to get that "damn idiot" out of the house before her daddy shot a hole straight through him. Tom grabbed ahold of Adina's hand, and told her to quickly go and pack a bag; that he would just take her away right then and there, permission or no permission.

Adina had a sickening fear in her heart, knowing well how violent her father could be, and fully aware that his threats were not empty.

"Tom, you'd better go or my father *will* kill you."

One after the other, he heard Ray loading shells into his shotgun which finally made him come to his senses and leave as spontaneously as he had come. As he hurried out the door, he promised Adina that he would be back in the morning to talk things out with her father. As she watched him drive away, she knew that he would never be back. In retrospect, she always wondered what her life would have been like if she would have said yes to him. At the time, she was upset not knowing the reason that he never returned, but later when she thought about what it would have been like being married to a man who loved himself more than anyone else, she was thankful that she didn't jump off of that bridge. To be honest though, she would have married Tom that night if her father would have agreed. She repeated many times how thankful she was that her daddy didn't say yes, and fully realized that even though half drunk at the time, he had great wisdom at that moment. Ray didn't make very many good decisions in his life, but that one saved her from a huge mistake.

Several months later, as Ray was traveling west headed for California carrying a full load of Angus, he stopped as he usually did at Maggie's Diner on the outskirts of New Mexico. His mouth had been watering for the past two hundred miles just thinking about "Maggie's Special." Whenever Maggie would see Ray walk through the door, she would yell to the cook, "Drop a steak in the lard. Texas is in the house!" Like clockwork, Ray would follow her instruction to the seasoned cook with, "Double size that, Ernie. Everything's bigger in Texas!" Within a few minutes, Maggie would proudly deliver a grand platter, filled with chicken fried steak, mashed potatoes, and green beans, all smothered in white gravy and homemade biscuits and butter to her all-time favorite customer.

Ray always sat in the same place, third chair from the wall, directly in front of the coffee pot. Sitting one seat away was a young man finishing up his piece of coconut cream pie and cup of coffee. After they began a friendly conversation, mainly about Ray's impressive big rig, Ray discovered that this fine fellow was in the Navy and on his way to Long Beach where he had recently been stationed. Carson York was a specialty mechanic for the U.S. Navy. One of the *best* and highly coveted mechanics, to be exact. He had just finished two months of top secret training in the most cutting edge field of mechanical technology available. Time flew by as Ray and Carson sat at the lunch counter together talking endlessly about Ray's truck and Carson's experiences thus far in the Navy.

All of a sudden, Carson frantically glanced at the clock on the wall, realizing that his bus was leaving in ten minutes. Ray had also stayed longer than he should have, and had to get on the road as well. As they were shaking hands and saying their goodbyes, Carson noticed that one of the tires on Ray's big rig had gone flat. Carson had ample experience dealing with trucks of all sizes, and was glad to help change the tire. Because the process was extensive and time consuming, Carson ended up missing the four o'clock bus into Long Beach. Ray insisted on giving him a ride anywhere that he needed to go, which ended up being an ideal situation as they were both going in the same direction. Besides, it would be a nice change to have someone to talk to.

"Son, I'd be honored to give you a ride home. You can tell me more about your job!"

The two thoroughly hit it off, and enjoyed one another's company all of the way to the west coast, talking the entire time. Ray was impressed that Carson had been all around the world, mainly working on top secret pieces of machinery. His life seemed more like something you'd see in the movies, rather than real life. During his global travels, he had learned the latest technologies from the most skilled machinists in the world.

In the middle of a discussion on the inevitable entry of the United States into the war, a single photograph on Ray's dash caught Carson's eye. It was of a beautiful girl with brown wavy hair and blue eyes. From that point on, he didn't hear a word that Ray was saying, but was fixed completely on that photograph. He tried not to stare, but was mesmerized by the stunning girl. When he couldn't stand it anymore, he asked who she was. Ray was proud to tell Carson that it was a picture of his oldest daughter, Adina. Carson couldn't take his eyes off of her, and for the duration of the trip, Adina became the new topic of their conversation. By the time they arrived in Long Beach, Carson felt as if he knew her, and he asked for permission to start writing letters to her. Ray readily agreed, and was thrilled at the notion of his daughter and this young man getting together. He liked Carson, and believed that any man that could change a tire on a semi-trailer truck of this magnitude, was surely capable of taking care of his daughter. When finally they arrived at the naval base in Long Beach, Ray got out of the truck to say goodbye, and when Carson went to shake hands, he got a big hug from Ray instead. (As most people came to realize after they got to know Ray, when he wasn't drinking he was a friendly man who would give the shirt off his back to anyone who needed it. Liquor was the Hyde of his Doctor Jekyll.)

When Ray arrived back in Texas, Adina had already received three lengthy letters from Carson. She was so upset that her father had given him permission to contact her, and was completely uninterested in the idea of corresponding with a complete stranger, especially one of her father's choosing. In one of the letters, Carson enclosed a photo of himself. At first glance she was not impressed, nor for that matter, very attracted to him. He was certainly not as handsome as the tall, dark Tom. He was, however, a bit taller and more muscular, but had an entirely different look. It was difficult to distinguish his hair color from the small black and white photo, but when Ray informed her that his crown of glory was red, she immediately placed the image back into the envelope, vowing to never look at it again. Although she refused to ever think of him, she didn't realize that she was actually spellbound by his face, and his eyes; his amazing eyes! It didn't matter that the photo was colorless. She could tell that his eyes were blue, crystal blue and piercing.

Adina discovered very quickly that Carson was a wonderful and romantic writer, very thoughtful and smart, but he also had a fun sense of humor and a great personality. She responded to each of his letters, but never really believed that anything would come of their communication. He asked many questions of her, such as what was her favorite color and song? What did she do in her spare time? He was the most inquisitive person she had ever interacted with, completely interested in everything about her. At one point she asked him if he was writing a book or something, and he responded in a way that she didn't expect. "My beautiful Adina, how did you know? Yes, I am writing a book as a matter of fact. It's a love story, *our* love story!"

As weeks turned into months, they grew to know each other more intimately through their letters. Carson faithfully wrote every single day; Adina not quite as often. He told her that he looked forward to getting home each night to record the thoughts of her that had consumed his day. Sometimes, he would sit on the sand and write to her, imagining that she was sitting next to him. He saw her blue eyes in the color of the ocean, the warmth of the sun setting made him feel as if she were near, and the breeze on his face had him fantasizing about her breath on his skin. Adina had never even been close to the ocean, so when she asked him to describe every detail, he was more than happy to oblige. Each letter would end in the same way,

"Forever Yours, Carson."

Later Adina would say that she fell in love with his heart, the place where his sincere and beautiful thoughts of love for her were born. It amazed her that anyone could fall in love with a picture, and she told him that in one of her letters. His eloquent and visionary response captured her heart completely.

"It wasn't just a feeling that came from a photo, Adina. From the moment I looked at your picture, I saw you belonging to me. You know that I have traveled all around the world, and in all of my travels, and of all the people that I have met, I have never experienced that feeling for anyone else. Adina, I am so in love with you!"

After six months of exchanging letters, Carson asked Adina to marry him. She was only 17 at the time, but quickly agreed to become Mrs. Carson York, and Ray gave his blessing without reserve. On the other hand, Molly did not share his enthusiasm, and spewed out caustic words of hatred towards them both. Even as Adina walked out to leave home and meet Carson, her mother shouted out a final warning, that the fate of her siblings was now on her head. What should have been a joyful event, was instead sorrowful. Although she was thrilled to finally be leaving Texas and the dead-end situation that restrained her freedom, she loved her brothers and sisters and was heartbroken to leave them behind. Her departure was cutting, but at the same time she had an indescribable peace within her that she was doing the right thing. There was no doubt in her mind that moving to California and marrying Carson was her destiny. Even knowing all of that to be true, the most bitter pill of all was leaving Rich. He was still just a baby and wouldn't understand why she was gone. She only hoped that her momma and daddy would finally step up and be the parents. Her days of nurturing, for now anyway, were over. Later she would learn that both of her sisters and her youngest brother, Rich, never forgave her for leaving them. Her brother, Wil, was the only one who understood why she had to go.

With a suitcase in one hand, and her sewing machine in the other, she took off for the bus station alone.

Chapter 3

Journey Chronicles

When Adina arrived at the bus station, to her dismay she discovered that it would take every penny that she had to buy a bus ticket to Long Beach. Not only did Ray and Molly fail to come and see her off, but they refused to give her even one dime to help with the expenses of the trip. Carson offered to pay her way, but she stubbornly insisted on doing it herself.

As she was sitting on the splinter-filled bench, feeling rather hopeless about her situation, an elderly lady approached her and inquired as to where she was going. Adina explained that she needed to get to Long Beach, California. The woman told her that she too was traveling west, to San Diego, and had found a couple who offered to drive her there for ten dollars (not including meals) if she could find another -passenger to come along and help pay for gas expenses. It sounded like an answer to her dilemma, so Adina made the decision to travel with the trio of strangers. Edith Irene informed the couple that she and Adina would agree to pay them ten dollars each for passage to Long Beach and San Diego. Their arrangement with Ed and Betty Curwood was to pay half upfront, and the other half once they arrived at their destination.

Edith and Adina loaded their suitcases into the trunk of the 1927 black Pontiac Coupe, hoping that these two seemingly normal looking individuals were on the up and up. As they headed west, Adina poured out her unconventional love story to Edith, explaining how she was going to marry a naval officer whom she had never met. Edith Irene, who reminded Adina of her grandmother, revealed that she was recently widowed and headed to San Diego to live with her daughter and son-in-law. As the trip progressed, they began to notice that Ed and Betty were showing signs of double-dealing as their increased pattern of dishonest activities was coming to light. Each time they stopped for gas, the couple would gouge Edith and Adina for a few more dollars, assuring them that the advance would be deducted from the final amount owed. At first, they agreed, but then noticed that the Curwoods were using the money for booze and gambling every chance they had, and not for fuel. It was apparent that this arrangement was a huge mistake as driver antics worsened with each mile, crushing the hopes of the desperate passengers. Edith and Adina were fearful

of shutting their eyes for even a moment. They agreed
that neither would sleep at the same time as the other -
one would always be awake - and both of them would sit
on their purses so that the couple would not be able to
steal their money. Finally, after being left in the car for an
entire night in what seemed to be the most depraved area
of Tempe, Arizona, Adina and Edith Irene concluded that
this travel plan was no longer safe or acceptable, and they
would both need to find another method of travel to their
destinations. As a last resort, Adina called Carson and
explained her predicament. Without hesitation he wired
her enough money to get a bus ticket that would take her
the rest of the way to California. He couldn't believe that
she had chosen to travel with complete strangers rather
than asking him for money. Edith Irene stayed in Tempe,
as her daughter agreed to come and pick her up. She had
also offered to give Adina a ride, but Carson couldn't
stand to wait even one more day for her arrival. At that,
they said their goodbyes, and Adina boarded the
remarkably comfortable bus and slept all the way to Long
Beach.

　　　　Carson told Adina that he'd be at the bus station
to pick her up, and just in case she didn't recognize him,
he would be holding a red rose so that he would stand out

from among the crowd. She told him that she would be wearing a navy blue suit with a white blouse, and a gold butterfly pendant. This pendant, her sewing machine, and a simple strand of pearls were left to Adina when her grandmother died. Her grandmother was her rock, and when she died Adina felt as though she didn't have anyone left who really cared about her. The gold butterfly pendant covered in an array of colorful rhinestones, with one solid pearl in the middle was her all-time favorite piece of jewelry. When Adina was a little girl, she would sit in her grandmother's lap, and ask to hear the story of the butterfly. Her grandmother would reach over to her tarnished silver jewelry box, lined in tattered red velvet, and pull out her butterfly pendant.

"Sweet thing….butterflies you see are a picture of a journey. The journey begins with the death of one life and the birth of another. The butterfly starts out as a little caterpillar who lives its whole life in one little patch of yard and believes that its life is grand. As far as this insect is concerned, it can see the whole world, and it appears to be a wonderful world. After all he has so many legs to carry him wherever he wants to go. But truly this little creature is in captivity within a jail of green blades. But oh my goodness me! When that little creature awakens from its death-like sleep, with wings named freedom, this grand monarch will no longer be bound by gravity, but instead will travel to the heights of the heavens. Adina, every time you look at this butterfly, remember and find hope in knowing that someday you too will have wings and go places far beyond your imagination."

She did feel hopeful as she looked at her pendant and remembered her grandmother's story. For the first time ever, she felt like the butterfly who had just been set free from the jail of green blades, hopeful that she would soon have a new and happy life. She would miss her brothers and sisters, but she would not miss her life in Texas. Before she even realized it, she had arrived in a place that felt like a new world, that revealed a mass of blue waters that looked to have no end, and she was consumed by every element. Just like Carson knew the moment he saw her photograph that his life would never be the same, so Adina knew that she was no longer bound by the subjection of gravity, but she would now take on the life of the monarch.

While lost in her reflections, the driver made the announcement that they would be arriving at the Long

Beach Bus Station in twenty minutes. Adina began thinking about meeting Carson for the first time, and found herself feeling anxious. Opening her purse and pulling out her compact mirror, she assessed the toll that the past few days of traveling had taken on her. She powdered her face and pinched her cheeks for a little bit of color, then touched up her deep red lipstick, and perfectly-chiseled eyebrows. Running her fingers through her hair to fluff it up a bit, she just stopped and thought to herself, "Well, this is as good as it gets."

When the bus pulled up to the station, Adina sat frozen in her seat, clinging to her bag, and looking straight ahead. She knew that when she got off that bus she would be walking into a new "everything." A new place, a husband, "a husband?" Panic once again overwhelmed her as she wondered if she even knew how to be a wife. Molly was such a poor example of what a wife and mother should be. Adina always wondered if perhaps Molly started out as a good wife, and a good person, but the many years of abuse, bitterness, and resentment possibly altered her character. Maybe Ray took a perfectly sound woman and ruined her as he broke her little by little each day until she didn't know who she was anymore. Adina imagined her mother as an exquisite fragile vase that was once flawless, but gradually and tragically, hairline cracks in the vase turned into pieces of glass lying on the floor, barely resembling the lovely vessel it once was. Adina made a decision right then and there that she would stay strong and never allow a man to break her or prevent her from experiencing all of the exciting things that her life would hold. Of course she wanted to be a good wife, but also an exceptional person who would never be alright with a mediocre life.

After the other passengers had departed from the bus, Adina stood up and began to walk down the center aisle. The closer she got to the door, the more she could smell the fresh sea air. As she looked out the window, she was met by not one, but a bouquet of red roses held by a gentle-looking man with clear blue eyes. Those blue eyes had followed her every movement from the moment she stood up on the bus. One look at Adina left Carson weak in the knees and short of breath; he couldn't believe that she was finally there. He met her at the stairs of the bus and held out his hand to help her down the steps. Not watching her own step, but instead captivated by Carson's intense stare, she tripped, dropping her purse, and nearly falling face first onto the pavement, but Carson was there to catch her. As he caught her, he held her tightly and whispered in her ear, "I will never let you fall. You are even more beautiful than your picture!" and then he kissed her cheek. At that moment, Adina was at a complete loss for words, being so embarrassed that her first encounter with Carson made her appear so clumsy. In an effort to get past the tripping episode and make Adina feel more comfortable, Carson changed the subject.

"You must be hungry!"

"I am starving. I haven't really eaten much since I left home three days ago."

He handed her the bouquet of roses, and Adina took them and inhaled the lovely fragrance.

"They're beautiful - But I was only expecting one."

"I know", said Carson, "but one just didn't seem enough. A dozen seemed much better. I got a little nervous when everyone else got off the bus except for you. I thought for a moment that you may have changed your mind, but I am so glad you didn't. Uhh, which ones are your bags?" Adina pointed to her one small suitcase and the wooden box that held her sewing machine. "You didn't bring much, did you?"

"Well, I didn't have much, but I brought my sewing machine. I can sew all of my own clothes you know." Carson smiled as he watched the words come out of her mouth, but heard nothing that she said. He was enamored by her adorable accent, as if he needed one more thing to love about her. The first time they ever spoke was when Adina called him from Arizona, and at that time, he didn't notice her captivating southern tone. He continued asking her questions just so he could hear her talk, all the while watching her lovely mouth move and the expression in her eyes. He paused for a moment and had to look away, as his heart skipped a beat merely by being in her presence. He took a deep breath and began telling her that she would be staying at the Admiral's home for a few nights, and then they would be married on Saturday. "Jillian, the Admiral's wife can't wait to meet you; I've told her all about you." Adina smiled at him, and thought to herself, "Hope she's not disappointed."

The house where she was staying was within walking distance of the bus station. Carson carried

Adina's bags, and they made small talk with one another until they arrived at the home of Admiral Wesley Bryant. He and his wife, Jillian, had lived there for the past twenty-five years. As they walked into the house, Adina was met by the aroma of something wonderful cooking. Jillian excitedly came out to welcome Adina, and give her a big hug.

"Oh my goodness, you are so young. How old are you?" Adina told her that she was seventeen. "Well sweetheart, I wasn't much older than that when I married the Admiral, and look at us today. Everything's gonna be just fine. I'm sorry, here I am rambling on, and you look famished and tired. Come with me!"

Jillian grabbed her two bags and walked Adina up the stairs to the room where she would be staying until her wedding. She told her to freshen up and then come down for dinner. Back downstairs, Jillian began gushing to Carson about how sweet and beautiful Adina was. She then began counseling Carson that he needed to be extremely kind and gentle with her.

"Carson, you're older than she is, and everything for her is new. She's probably feeling a little overwhelmed."

"I know. Jillian. I'll be gentle."

"Of course you will, honey. She doesn't know yet what a catch you are. She's a very lucky girl."

Adina changed out of her suit into a turquoise dress that she had sewn. This dress that matched her eyes, along with her always great, go-to pearls and cream pumps, unfailingly made her feel good about herself. To her new acquaintances, her entrance into the room revealed her overwhelmingly stunning beauty. Carson couldn't believe that Adina was finally here, and almost his.

"Adina, honey, what a beautiful dress. You come sit over here, across from Carson."

The four of them sat down at the dinner table; Carson being thrilled to be sitting right across from Adina, giving him an excuse to stare at her. Adina, on the other hand, had never seen such a beautiful room filled with such elegant furniture. The dark walnut table was covered with a white lace cloth, and the fine china was brilliant white and gold. It was obvious that Jillian and the Admiral entertained many high-ranking officials. From the corner of her eye she could see the cook standing at the kitchen door, overseeing the two servants as they brought out roasted duck, mashed potatoes, and peas with pearl onions, and even served perfectly sized portions onto her plate. The smell of the yeast rolls filled the house, and when they were brought out, they were still steaming. Adina was so hungry, that she wanted nothing more than to put her face in the plate of food and scarf it up like a dog, but thankfully was able to contain herself. The Admiral thanked the Lord for the food, and then they all began to eat. Adina was careful to watch the manner in which Jillian ate her food, so that she wouldn't appear ignorant of proper eating protocol. At her first bite of the roasted duck, she took a deep breath and closed her eyes at the pure joy of the delicious food. The meal was finished off with fresh blueberry pie and homemade vanilla ice cream which was the Admiral's favorite.

Afterwards, the Admiral and Jillian excused themselves, and Carson walked Adina out onto the back porch that overlooked the Pacific Ocean. She was thinking that this was probably the first time in her life, that she didn't have to clear off the dinner table and clean up the dishes. Looking out over the water, Adina fell even more in love with the ocean. As she stood there with her eyes closed, feeling the cool breeze hit her face, Carson asked her what she was thinking about.

"I love it here already. No matter where we end up living, I hope it can always be by the ocean. I feel like for the first time in my life, I can breathe. The ocean is exactly like you described." In their letters back and forth to one another, she had asked Carson to describe the sea to her. Like all of his other correspondences, he also brought romance to his description of the ocean. Adina believed that he could make a brown paper sack romantic; he had the gift of bringing words alive with his zeal.

Carson was so thrilled that she already loved it there. It was obvious, even after a few moments together, that there was a fire and passion between them that had been developing through their letters, but came to realization at that very moment. They sat for hours talking, simply enjoying one another's company. Adina told him about her venture in the car on the way from Texas, and even though it was not the best situation, she had made a new friend in Edith Irene. She continued talking, more than she normally ever would, switching from one subject to another. Carson just enjoyed listening

67

to her, and drinking in every word she spoke. Adina had a tendency to talk a lot, especially when she was nervous. He just sat listening and staring at her, which didn't really help with her continuous babbling.

Carson's heart began beating so fast, that he felt as though he might explode.

Without warning, he interrupted and said, "Please forgive me!"

"Forgive you for what, Carson?"

"I just can't take my eyes off of you, and I can't help it. I'm not trying to make you feel uncomfortable. I'm sorry."

Adina looked at him with a huge grin.

"No one has ever apologized for staring at me, and don't worry, I do feel comfortable with you. I'm just a little nervous. When I get nervous, I tend to talk too much, but I'm truly happy to be here with you, Carson."

He was so filled with emotion at her words; just the fact that she wanted to be there made him so happy. He gently took hold of her hand and caressed it, bringing it up to his face, and turning her palm to his mouth. He began kissing her fingers and then stroking her arm with his opened mouth.

"I love your smell! The letters that you wrote to me had your scent on them. You may think I'm crazy, Adina, but I kept your letters tucked in my pillowcase. Your fragrance was the last thing I smelled before going to sleep and the essence of my morning. I've been looking forward to the day that I could touch your skin, and breathe in your fragrance, and here you are!"

As he continued to lightly send kisses up her arm, inhaling deeply her scent of vanilla and ginger, he shifted closer to her, gazing at her with his crystal blue eyes. "I have waited for you my entire life. Honestly, I was starting to feel like I would never find you, and then I saw your picture in your father's truck. I'm not normally so sentimental, but when I saw your picture, I knew." He began stammering and felt that he had no more air left to speak. "I, I just knew that you were the one."

He began laughing at himself, shaking his head, "Seriously, I'm generally a very level headed person who wouldn't fall in love with a photograph, but I did. Actually, it wasn't something that I merely felt in my heart, but it came from a place much deeper, I felt it in my soul. I have never felt this way in my entire life. Until you, Adina, my soul within me was dormant. But now, I feel completely alive, almost as if I've been walking around not realizing that half of me was missing, that is until I found you. You make me feel alive." Hoping not to scare her away with all of his irrational talk, he continued pouring out his heart to her. "Please don't think me foolish to talk about such feelings of intimacy, I'm just being honest with you. I realize that there's still so much that we don't understand about one another, and all that we do feel, are just bits and pieces from our letters. But you must know that there has not been one second that's gone by that I haven't thought about you. I don't know exactly how you feel, I can only speak for myself. *I am willing to spend the rest of my life getting to know every part of you.* I guess what I'm trying to say, is that I hope you feel the same way. At the prospect of sounding like a total loon, even before I saw your picture, I knew, I knew."

Carson struggled to find the right words, and then Adina looked at him in a confused manner. "You knew what, Carson?"

"I just can't wait to marry you, that's all. I can't wait for you to be mine."

Adina sat speechless as no one had ever spoken to her like this before.

He stared at her intensely with tears in his eyes. "Adina, after coming here, after seeing me, do you still want to marry me?" He then said something that she didn't expect, as all she had ever known as an example of what a man should be, or say, was her father.

"I don't want you to feel like you have to marry me if you wouldn't be happy. I want you to be happy, and I promise that I will spend the rest of my life making you happy. Everything I have, everything I am, is yours. My love for you will always be a bouquet, not just one flower."

His beautiful blue eyes and the love that poured up from his heart through his words made Adina fall from *like* into *love* with Carson. She couldn't help but notice how much more attractive he was in real life than in his photo. The more he spoke, the more attractive he became. She kept remembering how warm and soft his lips felt on her skin, she looked forward to kissing him. She raised her hands up and held his face, which seemed to conform to every crevice of her hands.

Their eyes, staring into one another's, "I do want to marry you, Carson, and it's also my desire to make you happy. I just hope that I can."

He took her hands from his face and cupped them in his own. His mouth moved so close to hers, yet they didn't touch. Instead, Carson moved his mouth to her ear, skimming her face with his lips and whispered, "Please let me kiss you."

Carson presumed nothing. Adina hadn't known anyone in her life that would first ask for permission to kiss her, and this measure of consideration was intoxicating. He was completely gentle, and overwhelmingly concerned about making her feel at ease. She moved a step closer to him, and he tenderly held her face in his hands. "Yes, always, yes!" With her earnest consent, Carson kissed his beautiful Adina for the first time. Feeling warm and bewitched by the taste of his lips on her skin, she closed her eyes so not to miss even one detail of his lips. When she once again opened her eyes, his glare was so intense that she felt as though he could see right through her.

His hand slowly moved from her face, and began caressing her shoulders, then skimming every curve of her body. Feeling as though a Pandora's Box had been unlocked, her kiss being the key, Carson lost complete control, and pulled her feverishly into himself. He began kissing her lips, her cheeks, her eyes, then he let out a heavy sigh, moved his face away, and took a step back only staring at the wood planks on the porch floor.

"Adina, I'm so sorry! I have waited my whole life to be with you. I can wait a little longer." He then laughed quietly and said, "Well, at least until Saturday."

Adina smiled, and gave Carson one last kiss. "Until Saturday then."

Carson knew that Adina was tired, and needed a good night's sleep. "I think it's time you went to bed, young lady." They stood up, and he embraced her, pulling her body to his. For that one moment, Adina couldn't tell where his body ended and hers began. His muscular arms and the warmth of his touch made her, for the first time in her life, feel safe. He took her hand, and walked her up the stairs to her room.

"Goodnight, my beautiful Adina."

'Good night, Carson. Thank you!"

"For what?"

"For choosing me."

Adina closed her bedroom door, and leaning against it, slid like a rag doll onto the floor, staring straight ahead. The window on the other side of the room faced the water, and the moist ocean breeze felt incredible as it filled the room with the fragrance of salted spice. With a heavy sigh, and a rather ill sensation in her stomach, she wondered if she was getting sick, or if this was simply what love felt like. It was a very odd commotion of feelings, but in a good way; this marvel of unleashed senses in the pit of her stomach was both sweet and agonizing all at the same time, a once in a lifetime thrill that she had never experienced until now. She had been infatuated before, but Carson wasn't like the boys at home. He was a man, a truly wonderful man. Even though uncomfortable, she felt incredibly blessed and hopeful about her future, and couldn't help but smile every time she thought of him.

She hadn't really noticed earlier, but this ocean view guest room was absolutely lovely. Like the rest of the house, the floor was a deep rich brown wood, covered with a large Persian rug in deep red and gold. The down comforter on the bed was pale yellow with navy blue pinstripes. All of the furniture was rich with dark hues, and covered in gold and cream tapestry. Jillian definitely had a liking for the nautical flare. It was perfect! Adina felt as though she was smack dab in the middle of a fairytale, and this room was her own private chamber in a castle. Truly, she had never seen such extraordinary furnishings, except maybe in a movie.

Suddenly it occurred to her that this would be the first time she slept in a bed alone without her sisters. Sadness fell upon her as she thought about her family and how they hated her for leaving. By the time she walked out the door to leave for the bus station, not one of them except Wil, said goodbye. She was grieved that no one that she knew or loved would be at her wedding. Her father wouldn't be giving her away, her mother wouldn't be helping her get ready, her sisters wouldn't be walking down the aisle with her, and her brothers wouldn't be standing with Carson. Instead of feeling gloriously happy like a bride should, Adina laid on the bed and cried herself to sleep.

The unfamiliar sounds of seagulls cawing and powerful waves battering the rocks woke Adina from a deep and much needed sleep. As she sat up, she was delighted by the gentle ocean breeze that wafted through her room. The tranquil beach noises that she already loved, along with the wonderful aroma of coffee brewing downstairs, reminded her that she was not in Texas anymore. Feeling a bit foggy, she laid back down for a few more minutes of rest. Images of Carson ran through her mind, and she couldn't help but smile, thinking about their time together last night. It was hard to believe that in two days she would marry him, a man she hardly knew, and start a life that was completely different than anything she had ever known. She was ready though. She would always miss her family, but would never miss her situation there.

Rest became impossible as her mind went crazy thinking about the wedding, knowing that there was probably so much to get done. Generally it's the bride who plans and prepares for her wedding. The only thing that Adina had prepared for her wedding day, was her gown.

A few months back, when Adina's mother was home and having a *good* day (which didn't happen very often), Molly unlocked her cedar hope chest that Ray had purchased for her the day they got engaged, and pulled out a large wooden box. Within the aged container, wrapped in tissue paper, was the wedding dress that Molly wore when she married Ray. She handed the box to Adina and told her that this was now her dress to wear when she got married. Molly had no idea that giving Adina the dress was a slight prediction of a time very soon to come. Quite honestly, Molly had no intentions of letting Adina leave, as her absence would only force her to take on the parenting role that she had shrewdly avoided for years.

Adina appreciated the dress, but could instantly envision changes and alterations that would need to be made. She loved the fabric, but the style was sorely outdated, and assumed several weathered stains. It promptly developed into a most significant project to remake this long-sleeved ivory satin dress that her mother wore in 1918. The ingenious feat began by taking straight pins, and attaching the dress onto her wall so that she could analyze every inch, and create a well thought out pattern, and plan of action. Not having a dress form was

77

very inconvenient, but her lack of proper tools only spurred her creativity. She dreamed of the day that she would have the basics that every seamstress should possess; perhaps even a room used strictly for sewing. Night after night as her sisters slept, she would sit on the floor sizing up the long-sleeved, simple neckline, full-skirted wedding dress that hung on her wall. Once a complete idea was formulated, she began to draw a sketch of how she envisioned the finished gown to be. Adina had an eye for simple straight-lined fashion, so the full skirt would have to go. Her sketch showed a plunging V-neckline that would be fitted on the bodice and the hips. The bottom of the dress had a flowing tulip shape that barely skimmed the floor in the front, but had a short train in the back. The entire dress would be made of the original satin, *minus the stains*. The straps over the shoulder were made from the original lace, which would also overlay the rest of the satin. She made a pattern out of flour sack fabric, instead of her usual patterns made of newspaper, not wanting to risk getting any ink on the satin.

Over the next several months, Adina carefully cut apart the seams of her mother's dress. She re-cut and remade every inch of the outdated garment, taking her time to make it perfect. There were times while working on it that she wondered what it was all for, assuming that she would probably never get married. She couldn't even fathom falling in love, let alone finding someone around Belin, Texas that she wanted to marry. After watching her mother and father, she decided that she would rather be single till the end of time than marry the wrong person.

She worked on the dress for many hours, mostly at night when everyone was asleep. Once it was completed, she pinned the finished product to her wall once again, and sat on the bed admiring her work. This sleek and form-fitting dress with its plunging neckline would show off Adina's lovely and voluptuous figure that most commonly hid beneath plain dresses. She was so excited at the thought of one day wearing it at her own wedding. It turned out even better than she even imagined it would. She often found herself lost in daydreams, visualizing herself walking down the aisle in her elegant one-of-a-kind. She even had a picture in her mind of what her veil would look like; simple but elegant made of tulle that would drape down only to her chin line and be pinned in the back of her pulled-back hair with a comb. Of course, to finish it off, she would sew on tiny individual pearls that would complement her grandmother's pearls. Even though her mother would not appreciate the remake, she knew that if her grandmother were still here, that she would absolutely love it, and would be thrilled that her little Singer mastered such a work of art. It was only *because* of her grandmother that she learned to sew, and for that matter accomplished or held anything of value.

She made sure to also sketch out a picture of the veil, even though this part of the ensemble would have to wait until later. Knowing better than to show her mother how she had remade the dress (aware that she would probably be upset for not keeping it as it was), she tucked the vision of her veil and the dress back into the wooden box, and slid it under her bed until the day she would need it.

Placing her suitcase on a stand at the end of the bed, she began to unpack the few items that she brought with her. Situated on the very top of her things, wrapped in a silk pouch that she had made from the extra fabric, was her elegant wedding gown. Pulling a fabric covered hanger from the closet, she gently positioned her dress on the back of the closet door. Just then, she heard a knock, it was Jillian.

"Come in!"

"Good morning, Adina, how did you sleep?"

"I slept very well! I think the combination of your delicious dinner and the ocean breeze helped me to sleep better than I have in a very long time." Jillian glanced over at Adina's dress hanging on the door, and her mouth fell open.

"Good Lord, Adina. That is….well, that is the most beautiful wedding dress I have ever seen! Where did you get it?"

"Well actually, I made it! I mean, I remade it from my mother's old wedding dress."

"You must be joking! Are you sure that you're only seventeen years old? I am truly amazed at this dress. You are a wonder for sure."

Adina smiled, as she honestly felt much older than seventeen. Her life experiences had made her older than her years.

"Well, Jillian, I've always been a bit of an old soul. I used to sit for hours helping my grandmother sew, and watched and learned from her. When she died, she left me her sewing machine, and I've used it ever since."

"Well honey, that is a wonderful gift to have."

Jillian then told Adina that she had been helping Carson with the wedding arrangements, and that she would like to help Adina get herself ready for the wedding and, of course, for the honeymoon.

"Honeymoon? We're going on a honeymoon?"

"Why yes, honey. The Admiral called in a few favors and got you and Carson a cozy little bungalow right down on the sand for a few days. Usually, these bungalows are reserved only for high ranking officers and visiting officials, and only they are allowed to stay there. But Carson is like a son to us, and well, we wanted to do this for him and for you."

Adina really didn't expect a wedding ceremony that would require anyone to have to bother with planning arrangements, or a honeymoon for that matter. She figured that they would probably just go before the Justice of the Peace, or something very small and simple. Upon hearing all of this new information, she got a panicked look on her face that Jillian recognized immediately. Adina threw herself onto the bed.

"What's wrong, honey?" said Jillian.

"I….I only have my dress. I don't have even a bathing suit or beach clothes. And I haven't had any time to make a veil."

Jillian looked at her with eyes of compassion and a big grin on her face. "Well, that's why I am here! I'm going to help you get ready. My people are from the south, so while you are here, and even though we're in California, I'm going to smother you with some real southern hospitality, whether you want it or not."

"Thank you, Jillian!" It was as if her new friend knew exactly how she felt and exactly what she needed.

The Admiral and his nurturing wife knew that this would be a huge transition for Adina, and when they heard her crying through the night, he told Jillian to do whatever she needed to do to help the girl realize that she wasn't alone in all this wedding business. Adina felt so blessed to have someone care about her, and of course Jillian was thrilled to have a mission. Adina quickly found out that when the Admiral's wife was involved, "simple" was out of the question.

At breakfast, Adina was amazed at a new kind of concoction that was being prepared before her very eyes. Something wonderful, called an omelet. Of course she had eaten eggs before, but never made like this. She watched in wonder as Jillian shredded, sliced, and diced mushrooms, peppers, and cheese and then stuffed them into an egg pancake. She decided that this was her new favorite.

When they were finished eating, Jillian asked if she was ready to go shopping for her trousseau. Adina wasn't exactly sure what a trousseau might be, but whatever it was, she knew that the small amount of money she had left over would probably not be enough to cover the cost.

"That's ok, sugar. Carson will take good care of you. He gave me money, and said he wants you to get whatever you need. If we spend all of his cash, I've got a stash of mad money that I've been saving for such an occasion. This will be the perfect opportunity for me too. I need a dress for your big day; the Admiral will be wearing his dress blues, and he can't be more handsome than me."

Adina loved how Jillian laughed at herself, and her laugh was contagious. Even if what she said wasn't very funny, her laugh was so joyful that it made Adina want to laugh too.

"Now go get yourself ready. We've got a big day ahead."

Adina ran upstairs and slipped on her navy blue pants, and a white sleeveless turtleneck sweater. She pulled her hair back in a ponytail, put on some flat slip-on shoes, and she was ready to go. She didn't realize it about herself, but she was one of those people that always got a second look because one wasn't enough. As she came downstairs, Jillian told her that she could put on a gunny sack and look like a million bucks.

"No wonder that boy is so head over heels in love with you!" It always shocked Adina to hear people say such things, as she never felt very beautiful at all.

Their first stop of the day was to find all of the makings for Adina's veil. Adina knew exactly what she wanted, because she had envisioned it when she made her dress. She picked out some French silk tulle and miniature pearls. Next, they made their way to Mackenzie's to buy her some clothes. She had never really picked out ready-made clothes before, so she stood in the middle of the store not knowing where to begin.

Jillian coached her through the process. "Ok, let's think about what you're going to need! You'll want a

bathing suit, some beach clothes, and what about a
negligee for the wedding night?"

Adina was initially embarrassed over the idea, but
then wholeheartedly agreed. "Yes, I suppose Carson
would appreciate that."

"Oh believe me honey, Carson will definitely
appreciate it."

So, they spent the next three hours picking out
new clothes and a beautiful white sheer gown for the
wedding night.

For the next few days, Adina and Jillian spent
practically every waking moment together, not only
taking care of last minute arrangements for the wedding,
but having deep-seated discussions about their past,
present, and future lives. The hours were filled with many
tears, but mostly laughter. When their talks began to get
too heavy, Jillian would immediately bring up silly
anecdotes on how to keep your man happy, do's and
don'ts, and her personal ideas and secrets about marital
success.

"You know, the Admiral may be a powerful man
in his profession, but when he gets home, he's mine.

Even though we've been married for 27 years, I make sure I keep that fire alive. Call me a romantic, but I say we get you a few more little nighties. If you *feel* sexy, you'll be sexy."

The thought of actually having sex made Adina very nervous, but somehow the way that Jillian talked about it being a normal blessing and privilege of marriage, put her at ease, making her feel that in time everything would fall into place.

They finished their last day together before the big day, by going and getting their nails done. That evening they gave each other pedicures, and used all sorts of facial masks and beauty treatments while drinking champagne and eating chocolate on the back porch. Adina loved Jillian's attitude towards life. She had been a Navy wife since she was a young girl, and she knew how Adina felt. Her final and most powerful word of advice for Adina, was that nothing is ever so bad that champagne and chocolate won't fix it.

Chapter 4

The Wedding

The day of the wedding had quickly come. Two
days to prepare for such an event was unthinkable, but
Adina had loved these few days with Jillian; at this point,
they were the best of her life. Only because of Jillian did
Adina feel ready for this day, well as ready as she would
ever be. She sat up in bed, and wondered where she
should start. She felt a little hungover and slightly
nauseous from all of the chocolate and champagne. As
she was lying there, she began to panic when she realized
that she didn't have a ring for Carson. She felt horrible,
like she was the worst person, coming to this place to
marry him, completely unprepared. There was no way
she would ask Jillian for one more thing, but she had no
idea what she would do. She could sew just about
anything, but her creative skills couldn't make a ring out
of nothing.

Jillian busted through the door and plopped
herself on the bed. "Happy Wedding Day!"

Jillian was old enough to be Adina's mother, but she didn't seem old. She was more like what a sister or best friend would be. She had figured out even after knowing Adina for such a short amount of time that she wore her feelings on her sleeve. It was obvious from the moment she walked into the room, that something heavy was weighing on her mind. Jillian was a fixer, and was not going to allow anything to ruin this day for the bride.

"What's wrong, honey?"

"Nothing, I'm fine."

"We've come this far and covered a lot of bases in just a few days. You better tell me what's wrong before those worry lines become permanent. No one wants to see a bride with worry lines all over her face!"

Adina fell back on her pillow not wanting to burden Jillian with one more thing. "I don't have a ring for Carson."

Jillian smiled, "I have a ring you can give him. It belonged to my father."

"I can't take your father's ring. That should go to your kids or someone in your family."

89

"Adina, the Admiral and I were never blessed with children. This time I have spent with you has felt like how I imagined it would have been to have a daughter. I don't have anyone to leave the ring to; I want you to have it to give to Carson. We think of him as a son, and there is no one that we would rather give it to."

Jillian bounced off of the bed, and told Adina that she would be right back, and then raced with excitement out of the room. Adina still felt as though none of this was real. In her entire life, no one had treated her as special as she had felt these past few days. It was like being in another world that she didn't even know existed. When Jillian came back into the room, she was holding a small green velvet box rimmed in gold.

"My father was a wonderful man who loved his wife and loved his family. Carson is such a man! He truly is special, and like my father, will cherish you, and love his family. I know that you just arrived here and are even now getting to know Carson, but Adina, he loves you and will always take care of you. You deserve one another. Carson has had many opportunities to date many girls, but he always told us that only one girl would do. For so long we didn't think there was such a girl, until you. The day he arrived home after seeing your photo, he told us that he had found the girl he was going to marry, and that girl was you."

Jillian's depiction of Carson made Adina's heart beat so fast, that she became dizzy, and had to lay down with her feet propped up.

"Jillian, I can't breathe!"

"Sure you can, honey. If you can talk, it means you're breathing! You're just a little nervous, and that's ok. If you weren't, there'd be something wrong with you."

Jillian began lightly combing her fingers through Adina's hair. "You feelin a little better now?"

Adina inhaled deeply, "Yes, thank you Jillian!"

"Ok, now sit up honey!"

She handed Adina the box and smiled. Adina opened the box and just stared at the ring without saying a word. She pulled out the heavy gold band that was embellished with two gold cords that crossed in the center. At the crossing point was a sizable diamond.

"I love it, it's perfect. Thank you so much." Adina looked at her new dear friend Jillian and asked, "How can I ever repay you for all that you have done for me?"

Jillian smiled, "Well, I am glad you asked. I can't do a thing with my hair, and I hate going to the beauty shop by myself, all those gossipy women. Come with me, and let's get our hair done."

Adina looked at her, not expecting that to be her response to the question of how she could pay *her* back. No one had ever pampered her the way that Jillian had, but she highly enjoyed every moment of it.

As they sat together getting their hair done, Adina thought to herself, "Another first." Her days here had been filled with new and amazing experiences. It was as if someone finally switched on a life that had once been dark.

After an hour in the chair, and a final coat of hairspray, Adina looked at herself in the mirror with her hair in an up do, somewhat resembling a movie star. She couldn't believe how beautiful it was, and how much older she looked. She looked like a woman, not a girl. Her hair was gently pulled back off her face with large waves of curls forming a low bun.

"This will be perfect with my veil."

Jillian grabbed her hand and said, "We better get going. You're going to be late to your own wedding if we don't get moving."

When they returned home and ran through the front door, Adina hurried upstairs, but stopped in her tracks as she saw herself in the long mirror at the top of the stairs. For the hundredth time she had to remind herself that this was all real. She stood in front of her dress, and began carefully slipping it off of the hanger. The dress lay perfectly smooth as it fell over her new corset and silk stockings that Jillian insisted that she must have. The dress fit like a glove, and Adina looked beautiful in it. The ivory satin and lace next to her ivory skin was a stunning combination. Jillian helped her to pin on her veil and close the clasp on her pearls, then stood back tilting her head and holding her chin.

In a bothered tone she said, "It's almost perfect, but you're missing something!"

"What?" asked Adina, feeling a bit insecure.

Jillian handed her a small box with a card attached that she had been holding behind her back that read:

"Adina, in only a few hours you will be mine. I am the happiest man on the face of the earth. You are more valuable to me than precious stones, but I got you pearls because I know that you like them the best. I will see you in a little while, my love. Carson   P.S. This is your "something new."

Adina opened the box and saw two beautiful pearl earrings that matched her grandmother's strand of pearls. "Oh my, how thoughtful. I love them!"

After Adina put on her new earrings from Carson, Jillian handed her yet another box. "This one is from me, something blue." Adina opened the box, and inside was a cluster ring made of aquamarine stones and pearls. "Aquamarine is the March stone. Since you're getting married in March, it's only appropriate for your blue to be aquamarine; and the Admiral and I heard from a little birdie how you love pearls."

Adina slipped it on her right ring finger, and it fit perfectly. It was a thing of beauty. She gave Jillian a huge hug and said, "I will forever cherish this. Thank you so much!"

"And finally, something borrowed!" Jillian took out a small satin box that held a very rare and expensive bottle of gardenia perfume which the Admiral picked up while in Hawaii. She dabbed one drop behind each of Adina's ears, and also on each of her wrists. "There, you're perfect. A vision!"

Just then, the Admiral came in dressed in his highly decorated dress blues. When he entered, his eye looked first at his precious Jillian, and he said, "Jils, you're a sight to behold," and he kissed her. "You ladies ready to go? Adina, you are a sight to behold. I hope the boy doesn't faint when he sees you."

"Thank you, Admiral. Thank you both for everything! There are truly no words that I can say to thank you for all that you've done."

Just then, there was a knock at the front door, the Admiral answered it, and there stood a young man standing at attention, and then quickly saluted. "Your car is here, sir!"

"Well, ladies, let's go!" the Admiral said with authority.

As Adina walked down the steps, she was shocked to see something that she had never seen before. It was no regular car waiting to take her to the church, but a beautiful shiny black limousine with white wall tires. She could tell that this was a common occurrence for the Admiral and Jillian, but as far as she was concerned, it might as well be a glass carriage that was once a pumpkin.

"This has to be a dream!"

"Did you say something, honey?"

"No, I just....."

Adina couldn't seem to find any words to explain how she felt. She was in complete awe over everything that had happened, and was so filled with emotion, that the tears streaming down her face became her words. Jillian quickly grabbed a handkerchief out of her purse and handed it to Adina, then simply squeezed her hand, not saying a word. When the car arrived at the church, Adina didn't see one person standing in front of the lovely white wood building. The Church was surrounded by tall black wrought iron fencing, with a single gateway that was grand in stature. The doorway led to a cobblestone courtyard, centered around an ancient-looking water fountain that sat like an ornament in the middle of the yard. As Adina looked ahead, she saw two very large wooden whitewashed doors with huge wrought iron hinges and handles.

She and the Admiral walked up to the doors, and right then, the church bells began tolling in the steeple above. He took her arm and led her towards the door.

Adina stopped and made a request of this stately gentleman that was standing by her side. "Admiral, I know that I am not your daughter, but would you please walk me down the aisle?"

The Admiral's eyes teared up, " I would be honored, sweetheart. Thank you for asking me."

Just then Jillian walked over and handed Adina a bouquet of white roses tipped in red, then embraced her and whispered words of gratitude. "Thank you, honey. You have given the Admiral an experience that we both thought he would never have."

Adina grabbed tightly to the Admiral's arm as they headed towards the two double doors that led into the sanctuary. Together they stood beneath the rustic threshold, waiting for the grand reveal. As the doors began to swing open, she squeezed his arm and took a deep breath.

He looked at her with an expression of calm assurance. "You can do this, honey. Piece of cake!"

Adina was so glad to have a strong arm to lean on, but she was especially glad that she was not walking down the aisle alone. As the Wedding March began to play, the doors opened, and a church full of people stood up, all eyes on Adina. Her beauty mesmerized the crowd.

She, on the other hand, was taken aback by the remarkable room. It glowed from the countless candles, mixed with the afternoon sun that was shining through the mossy green and white stained glass window at the front of the sanctuary. There were three beautiful brass and crystal chandeliers that hung above the main aisle. They were crowned with white candles that illuminated the sweeping ceilings that were adorned with white washed beams running from one end to the other. The soft green glow from the stained glass window onto the cobblestone floor combined with the warm illumination of the candles created a nature-like atmosphere. It was like being outside rather than in a building. It was so beautiful, and Adina couldn't believe that all of this was for her.

As she looked around at the attendees, she noticed a sea of navy blue and white uniforms standing at attention for the bride, who was soon to be one of their own. The many faces that were staring back, looked at her as if they knew her. She had no idea that she had been the main topic of Carson's conversation with each person there. They all knew that this was the girl he fell in love with from the moment he saw her photo in Ray's truck.

Carson was madly in love with Adina, and everyone in the room knew it. Especially the Admiral and Jillian, who had sat with Carson many late nights listening to him read the letters from her. With each passing day, they could see that this young man, who had been so reluctant and picky with girls in the past, had fallen head over heels for a girl from Texas. Just as Carson came to know Adina through her letters, so also the Admiral and Jillian had come to know and love her long before they met her. Many times Jillian was a bit sad in hearing Adina talk about her home life, and couldn't wait until she arrived. She had been waiting months to finally spoil that girl! All of the planning that went into her arrival, and the preparations for the wedding, was all Jillian. Like a doting mother, she had poured everything into preparing for this moment.

There was only one couple in the room that stood out from among everyone else. They were sitting on the left side of the church, and seemed to be sizing Adina up as she walked down the aisle. Both of them made her feel terribly uncomfortable. The Admiral felt Adina fidget and knew immediately who the cause of it was.

He pulled her in closer and filled her in on the two solemn faces. "Ignore those two idiots. Jils told them the wedding was tomorrow. I guess they figured it out though."

Adina laughed softly. She would later find out that these two were Carson's mother and father, Reverend and Mrs. York. Bill York was a Baptist minister, and Barb was a stay-at-home supportive wife who obviously wasn't very happy that her Carson was marrying a girl from Texas. When Adina found out that Carson's father was a Baptist minister, it totally made sense to her as to why Ray liked him so much. Ray was a Baptist through and through, even though he never attended church and drank like a fish. He would stand on that Baptist soapbox until his last breath.

Adina looked away from this couple, and focused on Carson's friends in blue, refusing to let those two ruin this beautiful day. She was excited that Carson had so many friends; so many people who cared about him. Her hope was that his friends would soon be her friends as well.

Later, Adina said that she felt as though she lived her life backwards. She had parent responsibilities before she was even old enough to be a bride, and then her life truly began the moment she laid eyes on Carson.

Adina's gaze shifted from the room and the people, to her soon-to-be husband waiting for her at the end of the aisle. Likewise, Carson's regard had been on Adina since the moment the doors opened. His eyes never left her. As she walked up to meet him, and their hands touched, it took every ounce of self-control for him not to not take her at once and hold her in his arms. He had dreamed of this moment many times, but finally, today his dreams were coming true.

His mouth moved towards her ear and he whispered something that she would never forget.

"I hope everyone lives through the ceremony!"

"What? What do you mean?" Adina suddenly had a worried look on her face.

"Well you see my love, all of the air in the room is gone.... you have taken everyone's breath away, including mine."

With that one comment, she could feel blood rushing up to her face, and wondered if everyone could tell how nervous she was.

He looked with intensity into her eyes.

"Adina, you are gorgeous!"

If he was trying to sweep her off of her feet, it was working.

One after the other, they took their vows, carefully repeating the words of the pastor. Everything in the room seemed to disappear except Carson and Adina; it was a completely surreal and romantic moment for them both. As Adina was saying her vows and looking into Carson's eyes, she became distracted and enamored by this handsome man in his dress blues who was going to be her husband. Feelings of uncontrollable passion began to rise up in her; feelings that she had never felt before. A week ago she was a seventeen-year-old girl who lived in "Nowhere, Texas" and today she was in this beautiful place by the ocean, marrying a man who loved her. She really didn't know why he loved her. No one had ever loved her like this.

She placed the ring on his finger, and he looked very pleased, as he was not expecting such an incredible token of her affection.

He looked at it and then at her. "It's perfect!"

She was so happy that he liked it, and again so thankful for Jillian's generosity and kindness. Then the time came to place the ring on her finger. Adina didn't think about what he might get her, but to her surprise, he placed a single emerald-shaped diamond ring on her finger that was also perfect, and far more than she would have ever expected. Their gazes never left one another the entire time.

After all of the vows were sealed and official, and upon hearing, "Carson, you may kiss your bride," he placed one hand gently on the back of Adina's neck, the other around her waist, and pulled her to himself. With this complete kiss of passion, bodies coming together, they had finally stepped into a coveted season of uninhibited privilege .

"Ladies and gentlemen, I would like to introduce you all to Mr. and Mrs. Carson York."

The happy couple joyously walked down the cobblestone aisle, and were ushered into a small room with a stained glass window that extended from floor to ceiling.

Adina looked up at her husband with tears in her eyes and said, "I am in awe of how beautiful - I mean this whole thing - and I had no idea - thank you Carson!"

"Adina, I love you. Please know, I would do anything for you. You deserved all of this, and you deserve a life filled with happiness. I promise to make you happy."

"I am happy, sailor, and I love you too!

Chapter 5

A New Life

As the chauffeur drove them down the steep and curvy road that led to the honeymoon bungalow, Adina laid her head back on the seat and closed her eyes. Carson turned her face toward him and kissed her gently on the lips, and then followed her chin line down to her neck where he began to kiss her. She kept her head laid back and just let him. His lips on her skin felt incredible, and was like music to her soul.

"Here we are," said the driver. "Let me help you two with your bags. I hear there's a big storm comin' tonight. Better stay indoors."

Both Carson and Adina looked at one another grinning as if to say, "We have no problem staying in all night. Let it rain!"

"The kitchen's all stocked up compliments of the Admiral and his missus. Well, you guys have fun. I'll come pick you up on Wednesday around noon."

At that, he was gone, and they were finally alone. Not only were they alone, but now that they belonged to one another, there was nothing to hold either of them back.

Carson set their suitcases in the bedroom. As he looked out the French doors at the setting sun on the glistening ocean, he grabbed Adina's hand and said, "Let's go dance on the beach until the sun goes down."

They both kicked off their shoes, and ran down the sand to the shoreline. Carson held Adina so tightly, that she could feel every curve of his body through his clothes. He looked at her and said, "Mrs. York, may I have this dance? Dance with me until the sun goes down."

There they stood dancing on the shoreline with water flowing over their feet, his pants, her dress, but neither of them cared. The waves and wind along with the wind chimes hanging from the bungalow was their music. Storm clouds began to move in, and Carson, caressing Adina's arms, realized that she was cold. He took off his jacket and wrapped it, along with his arms, around her. She was completely enveloped by his jacket that was still warm from his body heat. He kissed her with a long, sensual kiss, and then swept her up in his arms and carried her back to the bungalow.

A bottle of champagne was chilling on the table by the door. Sitting by the silver champagne bucket were two long-stemmed glasses, both etched in gold, one with the letter "C" and the other with the letter "A." Carson gently lowered her into an oversized leather easy chair that was draped with a brown cashmere blanket. He pulled the champagne out of the ice, and opened the bottle with a loud "pop!" Adina was impressed that he confidently knew how to open a bottle of champagne, as if he had done it a few times before. The other night while she and Jillian were lavishing themselves with chocolate and face masks, she discovered that she truly loved champagne. She was very thankful that sparkling wine was coming, as she was quite nervous, and knew it would help her relax.

As she sat admiring Carson, she was reminded that he was a man who was nine years her elder, and he had in fact lived more life than she had. At this point, with the Navy, he had been almost everywhere in the world, and was extremely knowledgeable about many things. He had been a part of, and seen far more, than she had. Adina immediately began to feel frightened about the whole love and life thing, and that Carson may be expecting something that she didn't know how to do.

He poured her a glass of champagne, which she gulped down and then asked for another. He laughed at how absolutely adorable she was, and how her southern accent got a little stronger with each glass of champagne. Everything about her made him smile, he realized that from this point on, each thing that she would experience was probably for the first time. He was thrilled that all of her "firsts" would be with him.

He could tell that she was nervous, so he squeezed in next to her in the oversized chair, put his arm around her, and just held her. He continued reaffirming to her that everything was ok. "You're safe, Adina. Everything's ok. Don't you know that there is nothing that you could do that would make me love you less?" His words of love and assurance sparked a fire within her that melted away all of her anxiety. There was a new and unfamiliar kind of stimulation that rose up within her, which prompted her to please him in every way. The feeling became more intense as she was enraptured by the fervent heat from his body that seemed to naturally flow freely into her soul. "There's nothing to be afraid of, everything is ok my little Texas girl. Just know that I already love every part of you. You have nothing to be afraid of, we can just sit here for a while....no rush...no hurry." His words put her at ease, and she pulled herself up and sat on his lap facing him. She laid her body on his, sat her elbows on his shoulders, and began brushing her fingers through his hair. Gently, she touched her lips to his, and then without warning began kissing Carson in an amorous and aggressive manner that was both surprising and pleasant to her new husband. He held her tightly against his body, and then stood up. As he stood up, Adina embraced him with her entire body. To move her in even closer, he pushed her back against the wall, passionately kissing her while clasping both hands above her head, holding her captive to the lust that he had held back for so long.

Adina suddenly remembered the white negligee that she picked out especially for this night. "Carson, wait, I have something special for you. I promise you'll like it, and it's worth the wait." He reluctantly sat her down as the burning within him felt as though it was raging out of control. "You cool down now, sailor. I'll be right back."

Carson chuckled at Adina's fitting comment. Letting out a heavy breath. "I'm not going anywhere."

She went into the bathroom and struggled as she tried to get her dress unbuttoned. Jillian had helped her get in the dress, but it looked as though Carson would have to help her get out of it.

She opened the door, and when she did, there stood all six foot two of highly developed Carson standing with his shirt off and belt buckle undone, revealing for the first time to Adina, his marvelous body. She couldn't help but stare at him with wanting eyes, unembarrassed as she beheld the last of his uniform falling to the floor.

Realizing that the bathroom door was open and Adina was watching him, he turned around and began coming towards her. Without even realizing it, Adina began examining every curve of his body with her eyes, and Carson found great pleasure in the longing of her gaze.

"Done already, my beautiful girl?"

For a moment Adina said nothing; it wasn't until Carson said her name again that she answered him.

"Umm, no, no ... I'm sorry, I can't reach my buttons. Can you help me?"

He stood there looking at her with nearly uncontrollable passion, doing nothing to cover himself.

"Come over here, I can help you with that."

She walked over to him and turned around, pulling her hair out of the way. She felt him push his body to her back, and then his hands touching the top of her neck, sending chills down her spine. He ran his fingers down her back as he slowly unbuttoned her dress. Adina would later say that moment alone was one of the most erotic of her life, and that Carson knew how and where to touch her. After unbuttoning her dress, he put his hands through the opening onto her waistline, wanting her so badly that he let out an abandoned groan as he felt her bare skin for the first time.

She turned around whispering in his ear, "I'll be right back."

As the bathroom door closed, he went over to the dresser and lit a cluster of candles that had been left by Jillian, with clear instructions to Carson, which he followed to a T. After lighting each one, he turned off all of the lights, and stood in anticipation, waiting for her to come out. He was going to make love to her like he had so many times in his mind.

As the bathroom door opened, Adina stood in the luminous glow, dressed in a white silk corset with a sheer negligee. Her brown hair was down, her eyes blue like the ocean staring at Carson with a look of total surrender. As she walked over to him, he was spellbound by the beauty of his bride. He never took his eyes off of her; his eyes never closed. Carson didn't want to miss even one of any of Adina's "firsts." His hands slipped her negligee off of her shoulders, and as it fell to the ground, he slipped off the straps of her corset and began to kiss her mouth, her neck, her breasts. "Before this night is over I want to kiss every inch of you."

Adina touched his masculine chest feeling every ripple, every curve of his body. He put his head back with a heavy sigh, finding great pleasure as she touched his body. He picked her up and carried her to the bed looking intently at her, like a lion about to eat his prey, and then without any more hesitation he lunged his body onto hers. He passionately held and kissed her, and then one by one, he unfastened the silk buttons of her corset until her entire body, her beautiful voluptuous body, was uncovered. Carson did exactly what he said he would do. He kissed every part of her body and gently made love to Adina for the rest of the night.

112

For the next three days they fell completely and passionately in love with one another. Each time they made love, it was a new and exciting manifestation filled with intense passion. Carson was an exceptional lover, and even though Adina was a young, inexperienced seventeen-year-old woman, she learned very quickly how to love Carson back and keep him happy just like Jillian had told her that she should.

After the three amazing days at the bungalow, the happy couple went to live in a small house right outside the naval base. The next six months were perfect. Since Carson worked right on the base, he was able come home every night. Adina spent most of her days with Jillian, learning how to cook and keep a house at a whole different level than what she had done in Texas.

One night in late September, Carson came home later than usual and informed her that he, along with the Admiral and a few other men in his special unit, were to be stationed in Germany. They were assigned a special detail that was highly classified which would last for at least a year. He was given the option of either taking Adina with him, or having her stay in Long Beach.

113

Because of all of the conflict occurring with the new Nazi Regime in Germany, Carson was leery of her going.

"I am not staying here without you, Carson," Adina insisted.

He loved when she put her foot down about things as it made her southern accent (which he adored) come alive.

"Ok, my love, I'll let the Admiral know, and he'll make arrangements for you to go. Things are not like they are here though. Hitler is trying to take over the world, and it's ugly. My unit is completing a special mission that, hopefully, will help put a stop to it before it begins."

Things moved very quickly, and it was only one week later that Carson, the Admiral, and his unit left for Germany. For the safety of the mission, and Adina, it was necessary for them to travel separately. She was given a long list of instructions of what she should and should not do while there. The one and most important mandate was not to tell *anyone* that she was a U.S. Navy wife, *and secondly* that her husband was in Germany on a mission of aid and support. She was not even allowed to utter one word to anyone on her travel over. Carson warned her that the entire world was on the brink of war, and even though it would be difficult, she had to remain silent.

"Adina, people are not always what they seem. Watch out especially for those who try to be your friend. Error on the side of caution!"

Adina promised Carson that she would stay silent. She was prepared to set sail one week later, on the SS Meridian Cruise Liner. The SS Meridian was one of the largest luxury cruise liners of the day, and highly seaworthy according to the Admiral. He assured Carson that Adina's passage to Germany would be safe and comfortable.

When the day finally came for her to leave Long Beach and her dear friend Jillian, Adina felt great loss, and couldn't keep herself from grieving. Even with their age differences, they had become the best of friends. Jillian was the mother and friend that Adina never had until now. She had taught her all of the important things that a mother generally would teach her daughter. Leaving Jillian was the hardest thing that she had ever done, it was even more heart wrenching than leaving her family in Texas. They promised one another that they would write as often as possible, and then with the last call from the captain, they said their goodbyes. Jillian stood on the dock and watched as Adina waved goodbye from the deck of the ship. Adina stepped foot onboard with several trunks filled with clothes that would see her through all of the different seasons of the year. Carson knew that this particular part of Germany was generally cool, and most often cold. He had made sure that she had all of the warm clothing that she would need while living there. Because of Adina's affiliation with the Admiral, she would be dining at the Captain's table each night while on the Meridian. When preparing for her voyage, Jillian had helped her shop for several gowns to wear to dinner. Adina would have preferred to make her own formals, but there just wasn't time.

All of Carson and Adina's personal items that they had collected over the last six months of marriage were crated up and sent along with Carson and the Admiral on the USS Jefferson. A German counterpart secured a small cottage in Friedlich where Carson and Adina would live. The cottage sat on the outskirts of the Black Forest in the still-peaceful town of Friedlich.

Adina enjoyed her first cruise, and marked it up to another grand adventure. One of many yet to come with

Carson, but by the time she arrived at the Port of Breisach, and after many days of travel, she was ready to get off the ship, and reunite with her husband.

Carson was at the port waiting for her. She was scanning the crowd for her man in uniform, but didn't see him. From behind her, Adina heard, "Hallo, die Dame." She spun around and there was Carson, but he was dressed in civilian clothes - German civilian clothes. For a moment she was thrown off by his attire and hardly recognized him.

She smiled as her body fell into his and they kissed. He quickly swept her away from the crowd to a more secluded place where his truck was parked.

"I have a great little cottage for us to stay in. It should be safe. It's in a town that is still thriving, and still safe."

Adina looked at him with a concerned look on her face. It alerted and bothered her that he felt the need to say "it should be safe" twice. She wasn't sure if he was trying to convince her or himself.

"Carson, what exactly are you doing here? Are you ok?"

He gave Adina a reassuring smile, "Yes my love! Now that you're here, I'm great! I can't really tell you what I'm doing. The less you know the better, but I don't want you to worry! I've missed you so much!"

He loaded her trunks onto a flatbed truck, and they drove for two hours before they reached the small town of Friedlich. As they traveled through the outskirts of the German countryside, Adina was stunned as she saw the swastika flags and banners hanging everywhere. Carson told her not to make eye contact with anyone in uniform; to just keep her eyes looking forward.

"We'll be safe in Friedlich. The United States made sure to put us in the safest situation possible."

Chapter 6

Friedlich Chronicle

Carson and Adina's new home sat on the edge of
the city. On one side was the charming community of
Friedlich, which translated means "Peaceful", and on the
other was the wooded mountain range of the Black
Forest. For the moment, it was a peaceful town of people
who supported one another in their businesses and
community. Adina didn't know it at the time, but this
place and this period in history would change her life
forever. Up to this point, her life since leaving Texas was
in her mind, a fairy tale, practically flawless. She loved
her life, she loved her husband, and like every new bride,
she had visions of a perfect and long future ahead for the
two of them. This small family community was quaint,
but the people there didn't know exactly what to think of
the American girl that lived in the old Batton Cottage.
There was a fear in the air of Friedlich, one which the
community tried to avoid by staying busy and working
hard, hoping that the rumors of war would go away, and
that they wouldn't be faced with destruction or conflict.

Adina adored the little cottage, and spent her days and nights trying to turn it into a comfortable home. Unfortunately, she spent a lot of time alone. She had no idea when she arrived in Friedlich that Carson would be gone so much of the time. It was difficult not knowing from one day to the next if he would even come home at all. He told her that if he had not returned home each day by sundown, he probably wouldn't be coming home at all. Traveling at night was not safe, and never a good idea. Adina found herself throughout the day and into early evening, watching the front door, and waiting for a twist of the knob. Once the sun would go down without the appearance of Carson, she would be utterly disappointed. Most of her nights alone were spent studying and attempting to learn the German language. Many times she would write long letters to Jillian. When the letters were complete she would read them out loud, pretending that Jillian was there with her. Adina felt so lonely with no Carson, no Jillian, no friendly faces, nothing but the rustling sounds of the winds moving through the pines. Because Adina was not the kind of girl who was content with waiting at home, she knew that she would go absolutely crazy if she didn't find a productive way to spend her time. This waiting around for the doorknob to turn was for the birds! She resolved in her mind that she would no longer waste one more moment waiting for Carson as if she were a lost puppy waiting for its master.

Seeing an empty corner in the far side of the room, she decided to use it to set up her sewing machine. Her first task at hand was to make some curtains and throw pillows that would brighten up the little cottage, helping it to feel warm and cozy. Jillian taught her that any room could be made to look better and more inviting by simply adding a splash of color. Batton Cottage was old and small, but well-built and sturdy. Unlike her home in Texas, she was all too happy that there were no holes in the walls that needed to be patched up with pieces of cardboard. A fist being slammed through a wall was a constant occurrence in the Crawford house, an ugly result of Ray's drunken rages. During the winter months, cardboard worked wonders at preventing the cold winds from blowing through the room. Even having a stone floor rather than dirt was a blessing. She wondered what Carson would have thought if he would have seen where she came from.

The next day she went out all set to purchase enough fabric to complete her sewing project. She had already decided that she would choose a patterned cloth with tones that would complement the warm colors that mingled throughout her area rug. As Adina was walking towards the town market, enjoying the general splendor of the day and admiring the charming town of Friedlich, she couldn't help but notice a little girl and her mother quickly coming out of the town market. The little girl had bobbed blonde hair and big blue eyes that seemed mournful, and filled with sadness. Adina couldn't help but wonder why one so young would be so downhearted. Her dress and overcoat were dirty and worn, both bearing holes. When Adina passed by the two, she noticed the mother staring down at the ground, almost as if she were ashamed, purposely avoiding any eye contact. Upon entering the same store, the two shop owners were pointing and wildly gabbing in German *obviously* in regards to the mother and daughter who had just left so abruptly. Come to find out, the woman's husband had been taken by the new German regime in order to help in their efforts to grow and supply food for the government and the ever-growing armies that were rising up under Hitler's reign. He was chosen for this so called "honored" task because he was known throughout Germany as a highly successful farmer whose crops were more bountiful than any other in the country. He was not only a farmer, but also a chemist who created a fertilizer that would double, even triple, normal crop sizes. Adina found out that a few months ago, his wife, Inga, received word that he had died in an explosion in a lab. Since then, their farm had gone to ruins and Inga and her daughter Leta were poverty stricken.

Adina continued staring out the window at both mother and daughter who were standing on the corner, looking lost and rather hopeless. The brazen shop owners continued asking Adina what she needed. Not really even listening, she turned around and told them that she would be right back, in German that was not very good. "Ich bin gleich wieder da." That was the first time she had put her German dialect to use, and although she was quite pleased with herself, the two shop owners were highly entertained by her broken attempt to communicate. Adina quickly ran out of the store after Inga and Leta, and when she caught up to them, she wasn't quite sure what to say, so she opened her purse and pulled out her small notebook and fabric measuring tape. Inga, both startled and frightened, pulled Leta behind her. Adina backed

123

away, and pointed to herself, telling them her name, accompanied by a warm smile.

"I am Adina."

Then she held up her measuring tape so to let her know that she was a seamstress and all that she wanted was to take a few measurements of her little girl.

"Naherin, Bitte?"

Inga looked at Adina with tears in her eyes, lips quivering, and then set Leta in front of her, allowing this stranger to measure her daughter. Adina knew that desperate look that Inga wore, as she herself had worn that same expression on more than one occasion. It was the look of hopelessness, moved by someone's unexpected kindness. The bitter souvenir of complete humility by reason of uncontrollable circumstances that were as ample as a giant at the forefront of her life. The intimidation of a new day was never kind, but that of a monster shouting in a tone that wouldn't be hushed, offering nothing but a fear, a dread that seemed to never end. But suddenly, by a small act of kindness, the giant is taken down by a smooth stone marked by a labor of love. When she was done, Inga gave Adina a slight grin, grabbed her daughter's hand, and then walked away.

Adina went back into the market and not only purchased the fabric for her curtains and pillows, but additional material that would serve a much a higher purpose than decorations. Over the next few weeks, she kept herself busy sewing a new wardrobe for little Leta which consisted of five dresses and a wool overcoat. On the neckline of each garment, Adina embroidered one single red rose, as that was her favorite flower.

After many countless hours of sewing, Leta's lovely new wardrobe was complete. Adina decided that she would purchase two pairs of wool stockings that Leta could wear with her new dresses. Once again, she made her way back to the town market. In broken German, and with the help of her German/American dictionary, she asked the clerk if they carried children's shoes. The attendant just looked at her in an irritated manner and said no, "No schuh, no!"

Out of the corner of her eye, Adina noticed a woman enter the store who stopped at the doorway and began glaring in her direction. The power of this young woman's gaze was intense and made Adina feel anxious. However, she couldn't help but notice the lovely attire of this mysterious stranger who was dressed in a stunning blue suit with a matching felt side hat, covered in matching flowers with pearl centers. She was quite out of place in her stunningly elegant apparel that intensified her notable blue eyes that were peering from beneath the navy blue tulle. She was looking directly at Adina as if she wanted to say something, but only the continuous and awkward stare between the two remained.

Overcome by fear, Adina began wondering if the cover she and Carson had been working under, had been compromised. Her mind went in a hundred different directions, speculating on what she should do next. Was this woman the wife of a high-ranking Nazi official, who was sent to spy on her? Unexpectedly, the woman began walking over to the counter, clearly making Adina her objective. The closer she came, the faster Adina's heart began pounding within her chest. "Remain calm!" she thought to herself. With her eyes still on Adina, the woman lifted her arm and began pointing to her right, and uttered two words, "Schuh Coffee." She appeared to be even more nervous than Adina, and obviously ill at ease with all eyes on her. Putting her arm down, the woman in blue gave Adina a troubled grin, and then turned around and walked out the door.

Adina stood frozen for a moment, baffled by what had just taken place, but knew that "schuh" meant shoes. If she understood correctly, the woman was telling her that there was a shoe store down the street on the right hand side. Adina paid for the stockings, and walked out of the store half expecting to see the woman in blue somewhere in the distance. After all, she stuck out like a sore thumb, but she was nowhere to be found.

"Perfect," Adina thought to herself, Schuh Coffee was where she would go to buy shoes for Leta. Before stopping by this oddly named shoe store, that sounded more like a place one might go to get a cup of coffee and piece of pie, Adina first went home to pack up all of the items she would be delivering to Leta. She figured that she could go straight to their house after her shoe purchase, and drop everything off. Lovingly folding each dress and the coat, then placing them nicely in a small packing box along with the stockings, she was ready. With box in hand, Adina set out to the shoe store that was located in the middle of town that the mystery woman had told her about.

As Adina began to draw nearer to the store, she noticed a group of people standing out on the street pointing towards the end of town. They were chattering ceaselessly as if someone of great importance had just driven away, but she had no idea who. Obviously upset about what had just occurred, she could sense that they were also highly curious. Speaking so quickly, in elevated tones, she was unable to make out their fast moving gossip. After a few moments, one by one, each citizen began walking away and returning to business as usual.

A peeling chime rang out as Adina opened the heavy wooden door that led into Schuh Coffee. She was met by the overpowering bouquet of shoe wax and leather, accompanied by the faint aroma of peppermint. Remarkably, all of the scents combined were rather pleasant. At first sight the store appeared to be empty. In the back room, however, Adina could hear the rustling sounds of someone, most likely Mr. Coffee fashioning a pair of shoes. She waited at the counter, but the cobbler seemed to ignore the chime alert and continue in his task. As she waited, Adina was pleasantly surprised by the debut of the cuckoo from the clock that was hanging on the wall behind the counter. She began looking around the shop, and couldn't help but notice the array of framed pictures that lined the walls from floor to ceiling.

Strangely though, she noticed that some of the frames were empty, but were marked by a distinct area on the matting where a photo had once been placed. She thought it odd for empty frames to purposely be displayed; Jillian would definitely not approve.

The room was warm and inviting, bordered with wooden shelves filled with men's, women's, and children's shoes and boots, all stamped with "Coffee" on the inside sole. This cobbler's shoes were magnificently made, each one like a piece of artwork. It was no wonder he was unaware of the door chime, he was an artist engrossed in his most recent masterpiece. Because of Adina's humble upbringing, and the need to make the most of a dollar, she always tried to purchase items that would last and over time became proficient in recognizing great quality. Upon picking up a pair of Coffee shoes, she could tell that they were made to last a lifetime. On the far side of the room there was a separate large rack of high-lacing men's utility boots. They were tagged for pickup, most probably for German soldiers, as they were stamped with a swastika. The old wood flooring that flowed throughout the room was splattered with beautiful handmade-looking area rugs. Gray brocade-covered chairs sat in the center of the room, reserved only for patrons to convene as they waited to be measured for a new pair of shoes. In the far corner, surrounding a large stone fireplace, sat several comfortable looking wingback chairs that were draped with cozy throw blankets. This sitting area was clearly meant for the closest of friends who would most probably spend hours drinking tea from the black iron kettle that was wafting peppermint steam throughout the room.

Adina went up to the counter making sure to have her German/English dictionary readily available so that she could be prepared to ask for a pair of boots for a little girl. As she was flipping through the book, she turned and saw an older man with a head full of gray hair and bushy eyebrows staring at her. His eyes were curious, but kind. Mainly, she noticed that he seemed startled by her presence, maybe even a bit pale, and slightly out of breath at that. He stared at her, as if he knew her, but obviously this was first time either of them had ever met.

Adina made an attempt to communicate what she needed, "Uh, das boot, uh, schuh?"

"Ah, you are the one from America?" he said with a very strong accent.

"Yes, my name is Adina, Adina York, and I am looking for boots for a little girl."

"For your little girl?"

"No, I don't have any children. This is for a little girl who lives here in Friedlich."

"My name is Malachi Coffee, and this is your lucky day, my dear Adina, because your new friend, Malachi Coffee, speaks English and ....he also has boots for little girls."

The comforting tone of Malachi's voice made Adina feel welcome. Her new acquaintance was the first person that she had met since arriving in Friedlich that greeted her with kind words. Of all of the customs and traditions that had evolved throughout the ages within this charming little town, embracing outsiders was not one of them. But as for Malachi, everything about him made her feel warm.

"So, young lady, did you bring me a gift?"

She looked at him with a confused expression. "Excuse me?"

Malachi motioned with his eyes to the box that was cradled beneath her arm.

"Oh this, well it's really nothing. I just made a few things for a little girl that I saw walking around town who looked like she could use some new dresses."

"What girl?"

"Well, I only know her and her mother's first names, Inga and Leta."

Malachi looked down to the floor, and closed his eyes, nodding his head in sadness. "Yes, yes, poor Frederick."

"Who's Frederick?"

"Frederick's people have been here in Friedlich for many years. They were farmers, and very good ones at that! When Frederick was but 16 years old, he decided to go and study at the university. He was a very intelligent young man who loved farming and wanted to expand his understanding of agriculture and learn the science behind his craft. He did it all, however, for his family. He simply wanted to make a better life for them. He created a very good invention of fertilizer that made his crops grow large, and his farm became quite productive. Because of his impressive experiments, our little forgotten and slightly hidden Friedlich began to get much attention. Not good! Not good for anyone! Higher powers took note of his great success, and one day Nazi soldiers came and took him away from his family and made him work for Hitler's cause. The new Reich that is rising up, and this Hitler who wants to be emperor of all people, takes who and what he wants. So far he leaves me alone as long as I make his boots. He took Frederick against his will, he did not want to go. When he tried to escape and come back to his family, they shot him in the back."

"Shot? I thought that his death was caused from an explosion?"

"Well, Adina, you must know, the Nazis don't want people speaking the truth about those kinds of things. An 'accident' is much easier to justify to the people than murder, and they will stop at nothing to silence those who might say differently. You must not speak of this to anyone else, it's not safe. We are all so heartbroken about poor Frederick, but nothing can be done to bring him back....I fear that nothing can be done to stop this evil. All we can do now, is help care for Inga and Leta, and what you have done for Leta is a very kind thing. "Malachi walked over to his inventory of children's-sized shoes, and removed a small pair of fur-lined boots. "Here, take these boots for her. My gift."

Adina was thrilled! "These are perfect, Malachi. Thank you! I will let her know that they are from you."

"Adina, God knows - that is all I care about. No need to tell anyone else."

She sat the box on the counter and removed the lid, gently placing the boots on top of the clothing. She placed the lid back on top of the box and smiled at Malachi.

"I really love your store, and it was so nice meeting you."

Adina began walking to the front door, but before she could leave, Malachi said, "So, you sew?"

"Yes, I learned many years ago... from my grandmother. Just like making shoes is who you are, sewing is a big part of who I am."

"You think you can sew a shoe?"

She walked back towards him and said, "I can sew a shoe if you *teach* me to sew a shoe!"

"Ok, ok if you insist," he said with a twinkle in his eye and an ornery grin. "Be here at eight sharp, ready to work tomorrow. There is much to do."

Adina just stood there looking at him. "Did you just offer me a job?"

"Eight sharp, Adina. Don't be late!"

Malachi felt a stirring in his soul as he watched Adina walk out of his store. He knew that she was special and recognized that she had a caring spirit that is not often found.

Adina walked out of Coffee Schuh with a big smile on her face; she had a job, and couldn't wait to tell Carson. Up until this point, she'd wondered if she had made a mistake in coming here. Carson was never home, and she always felt so lonely. This was the first time that she felt like she may have a purpose in Friedlich.

The walk out of town began as a most pleasant and lovely experience, but as she journeyed deeper into the thick pines, the sun all but disappeared, allowing only slivers of light to shine through the dense clusters of needles. With a few scribbled directions that were vague at best, Adina felt a bit lost. As time passed, she began feeling more and more nervous as she moved further away from familiar territory in search of the home of Inga and Leta. Just as she was about to turn around and go back, she noticed that nestled behind trees and surrounded by an old rugged stone wall, was a tired looking house covered in wood siding that was once white, but like their situation, was now distressed and woeful in appearance. On each side of the house stood two enormous trees that looked as though they had been safeguarding the residence for hundreds of years with their massive and unyielding roots which reached deep within the rich soil that enveloped the property. Not only was the ground abundant in elements, but also in the history of Frederick's ancestors who tilled and prepared their family-owned land to be an agricultural heritage for their children, and their children's children. The boughs not only stretched up to the sky like walls of a fortress, but also sheathed every corner with its masses of timber shields. She could tell that this was once a grand residence that brimmed with joy and confidence at the prospect of the coming generations. But now, it was sadly a vapor of that dream.

She lightly knocked on the door, not wanting to disturb or scare them. After several moments of waiting, she gently set Leta's box of treasures by the front door.

Although she was a little bit more familiar with her location, the trip back into town seemed to take forever. Adina wished she had worn more comfortable shoes to make such a journey. Besides her aching feet, it was beginning to get dark and cold. To her great surprise, when she finally arrived at her cottage, there waiting at the door was Carson!

With her abrupt outcry of excitement, Carson was certain that she must have awakened the sleepy little town that latched their shutters at dusk. She ran towards him, and jumped into his arms, wrapping every part of herself around every part of him, and then kissed him without pausing for even one breath of air. It had been over two weeks since he had been home, and the agony of being parted from one another was unbearable.

"I was getting worried about you! Where have you been, you crazy girl?"

As she still clung tightly to him, Carson carried her inside and they dropped down together onto the fluffy down mattress.

It didn't matter how many times he looked at Adina, he was always taken aback by her beauty.

"How can you possibly be more lovely than you were the last time I saw you? I missed you so much! You'd better prepare yourself, my little Texas girl, because I have been strategically scheming this exact moment every second that I've been away from you."

Adina firmly pressed her body into his and kissed him.

"Have you now, sailor? Well in case you've forgotten, everything's bigger in Texas you know, and all of this belongs to you!"

He loved Adina's quick humor and playfulness. Then moving his body onto hers, it was all he could do to hold back the passion that was burning within him. He buried his face in her hair, inhaling as if only her fragrance warranted breathing, and then ran his lips over hers.

"Adina, oh God how I've missed you. The fragrance of your skin, how I feel when you touch me, I can't stand being away from you!"

With that, he slowly peeled back her clothing, taking his time so as to make this fulfillment of his imagination last as long as possible, inviting and then relishing her sounds of pleasure as he kissed every part of her ivory skin. For the rest of the evening they made up for the two weeks that they had been apart from one another.

As evening turned into early morning, Carson wanted to hear all about what Adina had been up to. He reminded her that he couldn't really tell her anything about his own goings on, so she began telling him all about Inga, Leta, and Malachi Coffee. She told him that the people in Friedlich were afraid of this new Reich that was rising up and taking over everything. They had no boundaries, and seized whatever and whoever they wanted. Already she had seen the remnants of their violent acts, which seemed to be accomplished without conscience or remorse for their ruthless acts of brutality.

"They are building their empire on the blood of their citizens... destroying families, murdering innocent people, and then lying about it. I hate it!."

She explained what she had learned about Frederick, who was a perfect example of what was happening.

"This poor family has been undone. Frederick was murdered by the Nazis, and his family was told that he died in an accident, but everyone knows the truth about what really happened to him."

Carson listened intently to every word that she was saying, remaining calm on the outside, while cringing on the inside over her newfound knowledge. She then excitedly began telling him about her new friend, Malachi, who owned a shoe store in the middle of town. She gloated about his ability to create the finest shoes she had ever seen. Suddenly pausing and looking sad, Carson asked her what was wrong.

"Malachi is the sweetest man that I have ever met, and I'm worried about him. I think that he's being forced to make boots for German soldiers. It makes me so mad how they use people! He offered me a job, you know...I start working tomorrow."

Carson was obviously troubled by Adina's knowledge and involvement. He remained very quiet, continuing to listen, and then looked at her with a somber stare.

"Adina, you have to be very careful what you say and to whom you say it. You can't trust anyone, not even Malachi. War is coming, it's coming here to Friedlich very soon. Once my assignment is finished, we have to leave. We may have to leave before then, I don't know. Until that time, promise me that you won't say anything to anyone. As far as the Germans are concerned, I'm here assisting in their farming efforts and helping to create machines that will make their agricultural department run more efficiently. Adina, I know about Frederick and Inga. Frederick was working with me and with the allies. Unfortunately, he got caught….and, well, you know the rest of the story."

Fully aware of this plaguing movement against humanity that had finally crept its way into Friedlich, Carson fully understood Adina's inner conflict because he felt the same. But getting involved and becoming emotional was unacceptable, and strictly against orders. He had been briefed and updated on all of the local citizens. including Malachi, but the thought of Adina getting mixed up in the mess disturbed him greatly, and for the first time, he wished that she would have stayed in the states.

Adina couldn't believe what he was saying.

"Carson, what exactly is your job here? I don't want to lose you like Inga lost Frederick! I guess I didn't realize how dangerous this was … you never told me how dangerous this was!"

Carson didn't want to worry her by the reminder that this was war, and that there is always an element of danger during wartime. This would be the first time since Adina arrived that she sensed an overwhelming fear of not only this place, but for Carson's safety. But the more she listened, the more she realized that there was nothing she could do to change the situation, and she refused to ruin their time together by worrying. At this point, she only hoped and prayed that this night wasn't the end, and that they would at least have a few more days together.

"So how long are you home for?"

"I have to leave at first light."

As hard as Adina tried, she wore her heart on her sleeve, and was greatly disappointed that Carson was leaving so soon.

"Please don't be upset, sweetheart I almost wasn't able to come at all, but I had to see you. I can't tell you exactly what I am doing, it's classified. But what I will tell you, is that the Germans have a new technology that no one else has. If we don't help combat the development of this weapon in the early stages, there will be no hope for the allies, or the world for that matter. Hitler is crazier than anyone knows, and he's gaining momentum, with an enormous following of patriots that are just as twisted as he is. The crazy son-of-a-bitch wants to rule the world, Adina, and will stop at nothing to do it. I'm doing everything that I can, along with many others, to undermine the progress. We're almost finished."

As if he were convincing himself as well as Adina, he dropped his chin to his chest and inhaled deeply.

"Everything's gonna be okay, I promise! Don't worry about me, my beautiful girl. Remember, the Admiral is here in Germany too. He's keeping abreast of all threats and military activity. If he hears that things are getting too dangerous, or that any vital information has leaked out that might put us in harm's way, we'll be gone before you can say 'everything's bigger in Texas!'"

Trying to make light of the situation didn't make the worried look on Adina's face go away. Carson wrapped his arms around her and held her tightly.

"Honestly, my love, don't worry, we have an emergency evacuation plan in place at all times. All you need to do is be ready if that time comes; be ready to leave at a moment's notice. I'll let the Admiral know where you'll be working, just in case."

Their conversation caused the mood to become gloomy, and Adina's initial excitement about the events of the day were replaced by concern. Although Carson could tell that she was trying to be brave with her false facade, he could tell that she was worried.

Kneeling down on the floor in front of her, he clasped her hands in his, staring at her with a loving and playful twinkle in his eyes.

"But you, Adina - what should I do with you? Who will keep you safe?"

He pulled her body onto his, and held her tightly.

"I'll always protect you, but I think right now, you ought to be a little afraid of me. For some strange reason, I just can't seem to get enough of you!"

Carson couldn't stand the thought of leaving without making love to Adina one more time. He rolled his body onto hers, with the sole intention of feasting on her beautiful body, total indulgence of his guarded passion. Simultaneously, she was more than happy to accommodate his furious appetite. Neither wanted the uncontrolled affections to end. Their oneness and sweet unity was a place where they were safe. While in this state of emotion, they journeyed far, far away where there was no war, no Germany, no fear, just pure unadulterated love.

In their last few hours together, as they held one another, Adina's mind couldn't stop thinking about him once again leaving. Resuming undercover status in a pit of danger, with people who would kill anyone who stood against them, upset her to a degree that he had never seen before.

"Please, Carson, don't go back! I think we need to leave ... I have a horrible feeling down deep in my soul. I don't think you should go back - I think we should go home!"

He held her even tighter.

"Don't worry another second, baby. everything's okay. I shouldn't have told you as much as I did. Everything's gonna be okay, I promise...we'll leave very soon!"

Mornings were generally Adina's favorite time of the day, but when Carson was home, the onset of daylight meant only one thing, saying goodbye to him, again. She was trying to make the very best of this arrangement, but whenever Carson was gone she felt as though part of her was missing. She was encouraged, however, that his job here was almost complete, and the opportunity to work with Malachi gave her a new sense of purpose.

Adina sat in the darkness of the morning with a cup of coffee in hand, watching Carson sleep. She had never loved anyone more, and desired to be a good navy wife who didn't complain. After all, she did insist on coming to Germany with him. No matter what, she would stay strong, not complain, and not make known to him the slightest inkling of how miserable she was without him. Their conversation made her realize the danger

146

involved with his mission, and she needed him to stay focused. As he continued sleeping, she sat there gazing at him. He was really quite beautiful, and every time she looked at him, she found a new feature to love. She laughed as she noticed some of the feathers from their down bed stuck in his hair. The bed was altogether comfortable, but had a tendency to leak feathers. In spite of the scampering fluff, the bed was quite cozy, and it kept her warm on many a cold night when she was alone, but nothing warmed her like Carson's body next to hers.

Adina had actually grown very fond of their little cottage that was made of red brick and embellished with green shutters, and a black front door. Her plan was to plant a small garden in the space outside of the front window as soon as the weather warmed up. But now, it was hard to say how long they would be here or when the war would come to this place. It was probably best not to make any long-term plans. Her heart grieved at the thought of Malachi, and how this war could destroy everything he held dear, including his shoe store. She was thankful to be privy to current events, but it was an oppressive burden to bear, knowing what was coming but not having the freedom to tell. In addition to everything else, Adina and Carson would have the privilege of being able to return to the "land of the free, and the home of the brave." These poor souls would be left behind, and enslaved to a crazed dictator. Yet, these good people of Friedlich who tried their best to carry on as normal, were far from ignorant. Their troubled faces were plagued by the anxiety and concern of veiled conversations filled with unbelievable rumors, now clanging certainties of the coming yoke of bondage. They knew that something terrible was on the horizon; they just didn't know when or exactly what that something would be.

Adina reached beneath her bed to grab her slippers, knowing that the stone floor was freezing cold and her feet already felt like popsicles. Thankfully, Carson had brought over the large area rug that Jillian had given to them as a wedding gift. It was thick and warm, not just with its fabric elements, but also aesthetically with its red tones that filled the plain room with pattern and style. Each time Adina stepped onto the carpet, she thought of Jillian and was reminded of how much she missed her.

Knowing that the morning send-off was inevitable, and also how she hated good-byes, it was time to get on with things. Letting Carson get as much sleep as possible, she quietly began making an omelet for their breakfast. Jillian always told her to make sure her man never left the house hungry. After last night, she knew that he would be starving, so along with the fluffy omelet, which he absolutely adored, she heated up sweet German ham, and then toasted several thick slices of cinnamon raisin bread and honey butter.

As always, they enjoyed their time together eating breakfast while sitting around their small café style table with matching chairs, located in the center of their even smaller kitchen. Adina had added her own touches to the cottage so that when Carson returned home, he would feel comfortable. She quickly discovered, however, that he was not very concerned with such things, but *she* was the only thing that he cared about seeing when he came home. He once told her that a cardboard box would feel like home as long as she was there. He did notice though, as he ate the last bit of his omelet, that she had set up her sewing machine in the far corner of the room under the window that looked out over the forest of pine trees. It was apparent by the display of new cushions, that Adina had been busy sewing. But after Carson's blatant warning about staying unemotional and indifferent, she thought it best not to say anything about the clothes that she had made for Leta. She did express her excitement about her job, and he just reminded her to only say that her husband is helping with the agricultural success of Germany. He warned her emphatically to not say a word to anyone about his being in the United States Navy.

With the rising of the sun came the dreaded moment of saying goodbye again to Carson. Adina had discovered that saying goodbye was one of her least favorite things; as a matter of fact, she hated it. They embraced, neither one wanting to let go of the other. He gave her one last kiss, and felt himself wanting to ignore the job that was waiting for him so that he could stay with her.

"It's only for a little while longer, my little Texas girl! This mission will end soon, and then we'll go back to the states where I can be stationed in a place where I can come home to you every night. It will be like it was before, I promise. I know this is hard, Adina, it's hard for me too. I ache for you every moment that we're apart, but it's just for a little while longer."

He kissed her once more, held her tightly, then reluctantly turned and walked away. Adina stood and watched as he walked out of town, where he was picked up by a work truck and taken to a destination unknown to her … not knowing when they would see one another again.

Chapter 7

Schuh Coffee

Malachi Chronicle

The hazy image of Adina's reflection in the old foggy mirror that leaned against the wall, was distorted, and did not truthfully reflect her beauty. This first day of work at Malachi Coffee's shoe store was exciting, but she had no idea what all it would entail, and if Malachi would even like her. It seemed a bit odd that he would hire a complete stranger, especially an American that he hardly knew. He was different than the other residents in Friedlich; they embraced their own, but were not so keen on the presence of outsiders. She wondered, now that she was employed by Malachi, if the people of the town would perchance accept her.

Staring into her dress cabinet, she wondered what she should wear. "What does one wear to make shoes?" she thought as she brushed her hair, and freshened up her lipstick. After a long deliberation, she pulled out a simple black dress, cinching in her waist with a matching belt, and then slipped into a pair of her most comfortable flat shoes. If she was going to be on her feet all day, heels were out of the question. "Well", she considered as she glanced once more into the mirror, sizing herself up, "this will have to do!" This area of Germany was always a little chilly, so she grabbed her gray wool coat and hat, and started on her way to her first day of work.

Each time Adina walked through Friedlich, she would notice a new incredible piece of art or architecture that she had overlooked before. This was a place filled with deep-rooted history that had been built and kept by exceptionally skilled craftsmen. These fine artisans of old did not just erect buildings, but works of art. This was the first time that she had left her cottage so early in the day, and with the quiet of the morning brought some new found ornaments to life, that seemed to flow like a river of colors. For the first time, she noticed that each of the doors that lined the city street were uniquely carved, and painted in various jewel-toned shades. Later she would discover that each of the carvings represented a particular family lineage and their story. These story doors, represented family trades in Friedlich that had been passed down from generation to generation, and the carvings, or the stories on the doors, were treasured reminders of the exalted significance of their family legacy to those who still occupied the dwellings.

The door that led into Malachi's shop was stained in a muted emerald green. The cameo that embellished his door was more simple than the others she had seen along the way. Dozens of chiseled cords ran down each side of the portal, all joining together to form a large decorative knot at the bottom. Upon examining the carvings, she was filled with emotion as it occurred to her that each cord represented a member of his family whose life would forever be intertwined with the others. Somehow this particular emblem made her miss Carson even more. She had never experienced that kind of relationship with her own family, but it was her hope to experience it with Carson.

Glancing at her watch, she saw that she was five minutes early, but lightly knocked to see if Malachi was there. After waiting a bit longer, she noticed the handle jiggling, and the sound of someone unbolting the latches on the other side of the door. When the doorway opened, there stood a short gray-haired woman wearing a blue dress and white apron.

"Hello, you must be Adina. I am Estee, Malachi's sister. Malachi is still upstairs, but will be down in just a moment. Please, please come in! Adina extended her hand to Estee, but instead, Estee grabbed Adina's hand with both of hers, enveloping it tightly.

"Malachi has never hired anyone to come in here and work with him. Many have tried, but you, my dear, are the one that he has been expecting."

Adina was taken aback by her words, and didn't know what to say except how happy she was to be there. She figured that Estee's English was probably a bit unsound, which in turn, confused her word choice. Of course he had been expecting her! After all he did hire her just yesterday. As she walked into the store, impatiently waiting in the wingback chairs arranged around the fire, were two gentlemen. They both stood up and smiled excitedly as she walked towards them. Estee introduced them as Lavi Blum, the town butcher, and Ira Sisken, who owned Germany's finest bakery. Lavi's butcher shop was directly next door to Coffee Schuh, and across the street on the corner was the bakery. Ira and Lavi both seemed jubilant to finally meet Adina.

Apparently Malachi had been talking about her nonstop even though he had just met her the previous day. He spoke to his two friends about Adina as if he knew more about her than he should have in the short amount of time they were together. Lavi the butcher was a tall but portly man who was bald on top with gray shaggy hair projecting from each side, like smoke billowing from windows, and was wearing a bloodstained apron with "Blum" embroidered on the front. He grabbed Adina's hand and kissed it.

Still holding her hand, he said with a thick accent, "You are lovely, my dear, so lovely."

Adina noticed that his eyes smiled even when he didn't. His hands were large and calloused, most probably from his trade as a butcher, working with and cutting up meat since the time he was a small boy.

Ira was a plump fellow, as wide as he was tall, with a head full of white hair that stuck straight up, giving him an almost eccentric look.

"I am happy to meet my Malachi's Adina. Come sit down. I have made Estee's favorite Franzbrotchen. We shall have it with peppermint tea."

Upon Adina's first bite of the mouthwatering delight, she understood why this sweet pastry made with rich butter and cinnamon was Estee's favorite.

Malachi came down the stairs from the small apartment that he an Estee called home. Seeing her new boss walk into the room, Adina quickly put her teacup down, and walked over to where he stood.

"Eight o'clock sharp, just like you said. I'm ready to work - where do you want me to start?"

"First we eat and talk. There is plenty of time for work later...we want to hear all about you. In unison, the other three sat their teacups down onto their saucers with a clang, so not to miss a word. Adina squirmed in her chair and appeared uncomfortable at his inquiry, and general interest from the group. Malachi could tell that she was ill at ease, so he decided to change the direction of the conversation.

"Do you like the Franzbrotchen? Ira Sisken is the finest baker in all the world... people come from everywhere for his tartlets and pastries. You know, the good book says that 'man can't live on bread alone,' but I don't think the good Lord had every tried Ira's Franzbrotchen!"

In one voice, Lavi and Ira proclaimed an "Amen",
and Adina laughed out loud at his words of wisdom.

"I think you're right, Malachi. I'm certain I could
live on Ira's Franzbrotchen alone!"

Adina began to relax. She wholeheartedly enjoyed
sitting and talking with her new friends, and was glad to
have people around her to laugh with. It had been a long
time. Because of the warning that Carson had given her,
she didn't feel free to say too much. It was difficult
indeed to carry on a conversation while trying to
scrutinize each thought before putting it into words. This
whole process of having to hold back made her nervous,
but she didn't want to reveal any information that might
put her or Carson in danger. She kept reminding herself
to be very careful what she said. They asked her all about
her life, marriage, and how a Texas girl ended up in
Germany. Malachi, Ira, and Lavi all took turns pretending
to talk like a Texan as they held a match between their
teeth, and bent one of Malachi's hats to somewhat
resemble that of a cowboy. Adina loved their sense of
humor. They made her laugh so hard that her sides hurt.
When they would ask her questions, she mostly told them
the truth, except for the "Carson-being-a-Naval-officer"

part, and the part about him trying to sabotage the Nazi efforts. She always made sure to reiterate that he was an agricultural expert; telling them that he was here to help the people of Germany. She could tell by how they responded to her answers that they didn't exactly believe her story. It was obvious that they knew she was holding something back. This façade of lies made her feel terrible, and she wanted so badly to tell them the truth about everything, but she knew that she couldn't.

As she began to know Malachi better, and watched and worked with him day after day, it became obvious that making shoes was a very big part of his life, but there was something mysterious about him - something else in his life that took priority even over shoes. This something else, this unidentified secret, made Adina both curious and troubled at the same time. She couldn't help but wonder if he was possibly a spy. Considering the notion that he only hired her (an American) so quickly, and without reservation was because he was an undercover informer, had definitely crossed her mind. Whatever it was that was going on with Malachi went much deeper than just shoes.

After a few months of learning the ingenious craft of shoemaking, Adina began to notice that Malachi would sometimes disappear without warning, and then be absent for days at a time. That was never the case with Lavi and Ira or even Estee. She would see them working every day from morning till night in their shops without fail. But Malachi, that was a different story. He was nowhere to be found. His truck would remain parked behind the building, so she knew that he hadn't driven anywhere. If he was a spy, maybe he walked to the outskirts of town like Carson, and then got picked up? When Adina would inquire as to Malachi's whereabouts, Estee would say that he was upstairs not feeling well, and shouldn't be disturbed. Adina discovered that to be a fabrication when she checked his room herself after Estee had left for the market one day. Just to be positive, she scoured the entire upstairs, discovering that not only was he not there, but his bed was neatly made, and all of his personal belongings, such as his watch, gold ring, and wallet, were sitting on his dresser. It seemed very odd to her that Malachi would leave and not take at least his wallet with him. Yet many other times, he was there, but in a state that required bed rest for several days. When she would interrogate Lavi or Ira, they would say that he often went for sabbaticals in the Black Forest, and then they would quickly change the subject. They were obviously part of whatever it was that was going on. On several occasions, the result of Malachi's "absences of secrecy" would be dreadful injuries including a black eye, a broken arm, or sometimes cuts and bruises. When she would ask as to what happened, Malachi would say that he was chased by a wild boar, or that he tripped in the night.

Regardless of the mystifying deception that was ongoing, Adina grew to love and cherish Malachi, Estee, Ira, and Lavi. Days turned into weeks, and like the wind, months blew by. Malachi taught Adina the art of shoemaking, including *all* of his personal "tricks of the trade." Applying her creativity as a seamstress, Adina created many new designs for footwear that she would first sketch out and then pass on to Malachi. On one such occasion, Malachi surprised her by bringing to life the drawing of her rather fashionable navy blue pumps, knowing that particular one was her favorite. He wanted nothing more than to make *all* of them for his Adina, but because war was inevitable and winter was right around the corner, he spent all of his time and resources producing warm winter boots for the people of Friedlich. But even that came to a screeching halt as orders were sent to Malachi demanding that "normal retail business" must halt immediately.

"Your allegiance to the Fuhrer is now required!"

He was firmly instructed to cease making anything other than military grade boots for soldiers, and not just any soldiers, but Nazis. As Hitler's armies grew, the demand for more boots, *more everything,* increased. With all of the additional work, Malachi was very thankful to have Adina's help. There were times when even Lavi and Ira would graciously come and assist in fulfilling the impossible orders. Every other day, shipments of leather and needed supplies would arrive at Schuh Coffee by another enlisted subordinate of the Third Reich. Apparently this man who dispensed containers of supplies that were branded with the bent cross, had until now, devoted his entire life to delivering milk and butter to the citizens of Friedlich. His demeanor seemed as if he were grieving for the loss of a loved one, but instead his life's passion had been ripped from him, leaving him completely uncommunicative. Identical to Malachi and many others, he had been made into a delegate for a cause that he didn't believe in. Like clockwork, the boots would be picked up at the appointed

162

date, at which time, a new, and usually larger order was left, giving a ridiculously short amount of time in which to finish them. No one wanted to say it aloud, but they all knew that the beginning of the end had come.

Carson's visits home became fewer and further between. On the rare instances that he was able to return, it was he who fell into Adina's arms knowing that she was remedy for what ailed him. She was concerned by his noticeable weight loss and dark circles under his eyes; disturbed that he was overworked and under rested. For whatever amount of time he was able to stay, she insisted that he remain in bed and rest. He agreed to abide by her request if she would stay in bed with him. Except for preparing omelets and hearty stews that would help him regain his strength, Adina was more than happy to oblige. Malachi understood that she would be absent when Carson was in town; in fact, he insisted on it. Not only was Carson physically affected by obvious fatigue, but he assertively and uncharacteristically voiced his concern for not only the future of Germany, but the world, and what was about to come. Somehow he knew what lay ahead. He tried to convince Adina to leave and go back to the United States, but she refused to return without him.

It was true that she couldn't stand the idea of leaving Carson, but she knew that she could never live with herself if she abandoned her new dear friends. Like Jillian, Malachi, Estee, Ira, and Lavi, had become the family that she never had. They would always tell her that she needed to have companions her own age, and not just spend her time with a bunch of "Alte Kauz", or old codgers, but she really never thought of them as being old. With her whole heart she cherished her time with the quartet of patriarchs. Age truly had no bearing on the love that she felt for them. It killed her not to be able to discuss updates about their country as she would hear them from Carson. At this point, she truly believed that they were friends who could be entrusted with her deepest secrets, but still she remained faithful to Carson's request to stay silent. She never let her conversations with Carson about what was inevitably coming to Germany go any further than the four walls of their cottage.

Spring had come and gone, and the weather began turning cold. Friedlich was never warm, even during the summers, but the winters consisted of many cold and dreary days with no sun at all. There were some days that seemed overwhelmed by darkness. Not just cold, dark weather, but a darkness that loomed above Friedlich.

Adina felt apprehensive as she walked to work this day. Perhaps she was just missing Carson, or perhaps the gloom in the air was taking its toll on her. Something was bothering her, but what it was, she didn't know. She recalled a dream that she had during the night. It was a dream, but seemed so real at the same time, and it continued to haunt her as she walked down the street. She dreamed that Malachi was walking up the stairs to his apartment, dressed in his best suit and wearing his finest black hat. He looked at her, not saying a word, only motioning with his hand for her to come with him. She then began to follow him up the stairs. Walking into his study, she was met by a huge wall covered in frames, and she began to look at all of the people in the photos. As she had so many times before, she examined the pictures within the frames. But they were different this time. Instead of being filled with faces of strangers, to Adina's disbelief, they was filled with pictures of her! Dozens of ornate, golden-framed photos of her life. Included were those of her working in the movie house, dragging a Christmas tree home on Christmas Eve, marrying Carson, and then a picture of her in a place she had never been before. She was standing in front of a lighthouse alone, staring out at the ocean. It was a beautiful place, but she noticed that her countenance was sorrowful.

She called out to Malachi, asking where he got these pictures of her, and why they were hanging on his wall. He just smiled at her and began putting an empty frame that was old and worn in his suitcase, as if he were leaving. Suddenly, the smile left his face, he looked up at Adina, and said in a serious tone, "Tempus Vector." As soon as he closed his suitcase, and the clasps snapped, Adina woke up, gasping for a breath of air.

When she arrived for work this day, Malachi was sitting in a wingback chair, alone. Usually the day would begin with Lavi and Ira there to greet Adina as she walked through the door, but not today. The fire wasn't lit, the teapot wasn't wafting. For the first time, the store felt lifeless. Malachi was alone looking straight into the cold fireplace. He was obviously preoccupied and bothered over something. At first, she only noticed his strange behavior, but as she looked across the room, she observed that all of his framed pictures were gone. The wall was completely empty. As she took a more thorough look around the room, she was alarmed to see that not only were his pictures gone, but all of his machinery, tools, and supplies were either missing or had been destroyed. Pieces of broken tools and machinery were lying all over the floor, along with remnants of shoes that he had made. She walked over to where he was sitting to see if he was alright.

"Malachi, it's Adina, are you alright?"

At first he said nothing, not giving one indication that he could hear her. As she moved closer to look at him, she noticed a gold star made out of cloth that was pinned to his jacket. It seemed as if he were in shock, as his gaze never departed from the old rugged fireplace, even as he began to speak.

"Adina, come here, I must speak with you."

She immediately went over and sat next to Malachi. She put her hand on his arm.

"What's happened here?"

"What has happened here is not important, it can wait! You must listen. There is something that I need to tell you. Something I know that you have been wondering about for many months now."

Adina knew what he was talking about. Where did Malachi go for days at a time, and what was the significance of all of the framed pictures? And for that matter, why did some of the frames, which had obviously at one time held pictures, now hang empty?

He pointed to the wall where the frames once hung. Adina had looked at those photographs a million times, and often wondered who the people and places were, and how they were connected to Malachi. She had thought it strange that the pictures were important enough to shroud the worn stucco, while not containing any personal remembrances of his family, friends, or even local citizens of this city.

"I actually dreamed about you last night and your framed wall, and I feel terribly worried and disturbed about something, but I can't quite put my finger on it."

"Adina, pictures in frames are like a soul in a body. They tell a story; they are the substance and purpose for the structure. Many times that one picture tells the story of a complete life. All of those pictures that you once saw here were not only their lives, but moments of mine as well. I played a part in each of them, accomplishing something that was important and meaningful, even though it wasn't my life."

Malachi's words didn't give Adina any comfort, or seem to make any sense, but only made her feel more confused and anxious.

"The empty ones, however, well they are a different story. The empty frames are my regrets. I have run out of time. These regrets can never be fixed by me. I can never go back and undo what was done."

"Go back? What do you mean 'go back'? Go back where, Malachi? You're speaking in riddles!" She looked deep into his eyes, trying to understand what he meant.

"Adina, you must listen to me. There is not much time, and this lesson, this information has nothing to do with shoes."

As always, Adina listened very carefully to what he was trying to tell her. She had learned so much from him, and she knew that he was very wise in his teachings and explanations of things. He had been a perfect example of what living a meaningful and productive life looks like, unselfishly putting others' needs above his own. What Adina didn't realize is that the day she and Malachi first met, he saw these same qualities in her; they were kindred spirits. All she knew, aside from Malachi's fine character and giving spirit, was that there was something else, something invisible, almost magical about him.

"Hitler is looking for a weapon. This weapon is not made by men, but by divine powers. If this weapon were to get into his hands, he would have a power that could destroy far more than bombs or rifles or armies could ever accomplish. The Nazis came in and took everything I have, destroyed everything, looking for this weapon, but they will never find it. I have made sure of that. Adina, I know life has not always been very kind to you, and I wish I could tell you that from now on life would be without sorrow. I can't explain everything right now. Just please remember, no matter what happens, you are never alone."

Adina sat at Malachi's side, trying to make sense of what he was saying.

"I, I don't understand."

"You don't now, but you will later."

As Malachi began to explain, the door opened, and along with a cold gust of wind, the Admiral came in with Estee by his side.

Adina stood up, "Admiral, what are you doing here?"

He looked at her with tear-filled eyes. "Adina, there has been an accident, Carson is ... the plane he was in ... was shot down."

"The plane, what plane? Why was he in a plane? No! You promised! You *promised* you would take care of him. Where is he? Is he, is he ... dead?"

"Come dear, we have to leave now. It's not safe anymore."

Malachi looked at her with eyes filled with sorrow. His blue eyes that normally smiled, were gray and dim.

"Go, my daughter. You must go now, but before you do, let me empower you with a blessing of grace, so that you can be successful in accomplishing the task before you."

Adina dropped to her knees, weeping before Malachi as he put both of his hands on her head and said, "I invoke upon you this blessing by the grace of God, that you will be empowered, and that you will come to realize and achieve your destiny with great wisdom. I commission you now with the heritage and tradition of those of us who have been sanctioned before you, the generation that has gone before you."

He then lifted her head and said, "Do not spend your time mourning what you have lost or do not have, rather pursue with all wisdom the journey that is before you. You will never be alone. At times, you may feel like an orphan, but those of us who have gone before you will be with you."

With tears running down her face, Adina looked at her friend, her mentor, her father. "I love you Malachi."

"Goodbye, my Adina. May the Lord bless you and keep you and give you strength. Before you go, my dear, take my coat. It will keep you warm, and remind you of me." He wrapped his coat around her, and then held her face in his hands, taking one last look at his Adina. "Go now!"

She turned around and ran out the door, weeping over this devastating loss of Carson and Malachi and Estee. She felt numb, as if she couldn't move. But the Admiral at her side became her legs as he held and carried Adina out of her beloved town of Friedlich.

Together they hurried to the edge of town where a covered truck with armed soldiers was waiting for them.

The Admiral sat there with his hand on her back, trying to comfort her as she wept. "I can't go without Carson! I can't leave him. Are you sure? Are you sure he's dead?"

"He would want you to go, Adina. He would want you to live."

"What's happening, Admiral?"

"It's begun. These poor people will be ripped from their homes and businesses and forced to serve under Hitler … or worse. Jews especially are being hunted, just because they are Jews. They are being forced to wear a yellow star on their chest. This makes it easier for them to be found. It's a horrible thing. The U.S. is gonna have to get involved and help these poor people, but for right now, we can't do a thing. Carson did some miracles that will help, but this is just the beginning."

Adina stood up in the truck and frantically told the Admiral to let her out, that she needed to help Malachi and Estee, and warn Lavi and Ira.

"You can't leave honey. I have strict orders for us to exit Germany *now*."

Adina turned and looked at the Admiral with panic on her face, sobbing, "You don't understand! I have just lost my husband! My God, my God…. Malachi, Estee, Lavi, and Ira, they are all Jews. I have to warn them. Oh God, Oh God, what have I done? I've known this was coming, but Carson told me not to say anything. I have to warn them."

The Admiral grabbed her, "No, Adina, you can't. Stop!"

Adina struggled and began hitting him all the while he held her. She fell to the floor of the truck sobbing.

The Admiral gently picked her up and held her tightly. "Adina, listen to me. There's a plane waiting for us in an open field an hour from here. We have to be on it. We can't go back. We *have* to get to that plane, do you understand?" As he held her, he told her that he would try to send someone to help those left behind.

Once she and the Admiral arrived at the plane, he got word that in one swift onslaught, the town had been emptied of all Jews, and everything there was being destroyed. He stared at the ground in sorrow and disbelief and began walking toward Adina. She could tell by the look on his face that the news wasn't good.

"I'm sorry, honey, there is nothing we can do. All of the Jews were gathered up right after we left, forced out of their homes and put on trains. I don't know where they took um."

Adina sat down, looking straight ahead, tears flowing from her eyes. Her husband was dead, Malachi, Estee, Lavi, and Ira probably dead too. Her world had just collapsed, and she felt as though there was nothing left for her. As the cargo plane began to take off, she stared hopelessly at a soldier sitting across from her, wondering how she could ever go on living when everyone that she loved was gone. She could have warned them, but chose not to. She could have begged Carson weeks ago, demanded that they leave, but she didn't, and now he was dead. How could she ever forgive herself for not warning her friends that a holocaust was coming? For holding back information from them that could have saved their lives? She wondered why they were all gone, and she was spared? She clutched Malachi's coat, and buried her head in the wool tweed that smelled of shoe wax and peppermint. Losing all control, she began weeping and felt as though a dagger had pierced her heart. Many of the soldiers on board the plane knew Carson well, and knew how he loved Adina. They sat in silence as she wept and grieved.

Upon return to the United States, Adina didn't want any part of the life she once shared with Carson in Long Beach; it was just too painful. Returning to Texas was out of the question. She would never go back there again! Her goal was to get as far away as she could from both places. She wasn't yet twenty years old, and had already begun and ended two completely different seasons of life. The first season was difficult, but molded and made her into the woman that Carson fell in love with. The second season was beautiful, for a moment, but then suddenly turned somber and hopeless. Carson was the perfect man for her, and no one else would ever come close. She vowed to never marry again as he was her one and only true love. She found herself in a daily battle for her soul, fighting the root of bitterness. She just couldn't understand why her blessings had so quickly turned to tragedy. It wasn't until a month after her return that she had an epiphany while reading a newspaper that was left on the counter of Sal's Coffee Shop. The article and picture on the front page of the *Bar Rousse Gazette,* spoke of an abandoned mansion in Bar Rousse, Maine, that was over a hundred years old. It was scheduled to be torn down, and the property made into a park that would overlook the Atlantic. Adina gazed intently at the picture, and recognized the lighthouse that sat by the mansion. It was the beacon in the photo from her dream, the one she stood next to in the prophetic framed picture on Malachi's wall. She couldn't believe her eyes! At that very second, she knew without a doubt that Bar Rousse was where she was supposed to go. Not wasting a moment, she made arrangements to buy the property, and two days later she loaded up her car and began her drive to the east coast into the next season of her life that would begin and end in Bar Rousse, Maine.

Chapter 8

Sentimental Journey

After sleeping the entire way to Bar Rousse, I felt more rested, but groggy. As the plane came to a stop, and I remembered where I was and that Adina was gone, I was overcome with grief. Generally when a six-hour flight comes to an end, passengers are overjoyed to finally escape the confines, kiss the ground, and enjoy their anticipated destination. In my case however, I felt rather uneasy about the imminent future, and I remained sitting in my seat even after everyone else exited the plane. Looking out of the hatch onto the ever familiar lush airport setting, and within the borders of my mind, I began my sentimental journey back to Bar Rousse that I had dreaded far longer than I realized.

My apprehension had not just begun today, but had been weighing on my mind and heart for many years now. My life in Bar Rousse was intertwined with many happy memories, but shrouded by the absence of my father. Adina had tried to fill that void as best she could, but this place was a constant reminder that I was left as an orphan not by death, but by total abandonment. In

178

addition to my lack of enthusiasm to revisit the past, was also the fact that it was my desire to be one step ahead of any situation, and always know what's coming. Because I was walking into the unknown, compounded by the guilt of staying away from Bar Rousse and Adina for so long, I was nervous to say the least. It seemed like the longer I stayed away, the easier it became to be absent from this world. My list of shallow reasons that prevented me from returning all of these years, continued to whirl through my mind like a jagged top that slashed through my validations, leaving them in shreds. Why didn't I go and visit Adina? I know it would have meant so much to her if I would have visited. I came to the conclusion that my biggest and most bothersome issue was guilt. The bottom line was that she had always been there for me, and I abandoned her, just like my father did me. Ironically, she never made me feel guilty. My continuous dismissal and rejection of her invitations were always met with kindness and understanding.

I stood up and grabbed my bags, and began my slow walk off of the plane, feeling as though a cloud of grief and regret was hanging over my head like a dark cloud. I knew however, that Adina wouldn't want me to feel this way; she always reminded me that grief and worry were simply thieves of joy. I found a bench outside of the airport entrance and sat down feeling exhausted. I had slept the entire flight, but within minutes of anguishing, I felt completely worn out. My tendency to overthink everything and exhaust myself in the process, seemed to be my calling card. Adina knew this about me and was always good at talking me off the ledge of my own making. I realized that I was currently standing on that ledge and needed to move past my childhood that was causing this juvenile behavior, and begin acting like a grown up. I made a decision right then and there, that I would go forward and do what needed to be done in order to honor Adina's memory and the impact that she and she alone had on my life.

I purposely didn't tell any of the Bar Rousse folks, mainly my Uncle

Wil and Aunt Angelina, exactly what time I was coming as I didn't want anyone to fuss over me. That was one quality that Adina and I shared. She never wanted anyone fussing over her either.

I caught a cab outside the airport, "Please take me to 52 Backshore." I knew this drive well, as I had taken it many times before. I closed my eyes and remembered

Adina waiting for me at the bottom of the escalator at the airport when I was a little girl. She would always greet me with a huge bouquet of wildflowers and a warm hug to match. On the cab ride to the estate, I would anxiously gaze out the window, brimming with anticipation for the first glance of the lighthouse, my symbol of home. Like clockwork, I could always count on Killen, Mari, and Carig, to faithfully be waiting for me with smiles and a warm Scottish welcome. To celebrate my homecoming, Mari would prepare Cullen Skink, which eventually became a tradition that we all looked forward to. Cullen Skink was customarily a creamy fish and potato Scottish stew, but Mari remade the recipe to include Maine's finest clams. All of Mari's cooking was exquisite, but her Cullen Skink was something I looked forward to upon each return. This feast of stew was such a happy memory; we would sit around Adina's table talking, laughing and enjoying Mari's wonderful chowder and homemade Scottish Soda Bread and butter. There would not be such a homecoming today, everyone was gone.

Maybe it was because it had been so long since I had seen the Bar Rousse countryside, but the drive was even more beautiful than I even remembered. The long beach grasses that were blowing in unison with the purple wildflowers reminded me of the times Adina and I would walk down to the beach as we often did, picking full bunches of flowers and taking them back to the house. Many times we would hang them upside down, allowing them to dry on the porch. When I would come to visit in the winter, she'd have the dried flowers in vases, sitting all around the house. She knew that I loved wildflowers, but Adina's favorite bloom was the red rose. Red roses were her signature flower and emblem that she embroidered on any garment she would sew.

There was a bit of a chill in the air as summer was ending and fall was upon Bar Rousse. Autumn had always been my favorite season, and now that it was October it wouldn't be long until the cold winds of winter would come. As the cab approached the house, I was taken aback at the mere sight of Adina's spectacular estate which had encompassed Pebble Cove for over 160 years. Her lovely gray wood-sided home with white shutters and an eye catching red roof seemed even more beautiful and immaculate than I remembered. All of the fences and trellises were blanketed with red and white climbing roses. Just above Adina's garden was a carved wooden gazebo that Killen had made for her, which was also covered with flowers.

182

The three acres that made up Pebble Cove were purchased in 1853 for six-dollars an acre by retired sea captain, Clarence B. Smithy and his wife, Etta. He and his son, Jonathan, immediately began building the home of their dreams, and finished both the estate and the lighthouse in 1855, just prior to the Civil War. He added the lighthouse mainly for the purpose of daily standing watch on the catwalk with his draw brass and leather telescope keeping tabs on the vast blue sea, which was of course, his first love. Once the war began, the lighthouse was used by the U.S. Army to keep watch for incoming ships and ground troops that were a threat to the great state of Maine. When his son was killed in the war, and Etta died of influenza, Captain Smithy could no longer bear staying in the house that they had built together, and decided to leave. One day, he left on his small vessel named "The Etta" and never returned to Bar Rousse.

When Adina moved back to the United States from Germany after losing Carson, she wanted to get as far away from California as possible. Like Captain Smithy, she couldn't stand the thought of staying there even one day without her Carson. Not even Jillian could console her or convince her to stay.

Because Carson had left Adina everything he owned, along with a very large insurance policy that he set up the moment he found out that he was being stationed in Germany, she had the freedom to relocate to anywhere she desired. With the approval of the Bar Rousse City Council, Adina was given permission to purchase the estate which had been abandoned and left to ruin for almost a hundred years. Upon arrival in Bar Rousse, she moved into the broken down muddle. There was only one room in the entire estate that was completely intact without a leaking roof, and holes in the wall, which was where she decided to stay during renovation. Ultimately, this particular area became her sewing room. Once Adina had settled in, the Admiral and Jillian personally accompanied Carson's body to her new home where they laid him to rest. They stayed with Adina for a few weeks, but had to return to Long Beach to pack and prepare to move. After Carson's death, the Admiral had put in a request to be transferred to Honolulu, Hawaii. Like Adina, they needed a fresh start so that they could begin to heal from their overwhelming loss. Little did they know, that within a few months, Pearl Harbor would be attacked by the Empire of Japan.

Soon after getting herself settled, a young Scottish man named Killen Hammel and his wife, Mari, who had recently moved to Bar Rousse from Scotland, were desperately in need of a job and a place to live. While in town, Adina overheard Killen asking the market owner if he needed an assistant in his store. At a point when Killen and Mari felt as though it may have been a mistake to come to America, Adina approached them with an offer that would help both parties. As it turned out, Killen was a builder and craftsman back in Scotland, and Mari was an excellent cook and housemaid who had managed a prominent household there. Adina knew that her house and all of the repairs were too much for her alone, so she offered them jobs at her estate, fixing up and repairing the house and lighthouse. She didn't merely offer a fair salary for their work, but Adina told them that they could make their home in the lighthouse and live there at no charge as well.

Killen and Mari very thankfully moved in the lighthouse, and spent the next five years helping Adina restore every inch of the estate from the floorboards, all the way to the roof line. It, along with the main estate. needed vast repairs from the floor up. Killen's master craftsmanship skills allowed him not only to repair and restore the original beauty of the house, but also into the hand carved ornate ceiling beams, chair railings, and climbing roses on the white pillars that stood around the porch. His repairs also included all of the inner workings of the lighthouse, reestablishing the beacon on Pebble Cove. He created a comfortable and whimsical home within the watchtower keeping the original paneling and distressed brick and stone. *As a little girl I would always pretend that I was a princess in this fantastic tower, being held by an evil king, awaiting my knight in shining armor to come and rescue me.*

When I was six years old, Killen and Mari received word that their son and his wife were both killed in a car accident. Their grandson, Carig, was also in the car, but he survived the tragic incident. They decided to bring Carig to the United States to live with them; he was only eight years old at the time.

As usual, Adina jumped in with both feet to support Killen and Mari through this difficult time in their lives. They were both so heartbroken at the loss of their only son that they felt as though they would never recover. Adina grieved with them both as she knew how it felt to lose someone that you loved so much. She assisted them with all of the legal processes needed to adopt and bring Carig to the United States, and even Adina helped pay for their to travel to Scotland to pick him up, and bring him to his new home in Bar Rousse. Together the three of them bonded and healed over time.

The faithful friendship between Adina, Killen, and Mari only grew stronger throughout the years, each considering the other a godsend. As for Carig and myself, we were childhood friends, but it had been years since I had seen him. The last time I remembered was the summer before I left for college, so I guess it had been about seven years. I chuckled as I recalled how annoying he was when we were kids. He would always chase. and usually catch, me. Even though he was skinny and scrawny, he was fast. Carig was always kind of quiet, never talking too much. When he would catch me, he would hold me down and tickle my ribs until I agreed to dance with him on the beach, like I often would with Adina. He was unique in that, from a very young age, he had an incredible work ethic that he learned from his father. As a matter of fact, he became the right hand of his grandfather, Killen. Each day Killen would instruct and demonstrate to his inexperienced apprentice the skills of an artisan. Carig caught on very quickly, showing a natural ability in woodworking and carpentry.

The moment Carig arrived in Bar Rousse, Adina didn't waste any time in getting him acclimated to his new life. She knew that in order for him to move forward and begin feeling like he belonged here, putting down roots and becoming a citizen of this community was imperative. She enrolled him in the third grade at Bar Rousse Elementary. He was very bright, but had a few setbacks due to the culture shock of a new place and the recent loss of his parents. It took Carig weeks of living in Bar Rousse before he would completely unpack all of his clothes.

When I came to Adina's that Thanksgiving break after he arrived, she told me that they were all concerned, because Carig was still struggling, and that he still insisted on living out of his suitcase. Killen and Mari had said all that they could to ensure Carig of how happy they were to have him there, but at that point he was just not capable of calling this new place home. At the time, I went up to his room at the top of the lighthouse to try and talk to him about it. I was even younger than he was and going through my own issues with my father, so I figured if nothing else, we could ache together. I plopped myself on the edge of his bed and just made small talk. I could tell he was grieving, and that he didn't know quite how to get through it or how to feel better.

Looking down towards the floor at his fully packed suitcase, it seemed a good idea to offer my services as an already-skilled unpacker.

"Hey, you want me to help you put your clothes in your drawers?"

In a totally panicked tone, he said "No, don't touch them!"

He sat there looking out the window of his room with tears streaming down his face. He told me that once he unpacked, everything would become real, everything was final. I will never forget the pain I saw in his eyes. He just wasn't ready to accept that his mother and father were really dead, that the home he knew in Scotland was gone, and that this foreign place was where he would be forever.

I sat there holding his hand, and told him in my childlike wisdom, "Carig, sometimes things change that we don't like. My father is alive, but he doesn't want me,

I don't know why. But Adina does want me and does love me, just like she and your grandmother and grandfather love you. I'll tell you what, let's take a few things out of your suitcase today, and maybe a few more tomorrow. Then we can go into town, have my Uncle Wil pack us a picnic, and we'll go on an adventure."

I'm not sure what I said that helped, but after that, Carig fully unpacked all that he owned, placed his empty suitcase under his bed, and as far as I know, has never strayed very far from Bar Rousse since.

Carig and I became the best of friends. When I visited Bar Rousse each summer and during the holiday breaks, he would faithfully be standing at the house waiting for me when I arrived. Carig had red, curly hair just like his grandfather, Killen, and tons of freckles - which were adorable on a little boy, but as we got older, just did not appeal to me. When I was 13 and he was 15, he asked if when we grew up I would I marry him. I thought he was kidding, and laughed and told him, "Never!" He even told me that he loved me. I in return told him that he was simply infatuated, and that I wanted to marry a man that looked like Omar Sharif and was a perfect gentleman like Mr. Darcy. I didn't know it at the time, but he was serious, and I broke his heart.

Adina loved Carig like a son, and she would always tell me, "Someday that boy is going to lose his freckles and you're going to be sorry you broke his heart." My ideas of love and friendship and Carig's clashed and changed everything. From that time on, when I would come for my visits Carig would no longer be standing at the house waiting for me. I was far too stubborn to ever say anything about it, so instead, I just became indifferent towards him as if I didn't care, but I really did. I never told him, but when the car would pull up to the house and I didn't see him there, I was truly disappointed. Sensing my indifference, Carig also didn't pay much attention to me. Most of his time was spent working wood and helping his grandfather. He was cordial, but our friendship ended on that day.

I hadn't really heard of what became of Carig since his grandfather passed away four years ago. Probably by now he was married with a bunch of red-haired kids running around everywhere.

I walked to the front of the house that faced the Atlantic and sat on the porch swing. This was one of my favorite parts of the house where Adina and I spent many of our summer days and nights. As the cool ocean breeze gently swept over my face, I could not only feel her sitting next to me, but also hear gentle whispers of her voice welcoming me home. It had been one of Adina's favorites too. Killen built this spectacular area that wrapped itself completely around the house, finishing it with climbing wood roses on the pillars that supported the portico which added a rich elegance to the house. In the late afternoon when the sun was setting, we would settle ourselves for the evening and drink iced tea and eat Adina's remarkable cheesecake, which she knew I adored. (The recipe and expertise to make this melt-in-your-mouth elegance was given to her by a baker in Germany named Ira.) This, along with a great book, made for a perfect evening together.

Many times as the sun was about to set, Adina and I would take the narrow dirt path that led down to the beach. On our way down to the water, we would kick off our shoes and dance on the shore, allowing the waves to consume us. Every 4th of July, we would dig large pits in the sand and cover them with blankets. We'd lie in our strategically-formed sand trenches, watching the fireworks explode over the water. For hours afterwards,

192

we would remain there together surveying the looming smoke in the sky, waiting for the stars to make their debut.

The lighthouse up the hill from the estate still remained as a spectacular beacon of safety that Adina had loved. She treasured and respected this stronghold which was an illumination of hope for those who had lost their way. I walked over and stared up at the tall red brick lighthouse with the glass and metal room at the top. It was always great fun to run as fast as I could up the twisting metal stairs to the top of the tower and hide, most of the time from Carig. As I stood gazing up, in the distance I noticed a tall muscular man with auburn hair chopping wood on the opposite side of the lighthouse. I figured it must be a new groundskeeper that Adina had hired to help keep the place up. After Killen's passing, Adina hadn't been sure at the time who she would hire to maintain things the way she liked. After 60 years of living on her estate, only Killen really knew how to keep things running like a well-oiled machine.

I walked over to introduce myself to bare-chested figure of a man who was dripping with sweat.

"Hello?."

With a loud grunt, he chopped one last log, making the task appear effortless, and then slammed his ax into the tree trunk. He stopped, stared straight ahead, pausing for a moment, and then he slowly turned around. His green eyes gazed right through me. He took a deep breath.

"Beni? You came!" said this man with a Scottish brogue.

"Carig? Oh my gosh, is that you? I had no idea that you even still lived here!"

"Aye, I do. I made a vow to me gran that I would carry on with this piece of land, and always be close at hand to take care of Adina."

"Wow, how thoughtful of you! I'm sure this isn't really where you wanted to stay, but I know that Adina cherished you and your grandfather and grandmother. She considered all of you her family."

"Actually Beni, this is my home and there was never any other place that I wanted to be. I have *almost* everything that I could ever want. It was my choice to stay. I could have left long ago, but I love this piece of land … it holds many memories for me."

194

As he spoke I found myself captured by his eyes, his lips, his body. This was the first time I had really ever found myself lost in anyone, and of all people, Carig! I hoped that he couldn't tell that I was completely mesmerized by him, and of course indiscreetly checking him out. I would have never admitted it to anyone, but he was the most gorgeous man I had ever seen, all six foot four of him, with shoulder-length auburn hair and piercing green eyes. Carig was no longer scrawny and skinny with freckles, but instead had a bronzed glow from spending most of his days outdoors, and a strong chiseled jawline just like his grandfather. When we were kids, I made fun of his accent, even mimicked him a few times, but now the sound of his voice and his dialect only added to his overall charm. Adina was right as always, he did grow up and lose his freckles, and if I were to be honest, I regretted how I had treated him when we were children. I wondered to myself if he was still mad at me for not agreeing to marry him.

"I was so sorry to hear about your grandfather, and....I'm *really* sorry that I didn't make it out for his funeral. He was a wonderful man, like a father to me, I'm so very sorry!"

As soon as I said it, and observed the transformation of his demeanor, I wished that I could have taken it back. It was stupid of me to mention his grandfather's name today of all days. Reminding him that the man whom he loved most in the world was not there to comfort him or talk him through the obvious grief of losing Adina.

His brilliant green eyes, turned gray, as he was suddenly laden with sorrow. "Aye, I miss him more than I can say. Now that Adina's gone, I'm the only one left here. I made a vow to him though before he died lass, and I intend to keep it. I promised to stay here, and carryin' on with the work he began. Gran loved Adina as if she was his own blood, and he promised her that a Hammel would always be watchman over this place. He laid deep roots that won't easily be moved. I mean look around Beni, there's pieces of him everywhere."

He was absolutely right. Every inch, all the way from the floorboards of the house to the trellises in the garden had been touched, molded and made by Killen. My eyes filled with tears as I noticed the pain on Carig's face. It was the same sadness and hurt that he bore when he arrived here from Scotland after losing his parents. He

196

had certainly had his fair share of loss. His grandparents and Adina meant everything to him. As a matter of fact, he was completely committed to her just as his grandfather was, and now that they were gone, he seemed a little bit lost.

"He's buried next to my grandmother out in the yard under the maple tree. When they first moved here, they planted that tree showin' that this was the place they'd be puttin down roots; the kind that would go down deep, and not be shaken even through the worst storms that life might bring. Once it grew a bit, he built her the bench that circles round it. He said that bench was like their love, never endin'. Bein' the romantic he was, he carved their initials in the tree in such a way that no amount of wind or rain could ever change it. I often come out here and talk things over with my gran. Just makes me feel close to um somehow."

Suddenly Carig stopped talking and walked over to where I was standing, slightly entering my personal space. He came so close that I was all but taken by his musky fragrance and the droplets of sweat that were suspended at the tips of his auburn locks.

"So, Beni, are you here to stay?"

I felt embarrassed, ashamed really, to tell him that I was only going to stay until I got Adina's affairs in order. Here was this man standing before me that wasn't even related to Adina, but had committed his life to her, and I was the one who left and would be leaving again.

"No, I won't be staying, I'm just here for a few days."

It was apparent by his look of annoyance, that he was not pleased with my response. "Well then, that's too bad."

"Yea, but I'll stay as long as I need to."

I began feeling uneasy, as he just stood there staring at me. I didn't know what else to say. I had made a life for myself in California, an important life, and I needed to return. To my relief, and out of the blue, I heard my name being called.

"Beni! Beni!"

Quickly turning around to that wonderfully familiar voice, I saw my uncle Wil coming towards me.

"Hey there, jaybird!" As long as I can remember, Wil referred to me as his jaybird.

I looked once again at Carig and told him that I would see him later. Obviously upset, he nodded, turned around, and started chopping firewood again. Uncertain of exactly what his problem was, and feeling a definite barrier of dissension between us, I turned around and walked away. Not only was he still mad at me, but I was pretty sure that in a roundabout way, he had just reprimanded me for leaving Bar Rousse, and not staying like he did. Thankfully, I wouldn't be here for very long and wouldn't have to deal with his cold manner, served up with a large helping of guilt.

I gave my Uncle Wil a big hug, and he kept his arm around me as we walked towards the house.

"How ya doing, Uncle Wil?"

"Oh Beni, Adina hadn't been doing so well for quite some time, but she wouldn't let me tell you. She always hoped, though, that she would go in her sleep, so it's a blessing that she did."

He started to cry as he continued talking about his beloved sister. I hated to see him so upset; he was always so happy, and quite a jokester. After all, aside from Wil's wife, Angelina, Adina was his best friend and his hero - it was she who saved him.

Chapter 9

Sweet Wil

Several years after Adina returned from Germany,
she, Killen, and Mari were working incessantly restoring
the old estate. One day, as they were in the thick of it all,
a telegram of the highest importance was delivered to her
door from an orphanage in Santa Fe, New Mexico.
Apparently her brother, Wil, had been taken to this
facility after Ray suffered a massive heart attack while at
a bar in this, *of late,* booming city.

Ray had decided that Wil had experienced just
about enough "education", and decided to teach him the
trucker trade first hand. As far as Ray was concerned,
experience was the "best way of learnin'", so he decided
that Wil would accompany him to the great state of
California to make a significant angus delivery. One
afternoon, after a long day of driving, Ray stopped at a
familiar bar to quench his thirst with an amber brew of
liquid courage. He told Wil to stay in the truck, and he'd
be back in a while. Before leaving, he warned him not to
open the door for anyone. Wil stayed in the truck, just as
his father had instructed; he knew better than to disobey

him. Hours went by, and poor Wil sat in the cab alone waiting for Ray to come out, while at the same time dreading his state of drunkenness when he finally did emerge.

Only moments after his boredom turned to slumber, Wil was aroused by the sound of sirens in the distance. As he focused on the outside goings on, he saw an ambulance racing towards the direction of the bar, and then watched as it turned into the bar parking lot. Next thing he knew, he saw his father on a gurney being put in the hospital wagon, (as he would call it) and rushed away.

With hands pressed against the window, he began crying out, "Daddy! Where they takin' you?"

When Wil was spotted in the truck, he was persuaded by the police to open the door. At first he refused, but then when they promised him a cheeseburger, french-fries, and a vanilla malt, he opened the door because the poor little thing was hungry. He was taken to the police station where they tried to contact his mother, Molly. When they finally got in touch with her, she told them that it wasn't possible for her to come and get Wil and that they would have to take care of him. That evening, he was taken to The Santa Fe Boys Home.

Three months passed with no contact from his mother, and in desperation, the SFBE notified Adina and told her the story of what had happened, and how long he had been with them. They told her that Wil's parents refused to come and pick him up, and that the state was about to deem him an orphan, making him a ward of the court. Adina was their last hope before this action would be taken.

Without a second thought, Adina jumped into her car, drove to Santa Fe, picked Wil up from the Boy's Home, and brought her ten-year-old brother back with her to Bar Rousse. She expected Wil to be broken and angry after being left there for so long, but to her surprise, he told her that those were the best three months of his life.

"I had my own bed, three squares a day, and they let me play baseball from mornin' till night instead of going to school!"

Adina was glad that he wasn't too scarred over the whole ordeal, but it grieved her that Wil was happier in an orphanage than in his own home. She completely understood his feelings on the matter though. After living in the Crawford home herself for so many years, she knew where he was coming from.

It took a great deal to make Adina fume, but this incident of desertion made her so angry that she could hardly see straight. It took a while, but when she was finally able to get ahold of her mother and father, she discovered that Molly had traveled to Santa Fe to check Ray out of the hospital, and they collectively decided to leave Wil. The words that poured out of her mouth to her parents were filled with venom and fury. After that point, she never spoke to either of them again, and she raised Wil on her own.

At the age of 21, Wil joined the Marines against Adina's wishes. The night before his first deployment to Korea, he met Angelina, the love of his life at a dance at the Bar Rousse Country Club. Angelina was there with another man, but she recognized him from the grocery market in town where he worked.

She came up to him and flirtatiously declared, "You don't know me, but I know you." Wil was instantly smitten with her and her witty personality. Even though he didn't know her, he was certain at that very second that he wanted nothing more than to spend the rest of his life *getting* to know her.

There was no doubt about it in the minds of everyone present that evening, that Wil carelessly and completely fell head over heels for her, and never looked back. It was always funny hearing Wil tell the story of their first meeting, as he was also there with another girl. Against his better judgment, he had been persuaded by his employer, Mr. Hughbert, to attend the dance with his only daughter, Daisy.

Mr. Hughbert's Darling Daisy, who was a large unattractive girl, was his pride and joy. She was constantly in the store flirting with Wil, who would inevitably attempt, no matter the task, to keep himself busy so that he wouldn't have to engage in conversation with her. Over the years, Wil's description of Daisy became one of being taller, larger, and more unattractive each time he recounted the saga. When I first heard the tale of that starry night at the country club, Daisy Hughbert stood only six inches taller than Wil. But throughout the years, she became a seven foot giant that outweighed him by a hundred pounds, with exaggerated yarns of how he nearly died on the dance floor that night as Daisy swung him around like a rag doll. Whatever the exact story may have been, it was in fact a long and painful evening for Wil.

There would be no sleep for him that night, as he spent the twilight hours writing a letter to Angelina. The next day before he left, he delivered the love struck epistle along with a single red rose from Adina's garden, to Angelina Horton who lived in Braydon, the next town over. This very romantic gesture captured her heart, and at his request, she pledged to wait for him.

For the next two years they faithfully wrote to one another. When Will returned home after a two-year absence, they were married on Adina's estate. Wil and Angelina purchased the Bar Rousse Market in 1960, and have owned and run it ever since. Daisy never quite recovered from the fact that Wil married someone else, but on her behalf, her father stepped in, and strategically made a deal with his meat vendor - something to the effect of, "You marry my daughter, I'll buy your meat!" To this day, Wil continues to buy meat from Daisy's beloved, Irvine Bannister, who believes that the sun rises and sets upon Daisy's blonde curls and false eyelashes. As for Daisy, she remains the sole organist at church where her large disposition spreads proudly over the entire organ bench.

Wil always knew that Adina saved him on that day when she picked him up from the orphanage, and it was only because of her, that he was given a chance to have a full life, a life that he loved.

As Wil and I stepped into Adina's house, we were both tormented by pangs of sadness. Her home still looked the same, and it felt as if any moment she would fly down the stairs with her arms opened wide, ready to welcome me home. This house not only brimmed with sweet memories of times together, but also with a rich history set in motion by the original owner who handcrafted the breathtaking ceiling that was elevated to great heights, swirling with seafaring embellishments. The walls still covered in time worn paneling, had been infiltrated by the aroma of dried roses and lavender. The room directly to the left was the library. It was difficult to see past the burnished chandelier that was colossal in measure, grandly marking the center of the room. The amber-colored bulbs that sat within the waves of metal strips, illuminated the entire area with golden gleams of light. When I was a child, I would lay directly beneath the glowing crown, and pretend to be a character from one of Adina's yellow-stained photographs that hung on her wall. For hours, I would imagine dozens of plots that were both mysterious and romantic, leading me into another time; a curious photo mixed with my nonsensical imagination was an ideal playground where exceptional stories came to life. Rising up from the floor was a full wall of built-in shelves that were lined with books. Facing the fireplace were two wingback chairs covered in a green and burgundy floral, and sitting on the side table was a half-read book with Adina's glasses resting atop. A massive French casement eyebrow window on the opposite wall was the crowning achievement of the room. It framed both sky and ocean, resembling a looking glass that was peering into an ultramarine world. The original walnut floors flowed gracefully throughout the house, with every room displaying a notably and perfectly chosen Persian carpet to embellish each area. To the far right was a spiral staircase with a dark wrought iron railing and stairs that were lavishly sculpted. As I made my way to the top of the stairs as I had so many times, there it was, *the room*! Most people would view this space as simply a sewing area. But it was special. This was our sanctuary where Adina and I would spend countless hours together. While she would turn out an array of incredible garments, I would read aloud to her, bringing to life the characters in my stories. In all of the years since I had been here, Adina never moved my books. There they stood, still side by side, held up by the bright blue-and-white-striped ceramic mug that I made for my father which was overflowing with bookmarks. Any time Adina would see an interesting bookmark, she'd would buy it for me and place it in my mug. Most would have thought me to be the oddest child and teenager, getting so lost in my stories, but not Adina. She was more than happy to escape with me into the thrilling world of literature

Various wooden tables were set up throughout the room, each one containing a particular sewing machine that was used for a specific purpose. In the far corner sat her favorite, her grandmother's pedal sewing machine that she continued to use throughout her entire life. There was a time that she was doubtful that she would ever see that machine again, as she was forced to leave it behind on that dark day in Germany. But somehow, unbeknownst to me, that priceless treasure was returned to her.

In the center of the room, a huge table was set up where she would do all of her cutting and pinning. Many dress forms of all shapes and sizes throughout the room made it seem as though it was filled with a gathering of headless models. In the corner was a bay window seat that had a perfect view of the Atlantic where I would sit for hours as a little girl, and read anything and everything that I could get my hands on. From that room, I suffered with Hester Prynne as she was being prosecuted for adultery in *The Scarlet Letter*, and then fell in love with Mr. Darcy in *Pride and Prejudice*. But my love of literature and the adventures that changed my life, truly began at the age of seven as I came alongside Nancy Drew, helping her unveil and solve the mystery of the day. Time seemed inconsequential while in this room. Not just this room, but this house, this place. For the first time ever, I realized how totally blessed I was to be raised by someone like Adina who allowed me to spend my days with her, diving headfirst into chronicles that would become the staircase to my future. This unique space also served as a photo gallery of sorts, being that the walls were covered from floor to ceiling with picture frames filled with black and white photos of people and places unknown to me. As long as I can remember, some of the frames have hung empty, bearing only a darkened area where a photo once rested. I used to love to look at the pictures and make up stories of my own about the images within the photos. Adina would laugh as she heard me create historical anecdotes about the strangers in the pictures. Sometimes however, I would notice Adina staring at the pictures with a far-off look on her face; she seemed to get lost in her memories of the photographs.

A twisting metal staircase at the far end of the room led to the third story of the house. Upon ascending up to this unusual but remarkable room, one is welcomed by an entire wall brimming with assorted hats hanging on hooks. Many of them were very old which Adina had from the time she was young, and some I recognized as I had helped her pick them out. She always thought it a good idea to be prepared with a hat for every occasion. Those on the lower hooks were the ones that I could wear and play with as a child. Those further up on the wall were reserved for Adina only. On the other side of the room was a group of enormous wooden wardrobes that ran the entire length of the wall, with a section reserved for me. When I would come to her house and the sewing began, each finished garment was placed in my wardrobe. Every closet space served a purpose and held particular garments; this was one thing that she was adamant about. When it was time for me to return to school, Adina would gather my clothes from my wardrobe and place them in garment bags so that I could easily transport them back to school.

Next in the room, was a wall covered in mirrors with a stepping stand placed in front where a finished product would be modeled and hemmed. The last wall in the room was nothing special really as it was left plain, and only had a French glass door that led out onto a balcony overlooking the ocean. This balcony was off limits. Adina told me that Killen was never able to reinforce it properly, so it was not safe, and an awfully long drop from the third floor. As Uncle Wil and I were walking through the house reminiscing about Adina, he informed me that I, and only I, had an appointment set up in the morning at 9:00 a.m. to meet with Adina's attorney regarding her estate. I thought it rather curious that Wil emphasized that only I could go to that appointment. In all honesty, I wished that he could go with me; I really didn't want to go alone.

Before we realized it, the sun had gone down and night was upon us.

Uncle Wil yawned and said, "Well Beni girl, I'd probably better get going. I've got to get the chickens in." Even though he didn't have any chickens, this funny antidote was his exit call. I loved and adored my Uncle Wil, he could brighten up the darkest room with his wonderful sense of humor and kind spirit.

I walked him down to the front door and gave him a big hug. "Oh, if I forgot to mention it, the attorney you will be meeting with is named Mr. Peevey." I looked at him perplexed.

"How did this Mr. Peevey know that I would be here in time for tomorrow's appointment?"

"I don't really know, but he came by and saw me at the market today. It was actually him that told me you'd be flying in this afternoon, that's why I came over. He's going to review all of the arrangements with you that Adina had in place for her funeral. Oh, I also asked him what day we're gonna have Adina's funeral, and he said Tuesday of next week, but that's all I know. Alright, jaybird, come by and see me after your appointment tomorrow, let me know how it goes, and if there's anything I can help you with." He looked around one more time, "Good ol' Didi! (Didi was Wil's pet name for Adina.) She was organized alright, and never missed a beat. I'm sure that everything will go smoothly. Don't worry about anything." Wil kissed me on the forehead and began walking to his car.

"Ok, I won't. I'll see you in the morning. Hey Uncle Wil, was Adina disappointed in me ... that I haven't been here in so long?"

"Listen, jaybird, Adina was only proud of the woman you became. She wouldn't want you to think about anything except how much she loved you." Wil always knew just what to say to make me feel better.

After such a long day, I was exhausted, and just wanted to go to bed. I began walking up the stairs to my room, when I heard a knock on the back door of the kitchen. Flipping on the porch light to see who it was, I was surprised to see Carig standing there.

"Hello Beni, sorry to bother you lass, but I thought ye might be a bit hungry." In one hand he was holding a black iron pot, and in the other was a loaf of bread wrapped in a white cloth.

"What's this?"

"Just some soup."

"Would you like to stay and eat with me?"

"Nah, I've got to be gettin' back, but I'll see ya tomorrow."

"Ok, thank you, Carig!"

The kitchen door closed, and I watched as he walked back to the lighthouse. There was a troubling barrier between us. I had a difficult time believing that he could still be upset over a silly teenage rejection; it had to be something else. Maybe the unseen wall that was built up between us had been growing since I left, created by the burdensome blocks of absence.

I opened the lid and was invigorated by the familiar aroma of Cullen Skink, just like Mari used to make. Sitting at the table alone, that once was filled with my family who would celebrate my homecoming, was disheartening. But after ladling myself a bowl of chowder along with a piece of the still warm bread, I felt revived. One moment I was so worn out, but after a bowl of chowder, I felt as if I had been brought back to life. It was even better than I remembered. I thought to myself, "Great, he cooks too! What doesn't he do well?" Dragging my sleep-deprived self up to my room, I was amazed that It still looked the same as it did last time I was here. I surrendered myself into the arms of my fluffy white down comforter and fell asleep.

Chapter 10

Adina's Legacy

I woke up to the sound of a horn blowing outside of my window; blaring like a trumpet from a fishing vessel that was venturing out to sea for the day. As much as it alarmed me, I was glad it sounded, being that it was 8:30 and my appointment with Mr. Peevey was at 9:00. I hurried up and got myself ready. Slipping on a pair of holey jeans and an oversized cream sweater, I felt a bit underdressed for an appointment with a lawyer. I didn't have much time, so I pulled my hair back in a ponytail, grabbed my purse, and ran out the door. I could have taken Adina's car, but after sitting on a plane all day yesterday, the walk in the brisk morning air would definitely do me some good.

The dirt path leading towards town was lined with beautiful oak trees adorned with leaves of orange, rust, and gold. This array of colors combined with the fragrant ocean breeze was the reason that I fell in love with fall. As I entered the little community of Bar Rousse, I was reminded of the friendly quaintness of the red, white, and

216

gray wood-sided buildings that made up the town. This was a place where everyone knew everyone, and it felt warm and inviting.

Mr. Lewin Peevey's office was at the end of the town in a newer building. I walked in the door and was met by his secretary, Miss Louise Brown.

"May I help you?"

"Yes, I am Beni Crawford. Benidette I mean. I have a nine o'clock appointment with Mr. Peevey."

"Yes, you certainly do. I have heard a lot about you. I am very sorry for your loss."

"Thank you." Miss Brown was very kind and had worked at Mr. Peevey's side for just under 40 years. It was only five years ago that he decided to move his practice to Bar Rousse.

"Have a seat, sweetheart. Lew will be with you in in a few minutes. Can I get you anything? Coffee? Tea? Water?

"No, but thank you."

As I pulled my phone from my backpack to check my messages, I was interrupted by the voice of Adina's

lawyer and friend who was undoubtedly very important
to her.

"Hello Beni, I'm Lew. Come on in." Mr. Peevey
was a tall gray-haired man with black horn-rimmed
glasses. His gray hair was slicked back, and he was
wearing a charcoal colored suit with a white shirt, and a
black and gray striped tie. We went into his office and he
shut the door.

"I was so sorry to hear about Adina. You know, I
have known her for forty years. I'm grieving right along
with you - feel like I've lost a sister."

"Excuse me, Mr. Peevey, but I have been coming
to visit my aunt since I was five, and pardon me, but I
don't remember ever meeting you."

"Well, that's probably because we've never had
the opportunity. For most of my career I lived and had
my practice in New York City. When Adina would come
and visit you at school, she'd usually come by and take
care of some business with me. The thing you may not
know, is that most of the time the business that we
discussed was you. This may be our first time meeting,
but I do feel as if I know you."

"Oh, ok. I guess I didn't even know she had a lawyer."

"Yes, Adina wanted to make sure every last detail was taken care of." He pulled out a large folder stacked with papers, and dramatically dropped it on the table. "We have a lot to talk about." Mr. Peevey began by telling me that Adina wished to be buried alongside Carson on the east side of her property in the garden, by the gazebo. Adina would go there each day and sit on the bench that Killen carved out of a two hundred year old oak. "All of the funeral arrangements have been made, and her burial will take place next Tuesday at four sharp. She chose that time of day for a specific purpose. That was the exact hour, without fail, that she would walk up to her garden area and sit on her bench, and discuss the day's events with Carson until the sun went down. Now Beni, I'm going to say something to you that you may not be expecting to hear. Please don't make any quick decisions until you spend some time thinking about it."

"Thinking about what?" I immediately felt uneasy with his prelude of words.

"Adina has left you everything she owns. Her estate, all of her property, and all of her money. I have itemized everything for you in this book." Mr. Peevey handed me a leather-bound book which listed all of Adina's assets and worth. "Now I know Beni, that Adina never made any requests of you, but these last wishes for you are, in fact, an appeal from her."

I looked at Mr. Peevey, feeling a little perturbed that he was playing on my emotions and that his plea was driven by a hearty helping of guilt.

"You know, I would do anything for Adina. If it weren't for her, I don't know where I'd be today."

I tried to hold back my emotions, but I started to cry. I was so embarrassed to start blubbering in front of a total stranger. Usually my pride would keep me from showing any emotion to anyone. I knew myself well enough to know that once I started crying, it would take me a long time to stop.

Mr. Peevey got up from the table and left the room. A few minutes later, he returned with a box of tissue, and a glass of water.

"Are you ok, Beni? You know, everything is going to be ok. It is, I promise!"

While forceful in his resolve, Mr. Peevey was also kind, and his words of encouragement made me feel better and able to move forward. But how could he or anyone make such a promise? How could he know that everything was going to be alright?

"Ok then." Mr. Peevey paused and took a deep breath. "Ok, so here it is, she wants you to stay here in Bar Rousse, and continue."

"I'm sorry, what did you just say to me?" I sat there staring at him in astonishment, "Stay in Bar Rousse? But I live in California. I have a job there that I love - I can't stay here! No, my answer is no!"

"Beni, don't say no yet. Just think about it." As he was telling me to think about it, he handed me an oversized worn brass key. "This is a key to Adina's trunk that sits at the end of her bed. Do you know the one?"

"Yes, I know exactly which trunk you're talking about, but what are you asking me to do?"

"Well, I don't know exactly, this part is a mystery to even me. The only instructions she gave me in regards to the trunk, was to give you the key. Now, I can tell that you're a smart girl, and you'll have no problem figuring

221

out what she's trying to tell you." Mr. Peevey referred once again to a check off list of items that he needed to cover with me. As he reviewed the list, he nervously began twisting his eyebrows. "Um, um, um, ok. Now on a totally different subject, tonight is the Catwalk Masquerade Ball. Adina requested that when her time came, and she could no longer be present at this event, that I should make sure you would go in her place. Adina has not missed that ball since she came here, it was a very important part of her life. And likewise, it was important to her that you attend in her place."

"I can't go to that ball, Mr. Peevey, I didn't bring a dress, and ….?"

Mr. Peevey closed the folder of paperwork, and looked at his watch. "Well, that's it really. I believe we've covered everything we needed to go over for now anyway. I will have some papers for you to sign depending on what your decision is."

"Wait, we are not done here! For God's sake, I feel like I'm in the "Twilight Zone"! One minute you're telling me that Adina wants me to stay, and the next you hand me a key and tell me I need to go the Catwalk Ball tonight? I'm confused, Mr. Peevey, what do you mean 'depending on what decision I make?' There's no decision here. I can't, and I won't stay!'"

"Well, it's simple really. If you stay, the Bar Rousse Estate and Lighthouse will continue to run as it presently does, and you will have complete control of all facets of the estate. However, if you do not choose to live there, you will still own it, but it will be run and maintained by a real estate management company. They'll bring in all of their own people to take care of the entire property, and keep it running properly. Eventually, you would probably just want to sell it. It would be a shame for it to be empty though. Carig, of course, would have to leave unless the management company chooses to hire him on, but they generally have their own people to do those kind of things. Adina's wish was that you stay here. Be that as it may, that decision is completely yours and it can wait until later, but not too much later. Before you leave though Beni, I want you to promise me that you will do some profound soul-searching before you make any final decisions. I have both sets of papers ready to be signed. Think about it and then let me know. Here is my card. Give me a call if you need anything."

"Can't I just sign them now? I really will need to leave, probably by next Wednesday after the funeral. If those are my only two options, letting the management company run the house is the way I'll need to go. I'll still keep the house, I just can't live here."

"Let's not be hasty, Beni", Mr. Peevey said sternly. "Please!! Think about what this meant to your aunt. She loved you so much, but she also loved that house...it was part of her. Young lady, don't dismiss this as unimportant, it's of the utmost importance and a decision such as this should not be taken lightly. It would be a shame to just walk away from it. Take the key, see what Adina has for you in the trunk, and go to the Catwalk and have a good time. This would be a great place for you to live."

What in the heck was wrong with him? It was as though he didn't even hear a word that I said. I was completely annoyed that he had his own agenda, refused to hear me, and wouldn't allow me sign the papers of my choosing right then and there! Why was he trying to back me into a corner and tell me what I should do?

By the time our conversation ended, we were both thoroughly irritated with one another. If I could have done what I wanted to do, I would have stormed out without saying another word. But instead, like Adina, I chose the higher road.

"Ok, Mr. Peevey, thank you for your time. I'll be seeing you soon *to sign those papers*, and then I will need to leave."

"One more thing Beni, when I say 'soul-search', I mean search with the eyes of your heart and your soul, not too much with that hardheaded gray matter upstairs. Do I make myself clear?"

He did *not* just tell me to let my heart make this decision for me! It took every ounce of self-control to hold my tongue towards this man who was asking me to give up everything that I had worked so hard for.

"Mr. Peevey, I understand fully what you're talking about!"

I turned around and walked out his office, ready to spit fire. If I had to hear the patronizing tone of his voice for one more second, I would scream.

Resentment drove my steps, causing me to storm down the street. My mind was swimming with unending questions, such as why Adina would insist on me staying? I just didn't understand. No so called "soul-searching" was necessary - I knew what needed to be done. I *would* be signing those papers in favor of the management company, and *would* absolutely be returning to California, and there was nothing that was going to change my mind!

As I began walking towards Wil's Market, the colorful buoys of Jay's Lobster Shack caught my eye. Every Saturday night, Adina and I would eat at Jay's where we would feast on lobster tails, coleslaw, and cheddar yeast rolls. Jay's lobster was something that Adina and I craved on a regular basis, and having it once a week was hardly enough. Just walking by his lobster shack made my mouth water. That was one thing about California, there was no place there that served up a lobster like Jay's.

It was funny, even though I had been gone for seven years, nothing in Bar Rousse had really changed. A few new faces perhaps, but the buildings and shops were just as I remembered. I arrived at Wil and Angelina's market, still as always, stocked and organized with only the finest items. Their store did very well, but what they were really known for was their homemade brittle. They shipped unique brittles such as butter pecan and blueberry pine nut all over the world. Their little store had become a tourist hot spot because of their unique confections. The inviting aroma of their famous brittles welcomed me as I walked through the door.

Angelina ran with open arms from behind the counter and gave me a big hug.

"Oh Beni, you are so beautiful! You look just like your Aunt Adina, but even more lovely! Oh my goodness, you are so grown up."

"Thank you Ange, you haven't changed a bit either - still as spunky and cute as ever!" My Aunt Angelina was a petite woman with short blond hair and blue eyes. Even though her grandmother was a Cherokee Indian, no one would ever know by looking at her as she was so fair-skinned.

Just then, Wil walked out carrying a case of canned goods and began stocking a shelf. "Hey, jaybird, how did it go with Mr. Peevey? Or....should I even ask?"

Clearly he could tell by my expression that it didn't go very well.

"Well, I don't know really. He said Adina's last wishes were for me to stay here in Bar Rousse and finish."

"Hmm? Finish what exactly?"

"Well, I'm not sure. He gave me this key and told me to look through the trunk at the foot of her bed."

"You know babe, don't be discouraged. Adina had a purpose in everything she did. She was always like that. I think you should do what he says and look through the trunk. You and I both know how you love a great mystery!"

"He also asked me, well told me really, that Adina wanted me to go to the Catwalk Masquerade Ball tonight." It was ironic, I had waited my whole life to go to this ball, and now that the opportunity was right in front of me, I didn't really want any part of it. "You know Wil, I really just need to focus on finishing up everything here and get back home. Besides, I have nothing to wear. And you and I both know how people dress for this shindig!"

"I think I can help you, Beni girl. A few years ago, Adina thought that you might be coming out for the

228

Ball, but it didn't work out because you were going through all the interview stuff at the university. But you know her, the moment she found out that you *might* come, she started making a dress for you to wear. I never saw the finished product, but I do know that she wanted to make it really special since it was your first ball, and she knew how you had looked forward to going someday. She left it for you on the left side of your wardrobe in a silk garment bag. You put that dress on tonight and go and have a ball. 'Go to the Ball and have a ball!'" He laughed out loud at his own witty humor, but then became teary eyed and more serious. "Do it for Adina, it would mean so much to her!"

"Are you and Angelina going?"

"Na! Adina loved those things, but we gotta get home and bring the chickens in, and besides, I need my beauty sleep you know!"

There he went again, making everything ok with his unfailing humor that could always cheer me up, and put everything into perspective.

"Oh Wil, I just don't see how one extra minute of beauty sleep could make you any more handsome than you already are! Thank you for cheering me up!"

"I'm always here for you, jaybird!"

As I began walking out of his store, I remembered something that I needed to tell him.

"By the way, Mr. Peevey also said that Adina's funeral will be at four o'clock on Tuesday, in her garden."

Wil's eyes filled up with tears and he put his head down shaking it back and forth. "I still can't believe she's gone."

Angelina came over and began rubbing his back. "It's ok, hun! She's with Carson now, and she's happy. She's not alone anymore."

I gave Angelina and Wil a big hug, and began walking home. My mind was so preoccupied that I hardly remembered the walk back. The vibrant colors of fall that had earlier inspired, now seemed stripped of their rich hues. It was clear that this morning's affairs and the request to relinquish my life, had all but dimmed my vision. That one single meeting with Mr. Peevey made me feel as though everything had changed, and I was overwhelmingly troubled. Not only was I fighting the guilty reminders of how I had disappointed Adina in life, but now the thought that I was faced with doing the same thing when it came to her final wishes, was excruciating. Each step forward became more and more difficult, until finally I came to a complete stop. I was weighed down and heavy laden as if a satchel filled with stones was strapped on top of me. Every thought became an added weight, heavier and more difficult to bear. I was alone in all of this, and it seemed that there was no right choice. Any decision that I would make would leave someone upset and disappointed. But there was something else bothering me as well, something -Wil had said. He said that Adina was alone... was she alone? She had Killen and Carig and Mari, Wil, and Ange. She lived in a community of people that she loved, and who loved her in return. So on top of everything else, I was sure that she spent her last days hoping that I would come back home, but I never did.

I had to stop with all the guilt, or I was gonna make myself crazy. Adina may have been lonely, but at the same time, she loved her independence. It was her choice not to marry after Carson's death. She could have had anyone she wanted. I mean for goodness sake, she was only nineteen at the time. I began pondering the fact that I, like Adina, was alone. She, however, made a conscious decision to remain in her state of singleness. But I on the other hand, never really gave it much thought, until now. The idea of ending up alone bothered me more than I realized. Perhaps my trip here, and my separation from normalcy, had spurred me into a much needed reflection of my life. I wasn't completely pathetic though, I had dated a few times, but was just never impressed enough to move on to a second date. I would be the first to admit my hair-splitting pickiness, but even Adina continually declared that one should never date someone that they wouldn't marry. She even went so far as to say that it was far better to be alone than wed the wrong person. I knew that there was someone for me, I just hadn't found him yet, or maybe he hadn't found me. Honestly, my whole life had been spent on pursuing my education and career. Relationships for me had been placed on the back burner a long time ago. Bonds of intimacy were complicated, and left me feeling confused. Even though I promised myself that I would never be one of those people who blamed their brokenness on their parents, the truth in regards to my "complication" stemmed from my father. He was the man that I loved most in the world. Instead of returning that love though, he shattered my heart in such a way that I wasn't sure if it would ever fully heal. Anyway, who would even want a heart like mine that was still somewhat broken?

The ledger and brass key that were now in my possession were symbols of a life well-lived. I quickly determined that these deep-rooted pieces of legacy and tradition that she chose to hand down to me were completely undeserved. In comparing our approaches to life, it was painstakingly clear that I fell very short. Mine had been good and productive, but contritely driven by lofty goals and high ambitions. Hers on the other hand, had always been motivated by love. If I abandoned my life, gave up my profession, and came to Bar Rousse what would I do? What would my purpose be? What would I become? Like Adina, I too loved this place, but at the same time I was utterly passionate about my job and the lives that I impacted every day. The more I thought about the two of us, the more I realized how similar we were. Both driven by our passions, and both exceptionally stubborn with a hint of hardheadedness.

Although moved by Adina's generous inheritance, I was still offended by Mr. Peevey's bold impertinence of inviting me to give up everything. And the nerve of him to be upset that I didn't jump at the opportunity!

Honestly, the bottom line was that I was scared, and I hated my fear! I felt as if there was a battle raging within me, and I didn't know how to make it stop.

My thoughts detoured as my attentions turned once again to the brass key that I had tucked into my jacket pocket. It occurred to me that when I was a child, I would regularly beg Adina for just the tiniest peek in her trunk. She would always tell me, "No, not yet, my dear." Of course I didn't think about it at the time, but "not yet" didn't mean no, it meant later. I realized that later was now, and it was my hope that everything would make sense once I opened the aged locker that sat at the end of Adina's bed. I decided right then and there, that I would need to deal with one obstacle at a time. For right now, there were two things that I would focus on: Attend the Catwalk event in Adina's name, and secondly, heed Mr. Peevey's advice and do some soul-searching about whether I should stay or leave.

Chapter 11

Catwalk Masquerade

*The strong towers of the world that guide the lost home
would be worthless without those who keep the light
burning....Killen Hammel*

      Many traditions of grandeur often die through the ages. The only customs that remain and stand the test of time are those most worthwhile, that benefit and consider not only a worthy cause, but most importantly, people in need. The strong towers of the world that guide the lost home would be worthless without those who keep the light burning. The Catwalk Masquerade that assembled for the first time in the marble- covered ballroom of the Bell Cove Grand Hotel on October 6, 1900, was such an event, and what a grand event it was! Like many benefits, this splendid affair was set in motion after a near catastrophe occurred during the wee hours of an unfriendly September daybreak. Just after the first watch of the morning, as Captain Sean Scully stepped off of his catwalk, an enormous wave crashed down onto the lighthouse, ripping the entire walkway from the tower. He watched in horror as it fell off and plunged into the sea, almost taking him with it. Before the beastly swell was finished, the iron catwalk furiously thrust into the side of his tower, provoking endless blows of devastation. He was devastated knowing that he could not effectively do his job as keeper without a proper walkway and undamaged fortress. Scully Tower resided on the coast of Braydon, and had respectably been passed down to the Scully sons for decades. Even though his lighthouse was located in the next county over from Bar Rousse, proper working conditions of this particular tower were important for *all* of the surrounding communities. Every resident was fully aware that Scully kept the only sector lighthouse in the area whose main and sole purpose was to ensure safe passage for all incoming and outgoing boats through the shallow waters of the harbor. The mayors of both Bar Rousse and Braydon immediately assembled, along with other city councilmen and commissioners, to fashion a resolution. After hours of deliberation and determining that the repair costs were immense, they were at a loss. It was not until Lilabette Muller, wife of the Bar Rousse Mayor, walked into the meeting with lunch for the gathering, that a solid plan of action was revealed. She overheard them bickering back and forth about which city should furnish

236

and provide this and that; both arguing that the other should pay for the costly repairs. Setting down her basket of food, she staged a chair up to the table, and didn't sit, but stood on top of it.

"Hush, all of you. That is enough!"

Her husband, Jeremiah Muller, was just as surprised at her unexpected opposition as everyone else in the room. He couldn't believe that his sweet and always-appropriate wife would do such a thing. Somewhat disturbed, he awkwardly walked over to where she was standing and lifted his hand to help her down from her soapbox. With eyes focused on her audience, she ignored his gesture completely.

"I have a solution that should make all parties happy! A BALL!"

At those two words the men broke out in laughter at such a silly and "womanly" notion. After enduring a few moments of unkind bantering at her expense, she had heard enough.

"Excuse me! If you fine gentlemen are interested in eating, you *will* hear me out!"

Because they were all famished, mouths all but drooling from the tantalizing aroma of her well-known yeast rolls, they silenced themselves immediately.

"I propose a dinner ball, charging per plate to attend. I, along with accomplished cooks from both cities, will prepare and organize the food and decorations. The rest... music, and a location will be up to you. That is if you think you can come to an agreement without bickering for the rest of the day. But, if I were in charge of selecting a venue, I would designate The Bell Cove Grand as the location. As we all know, the ceiling is covered with dozens of the most unique chandeliers that once sat in the dining chambers of seafaring vessels around the world. Each one was appropriated for their ballroom upon retirement of the craft. I think it would be highly appropriate to have a maritime ball, whose proceeds will repair Scully's lighthouse, in such a room, don't you?"

As Lilabette began serving the food, the men who were quietly impressed by her idea appeared indifferent, except for low murmurs of approval, and questions of how to tag this amazing notion. Lilabette, rolling her eyes at their ridiculous and uncreative titles such as the

"Mayor's Ball" or "Dollars for the Lighthouse Ball", had finally had enough.

"No, no, no! If we are to charge a hefty price per plate, this can't be just some common thing, but completely unique. It will most certainly be a trend that others with copy, but will never fully attain. It not only has to be amusing, mysterious, and black tie of course, but be identified as exemplary and completely untypical."

At this point, they listened attentively and watched in anticipation as her deep thoughts manifested the trademark that would remain the christened name from that time forward.

"How about....The Catwalk Masquerade?"

She could tell by the symphony of smiles across the table that they not only loved the idea of the ball, but the ideal name.

"Well gentlemen, my job here is done. I'd say we should be ready for this shindig by.... October 6th? Yes, October 6th is perfect. We may even have a full moon by then. That will give us about two weeks to prepare. I'll make sure invitations are sent out by the end of the week. Good day gentlemen!"

The first dinner and dance was indeed held at the Bell Cove Grand Hotel, only because it was the largest venue between the two cities, not to mention the fact that Lilabette suggested it. Each attendee paid a whopping ten dollars per plate, donned their finest black and white attire and most elegant and mysterious of masks, thus setting a standard of superiority and excellence at the highest level. The event was a great success. Proceeds surpassed populace expectations, allowing immediate construction to begin on Scully's catwalk and tower. Within a week's time, the sector lighthouse was up and running. The Catwalk Masquerade soon became the social event of the year, and continually grew into a most enjoyable and profitable tradition for both communities.

Just as Lilabette predicted, The Catwalk Masquerade has never been paralleled, but has only become more respected and honored throughout the years. To this day, every dollar gained is not only used to benefit and keep up restoration efforts for *all* lighthouses along the coast of Maine, but also to benefit *lighthouse keepers* who are in need. This organization, for example, came alongside Killen and Mari, Adina's lighthouse keepers who needed help and support while traveling to Scotland to pick up their orphaned grandson.

Today the price tag to attend this prestigious event is a minimum of $500 a plate, with the exception of all lighthouse keepers, who are of course, free of charge. Customarily, very few keepers attend, as most of them are a bit rough around the edges and don't really enjoy that sort of thing. They would rather be *on* their catwalk than *at* the Catwalk.

When I was a little girl, I loved to hear Adina's rendition of Lilabette's story and how the Catwalk began. I never grew tired of the "tale of old", and hoped that someday I too would be brave, just like Lilabette Muller. Even after the horrible disaster that occurred in December 1924, nearly ending the Catwalk Masquerade Ball forever, Lilabette persevered in her convictions. Citizens from both communities stood in horror as they helplessly watched The Bell Cove Grand burn to the ground after a candle-lit Christmas tree caught fire. The owners were older and too heartbroken over the destruction to consider rebuilding. Lilabette convinced them to sell the property to the City of Bar Rousse, promising that the ball would continue to be held in the same location of Bell Cove. Since that time, this celebrated locale has become one of Maine's premier outdoor spots for public use.

Adina took me there many times. As we would sit on the well-loved inlet, she would illustrate every detail of the evening's layout and activities. For years I waited in anticipation to finally attend the Catwalk Ball, and Adina promised that when I did, she would create for me the most extraordinary "far beyond anything that I could ever imagine" gown. It's a well-known fact that two weeks prior to the big event, like clockwork, the cove is roped off in preparation for The Catwalk. Just as Lilabette promised, the site of Bell Cove has been, and always will remain, home to this worthy event.

At dawn on the first morning of set up, construction begins first and foremost on the celestial ballroom, the "Diamond" of the event. The floor of cedar that is laid directly onto the sand, is the cornerstone for everything else. At each of the four points, beams are erected where hundreds of strands of lights are latticed to create a heavenly ceiling. To the right of the floor, a tiered landing is perfectly placed to accommodate a full orchestra whose melodies can supposedly be heard across the great state of Maine. Directly opposite the bandstand, extensive banquet tables are arranged for the sole purpose of providing an uninterrupted flow of champagne, blueberries, and sinful white chocolate. The only decorations needed to create a magical atmosphere filled with beauty and romance are the star-filled sky, the glistening ocean, and of course the full moon that arrives each year without fail. The massive dinner tent which became the traditional gathering place after the fall of the Grand, is next on the agenda. Hundreds stand in awe as it is rigorously and impressively hoisted up to the sky. Its delicate and virtually transparent ceiling is unique to say the least. The once opaque roofing was replaced with fabric that majestically showcases the stars. Dawning from the center of the room, sheer light- infused swags are attached that run in every direction. Adina would often comment that it was difficult to tell where the lights paused and the heavens began. On its own, the canvas encampment is spectacular. As if anything could add to the embellishments already in place, the priceless chandeliers that were salvaged from the burnt rubble at the Grand, serve as lateral centerpieces, each one carefully suspended like a pendant above every table. Somehow, having a little piece of the Grand Hotel has always honored the tradition and legacy of the Catwalk's origins, and most definitely brings about an air of perfection to the night. Finally, and gloriously spread over each tabletop, are crisp white linens and vintage blue and white nautical china that have been the place settings of choice from the very beginning.

As long as I can remember, I had yearned for the day that I could attend the Catwalk. And now coming full circle, I could almost touch it, even hear it zealously calling my name. But somewhere in the past seven years, my fervor for this long- coveted possibility had been disengaged along with everything else here in Bar Rousse. To be honest, I had become completely disconnected from those who were once most important to me. The more I thought about it, the more confused I became as to why I had never returned. It was almost as if something had intentionally obscured my rationale. For the first time since I arrived, I felt certain that I was supposed to be here, but still uncertain as to whether or not I was supposed to stay.

Regardless of my inclination about attending the ball, I suddenly felt wildly excited to see the dress that Adina had created for me. But like an ever raging battle, my enthusiasm continued to be clouded by the uncertainty of whether I should even attend. Instead of looking at this through eyes of joy and opportunity like Adina would, I had a terrible habit of allowing my imagination to run wild with the worst of scenarios. My foolish wavering once again reminding me that I was without a doubt my worst enemy, and it had to stop!

"Come on Beni! This isn't about you, it's about Adina. It's time to grow up, and become the woman that she raised you to be!"

This would be the first time that I stood alone in the third story room, facing the wall of wardrobe thresholds that held Adina's works of art. Just being in the center of her most worthwhile achievements inspired and filled me with the same fire and passion for life that she modeled every day. It almost felt as if she was here, reminding me that everything was going to be alright. If even for a moment, all of my stubborn inhibitions and doubts seemed to fade as I opened the wardrobe and saw the ream of satin that held my dress. The eagerness that I felt as I unzipped the bag, ignited Christmas morning memories of zeal and enthusiasm for the lovely packages soon to be opened. The gown was more splendid than I could have ever imagined, and the awe that I experienced reminded me of Dorothy Gale's reaction as she beheld the Emerald City for the first time. I removed the rich jade-colored gown and hung it on a dress hook, unable to take my eyes off of the exquisite design. By far, this was Adina's best work. I wished that she was here so that I could tell her how amazing she was. It was evident that she created this plunging neckline masterpiece illuminated with glints of silver, to completely hug my body. She was forever trying to convince me to show off my figure and *icksnay* my blue jeans and oversized sweatshirts. But unlike her sense of style, comfort for me always took priority over glamor. Within the mantle of the wardrobe sat a large floral hat box that was labeled with my name. Sliding the snug fitting lid from the circular box, I couldn't help but smile as I caught sight of the matching shoes along with a translucent silver masquerade veil that was wrapped in white tissue paper. Finally, not forgetting a thing, beneath the shoes was hidden a velvet box containing a choker and matching earrings made of emeralds and diamonds.

It felt strange getting ready for the Catwalk and attending for the first time ever, and not being able to share it with Adina. If she were here we would have spent the day swimming in beauty treatments, manicures, and pedicures … oh how I missed her! After finishing my makeup and hair, which I opted to wear down, it was time to put on the dress. I had worn many elegant formals in the past, but this one far exceeded them all. It was apparent that Adina fashioned this constricting gown with the intention of being present to help me step in, suck in, and zip up. The low-placed zipper was practically impossible to reach, but after several awkward attempts of lengthening and compressing every muscle in my body, while of course holding my breath, I finally did it. Standing on the hem step, I was able to inspect every angle of this magnificent gown. I was truly amazed at the glove-like fit, and once I slipped on the stilettos I felt statuesque as well. Suddenly noticing the late hour, I quickly snapped the choker and earrings into place, and decided to carry my mask, putting it on once I arrived at the ball. I wished that I wasn't going alone, but once again reminded myself that none of this was about me.

Thankful to finally hear the blow of the horn from Bar Rousse Cab, I took one last glance at myself, and couldn't help but notice how tall I looked in these highly uncomfortable shoes. Adina would have been thrilled to see me in this dress, and would have proudly been by my side as I attended the ball for the very first time. I could almost hear her laughingly say that it took her having to die for me to finally put on a pair of stilettos. She was

247

right actually, and knew me very well. I would only endure such torture for her!

I had the entire evening mapped out in my mind. It was now eight-thirty, and the event had been in full swing since eight. It was my hope to walk into the ball unnoticed when everyone would be busy socializing, already half drunk, and I could move in under the radar. I would only stay long enough to make an appearance on Adina's behalf.

Unaware of what the nightfall watch would reveal, Carig followed his usual course to the top of the lighthouse for his evening inspection of the lantern room, ensuring that the beacon was lit and properly rotating. The next several hours of watching for changes in the tide, disruptive weather, or ships in distress would generally consume the twilight hours. But tonight the sea was unusually peaceful, and the skies strikingly clear and bright. The advent of the most full and kindly moon that he had ever observed, seemed to make a private declaration of vigilance.

"The watch is mine tonight, lad!"

Carig knew that such a consummation of elements was an omen to be sure.

"Change is comin' for certain, but what it may be, I don't yet know!"

In an attempt to ease the restlessness that was provoking him to, at any moment, leap out of his very skin, he tightly grasped the railing in frustration, trying to ignore the edgy intuition, while knowing deep inside who it was that held the key to both his irritation and salvation from this agony. It had taken years to try and forget her, to make peace with the fact that half of him would forever be missing, and that he would journey through the rest of this life apart from her. He wished that she had never returned because he couldn't stand the thought of watching her leaving again. On the other hand, she consumed his every thought. He shook his head and closed his eyes in frustration as he was pretty sure that the whole thing was going to make him lose his mind. Her being here clouded his discernment.

Distracting his survey of the sea, Carig spotted something unusual out of the corner of his eye that was beyond his normal charge. It wasn't just an individual that he could see, but an overwhelming allure, as if his very core was being influenced by a force greater than he. For the first time in many years, his glance was uninterested in the deep billows, but was furiously drawn to her. "Beni!" He whispered quietly to himself. He swore that he would never allow his heart to go there again, but as he beheld her standing on the porch wearing a dress that shimmered like the moon on the ocean, his hesitancy disappeared. He was immediately mesmerized, and discovered a new resolve within himself that would no longer feed off of the fear of losing her, but instead, was intent on doing anything and everything within his power to capture her heart. Even from a distance, he couldn't help but notice the way the dress embraced her body, and how beautiful she looked. He could always tell that Beni was near because her presence inescapably caused his knees to go weak. She didn't realize it, but he loved her; from the moment he met her, he loved her. Even when they were children, whatever she was doing, he just wanted to be near her. Whenever she would read to Adina, whether on the porch or in the sewing room, he would always be sitting somewhere close by just so that he could hear her voice.

Just recently he began dreaming about her more and more often, which made him both dread and yearn for sleep. The frequent visions always began with Beni standing on the beach wearing a white linen dress that would reveal the silhouette of her body, complimented by her lustrous chestnut brown hair blowing in the wind. Inevitably, he would walk up behind her, which took an enormous amount of effort to finally get to where she was standing. A strong power, like that of a gale, held him captive. When finally he would break free from an almost painful constriction, he found himself in her presence. Finding it hard to believe the evidence of his own eyes, he would reach out and touch her hair, then began sweeping it off her neck. Slowly drawing her nearer, fantasy becoming reality, he gently began kissing her neck and shoulders while breathing in the perfume of her succulent flesh. She wouldn't run away from him like she did as a child, but only abandoned herself to his affection. Suddenly, she would turn around and face him, returning his tenderness by caressing his face and neck which was a trigger of passion, then pressing her body into his. He would study her perfect features, touching each line with his finger, but always returning to her deep blue eyes that were the exact color of the sea. No words were ever spoken between the two, intensity was their conversation. As the dream would unfold into the reality of daybreak, his heart was left broken over tormenting images of void. The beautiful yet cruel delusions of Beni left his heart beating so fervently that he could scarcely catch his breath.

When she had unexpectedly arrived at the house, he thought for a moment that this was yet another one of his dreams. That is until he heard her voice. He stood there plagued by the question of whether her presence was good or bad. There was one thing he did know very well as he stood face to face with her, hoping that his knees wouldn't collapse from beneath him... his heart would absolutely not survive another goodbye from her. Adina had known how he felt about Beni, but he made her vow to never say a word to the girl who took possession of his heart long ago. It was very difficult for Adina, who was a "fixer," not to intervene. She knew the hidden evidence of his devotion. For example, every year in preparation for Beni's summer homecoming, Carig would spread wildflower seeds as far as the eye could see, so that when she got there, the fields would be teeming with complex colors and textures of all shapes and sizes that would blanket the customary beach meadows. He always believed that her favorite flower described her well, and it's how he saw her, like a wildflower. It's what he loved about her. She always had big dreams and big ambitions, and wasn't afraid to be planted wherever the wind would take her. Beni believed that wildflowers naturally grew rampant around Adina's house, but it was actually only because of Carig that they were everywhere continually.

The last time he had seen Beni, she was a young miss going off to college, but now she was a woman - a beautiful woman - and he still loved her; there was no doubt in his mind, he wanted only her. Of course he knew that she was used to having her independence, and he didn't want to take that away from her. But at the same time, these many years separated from Beni, made him feel adrift within the clenches of bondage. Holding on to the dream of Beni was like forever remaining on a carousel that was spinning round and round, but never going anywhere. Even though he had determined hundreds of times to never think about her again, he would dream of her or come across her picture in Adina's house that would once again, send him reeling. There were plenty of girls who zealously pursued the well-built Scot, but he paid no attention to them because none of them were Beni. He had waited his whole life for her, and there would never be anyone else for him. He vowed in his heart that he would rather spend his life alone if he couldn't be with her…for him it was Beni or no one.

Now that she was here, so close that he could touch her, he would have to move slowly and not say too much too fast. Beni didn't realize this about herself, but Carig knew that she had a tendency to run at the first sign of losing control of a situation. As difficult as this all might be, and no matter how it would turn out, he knew he had to try and not let the fear of a broken heart keep him from going after the one true love of his life.

His attention turned once again to Beni as he watched her drive away in the cab. He decided that this night would not end simply watching her from a distance, so he decided to seize the moment and attend the Catwalk Masquerade. He'd gone before with Adina, but had no plans of going this time, until now. He simply had to see her again - tonight. Knowing that she was here, but not being near her was excruciating. He also knew the "spoiled elements" that would be present at this event. Rich mamas' boys in white tuxes with quick tongues and wandering hands. Beni would not go unnoticed, and he couldn't stand the thought of anyone holding her except for him.

With that thought, Carig ran down the spiral staircase, quickly showered, and dressed in the black tuxedo that Adina had purchased for him to wear at last year's event. He vividly remembered Adina's comment to him as he stood in her doorway holding a rose corsage that matched her scarlet dress. "Good Lord son, you look like you just walked off the movie screen! You look like Bond! *Ginger* Bond!" If only he would have known that would be his last year with Adina. There were so many more things that he wished he would have said to her. But he remembered the old saying that "When God closes a door, somewhere, He opens a window." To his great sadness, Adina was gone, but Beni...she was his open window. As his thoughts turned to her at the Ball, his speed increased over the twisting roads that led down to the cove. He was anxious to arrive before she would have to walk in unescorted.

From a distance the soft warm lights of the ball illuminated the night, and I felt a tinge of excitement as my car pulled up to the entrance of the "116th Annual Catwalk Ball." As I walked down the stone walkway that lead to the dinner tent, it was like going down a lane of memories. Billboards lit by soft spotlights lined the trail. Each signboard contained a historical photo from previous Catwalk events. Adina was in many of them, looking ravishing as she always did. Upon moving closer to the tent, I spotted one standing photo of a group of people in the ballroom. Among them was Adina who was dancing with a gentleman who appeared to be more than just a friend. She was so young and beautiful in her violet gown. She could tell by how young Adina was that this photo was taken many years ago! Everyone else in the photo was full of smiles for the camera, but the mysterious and rather dashing gentleman with blonde hair and captivating blue eyes seemed to be entirely attentive to Adina, and she to him. The caption read "45th Catwalk Masquerade Ball - October 6, 1945." I was curious. I didn't know that Adina ever dated anyone, let alone was serious about any man other than Carson. I stood a little closer and tried to focus in on his face. There was something familiar about him, but I still didn't know who he was. I would have to ask Wil if he knew anything about it. The last picture was a single large painting of a woman in a most elegant silver lame dress and long white gloves standing in front of the Grand Hotel. The note below revealed the name of this stunning woman. "Lilabette Mueller, October 6, 1900 - The First Lady of the Catwalk Ball." I had only heard stories about her, but this was the first time I had actually seen what she looked like. As I looked a little closer at her face, I could tell by her spunky smile that she was a bit of a firecracker, and I would have definitely wanted to be friends with her.

Distracted by the intriguing images, I didn't notice the huge amount of people that were still lined up waiting to go in. "Say goodbye to your comfort zone, Beni!" Walking into a crowded room full of people, especially alone, was never my favorite thing to do. Although hesitant, I was in awe of the glorious beauty of the event. It was truly grander than I had ever imagined. Even though it felt a little silly, I slipped the mask on my face. Like everything that Adina ever made, it was so elegant and unique, and it made me feel beautiful. As I finally approached the front of the line and stepped inside, joining the mob of Maine's best, to my dismay the room seemed to stop and look directly at me … exactly what I did not want to happen. I wasn't sure if this had to do with me or Adina. But then I heard countless whispers of Adina's name rising up from the crowd, and fingers pointing in my direction. She was such a large part of everyone's life, and had been attending this event for years; how could I not have anticipated such a reaction? They, like me, were mourning her loss, and I was the one standing in her place.

From out of nowhere, an elderly gentleman swiftly approached.

"My dear, Benidette, you are simply stunning in that emerald gown. You certainly remind me of your Aunt Adina! Yes sir, you sure do! She would never wear the normal white or black traditional gown, but always stood out with color."

I laughed to myself, because it was so typical of Adina to make a green dress for me to wear, knowing that all of the other women would be wearing black and white. I was completely embarrassed as I looked around at the sea of customary attire, all together normal, and obeying the status quo, while I stood there in a shimmering green frock that might as well have had been equipped with blinking Christmas lights. After several minutes of countless stares and ongoing comments about my uncanny resemblance to my aunt, the crowd's attentions were swayed by the announcement that the silent auction was just about to begin.

I was just about to find my seat, when I looked over at the moon sitting on the water. It so reminded me of when Carig and I would sit on the shore as children watching the sun go down and the moon come up. When the moon would finally rise and reflect upon the water, he would say to me, "Beni, you want me to pull the moon out of the water for you?" Just to get rid of him, I would tell him to swim out to the moon and pull it to shore for me. Like a lunatic, he would go running into the waves and start swimming out to the reflection. Every time, however, I would lose sight of him, and would begin calling his name. When he didn't answer, I would, in a panic, swim out after him. Every single time he would be quietly waiting for me in the center of the reflection, laughing that I swam out to find him. He'd say, "Beni, you do care about me - tell me that you love me!" Then I'd get so mad at him for scaring me, and I'd tell him that the next time I would just let him drown. But of course, when the next time came, I swam out again. I started thinking about how I used to treat Carig when we were kids, even teenagers, and I felt ashamed of myself. After seeing him again and how he acted, it seemed as though any infatuation that he may have felt towards me was gone. It was almost as if he couldn't stand me at all, except he did bring me soup. Why was I suddenly consumed with his opinion of me? I really hadn't thought about him in years! But now I couldn't *stop* thinking about him. I don't know, maybe he was part of the reason

I hadn't been back in so long. I tried not to think too much more about him as it only left me feeling torn and confused, and I had enough conflict in my soul at the moment without adding any more.

Suddenly I was on the beach. There was nothing that could soothe my heavy heart like sand and water. Even though I was dressed in a sophisticated gown that screamed diamonds and champagne, I felt the need to take off my shoes and allow my feet to sink into the invigorating, coolness of the sand. Standing there by myself, it was as though all of the elements of the night, the full moon and the stars that filled the sky, combined with the sound of the waves dancing on the shore, encompassed me. Being out here was far more gratifying than if I had been in the midst of the ball. A few more minutes! Just a few more minutes, I thought to myself, and then I'll go back inside and do my duty.

My peaceful moment was interrupted by the arrival of three young men dressed in tuxedos who had apparently began their partying hours ago, as they were all clearly intoxicated. One of them was carrying an almost empty champagne bottle, and the other two had exhausted whatever poison that had unfortunately led to their altered state. As they approached me, one let out a drunken whistle, another was so drunk he could hardly keep his eyes open, and the last one was the apparent leader of the pack who they called Rade.

"Hey, lovely lady, why don't you come with us and have a lil fun?"

I immediately felt uneasy at the sound of his voice. "No thank you, I was just on my way back into the ball."

I began to turn around and walk away when Rade grabbed my arm. "That was not a question," he said pulling me toward him.

"Get your hands off of me!" I demanded. On my other side, I felt one of the drunk and disorderly grab my other arm, and I began to struggle, trying to get away from them. "Let go of me now, or I'll scream!"

Carig entered the white tent, focused only on finding a green dress with Beni in it. He looked back and forth, but didn't see a sign of her anywhere. He wondered if maybe she hadn't come to the Ball after all, but knew that wasn't possible. She had to be here, as this was the only event going on in the area that would require such a dress. He felt immediate disappointment when he couldn't see her, almost feeling a little panicked. He walked outside of the tent and looked toward the dance floor. Distant screams from the beach caught his ear, causing him to briskly walk in that direction. As he continued approaching the shore, he recognized that it was Beni's voice. With scarlet rage, he raced down the sand with every intention of ending the faceless dinner jackets that had hold of the one he came here for. Running towards them like a freight train, and screaming threats of permanent injury, quickly motivated them to release their grip and take off back in the direction from which they came. At first, Carig took off after them, still wildly furious. But because he recognized them, Rade and Owen Vaughn, and Jonathan Mitchell, all of whom resided in Braydon County, he decided that he would take care of Beni first, and deal with those idiots later.

He stopped and gathered himself, and then turned around and ran back to where I was standing.

"Are you ok, Beni? Did they hurt you?"

"I'm ok! No, they didn't hurt me, thanks to you. Thank you for helping me! When did you get here? I didn't even know you were coming!"

Carig gently wrapped his arms around me, and held me so completely, creating a shelter of safety. "I'll never let anyone hurt you lass ... I'm so sorry, I'm so sorry."

"Carig, it's not your fault, I'm ok really."

As he continued holding me, he too seemed entertained by the reflection of the moon on the water. I wondered if he was thinking about our endless hours together as children playing beneath this magnificent celestial body. Without fail, he would swim out to the reflection and try to pull the moon out of the water for me. If he could have, he would have. Honestly, I knew, I always knew that he would do anything for me.

Reluctantly parting from his warm embrace, I walked to the edge of the water, and then turned around and smiled in his direction. "Are you thinking about when we were kids?"

Initially, he didn't answer, but just stood there, staring at me. He appeared lost in thought, somewhere other than our conversation. With a yearning in his eyes, and lips open, ready to speak, he still remained silent. His unwanted hush seemed to frustrate him.

"How can I even answer such a question, she alone has consumed my thoughts since I was a lad? Would this radiant beauty standing before me run away if I told her that the moon lofted pale in comparison to her shimmerin' silhouette? Or that I can scarcely contain my longing for her? Faded memories of our childhood together have only now been stirred for Beni, but as for me, this bloody moon is just another reminder of the girl I fell in love with so long ago; an affliction that I will gladly bear, if it means being close to her. She consumes me, there's no doubt about that! Oh God Almighty, give me the right words that will convince her to stay."

"Honestly Beni, I don't just think about when we were kids. I think about you now! All the time, to be sure! You may not know it lass, but you left behind a gaping hole, that couldn't be filled with anything or anyone, it was just emptiness. When ye did leave, you let this place and the people here go, but we, *I* have never let you go."

I could tell by the look on his face that I had hurt him deeply. I had become numb over the years, but he on the other hand, had sustained a festering ache, brought about by time and distance. It was obvious that he wanted

264

to be close to me, but knowing that I would be leaving again soon, made this an impossible situation.

I didn't know how to make it better, or exactly what to say to him...I felt horrible that he thought I had just left everyone behind, and stopped caring.

"I'm sorry, Carig, I never meant to leave and not come back. I never meant to hurt anybody."

Carig could obviously see the remorse in my eyes, and could tell that the cold October breeze along with the uncomfortable conversation was wearing on me. Being the gentleman that he was, he took off his jacket, walked toward me, and then wrapped it around my shoulders. As he enveloped me with the black tuxedo coat that smelled like heaven itself, he stood only inches away from me. Holding each lapel firmly in his grasp, he gazed deeply into my eyes, not looking away for even a second. At first I thought that he was going to kiss me, but he just continued the intense stare into my eyes.

"Carig, what are you doing?"

"I'm looking at you, lass!"

Listening to his Scottish brogue I was no longer cold, but actually felt a peculiar heat rise up from inside of me. Moving even closer towards me, still not breaking his gaze, I couldn't ignore the fact of how incredibly good looking he was. It wasn't just his well-fitting tuxedo, but everything about him was charming and handsome. I tried not to stare back, but it was impossible.

In an attempt to make a fiery moment cool down, I tried to make small talk, "So what are you doing here? I didn't know you came to these kinds of things."

"I am here at the ball, Beni, because I was invited. All lighthouse keepers are. I saw you leave from the house earlier, and when I got here and didn't see you, I came out looking … just wanted to make sure you were ok, and I guess it was a good thing I did."

"Yes, it was a good thing you came, thank you!"

I turned once again to face the water. To my great pleasure, Carig once again moved into my space. "Would you like me to capture the moon for ye, Lass?

I turned towards him and laughed. "To be honest, I think I would rather go swimming like we used to, than to go into that ball."

Uncomfortable and wonderful all at the same time, his eyes wouldn't leave my face. There was

266

definitely a stirring heat that we both felt. Carig knew even now, as it seemed impossible to take his eyes off of her, that his initial idea of moving slowly, had already gone *out the window*.

"Here Carig, you can have your jacket back … I'm really ok, and you'll need it to go in for dinner. You know, when I was on my way here from the airport, I was wondering about you and what you were doing. I thought maybe by now you'd be married and have a dozen kids."

"No, not…. yet." Carig looked down at the sand and then looked straight into my eyes. "You look so beautiful tonight, Beni!" I was embarrassed at the compliment, and could feel myself blushing.

"Thank you, and you look beautiful, I mean...so-very-handsome! I guess we've both grown up since we saw each other last."

"Yes, I guess we both have." Still looking at one another, I had dealt with just about enough awkwardness for one night.

To break the cycle, mostly felt by me I think, I asked Carig if he'd like to be my date for the night?

"I was hopin' you'd ask!"

As he offered his arm, we made our walk to the dinner tent together. I felt completely graceless, between trudging through the sand in my much *too* high heels, and trying to control my racing heart. It was impossible not to be distracted by his extremely muscular arms that begged to be fondled. Carig on the other hand, seemed to have the gift of staying quite composed, and I wished that I could be more like him. What I didn't realize at the time was that he was able to maintain a cool composure, on the outside. But on the inside, he was just as restless as I was.

We entered the tent, and were advised that our seats were at the head table, *the mayor's table* to be exact. This was where Adina always sat, and ironically, both Carig and I were assigned to that particular table together, which was rather odd considering we both came last minute. The mayors of Bar Rousse and Braydon County, along with their wives, were included in our party. The group talked our ears off for a solid hour while dinner was served. Once the crowd had stuffed themselves on seared scallops and filet mignon, the endless thank you announcements began. The speeches were extensive and dramatic. At one point, I whispered in Carig's ear that I was almost certain that the Academy Award for "Best

Picture" would be announced at any moment. He laughed and nodded in agreement. After the acknowledgments honoring the many donors and most prestigious families concluded, music began to fill the room. Mayor Harvey went up to the stage and joyously announced that dancing had begun.

"Please everyone, make your way to the ballroom where Maine's finest champagne and blueberries will be served. Enjoy! Enjoy Enjoy!!"

Carig had heard enough of the empty talk, and was ready to spend some time with the one he'd come there for. He stood up with his face toward the room of people, but he only had eyes for Beni.

He put out his hand and took hers, "Dance with me."

I looked up at him from my chair. He was so tall and handsome. From this view, I was able to see his broad shoulders vividly and followed them down to a perfectly tapered waistline. In a moment of shameful lust, I recalled my initial "shirtless encounter" with him and couldn't help but recall the body beneath the suit.

"I would love to."

We were both more than ready to leave the mayor's table, as we'd heard enough braggadocios politics to last a lifetime. Following the sounds of symphonic melodies down to the dance floor, I was unexpectedly greeted by the melancholy tune that was forever Adina's favorite. Without warning, and feeling completely out of control, tears began flowing from my eyes, and the more I tried to make them stop, the worse it became. As we walked onto the dance floor, I put my head down so that no one would see. But then of course, Carig noticed.

"Beni, are you ok? What's wrong?"

"Sentimental Journey was Adina's favorite song. She always told me that it reminded her so much of her own life and travels with Carson, and any time she would hear it, the words and the sentiment would take her back to the day she got off of the bus and met him for the first time. She even said that the title was the sum of her life."

Carig pulled a handkerchief out of his pocket and wiped my tears away. I could tell by his sympathetic expression, that he couldn't stand to see me sad. Then with his fingers, he gently brushed my face, wiping the last of them from my skin. Lifting my chin up towards him, he reassured me that everything would be alright.

"Everything's ok, Beni. Everything's ok."

"Heaven help me! Handkerchief, wiping my tears, saying the *perfect*, and utterly romantic words in a most gentlemanly way! A 'Darcy moment' for sure!"

He placed both hands on my waist, then wrapped his arms tightly around me. I couldn't resist him, so I returned the gesture, and draped my arms around his neck; I loved the feel of his auburn locks as they swept over my hands. Without even realizing it, I began twisting and combing his hair through my fingers, and Carig let me. His eyes closed with pleasure at each caress, and he pulled me even closer and began whispering truths concealed, which had been hidden within his heart.

"Beni, can this really be happening? I have waited for this for such a long time. Your touch on my skin inflames me." In addition to just her mere presence, the incense of her skin drove him crazy. He had no choice but to bury her in his arms, making her feel safe and warm. His words of comfort were sincere, and she believed him. Carig had a way of making everything ok.

They melted into one another's arms, losing track of time. Even when the music stopped, they still held one another, slowly dancing in the middle of the room.

Not one thing could have been added to make our time together more perfect. I never wanted this moment to be over, but all good things come to an end at one point or another.

"Beni, are ye going to stay here, here in Bar Rousse?" He asked something of me that I couldn't answer the way he wanted me to. His ill-timed inquiry forced me to return to the reality of the situation. The question that had been looming in his mind, had broken the spell.

"No, Carig. I have a life and a job in California. I'm only here until after the funeral."

Realizing the intimacy that we had just shared and how far it had gone in such a short amount of time, I knew that I had to walk away right now. There was a deep connection between the two of us; one that generated an insatiable heat that was dangerous, to say the least. I would be leaving in a few days, and I didn't want to start something that I wouldn't be able to finish....I don't even know what I was thinking, allowing it to go this far.

Our wavering delusion quickly came to a halt, and yet I couldn't help but hold Carig's face in my hands and brush my fingers through his hair, knowing it would probably be the last time. He allowed his body to melt into mine, affirming that this was a difficult subject, one of no return for him. I could see that my touch was causing him to spiral into an unpredictable place of uncontrolled passion, and then he suddenly stepped back away from me. He also knew that allowing things to move forward would be too hard. I didn't belong to him, and he didn't belong to me....none of this was real!

"I think it's time for me to go home."

"Beni," grabbing my hand, "please stay."

"I can't. Carig, I'm going back to California, and this, whatever this is between us, can't be." I walked off the dance floor and out through the front entrance.

"Stop, let me at least take ye home. I mean after all we live at the same place." My heart was pounding so fast, and I felt as though I needed to get away from him at that very moment. If I didn't, I was sure that I would hopelessly fall into his arms and stay in Bar Rousse, for no other reason except him. I stood there for a few minutes waiting for a cab to come, to make the drive back with anyone other than Carig, but not one car drove by. He continued standing there looking at me until I turned around and agreed to let him take me home. The drive back to Adina's house was very quiet, neither of us saying a word to the other. When we arrived back at the house, I got out of the car and began walking towards the front door.

"Let me at least walk ye to the door, Beni! Why must ye be so stubborn lass?"

"I'm ok Carig, really. I had a wonderful time with you - thank you for being my date. Maybe I'll see you tomorrow?" He stood and watched her walk into the house, not believing that he'd allowed himself to fall again so quickly. This was not the first time that he had been victim to Beni's walls, and it irritated him to no end. He walked away frustrated and disappointed as he once again realized that his feelings for her far exceeded Beni's. He knew at that moment, that her feelings had not changed and he was once again disappointed at being second chair to her life pursuits.

Chapter 12

The Tempus Vector

I would let nothing wake me today. There was nowhere that I needed to be. I didn't have to teach, fly anywhere, go to any appointments, not even get ready for a ball. The ball ... Carig ... last night ... I was suddenly stirred by all of it, and the peace of the morning was feverishly aroused by the restlessness of my heart. The fragrance of his embrace was still fresh on my skin. The lingering aroma of spice and sandalwood rendered me deep in thought, and I loved it. It was almost as if he was there, right next to me; I could see his face, feel his hair, touch his body. This was a very strange and unfamiliar sensation. For the first time in my life, my thoughts were consumed by a *someone*. It was as if a spell had been cast, that could never be recanted...there was no turning back from this uncomfortable but heavenly state. Both my heart and stomach ached at the same time, as if I were ill. But this strange, unexplainable feeling of slight torment, infused with bliss was far from a calamity.

Distracted by the brass key that was peering at me from the corner of my bedside table, I was reminded of the task before me. For some reason, I dreaded the search into Adina's appeals and secrets that were intended *only* for my eyes. Perhaps I knew that whatever I would discover would determine my future, and I wasn't quite ready to surrender both life and liberty while also abandoning my own hopes and dreams. But procrastinating would only make things worse. I couldn't put this off any longer. As much as I would have liked to stay in bed all day, "It was time to get up and meet the new day head on", as Adina would always say. There was something that she wanted to tell me. Knowing that she was never one for frivolities or nonsense, I knew that this was important, and I would do it for her.

While slipping into some jeans and a t-shirt, I looked across the room and saw my emerald green dress hanging on the wardrobe. Motivated by the recollection of the most romantic evening that I had ever had, I couldn't help but grab a handful of the gown, and bury my face in the lingering aroma of *him*. I cringed, and let out a deep-rooted sigh as I glared at my reflection in the mirror, suddenly recalling the last incident of the night between Carig and myself. The flashback of the rather rude and thoughtless manner in which I informed Carig of my intention to leave, now haunted me. "Well, you told him the truth; you are leaving Beni. You have got to snap out of it!" It was so not like me to fall this quickly for *anyone*. But Carig wasn't just anyone, he was.....he was my friend, my family, and if I were to be perfectly honest, Carig had become or maybe always had been, the desire of my heart. And now ... I couldn't stop thinking about him, or the wounded expression on his face after I blurted out my plan to once again walk away.

I had never felt so conflicted in my life. On one hand, I wanted to be faithful to what Adina was asking me to do. But on the other hand, I had worked my entire life to achieve my esteemed career as one of the youngest and most successful college professors in the country. It almost seemed as though I was being disciplined for pursuing my life goals and plans. Even just trying to keep some kind of reasonable perspective about everything was making me feel guilty. But when it came to Carig, reason went right out the window. It was different with him, his was simply a matter of the heart, my heart! I could feel myself losing control of my life, slowly drifting into a place where I would surrender myself to a plan that would not be of my own choosing.

Because I hadn't eaten even a nibble of the mouth-watering food at the ball, I was starving! The wild events of the evening seemed to have taken my appetite away earlier, along with my snug-fitting dress and of course my unexpected date. "Carig......dammit, Beni! Why can't you just *not* think about him? Please stop thinking about him!" No matter how hard I tried, I couldn't keep my thoughts from revolving around him. In one bounding swoop, my heart, my mind, and my soul had been charmed by a Scottish boy who had now become a desirable man. Once friend, now lover? My sentiments quickly spun into daydreams about him, and how he held me on the dance floor. Even now, I was experiencing the same shivers up and down my spine, as I remembered him whispering my name.

I was temporarily distracted as he walked past the kitchen window and towards the lighthouse. More than likely he had been up and working since the crack of dawn. But there he stood, like a god, wearing Killen's leather apron, and just about to step into his wood shop, the place where he and his grandfather spent most of their days. I decided to say good morning, and ask if I could make him breakfast.

278

On my way out, the screen door shut loudly behind me. The sound of the slamming door made Carig quickly turn around. I smiled and waved, but he just looked back with no expression, making no friendly gesture, and then walked into his workshop. "Oh great, what have I done now?" Actually, I knew exactly what I had done. I seem to have a tendency when anyone tries to get too close to me, to just walk away. I'm not sure why. For some reason, I've mastered the art of sabotaging romantic relationships. Maybe it's because of the difficult relationship that I had with my father, if you could call that a relationship at all. Or maybe it was watching Adina grieve her years away over Carson, and never wanting to hurt like that. Maybe it was just a fear of loving anyone or being loved; my independence was both a blessing and a curse.

I went back into the house, grabbed the key, and went straight to Adina's room. I couldn't stand the closed shutters and windows, so I opened everything up, allowing the cool ocean breeze to fill the room. The sheets and blankets from her bed had been stripped, as this was the place where she had passed away. As I knelt down in front of the trunk, I ran my hand over the cedar wood, brass, and leather casing, first noticing the

unfamiliar initials "MC" on the brass band. "Hmm? Who
is 'MC'?" I went through the list of names in my head,
"Adina York ("AY"), Carson York ("CY"), Wil
Crawford ("WC"). The first thing that I surmised was that
this chest did not always belong to Adina - it had
belonged at one time to someone with the initials "MC." I
thought perhaps the "C" represented the Crawford name,
but who "M" was, I didn't know.

Upon opening the lid of the antique musty chest, I
first noticed a set of drawers on the left hand side. Sliding
them open one by one, I found it peculiar that each
drawer except one held cobbler tools, old cobbler tools of
heavy iron, that were painted black. The last drawer held
two stacks of letters that were faded and worn. They were
tied together with satin ribbon, crowned with pressed
flowers. Upon further examination, I was delighted to
discover that these were the letters that Adina and Carson
had exchanged back and forth during their courtship in
the months before they finally met and wed. In the larger
storage area of the chest, was a man's overcoat which I
figured to be Carson's. As I removed the soft tweed
cloak, revealed beneath were two old shoe boxes with the
word "Coffee" in black scripted letters printed on the top
of both lids. The first shoebox, however, was made of

wood. Oddly, it looked as though it had been buried at one point. Each nook and cranny was caked with cement-like mud, and the box had left scattered remnants of dirt on the bottom of the trunk. Within the wooden container was a seemingly brand new pair of navy blue women's shoes. The inner sole also said "Coffee." The leather pair was lovely, and seemed to never have been worn. There were no shoes in the second box, but instead a smaller case made out of wood, that was beat up and marred with deep scratches and dings. The hinges were made of brass, and in the front was a large keyhole, unusually large for a container so small. Because the case was locked, I began thoroughly searching through the trunk, but could not locate a key anywhere. Perhaps Mr. Peevey had this key as well, but forgot to give it to me. There had to be more than just these few items that supposedly were going to reveal hidden mysteries. I needed the key, as it seemed that the possible answer was locked in the small wooden box. Hopefully, it was filled with a precise explanation of why I should stay in Bar Rousse. And yet I wondered if it would be that simple and obvious? "Doubtful!" Up to this point, everything seemed like such a riddle to me. Why did Adina make this so difficult to figure out?

I became frustrated as the pivotal brass access was nowhere to be found, and I didn't feel any more enlightened than when I first began. I stood up and grabbed the coat to fold and return it to the trunk. When I doubled it over, the elusive key that I had been looking for fell out of the pocket and onto the floor! While picking it up, I noticed the corner of an envelope peeking out from the pocket. Like everything else, it was antiquated, but this was uniquely labeled with my Aunt Adina's name.

Without wasting another moment, I inserted the key into the eyelet of the small box. When I opened it, there sitting on a bed of maroon velvet was a rectangle-shaped wooden frame. The frame, like the box that held it, was scratched and worn. Nonetheless, its shape and the distinct symbols that were carved within the dense wood, were unusual. I had never seen anything like it before! On either side of the frame, were balanced cutouts that gave the appearance of two handles. The top of the frame had a rounded scalloped edge, while in the middle of the top of the curve, was another cut-out, etched with a half circle above and below it. The hollowed insert resembled a sun that was both rising and setting at the same time. Nearing the bottom of the frame was a symbol of some sort that had a well-defined significance. The figure of two loops locked within one another making a cross shaped knot was carved deeper and more vivid than the other markings. Thick lines resembling threads or maybe even cords proceeded from each endpoint of the knot, moving north, south, east, and west. These lines traveled up the sides of the frame and ended at the luminary cut-out. In the middle of the frame where a photograph would generally sit, was a rectangular area covered in worn green velvet. The center of the velvet, where a photo would generally be positioned, was several shades darker. The frame was nothing special, not even very attractive, quite plain actually. But because it was kept safely locked in its own case, then locked a second time in the trunk, I knew that it held great significance and was very important to Adina. She protected it as if it were a fine piece of jewelry or art. I shook my head wondering why it required such a safeguard. I mean, who in their right mind would ever try to steal an old wooden frame? Confounding me even further, was the fact that not only was it locked up twice, but the key to its access was kept in the most unlikely place, as yet another possible obstacle, intentionally hidden.

My empty gaze was an undeniable speculation of
my mind's eye. If it were even possible, I was more
confused than when I began. With each new discovery
within the trunk, I couldn't help but grow more intrigued
with the bits and pieces of information. But the task of
piecing together the evidence that had been revealed to
me thus far seemed impossible. This whole thing didn't
even seem real, and left me feeling as though I was a
character in the midst of a great and perplexing mystery
that would require the services of Sherlock Holmes and
Watson. "If only they were here to help me," I thought to
myself. "What would Holmes do if he were here? The
letter! He would begin with the binding evidence of the
letter." Before opening the dated parchment, I wrapped
myself in the overcoat that held both the key and letter, in
hopes that the old cloak would create an ambience of
yesteryear. The coat was purposely kept in the trunk,
making it a significant part of this historical charade.
Before opening the envelope, I called out to Adina, if by
chance she could hear me. "Ok Adina, I'm doing what
you asked of me. Now, what are you trying to tell me?"
As I carefully tugged the chronicle from its dwelling
place, I realized that it had remained untouched since the
day it was unsealed by Adina. Like me, she was probably

alone and curious to find out what it held. It was my
desire to read it, and then acknowledge its message with
the same heart and mind as my very wise aunt had. Little
did I know that this letter would bind together the
scattered clues, while at the same time, pull me into the
most fantastic account that I had ever known.

"My Dearest Adina,

If you are reading this, I know that you figured
out that both the key to the chest and the letter were
hidden in the shoulder pads of my overcoat. You probably
thought it strange that I gave you my coat as you were
leaving, but it was imperative that both letter and key
were safely given to you, and not left in the trunk. I knew
you were a smart girl and would figure out my clue.

I am sorry, Adina, that you must deal with such
great difficulties, but I had to be very careful. All of the
parts to the paradox that I am about to share with you
could not remain in one place.

I know you are confused, but very soon this will
all make sense. I know too that your heart is broken, but

remember, everyone is a little broken. God won't put these kinds of burdens on weak shoulders.

I have very little time to tell you so much. I wish I could have explained this to you as we all sat around the fire delighting in Ira's pastries and drinking peppermint tea. Maybe I should have. The past few months with you have been some of the best of my life. All of us, Estee, Lavi, Ira, and I adore you. We couldn't love you more if you were our own daughter. Don't worry about us, we will pray for you. Pray for us too!

What I am about to tell you, Adina, I wasn't sure of until this moment. As I was sitting here writing this letter, Estee got word of poor Carson's death. This may sound cruel, but I was not certain until all of the events of today came together. I knew this journey would not be possible if you still had Carson in your life. I know how much you loved him, and if he were still alive, he would be your priority. All I know, is that you are the one. You are the one! With this information, you are about to embark on a passage, and you cannot allow this tragedy to hinder you from moving forward. There is too much to be done.

Let me begin by telling you something about Estee and myself that you do not know. When Estee and I were but five and six years old, our father, Uri Hausemann, who was in the spice trading industry, traveled from Poland here to Friedlich. From here he intended for all of us to go to America for a better life. Remember how you were surprised that I knew how to speak English? Well, it's simple really. Our father had planned for many years to go to America, so he learned how to speak English and he raised us to know the language as well. The journey to Friedlich was difficult for a single father and two small children. From that trek, he decided that taking two little ones to America would simply be impossible. Once we arrived in Friedlich, he walked us through town with the sole purpose of finding a new home for Estee and me. To this day, I do not believe that he ever had intentions of taking us with him. For many years I did not understand what led him to Schuh Coffee, but now I know he was drawn there by something bigger than himself, just as you were.

On that day, he told Estee and me to wait outside while he went in to buy new shoes. I remember him saying that he couldn't show up in America looking like a pauper, or they would not let him in. We waited outside the front door for a very long time; it was so cold, so I put my arm around Estee to try and keep her warm. When my father came out, he was holding several shoe boxes that were tied together. He sat the boxes down on the bench, bent down and gave us farewell hugs, and said, "You need to stay here for a little while. I will send for you soon. Malachi, take care of your sister." I called out to my Papa to come back, but he kept walking, and never turned around - that was the last that we saw of him. There we sat on a small bench in front of Schuh Coffee. Yosef Coffee, a harsh looking man but gentle in spirit, came out and took our hands, and told us we would be staying with him until our father sent for us.

As weeks turned into years, both Estee and I knew, along with Yosef, that my father was never coming back. Yosef was kind to Estee and myself. He did his best to make sure that we received an education in school, as well as an education in shoes.

Years later, I discovered that my father, a master trader, exchanged us for two pairs of shoes and a belt. My father told Yosef that I was a good worker and could help him in his shop; he also said that when Estee got older he could find a rich family for her to marry into.

288

With this connection, he told Yosef that he could become a wealthy man.

Yosef Coffee was a good man, and agreed to keep us. You see, he never married or had children of his own. He always called the two of us his little blessings from God. He was more of a father to us than our real father ever was. The trade, you see, was very one-sided. Yosef knew our father would never come back if he had the audacity to trade us for shoes and a belt. I haven't spoken of this since I was a child. Yosef Coffee gave his name to Estee and to me. Along with his name and the craft of shoemaking, he gave me something else before he died. Yes, he passed his shop down to me, but there is more. Just as you have wondered where I disappear to for days at a time, I also wondered, where Yosef would go. He would tell us that he was traveling to other places to buy supplies for his shop, although his carriage and horse remained at home while he was gone.

Before he died, Yosef passed a secret on to me, a mystery, a gift, but also a weapon. Just as I told you before you left, I am passing on to you a blessing. It is a supernatural gift that must be carried on from one generation to the next. Before you left my shop, I blessed

289

you with the same blessing that Yosef gave me. Yosef
came from a very inimitable line of people known as one
of the Ten Lost Tribes. He descended from the Lost Tribe
of Solomon, and the gift of his tribe was wisdom. This
wisdom also had the ability to return back to particular
times in history and change mistaken events both small
and large. As I was not of his heritage or tribe, in order
for him to impart this supernatural gift to me, Yosef had
to transfer his natural ability into a supernatural artifact
that would carry and empower the bearer. The empty
wooden frame that hung on my wall is this artifact, it is
called the Tempus Vector. This frame carries the bearer
to another time in history, along with wisdom from
Yosef's people to correct certain events. This is my
warning to you, in the wrong hands, this could be a
weapon of mass destruction. Why do you think that Hitler
and the Nazi regime are looking so diligently for the
Tempus Vector? This is not a weapon of this world, such
as guns and bombs, but one not made by man. Like many
things that hold power, it must be left in the right hands.
It must be given to one who has a pure heart, and will use
it to accomplish only good. Yosef gave it to me, and now
I am giving it to you. It will consume your time, which is
why it is very difficult to bear the Tempus Vector while

*you have a family. For years, men like Hitler have
searched for this device in an effort to have a power
unlike any other. Just as evil power-hungry men have
searched for the Ark of God and Solomon's wealth, so
they also search for the Tempus Vector. Always keep the
rumor of the Tempus Vector along with the lost tribes a
myth and mystery so that the pursuit to obtain it will be
diminished to a falsehood. Yosef's tribe was not lost nor
exiled as rumors might say, but they were set apart and
chosen, even sacrificed for this journey, so that its
purpose may be fulfilled.*

    *Through the kindness of the Admiral, Estee was
able to ship a crate to you, undetected, through Navy
resources. Within it, you will find everything you will
need that was once mine. I know you are confused right
now, but very soon it will all make sense. Fear not
Adina, you have been blessed and empowered to
accomplish this task.*

I will love you always, my dear Adina,

Malachi Coffee"

As I finished reading the letter, it fell from my
hand. "Malachi Coffee - 'MC.'" This was his trunk. But
who was Malachi? Adina had never spoken of anyone

with that name, yet he knew her so well that he turned over something like this to her. I took the frame out of the box and ran my fingers over the etchings "this cannot be real." Even though Adina had a great sense of humor, she would never play a practical joke like this. She had a purpose in everything that she did. She would never make something like this up, and she would certainly never ask me to do something unless it was very important. Adina was the most unselfish person, she never put any expectations on me except those that would benefit my life.

I removed Malachi's coat and examined the shoulder pads. Sure enough, there were special compartments that had been sewn in where a key and this letter had once been placed. The letter appeared to be the last testament of Malachi Coffee.

I sat for hours inspecting the frame. The more I looked at it, the more confused I became. How did it work? How would I figure out how this worked? I'm not wise like Solomon… what if Adina made a mistake picking me for this job? All I know is that she never encouraged me to do anything that wasn't right and good, she only had my best interest at heart, always. This letter,

Adina's past that I knew nothing about, made me so curious that I began a journey of my own, looking through all of her old boxes of papers and pictures. I began doing research on the Ten Lost Tribes, particularly the Lost Tribe that descended from the house of Solomon. It was very interesting that the legends of the Lost Tribes had become myths, folklore at best. If this was in fact true, Malachi and Adina, along with those who had gone before them, had done an excellent job of keeping the lore of "The Lost Tribes" unknown. For the rest of the day and that night, I looked through every piece of information that I could get my hands on. I searched for even a shred of evidence that I could find in order to validate this saga.

I felt as though the endless hours of searching were fruitful, as they revealed glimpses of Adina's past. But exactly what any of this had to do with me, and how I would fit into this unraveling recital of events, I still didn't know. In spite of my uncertainty, I was inspired by Adina and Carson's love letters. Had I been *that* blind all those years, not seeing that I had spent them with a woman who had experience such a rare and deep-seated love? If I were to be completely honest, until now, I was skeptical that affairs of the heart such as theirs, even existed. But now, my perception was suddenly unclouded by their intimate accounts. Their love affair began as a small rosebud, but as the time came for them to finally be together, it had blossomed like a Grandiflora Rose. Carson was an absolute poet, and I hoped that someday someone would love me the way he loved Adina. I could see why she was so heartbroken over losing him. His letters of love would most certainly make the hardest of hearts melt. Mine was still slightly bewitched by his incredible bouquet of affections. I couldn't tell if my heart was beating erratically because of the remarkable love story I had just read, or because Carson and Adina's flaming passions for one another made me think of Carig.

I carefully positioned the frame back into the box and then placed Malachi's coat on top of it. I took the two keys, and placed them in the drawer in my nightstand for safe keeping. Night had turned into morning. This would be a big day. It was the day that we would all say goodbye to Adina.

Staying up all night, compounded by the east coast time change, left me exhausted. I laid down on my bed, hoping to get a few hours of shut eye before everything began, which was no easy task. The long list of things that needed to be accomplished spun endlessly through my mind. Adina's funeral, making my flight arrangements, and tying up loose ends so that I could leave by tomorrow afternoon, were but a few. Of course, the moment I closed my eyes the phone rang. It was Mr. Peevey. He was calling to let me know that flowers would be arriving for the funeral at twelve noon, and the caterer for the event would arrive at two for set up.

"Caterer?"

"Yes, Beni. Neighbors from all around Bar Rousse and Braydon will be attending a reception at the house afterwards. Your Aunt Adina wanted this to be more of a party than a funeral, and as easy as possible for you. You know very well how she was, she didn't want anyone fussing over her. For that reason, everything is taken care of, except you may want to have a few words ready to say at her gravesite."

"Oh yes, something to say at her gravesite, I'll make sure that I do!"

What could I possibly say that would even come close to explaining how I feel about her? He then asked me how everything was going, and if I had looked through Adina's trunk.

"So Beni, did you find what Adina left for you? Have you made a decision on whether you will stay here in Bar Rousse?"

I was silent for a moment.

"Mr. Peevey, I think I did find what Adina left for me, but what I uncovered may have to stay where it is. Even after going through her trunk, I still have every intention of returning to California. There's a flight leaving tomorrow at two in the afternoon, and I plan to be on it."

"Ok, Benidette. We won't mess with the papers today. I'll come by the house tomorrow morning, say by ten, and I'll bring the documentation for you to sign that will discharge and diminish your responsibilities regarding the estate. I can't tell you how sorry I am to hear that you have decided to leave. I know that Adina would be very disappointed too."

I could tell that Mr. Peevey was not only disappointed, but when he called me Benidette instead of Beni, I felt as though I was being scolded.

"I'm sorry, Mr. Peevey, but I'm expected back to teach next Monday. I really do appreciate everything you've done. I'll see you this afternoon at the funeral."

"Will do. Goodbye, Benidette."

By this point, sleeping was out of the question, so I decided to get online and make my plane reservations for the two o'clock flight the next day. As I sat there staring at my computer screen, trying to focus on what I was doing, the words Tempus Vector along with the information from Malachi's letter, continued flowing through my mind. Although I was a creative spirit and thinker, I just could not make sense of any of this.

When I finished purchasing my ticket, I began thinking once again about Carig. I wondered what he was doing and if he was still mad at me. It would probably be best for both of us to just get through this day and not really interact too much with one another.

I made my way upstairs to take a shower and get myself ready for the funeral. As the shower was running, something occurred to me that Adina once said. "Beni, when I die, don't wear black, it's too sad, and I don't want my funeral to be filled with a bunch of people wearing black. Wear something pretty and happy and joyful. After all, I will finally be with Carson again." I remembered that all I had packed to wear to the funeral was my black suit. I went up to the third floor and began looking through the wardrobes for something more suitable and joyful. I first looked through the wardrobe where my green dress had hung. There were other dresses and such, but not really what I was looking for. The fact of the matter was that I didn't really know what I was looking for. I figured I would know it when I saw it. I opened up one of Adina's wardrobes, and hanging in the back was a lovely short creamy white dress made of lace. The long sleeves were sheer, and all of the borders were embellished in charcoal colored velvet. It was a little old fashioned looking, but quite elegant and sophisticated; it looked like Adina. I decided that in her honor, I would also wear one of her favorite hats, and of course her pearls that she wore with practically everything. Scanning through the choices, I spotted one made with the same fabric, a lace veil, and one single charcoal flower with a pearl in the center.

Before changing out of the comfort of my 501's, I decided to take a quick jaunt outside to pick roses and wildflowers for a bouquet that I would carry as a mark of cadency. While enjoying the general splendor of a most beautiful day, I was interrupted by the sight of two men standing in the center of the garden resting on their shovels. It took a moment, but I soon realized that they had just finished digging Adina's grave. The sight of it made me sick to my stomach. It was a clear-cut affirmation that Adina was really dead and never coming back. In only a few short hours I would bear witness to her descent into the pit of the earth.

To my dismay, the grave diggers were only the beginning of the inevitable, as an entourage of delivery trucks began to arrive. An endless array of chairs and flowers were unloaded and set in place, creating a site that I could have done without. The entire area was bustling with strangers that had been given the green light to carry out all of Adina's last wishes. Suddenly and unexpectedly, in sacred unison, each and every individual stopped and stood still, as a black hearse slowly pulled up to the bottom of the garden area. As I observed the casket through the small side window, I felt as if a dagger was piercing my heart. I just couldn't do it...any of it! I dropped everything, and ran into the house. Aiming to hide from the rest of the world, I ran up to Adina's room, and sat on the floor directly in front of the chest at the end of her bed, vowing to never leave that spot.

Out of the corner of my eye, I noticed a brightly-colored picture sitting on the side table. Twinkling lights, and boughs teaming with shiny ornaments were the background of that evening. For hours we would sing our favorite Christmas hymns while excitedly airing our skillfully decorated gingerbread boy. It was our tradition each Christmas Eve to bake a huge gingerbread cookie that we would leave out for Santa to feast on, along with a glass of milk, sprinkled with cinnamon. For the rest of the night, we would eat cheese fondue, and drink sherbet punch. This memory, filled with joyful smiles, and a "soon to be eaten" reward for "Old Saint Nick", reminded me of Adina's God-given talent of making everything special. I squeezed the photo close to my aching heart, hoping that it would somehow ease the pain. I didn't want to bury her, I didn't want to say goodbye. From the moment I heard of Adina's passing, I refused to bear the cross of acknowledgement, never fully accepting that she was gone. The thought of mingling with all of those people, and trying to come up with the right words to sum up her life, seemed like an impossible task. I felt lost and alone. I just wanted to shut all the windows and doors and hide.

My grieving had finally begun, and I feared the weeping would never stop. But thank the Lord for elusive distractions, that in this case took the form of a mystical figment. Maybe I was losing my mind, but for a split second, I could have sworn that I saw Adina standing in the corner of the room. Of course when I whipped my head around to get a better look, she wasn't there. But the result of this phantom experience, left me with an all-consuming peace and prompting to get up and go forward. Maybe Adina wasn't really there, but I could hear her voice in my head. "Get up, Beni! There's much to be done- this is the beginning, not the end!" Adina was never one to sit around feeling sorry for herself, and she certainly would not allow me to be party to self-pity either. She was a woman of wisdom, who had lived a life worthy of praise, and worthy to be honored on this day. The more I thought about her, the more driven I was to be like her, but I knew that I had a long ways to go.

With my new found encouragement, I quickly got myself up and ready for the day. It made me feel happy that I was wearing something of Adina's. I laughed as I looked down at my bare feet, knowing that she would never approve of wearing such an elegant dress without pantyhose, let alone traipsing around shoeless. She most definitely would have considered the entire look "quite scandalous." But I was determined to take a quick walk to the beach before the services began, and shoes would only slow me down. As I stepped out the back entrance of the house, I looked over to the garden area, utterly amazed at the large number of people who had already arrived. Those who knew and loved Adina, were waiting to pay their respects, each one ready with a heartfelt story about their dear friend.

This favorite spot of sand, held memories of dances on the shore, picnics, and fireworks. I stood staring out at the waves, contemplating each word of my tribute to Adina, but was interrupted by the howling ocean breeze that felt as though it was sweeping through me, and repeating the same two words, "Tempus Vector." Like a beast of prey, it was trying to capture and entangle me with its persistent call that left me feeling confused and alone.

It had been Carig's goal since Adina's death and Beni's arrival to stay as busy as possible. He had diligently been working on property, trimming all of her roses, and making sure that everything was perfect. In addition, he had been working non-stop making a new bench that would stand as a memorial in the garden. This finely carved sitting area, made from aged oak, was inscribed with a meaningful and personal message from Carig. "Until We Meet Again." That was the last thing that Adina said to him the night she died. He had carried her up the stairs after they had shared a dinner of clam chowder and fresh bread. As he laid her into bed, she told him how precious he was to her. Carig had said, "I'll see ye in the morning, Adina", and she replied, "Until We Meet Again."

It was Carig who discovered that Adina had died. He had been concerned about her sickly state, and when he checked on her in the early morning hours, she was gone. After she was officially pronounced dead, and her body was removed, Carig was beside himself. For hours, he sat at the top of the lighthouse sobbing, and probably never would have come down if not for Wil. Wil partnered in his grief, and together they cried, laughed, and consoled one another with sweet remembrances of Adina. Family meant everything to Carig, and Adina was not only like a mother, but a friend, and he couldn't imagine life without her. Like his grandfather Killen, he would have gladly exchanged his life for hers. Not since the moment, that he lost his parents had he felt so alone, but little did he know, that in a few short hours, Beni would walk back into his life, restoring hope to his emptiness.

His grief over Adina was all consuming, but it didn't compare to the distress he was experiencing over Beni. He knew in his heart that he couldn't stand to watch her leave, but he also knew that she had every intention of doing so. It was a no win situation as far as he was concerned, but still, somewhere deep inside, he held a glimmer of hope for a more desirable outcome to their story. But time was growing short. He knew that she would be leaving the day after the funeral, which was tomorrow.

Carig had finally finished with all needed preparations, and went into the lighthouse to get dressed for this highly unpleasant occasion. He, along with Wil and a few others who Adina had requested, would carry her casket from the hearse up to the gravesite. He dreaded the foreordained task. He realized that there were particular moments in life which would seem grim and hopeless, such as losing his mother and father, and then his grandparents, and now Adina. He understood the sorrow that came with loss, but the deepest blow, the one that he would never survive, was the added loss of Beni.

Carig, looked out his window at all of the funeral commotion going on down below, and decided that he should probably go out and help where he could. When he went outside, he was met by Pastor Strong.

"Everything looks wonderful, Carig. You do such a great job with this place. Adina loved you so much, ya know!"

Carig didn't say a word, and wasn't really in the mood to engage in trivial conversation. He knew that if he tried, he wouldn't be able to hold back the tears that were rising up from his heart. Saved by a beautiful distraction that was standing alone on the beach, he excused himself, and began walking towards the brown haired girl in the white dress. He felt as though he were living somewhere on the cusp of a lovely but frustrating illusion; His dreams of her were so vivid, not unlike this very moment! He could hardly feel his legs beneath him, but nonetheless, he began walking down to the beach, still not knowing if he was dreaming or awake. Moving closer towards Beni, he noticed that she was arguing with the wind.

"What do I do Adina? I'm so torn! I understand that you want me to stay, but I love my job; you knew that I'd want to go back. I do want to go back, but I want to stay too. I have never felt so conflicted in my life Adina, and I don't understand any of this….the Tempus Vector, or what it has to do with me. And then there is Carig. He makes me feel like I've never felt before, and when I'm not with him, I ache. What should I do Adina? I wish you were here so that I could talk to you face to face, … so that you could tell me exactly what to do. If staying is the right thing, please give me a sign, something that I know is a confirmation from you."

Carig knew that it had to be a dream. It had to be, because he just heard Beni say that she thought about him, even ached for him. He couldn't believe that those words had just come out of her mouth. Just then, he watched as she fell to her knees holding her face and weeping. He hurried over to her, and lightly touched her hair just to make sure that she was real, and that this wasn't simply a dream. He too dropped down onto the sand, put his arms around her, and then held her tightly while burying his face in her hair. Together they wept. Although neither would admit it, their bodies were created to connect. For those few moments together they understood for the first time in their lives, what it meant to be complete.

Although he could have held her forever, Carig knew that it was time for the funeral to begin. "Beni, it's time. We have to go do this. Everything's gonna be ok lass. I won't leave you- I'll be with ye the entire time." Once again, Carig had a way of making me feel like everything was truly ok.

They both stood up, Carig with his arm around Beni, gently pushing her up the hill to the gravesite. Once they arrived at the garden, he sat her down in the chair that was reserved for her in the front row. Sitting in the very front, was a white metal podium where Pastor Strong stood. Above the gravesite was a beautiful trellis covered in white climbing roses. To the right was Carson's headstone, and to the left was Adina's empty grave. Pastor Strong asked everyone to please stand. As they stood, all eyes focused on the entrance of the garden, woefully observing as Carig, Uncle Wil, and four other gentlemen bore Adina's coffin. Carig and Wil were on each side in the front, both crying almost uncontrollably. Once the coffin was in place, they both came and sat down, Wil with Angelina by his side, and Carig by me, holding me so tightly, almost as if he were afraid that I would crumble if he let go. Pastor Strong shared with all who were present about the life of Adina. "Before I open up a time of sharing, I'd like encourage you all with Adina's favorite scripture found in the fortieth chapter of Isaiah, verse thirty-one. 'But those who hope in the Lord will renew their strength. They will soar on wings like eagles; they will run and not grow weary, they will walk and not faint.'"

After Pastor Strong concluded, one by one, citizens of Bar Rousse and surrounding counties came forward and shared their stories and memories of their beloved friend. One thing that each memoir had in common was that she had given unconditionally in some way to each of them, never asking for anything in return. Finally, after everyone had spoken, I walked to the front of the crowd, praying for the strength to keep myself together, and mainly to honor Adina with my words. I think Carig was a little surprised that I actually made it up to speak. I knew not to look at him if I was going to get through this.

"Thank you all so much for coming here today. As most of you know, I'm Benidette Crawford, Adina's niece. I didn't know exactly what to say to each one of you today. Sometimes there really are no words that can take away the sting from our hearts. We're just gonna ache for a little while, or maybe a long while. But as I listened, to those of you who came up and shared, I was overwhelmed by how Adina had touched, even changed your lives. But I also know that she sincerely loved each one of you, and you touched and blessed her life as well. As for me, I didn't know what unconditional love was until Adina came into my life. Without any expectations, she took me in as a daughter"

I had to pause for a moment as I felt tears burning in my throat. When I looked up, Carig was intently staring at me, and I couldn't help but stare back. I loved him! There was no doubt in my mind, I loved him!

"And Carig, I know that she loved you as if you were her own son." On more than one occasion, she said that if she and Carson would have had a son, he would have been exactly like you."

With those words, I could tell that he was struggling.

"It's hard to fathom a world without her. There are those like Adina who make such an impact, such a difference, that they should never be allowed to leave…but that's life isn't it? Adina had so many reasons to be bitter and spend her life mad at the world, but she did just the opposite. She lived each day to the fullest. I never had the opportunity to meet my Uncle Carson, and yet I know like her, he spilled over with love for others, but especially for Adina. Last night as I was going through some of my aunt's things, I came across the love letters that she and Carson wrote to one another. You may not know this, but they had only known one another through letters and pictures when they married. As I read through each one, I felt I was given a glimpse of what deep meaningful and unmovable love really is. And all I knew as I sat there absorbing every word, was *that* was the kind of love that I not only wanted to give, but also the sort of love that I desire to share with someone. I'm not really sure if this is appropriate or not, but I would like to share with you a small passage from one of Carson's letters to Adina. We may be sad today that she's no longer with us, but her husband who loved her more than life, is rejoicing that they are finally together again.

"My Beautiful Adina,

Please don't think me foolish, but from the second I saw your photograph, my world changed. It was as if a flawless looking glass had been set in front of blind eyes. For the first time, I can see. Everything around me is cloaked in beauty, simply because I see you in everything. You are the lens of my every sense. No longer do I see the waters of the ocean, but only your eyes. No longer do I hear the crashing waves on the shore, but only your laugh and whispers of our passion. No longer will my lungs be filled with sea air, but instead the essence of your skin. No longer will I be teased by the soft white sands, but consumed only by your caress. No longer will I feed on fine delicacies, but only the taste of your lips on mine."

Chapter 13

Leaving

It had been a terribly long and emotional day, and I was so glad that the funeral was over. Returning to my normal life in California was definitely at the top of my priority list. Be that as it may, the utterance "Tempus Vector" continued to run through my mind, not as a gentle tone but as a loud clanging noise that refused to be ignored. In spite of this constant flow of words, I made every effort to keep my focus on the task at hand which included tying up all of the loose ends here in Bar Rousse. I reviewed the itinerary in my mind, remembering that my plane would be leaving at two o'clock, so I'd need to leave here around eleven. I sat down at my computer, checked into my flight, and printed my boarding pass. Also, I couldn't forget that Mr. Peevey would be dropping by in the morning around ten, right before I left, so that I could sign all of the necessary papers. I knew that by signing them I was giving an outside company permission to take care of the estate. I felt confident, though, that Adina chose this company carefully, and that they would do a thorough and efficient job. Of course I planned on coming back every once in a while so that I could check on the estate, and I would also keep in close contact with Mr. Peevey who would be overseeing the property management company.

I went into my room, set my suitcase on the bed, and began packing. Looking over at my wardrobe, I couldn't tear my gaze away from the emerald dress that would forever make me think of Carig. I knew that I would probably have no occasion to wear something so elegant back in California, so I decided to return it to the wardrobe along with the white dress and hat that I wore to the funeral.

Unaware that I still intended to leave, Carig eagerly made his way over to see me. Even though (until now), he had never needed permission to enter Adina's house, he began knocking at the front door. From the time he was a little boy she made it clear that this too was his house and he could come and go as he pleased. After a few moments of unattended pounding, he opened the door and walked in.

"Beni, are you here?"

Hearing no reply, he continued looking in each room, still calling my name. As he walked by the computer, he noticed that there were papers sitting on top of the printer. Reluctant to pick them up, he began reading out loud. "Benidette Crawford, flight 145, departing at 2:00 p.m. from Bar Rousse to Los Angeles International….." Carig couldn't believe that I had really done it, and felt immediate anger rise up within him like he had never felt before. He crumpled the paper in his hand, and began bolting up the stairs. As he was racing up, and I was coming down, there was nothing that could have prepared me for the wave of fury that was about to strike.

"Carig, you scared me to death!"

"What are ye doin, Beni?"

"What do you mean?"

"After sittin' there at Adina's funeral, hearing the pastor talk about the life she lived so unselfishly for all of those around her- most of all you!- and after all the things *you* said, does it mean nothin' to ye? Really, Beni? You're still gonna leave?"

"Yes, I am."

I walked back into my room, and Carig followed.

"I don't know why you're so upset! Adina has a company that will come in and take care of this place. Everything will be fine!"

"It won't be fine, Beni. Why can't ye see that? Why are you so bloody blind? She wanted you to stay, she didn't want a company to take care of her house; she wanted you! It was her greatest fear that you'd walk away!"

"I know, but she set up an option number two for exactly that reason, to give me an option."

"Dammit, Beni, yer the most selfish, spoiled rotten person I have ever met in my entire life! Everything is always about you. You have no idea what Adina gave up for you. She left all of this to you - she has given you everything - and you won't stop long enough to open your eyes, and really look hard at what you're givin' up! What is wrong with ye? Yer like poison to yourself and those around you, sabotaging everything that's good in yer life."

Carig's destructive but accurate discourse cut through my heart like a dagger that penetrated deeper with each word.

"Ok, I get it, yer mum died when you were young and yer dad was an ass. Both my parents died, and I had to leave my home and the country that I loved. But once I was here, I was so loved by my grandparents and Adina, the same way they loved you, but it was never good enough for ye. All you've done all of these years is take. Once ye saw that there was nothing more you needed, you left everybody including me, and never came back. Do you know how badly Adina wanted ye to come and visit? Even when she asked, ye never did. Why did you even come when she died? You don't care. You haven't wanted to be here from the moment you arrived. Ye know what, forget it, ye don't deserve all of this. Ye don't deserve what Adina did for you, what she left for you; the calling of her life that she was compelled to leave with ye, Beni! There is one thing that yer right about, she *did* make a mistake. You were, and you absolutely are, the wrong bloody person. She made a huge mistake!"

All I could do was stand there in complete shock. No one, especially Carig, had ever spoken to me that way. I had never witnessed someone so angry, especially at me. Carig took the wadded up piece of paper and threw it as hard as he could across the room.

"I think ye need to leave right now, you are not worthy to be here! You didn't earn the right to have Adina or my grandparents in your life. And as for me, I have tried to love you, but ye don't want to be loved, you want to be alone. Well Beni, this is me leaving you alone, walkin' out of yer life forever. I will never be a part of yer absurdity again. And by the way, when you sign those papers for that company to take care of this estate, they will replace everyone that works here, including me." Carig turned and stormed out of the room, slamming the door on his way out.

I slid down the side of the bed and then onto the floor. Tears began flowing uncontrollably, and I began to sob. I knew in my heart that I had a talent for shutting the world out, but for some strange reason, I was hardly aware that anyone noticed. "Oh God, Oh God, I feel so lost! Adina, I wish you were here." I sat motionless on the floor replaying in my mind all of the things that Carig had said to me, and I knew that he was right. I did dread coming here, just like he said. As an adult, I don't really know what kept me from Bar Rousse, from Adina especially.

Even though Bar Rousse held such happy memories, it also reminded me of being abandoned by my father. Abandoned by my father? Thinking about him, what he did, felt like a dagger in my heart. There was a time when he treasured me, and then when my mother died, he abandoned me; he didn't even want to look at me. I think after my father, I had a true understanding, even at such a young age, of what it was to feel deserted. I had watched Adina grieve over Carson even after he had been gone for over 50 years. I just didn't want to hurt that way again, the way I hurt when my father refused to visit me at school. When I graduated from high school he wasn't there, he only sent flowers, so I thought. That summer after my graduation, I heard Adina arguing with him on the phone, and found out through that conversation that it was Adina who really sent the flowers and signed my father's name. I never heard from him after that; not even at my college graduation. But Adina tried so hard to make up for the areas where my father lacked, and I abandoned her. Instead of ridding myself of the dagger that my father pierced my heart with, I kept firm grasp of it, wounding all of those around me, especially Carig and Adina. I will never understand why they continued to love me and believe in me, and yet here

I am letting them down again. I couldn't bring myself to move from that spot on the floor, so I laid there for the rest of the night and cried myself to sleep.

When I woke up the next morning, I was still lying on the floor next to my bed. I sat up, feeling completely empty. Sleep didn't take away the ache that was in my soul. Carig had uprooted and unleashed a truth within me that has always been there, but that I've chosen to keep at bay. I was paralyzed by my circumstances, and utterly embarrassed and ashamed of how I had acted. It was clear that I had allowed bitterness to take root and grow inside of me. I had hurt all of those around me, and I knew now that if I didn't make some serious changes in my life, that resentment and malice would destroy me, just like it destroyed my father.

I thought of all of the things that Pastor Strong had said about Adina's life during her funeral, things I never knew. I did know that she sewed clothes for anyone who needed them. She couldn't stand to see a little girl or boy in ragged clothing. But what I didn't know, was that she worked at the convalescent home in town. She'd go there every week and visit with and cheer up the lonely and forgotten. If someone was sick, she would deliver a meal to their home. She was also at church every Sunday, serving and giving of herself completely. Thinking about her life and all that she did, all that she gave up, made me feel even worse. I made a decision right then and there, that even though I was going back to California, I would no longer find solace in my aloneness, but I will be like Adina and make a difference in the lives of others.

It was already eight-thirty, and I needed to finish packing and get myself ready. Reaching over, I picked up the picture of Adina and myself that was sitting on my bed stand. "Adina, I am so sorry that I wasn't here for you, please forgive me. I want to do better than what I've done. I don't want to live for myself anymore, and I don't want to be alone either. But if I'm meant to be alone, I want to change people's lives like you did. Mainly Adina, I don't want to disappoint you. You were the perfect example of how someone should be, and I want to follow in your footsteps. If you can hear me Adina, please, please help me to know where to start, what I should do." I put the picture in my suitcase to serve as a constant reminder of who and what I wanted to become.

Time was ticking away, so I began preparing for my long flight home. Finally, with the last snap of my suitcase I was ready to go. Since Mr. Peevey had not yet arrived, I decided to go into the sewing room, to just sit there, like I used to with Adina. I pulled down the book *"The Count of Monte Cristo."* Of all of the books that I would sit and read to Adina, this was my favorite story of all which was obvious by the tattered edges. Even though I had read it to her so many times, she would react as if she had never heard the story before. Together we memorized our favorite parts and quotes, and would often use them when we would feel very dramatic and silly. Even though this was a novel filled with action and intrigue, I loved it for its romance and longsuffering love between Edmond and Mercedes. But Adina loved how Edmond was transformed from a humble sailor into an intelligent and powerful count.

I began reading out loud just like I used to, adding a British accent and individualizing my tone to differentiate between each character. *"On the 24th of February, 1810, the look-out at Notre-Dame de la Garde signaled the three-master, the Pharaon from Smyrna, Trieste, and Naples. As usual...."*

321

"Beni, are you in here?"

"Yes, Mr. Peevey, in here!"

"Is someone in here with you?"

"No, I was just reading the *Count of Monte Cristo* out loud. I'm sorry that I wasn't downstairs to let you in."

"No problem at all. Ya know the service yesterday was just beautiful; it was exactly what Adina wanted. And you, well, you did a fine job!" He furrowed his brow and began twisting at his eyebrows. I noticed that this nervous habit was one that he practiced often, and it was amazing that he had any brows left at all. "So, let's get down to business here. Have you changed your mind about staying?"

"No, I'm afraid not, but I promise that I'll come often to check on things."

Mr. Peevey cleared his throat and in a very business-like manner, put his briefcase down on the table, and snapped open the locks on each side. He pulled out a manila envelope and sat it down on the table, sorting through each of the papers, setting them in a particular order.

We were both suddenly startled by the loud honk that was blaring from outside. "Oh, my cab is here - gosh, he's early. Will this take very long?"

"Well, there are a few things you need to read over and understand before you sign. These are important legal documents that shouldn't be signed carelessly."

"That reminds me Mr. Peevey, is it possible that Carig can still be left in charge of, and live in, the lighthouse? He's been here since he was a little boy, and no one knows that lighthouse and this property like he does."

"Well, see that's the thing, Beni. This agreement that Adina made with the management company is air tight. There is no leeway on the prearranged contract. It's a downright shame though. This will be an awfully hard transition for Carig.....downright shame! So, I have marked the pages where you need to initial and then sign on the last page."

I took the document and began reading it over, when the horn outside honked once again. "Let me just run out there and tell him I'll be a few more minutes."

"Fine with me, I'm in no rush. I have all day."

I ran down to where the cab was, and asked the driver if he would give me another ten minutes.

"Sure thing lady, but you're on the clock!"

I agreed, and then rushed back into the house, running up the stairs and then back down into the sewing room, still holding the papers to be signed. As I hurried down the stairs, my shoulder hit the wall and knocked down one of the hundreds of framed photos that was hanging along the staircase - it came crashing to the floor, then began tumbling down the steps, with glass breaking along the way.

"Damn it!" I picked up the picture, and then began to gather up the broken glass pieces. As I was placing the shards on top of the picture, I took a second glance at the gentleman in the photo. Quickly dumping the broken glass in the trashcan, I brought the photo up closer to take a better look. I was frozen where I stood, feeling the blood rushing from my face, unable to take my eyes off of the man in the picture. Immediately I began to feel dizzy, and the room seemed to spin out of control. I recognized the man in this photo! He was sitting in a chair wearing a black suit, bowtie, and hat. Like an old friend, directly beside him, sat a worn leather suitcase. "I've seen this man! I talked to *this exact man* at the airport when I was leaving California! He looked exactly like this, same suit, same hat, same suitcase, same everything." His eyes in the picture smiled just like he did as he sat at my gate. I removed the picture from the frame, and turned it over. Written on the back was: Malachi Coffee, Friedlich, Germany, 1939.

"Beni, you ok up there? What broke?" Mr. Peevey met me at the stairs where I sat in a state of shock, holding the photo, and staring at it.

I looked up at him, pale as a sheet, feeling as though I had seen a ghost.

"What is it, Beni - who is that?"

"It's Malachi Coffee. I met him at the airport in California when I was leaving to come here."

Mr. Peevey took the photo from my hand, "No, you must be mistaken … 1939? Good Lord, that would make him, well he's old in the picture, so that would make him about 150 years old. You must have seen someone that looked like him."

I continued studying the picture of Malachi and then began thinking of the letter he wrote Adina, and the

325

Tempus Vector. "It can't be, it can't be true! But I think it is true, it's all true. I didn't realize it, I didn't believe it until this very moment."

Another honk came from outside. "Beni, we've got to get these papers signed and in order. You're going to miss your flight, young lady!"

Like the first flame of dawn erupting into the reality of day, so a light had been switched on inside of me, creating an encounter of truth and understanding. I heard the tone of Mr. Peevey's continuous talking, but I had no idea what he was saying. I felt as though I had entered into a world that I had never seen before. Until this moment, I had dwelt in darkness with no direction. But suddenly I had a clear vision of what I was supposed to do. I stood up and looked at Mr. Peevey. "I'm not going back Mr. Peevey! I'm staying here. I won't be signing these papers, I'll sign the others that say that I'm staying in Bar Rousse. I'm staying!"

Chapter 14

Final Verdict

Mr. Peevey, still in shock, but thrilled over my change of mind, packed up all of his papers and told me to come to his office in the morning so that I could sign the other documents.

"This new decision, Beni, is a whole new ballgame. Along with these other documents that you will sign, Adina also left a small box full of information that is for your eyes only. I couldn't tell you about it until you made the decision to stay, and I have no idea what's inside.

He gave me a big smile and thumbs up as he left the house, happily taking care of the cab fare on the way out. My mind began racing around this new but ancient calling for my life. Even though I had no idea what it was exactly, or how it worked, I felt assured that Adina would reveal each chapter and verse in due time.

I phoned the university to inform them that I would not be returning. I couldn't believe that I was actually quitting my job! A career that I absolutely loved!

But surprisingly, once I'd made the decision to stay, making that call was not as difficult as I thought it might be. As a matter of fact, it was rather odd that my administrator seemed unsurprised at my resignation, almost as if he already knew. To compound my peculiar situation, the instant I hung up the phone I received word from Mr. Peevey that all of my personal belongings from California had been packed up, and would be delivered within the next week.

Normally, I would grieve such a loss as waving goodbye to my life's pursuit, but nothing about any of this was typical or normal. Like so many other things that had happened since I arrived, I chose not to scrutinize, but move forward. Making a beeline to my side drawer, with Malachi's picture still in hand, I grabbed both latchkeys, and hurried into Adina's room. Unlocking the chest, I opened the lid. This time, instead of being filled with dread at what I might find, my mindset and demeanor was one of excitement and enthusiasm for the task ahead.

With an attitude of reverence and awe, I once again removed Malachi's coat from the chest, reflecting on the mind-boggling reality that he had come and visited me. He somehow knew who and where I was, but I had just begun to learn about him. This time, as I threaded my arms through the silk-lined sleeves, I had an overwhelming sense of grief as I considered Malachi's sacrifice. He renounced everything that he held dear, even to the point of death, to assure that his life's work would endure. Carefully removing the Tempus Vector frame from the case, I thoroughly examined the entire wood form for the next few hours. Nothing out of the ordinary happened while I held it, and I didn't feel anything different; as far as I could tell, it was just a frame. I even put Malachi's picture in the center blank square, but still nothing happened. I guess I would have to wait until I met with Mr. Peevey. Hopefully, whatever was in the black box would give me understanding and direction.

I stood up and looked out Adina's window and thanked her. Even though I knew she was gone, I somehow felt that she was close by. "Thank you Adina. I asked for a sign, for confirmation, and this one (holding up the photo of Malachi), was exactly what I needed!"

So much had happened, so many things had changed since this morning, and through it all Carig was the focus of my thoughts. He had no idea what had occurred and that I had decided to stay. But the reality was this, he was the one that I wanted to share my news with. More than likely he heard the cab driver honking for me out front earlier, and as far as he knew I was on my way to California. Carig had always been the most level-headed person that I had ever met, until yesterday that is. I still couldn't believe how angry he was, I really touched a nerve. I wondered if he would ever forgive me. Either way, I knew that I needed to talk to him.

It was cold outside, so I decided to keep Malachi's coat on. I stepped out onto the porch and sat down for a moment just gazing at the tower. I was really nervous to go over and see him. What if he truly was done with me and had walked away like he said he would? I guess I wouldn't blame him. He was right in everything that he said about me. The fury that blazed from his lips had most definitely been bottled up inside of him for many years. His honesty hurt, but I appreciated it; no one had ever been that honest with me. His anger, I could tell, came from a very deep place inside of him.

Finally mustering up the courage, I went over and knocked on his door. There was no answer. I stood back and looked up, and saw him up on the catwalk looking out at the ocean. Since he was a little boy, the top of the lighthouse was where he would go when he wanted to be alone. For both Carig and his grandfather, Killen, the lighthouse was their sanctuary. Feeling a bit intrusive, I opened the door and began my ascent up the spiral staircase. When I reached the top, it was all I could do to stand still, and admire the man that Carig had become. As I neared him, he turned around quickly, startled, and looked at me with no expression.

"Please don't say a word, Carig. I have something to say to you." He turned around to face me with his back towards the water, not saying a word, just as I had requested. "I, I am so sorry. Please forgive me for how I acted - how I've acted these past few days - my whole life really. You didn't deserve it. You're right. You were right about everything that you said about me." Tears began running down my cheeks, and I felt that I may not get the rest of my words out. "I've been very selfish, and Adina gave up everything for me. I've sabotaged every relationship that I have ever had. I could stand here and give you a hundred reasons why I'm this way, but no more excuses. I refuse to be like I was. Anyway, I really just wanted to say that I'm sorry, really sorry! Please forgive me! By the way, if you don't already know, I'm staying. I'm staying here in Bar Rousse. I don't expect for you to be overjoyed, but I just wanted to let you know."

Carig looked up at me with a slight grin, still not saying a word. I began to feel uncomfortable at his silence.

"And when you talked to me the other day, I'm not sure, but I think you said that you loved me. I don't know if you do anymore, but I, I want you to know that I love you, I always have."

Carig remained still, just staring at me.

"Well, anyway, it's really cold up here, so I'm gonna go. I'll just uh, leave you alone. I'll see you later, okay?"

I walked into the lighthouse and hurried down the spiral steps. I felt so embarrassed at the completely one-sided conversation that I had just had, and I wanted to get out of there as quickly as possible. I couldn't believe that I told him that I loved him. But why not? After all, it was true, I did love him.

It would have been a complete lie if I said that I wasn't a little disappointed after that conversation with Carig. I guess I felt like it would somehow end a little differently. That was the first time that I can ever remember talking to him, and him not responding. I must have really upset him. He probably doesn't realize that I've never told anyone that I love them before. Not this kind of love anyway. The fact of the matter was that I was tired of hiding behind walls that kept me from telling the truth about how I feel. No more! I wanted to be free from those barriers that held me captive and the lies that I would live out trying to protect myself from getting hurt. I decided right then and there that I would rather be hurt in the process of living and loving than to never have lived and loved at all.

I felt lonely walking back into Adina's big house, and I wished that Carig was here, but I wasn't going to engage in another one-sided conversation with him. I had told him that I was sorry and asked for his forgiveness. I even told him that I loved him out loud. There was nothing more that I could do or say. The next move was gonna have to be *all* him.

It was hard to believe that this was my house. I wasn't just here for a summer break or Christmas vacation, but I was here to stay and my life was about to change.

Tomorrow couldn't come soon enough. I couldn't wait until my meeting with Mr. Peevey.

Chapter 15

The Black Box

I decided to take a deeper look around Adina's
sewing room where Malachi's picture had hung aside the
hundreds of others. Maybe there I would find another
noteworthy fragment that would help me to piece
together this puzzle. I slowly moved around the room,
examining each of the images which were hanging on my
aunt's walls, and I realized that I had seen these pictures
many times, yet never really looked at them. Every inch
of every wall was covered with framed photos. For some
reason, I never thought it odd that Adina would have so
many pictures hanging in one room, and most curiously,
of people I did not know or recognize. As a child I had
noticed, that some of the frames were empty, bearing no
picture at all, but never questioned it; I never questioned
any of the plethora of images that masked her sewing
room. I came to the conclusion that Adina must have held
dear the people and places in these pictures, or she never
would have displayed them. She had been many things,
although certainly not eccentric. So why the empty
frames? I didn't know the purpose for any of this yet,

nevertheless, I felt compelled to find out. Not only were these pictures of individuals that I didn't know, but the photos didn't even appear to be from this era. Their garments paralleled, and most resembled, eras falling between the 1800's and early 1900's. None that I saw were recent or of this time period.

My conclusions thus far still left me confused. I sat down on the couch and once again began looking at Malachi's picture. I was mesmerized by his image, and I think, just trying to find some kind of explanation for his mysterious appearance in my life. As I examined it more closely, I noticed that the paper it was printed on was old cabinet card stock that was most commonly used in the 1800's. Feeling a bit frustrated and overwhelmed by so many bits of information that just didn't fit together, I decided to stop searching for the night. It had been a long day, and bed was calling to me. I looked out my window and noticed that the lights were still on in the lighthouse, and that Carig was still awake. I couldn't help but want to see him, and I wondered if he was thinking about me. Lying in bed I tried to sleep, but all the facts of this unraveling mystery continued swirling around in my head; the letter from Malachi to Adina, the Lost Tribe of Solomon, the Tempus Vector, a calling, a purpose? I just couldn't think about it anymore, so I turned over and went to sleep.

During the night, I fell into a deep deathlike sleep that led me into a dream that seemed so real, so vivid. I dreamed that I was sitting on the swing on the front porch of Adina's house reading a book that was filled with blank pages. I became frustrated and confused as I swept through each page searching for text. I looked up, and Adina was standing in the doorway of the house looking at me. She said nothing, but only motioned with her hand for me to come with her. I followed her to the sewing room, and as we proceeded down the stairs, I looked over at the walls of pictures. The frames were no longer filled with people that I didn't know, but *all* of me, of my life. There was a picture of me as baby coming home from the hospital with my mother and father. In another I was standing at my mother's grave; and then my college graduation. They were all pictures of me and different events in my life that now filled the walls of Adina's room.

I looked at her and said, "Where are the pictures that were here? Where did these come from?"

She looked at me, only whispering two words. "Tempus Vector."

As she turned around to walk away, I yelled out her name. "Adina! Please come back. Don't leave me - I don't understand!"

She stopped and slowly turned around. A ray of light entered the room, and lit it so brightly that I could hardly keep my eyes open. Upon her turn, I noticed that she was no longer old, but young like me. Exactly the way she looked when she married Carson. She uttered some all too familiar words, the same that Malachi spoke to me at the airport.

"You're not alone."

As those words echoed through my room, I quickly sat up in bed, gasping for air, and feeling as if I had been holding my breath. "What a strange dream that was!" I wondered what it all meant. I shook my head and laughed. Wonderful! One more element of this mystery to multiply my confusion. It was, however, the first time I had ever dreamed of Adina.

Still feeling uneasy over the alleged haunting, I got up, got dressed, and made my way to Mr. Peevey's office. His assistant wasn't there this time, but instead, he was standing at the door waiting for me. When I came in, he pulled down the front blind, and locked the door.

"Mr. Peevey, is everything ok?" I felt a little unnerved, almost as though he had locked me in.

"Everything's fine, Beni. Just being cautious. Come with me."

He was not jovial like he had been before, but quite serious. I followed him into the very back client room, where he closed the door behind us. He motioned for me to sit down at the end of the long wooden table surrounded by chairs.

"The items that I am about to give you, I promised Adina that I would distribute in a completely private setting. First, let's get these documents signed."

He brought out a thick stack of papers that were marked with tabs where I should sign and initial. He and I went through each of the documents while he explained each one thoroughly before I signed.

When we finally finished, he commended me. "Congratulations, Beni. Adina's entire estate, house, lighthouse, property, and assets are yours. Also, she left you a trust fund so that you won't have to worry about anything."

I felt blessed to be sure, but also still so confused over any and all expectations of me.

Just then, Mr. Peevey brought out a black metal box and handed it to me.

"This part of it, I can't help you with. I don't know what's in it, and she didn't leave the key with me. Adina didn't want the key kept with this box."

I asked him where I could find the key, and he answered "Carig, Carig has the key. You see, Beni, Carig's grandfather was Adina's greatest confidant. He carefully guarded all of her secrets. Once he died, all of the mysteries that surrounded Adina were left to Carig, and now to you also. I am thrilled that you decided to stay and take up where Adina left off; it was always what she wanted. If you need anything, I will be here for you, just like I was here for Adina."

"Speaking of Carig, Mr. Peevey, I would like for you to do something for me."

"Of course, what do you need?"

"Well, first of all, I want you to know that I am very thankful for all of this. I really don't deserve it, but Carig does! I want papers drawn up that make him beneficiary If anything ever happens to me. He is truly a remarkable person in every way, and he would spend his life honoring Adina's memory by using it all for good. Can you do that for me?"

"I absolutely can. I'll get that written up, and all it will take to make it a done deal is your signature. But Beni, I am sure you are going to live a very long life, just like your aunt."

"Thank you, Mr. Peevey! May I stop by in, let's say, an hour and finish this up? I think I'm gonna walk around town for a bit, and then I'll be back."

"You bet! I'll see you in about an hour."

I took the black box and placed it into my messenger bag. For some reason I felt uneasy even carrying it around town. My apprehension stemmed from Mr. Peevey's own fearfulness as I arrived, making certain that the two of us were isolated and unnoticed. After picking up a few items at Wil's store and visiting with he and Angelina, I headed back to Mr. Peevey's office and

341

signed the paperwork, assuring that everything I have would go to Carig if anything were to happen to me.

Chapter 16

Devil's Knuckles

My walk home was shaded by the haunting recollections of my peculiar dream. Adina seemed so real, but rather than joyful and lighthearted, her demeanor was rather somber. It was as if she were having a serious conversation with me, echoing the importance of the message. I was also distracted by the truths held back by Carig. He had obviously been privy to the goings-on of my Aunt Adina, but he never said a word to me about any of it. That did, however, explain why he was so passionate about the legacy that she had left for me. His furious passion now made more sense to me.

When I arrived back at the house, I set my messenger bag and black box on the kitchen table. Of course I was curious as to what exactly was in it, but I had no intention of approaching Carig again, even if he was the one who held the key that would open it.

With the pulsing sound of the grandfather clock as my only companionship, I felt myself growing curiously impatient. Waiting was futile, and a complete waste of

343

time. I didn't even know what I was waiting for....this was ridiculous! My ever familiar stubbornness was proving to be just as ineffective as gaping over this black box.

It was decided, I would go and talk to Carig *again,* and try to sort all of this out. Our roles had reversed; him being the stubborn one, and me trying to make amends. I knocked at his door, but he didn't answer. I knew he was there, and obviously still didn't want to talk to me. For the moment I was at peace with just letting him be, and decided that I would just try again later.

It was such a beautiful day, and I could see clouds forming in the distance that were sure to bring rain later in the afternoon, so I took a very familiar walk down the beach that would eventually lead me to Devil's Knuckles.

A half a mile away from the estate lies a threatening rock formation called Devil's Knuckles. It resembles two fists shooting out from the earth, joined by knuckles that are pushed together. Hundreds of years ago, the place was given this chilling name because of the strong surges of water that explode through the opening below the fists. Ironically, the formation of flat rocks that surround the knuckles is called Devil's Skin. It acquired this name because the rocks are flat and *appear* smooth, but are actually very sharp and rough. One fall on Devil's Skin can cause considerable bodily damage. When Carig and I were children, we used to play on the rocks for hours and climb all over the knuckles. Once we would climb up to the opening of the knuckles, one of us would dare the other to stand up with our arms outstretched and eyes closed, moving at the last second before the wave could knock us down. Many times we went home with bloody knees or elbows from the jagged rocks, but we didn't care - we would still go back again, it was thrilling. The open gap beneath the knuckles, where the waves would shoot through fiercely, was called the volcano. If you could get out of the way right before the volcano erupted, you would earn the prized name of "Mighty Conqueror." Today, I felt ambitious, and decided to climb up to the knuckles. The air was chilly, but I didn't care. I took off my shoes so that I could feel the sand between my toes, and began climbing.

Beni was right. He had ignored her knock at the door, only watching her through his window as she walked down the beach. He made his way up to the catwalk, just so he could have a better view. He was still upset with her, and for some reason was having a difficult time letting his anger go, but down deep inside he knew that his atypical stubbornness was simply a precaution to guard his heart. She kept walking, further than her normal walks would take her, and he knew that she was headed for Devil's Knuckles. He felt uneasy and knew that this was not a very good time of year, or time of day, to go around the rocks, with the tide higher and stronger than normal. His eyes never left her, as she walked along the shore dancing in the waves. She captivated him with her playfulness and joy, and he couldn't help but be pulled into her world. When he was a little boy, he used to sit on the path and watch her and Adina dance and laugh, just like she was doing now. It had been years since he had seen her so free.

He regretted his outburst of anger, and cursed the bitterness that robbed him of time with her. Never had he been that cross with anyone before, but his passion combined with Beni's pigheadedness, caused his dormant Scottish temper to rage. But now, the soft tone of her voice, the words that she had spoken to him, continued echoing through his mind, the words that affirmed her love for him. "I love you, I've always loved you." Quite honestly, he wasn't trying to be rude or insensitive when she was talking to him at the lighthouse, but he was genuinely overwhelmed and speechless over the three-word phrase that caught him off guard. He had loved Beni as long as he could remember, but he was unsure that she would ever love him back. He wanted nothing more than to be with her always, and when she told him that she had decided to stay in Bar Rousse, his heart leapt within his chest, he had never been happier. He wanted to take her and hold her in his arms and never let go. He suddenly became furious at himself. Why didn't he? He knew what he wanted, and he wanted Beni, but Carig had learned, not always the easy way, that he needed to move slowly when it came to her. As difficult as it would be, he decided that he would begin by just being a friend to her. Living here and giving up her other life would be an adjustment and it would take time for her to assimilate. She wasn't used to staying; she was used to running, especially when it involved relationships.

He recalled a time when he and Adina had one of their many long conversations about Beni. Carig openly acknowledged complete and utter love for her, and Adina assured him that a moment would come, at the perfect time, when Beni would be ready to love him back in the same way he loved her.

For Carig, the lighthouse and the ocean had always been places of safety, a retreat where he would escape, to sort things out. It had been the same with his grandfather who understood the medicinal benefits of an endless blue serenity and sea-filled air. When Carig was just a boy, and his heart was grieving, Killen would encourage him to climb to the top of the tower and call out to the sea.

"The sea is like a lifelong companion lad, always there and never changin', with ears always ready to listen. There's nothin' that will fix what's ailin' ye like this faithful friend."

Adina was always impressed by Killen's theory about the ocean, and how it really did seem to help Carig heal from the loss of his parents. Nothing would ever replace the long conversations and relationships that Carig had with his grandfather and Adina, but his refuge at the top of the lighthouse came awfully close.

"Adina, that lass is as stubborn as a mule. I know that I promised ye that I would watch over her and take care of her, and I intend to keep my vow, but she doesn't make it easy to be sure. Now that she's decided to stay, I guess I'm just needin' a little help understandin' my own calling … you know, make sure that I do it right an' all. Ye know, Adina, Beni makes me crazy. I can't even see straight when I'm with her, and I feel like I'm suffocating when were apart.

Carig was suddenly distracted and anxious by the threatening tempest that was quickly moving towards shore; he sensed that something terrible was approaching.

"Adina, I can't put my finger on it, but there's a storm coming, I feel it."

Carig watched as Beni moved further and further down the beach, when unexpectedly, she stopped, turned around, and began looking right at him. Making no movements at all, with her eyes fixed on his, she unexpectedly lifted her arms in the air, and began gesturing for him to come and dance with her. He knew exactly what she wanted, and wasted no time running down the spiral stairs of the tower and onto the beach.

After a few minutes of waiting with no sign of Carig, she assumed that he wasn't coming and continued walking towards Devil's Knuckles. She climbed to the top of the rocks, and with her back facing the water and eyes closed, she swore to stand there, unmoved, until she would see Carig coming towards her. She would not fear the waves, even with their thunderous resound. But then with the eyes of her soul, she could see him nearing her. Beni knew if he was there, everything was alright and there was nothing to fear. Never in her whole life did he let a wave hit her, he would always pull her to safety before the water could touch her. This would be the day that she danced on the beach with Carig, the only man she had ever loved. Even though they were still so far from one another, she purposely faced him and looked at him once again with outstretched arms. For those few moments she looked free, not bound by a calling or any rules.

Carig couldn't help but be enraptured at the mere sight of Benidette, and he hoped that one day she would surrender to him in that same way. His trance was suddenly shattered as he saw a massive wave in the distance that was making its way towards the Devil's rock. He began yelling her name, but she was still too far, and he couldn't be heard over the roar of the surf. Carig knew that unless she moved quickly, she would certainly be swept away and swallowed up. He began sprinting towards her, not averting his eyes off for even a second so that he wouldn't lose sight of her if she was hit. He continued shouting her name as loud as he could, but she didn't hear him. And then right before his eyes, and him being completely helpless, it happened. He watched in horror as the wall of water broke over her and consumed her.

"No! Beni! Beni! Oh my God, No!"

He continued running towards her, screaming her name. At first, he didn't see her anywhere until, with the sweep of another wave, he spotted her limp, lifeless body slamming against the side of the giant rock. As a last attempt to take her, the hostile waters shrouded her body, and then began to pull her out into the abyss. Carig dove into the waters, grabbed hold of her, and then ripped her body from the strong clutches, pulling her out of the water and carrying her up to the sand.

She was limp and unresponsive. "No, no, no, Beni!" He laid her in the sand and felt for a pulse. It was faint, but she had one. There was a large gash on the back of her head that was bleeding profusely. He pulled off his shirt, and tied it over the wound. He needed help *now*, but there was no one else there. His only alternative was to get up to the house and call 911. He picked her up and carried her tightly in his arms. "Stay with me Beni, don't you dare leave me!" Finally arriving at the front of the main house, he laid her on the grass. For the second time in a week, in a complete panic, he had to call for an ambulance. He had lost Adina, he couldn't lose Beni too. He ran back outside where her body lay lifeless, and covered her with a blanket, then held his warm body against hers. "Beni! Beni! I'm so sorry, I'm so sorry! Everything will be ok lass, help is on the way!"

Within a few minutes Carig heard the sirens from the firetruck and ambulance that were quickly moving up the drive that led to the house. Immediately, the medics began working on Beni. Communications between the paramedics and the hospital were of a critical nature. They informed them of the serious condition of this 25 year old female with severe head trauma. Carig backed away, stunned and afraid. There was blood everywhere, and the medics looked at him, and then at one another, with a look of despondency. Within seconds they had her on the gurney and in the ambulance. Carig wanted to stay with her, but they wouldn't allow it. He was advised to follow them to the hospital. So as quickly as he could, he ran to his car, and began following.

Still in shock himself, Carig couldn't even fathom that this was real. He hoped and prayed that he would wake up from this awful nightmare, but to his dismay, it was true. Before arriving at the hospital, he placed a despondent call to Wil to let him know what had happened. Wil assured Carig that he and Angelina would meet him at the hospital. As the ambulance sped up to the emergency room doors, a crew of doctors and nurses were waiting and prepared for Beni's arrival. They told Carig that he needed to stay put in the waiting room, and they would come and talk to him as soon as they knew anything. He sat in stunned silence, overcome by the whole ordeal.

A few minutes later, Wil and Angelina rushed in.

"Carig, what happened? Where is she?"

"She went to Devil's Knuckles, and got swept from the rocks by a giant sea swell. I couldn't get to her... I couldn't reach her....I, I tried to call out to her, but she couldn't hear me."

Carig could hardly speak, and the words that did come, were broken, and filled with agony.

"She was....... pummeled into the rocks at least twice, maybe more before I could get to her."

He cringed while replaying the horrible event in his head, and was forced to sit down as shock began to set in. He stared intently at his bloodstained hands that were now shaking.

"I don't know how bad she is... there was so much blood coming from her head, and she didn't come to. Oh God, Wil, what if she never wakes up? I'm so afraid ... I can't lose her!"

Wil too was distressed over Beni, but he was most concerned about Carig.

"Son, you've got to keep the faith! She's in good hands, and at this point, there is nothin' that we can do for her. You have two choices here, worry and grieve, or cry out to the God who created that girl in there. He's the one that keeps her heart beating .... right?"

Even after his words of encouragement, Wil witnessed Carig going deeper into a pit of despair. It hadn't even been a week since Carig found Adina, and Wil would never forget the toll that it had taken on him. At one point, Wil didn't know if Carig could even be consoled as Adina was the last bit of family that he had, and his family meant everything to him. But the day Beni showed up, Carig came back to life. He seemed to be suddenly freed from the harrowing grasp of lonesome shadows. But now, Carig was shivering, pale, and consumed once again by a veil of darkness, and he feared that if Beni didn't make it, Carig might be lost forever.

Carig held his head in his hands and cried. The one person he loved most in the world was barely hanging onto life. The three of them waited for what seemed like an eternity. More than once, Carig marched over and demanded to know what was going on. Each time they replied in the same way. They were still examining her, they didn't know anything at this point, and he would have to wait until the doctor came out. Several hours later, a man wearing light blue scrubs finally approached them.

Carig attentively stood up, and met him halfway. "Is she okay, doctor?"

"Well, we don't really know everything yet. She's being prepped for surgery right now. But what we do know is that she has a ruptured spleen, and has lost an awful lot of blood from both the internal bleeding and of course from her head wound. She's also suffered a fractured arm, and is pretty banged up all over. Our main concern at this moment is the traumatic brain injury that she's sustained, and secondly, getting her safely through the surgery. Due to the considerable swelling in her brain, I thought it best to place her into an induced coma that we will continue to monitor very closely. Once the swelling subsides, we'll slowly bring her out of it. We're doing everything we can. It's truly a miracle that she survived; she must have had a guardian angel watching over her."

This older African American doctor, who seemed to have vast experience, and confidence filled wisdom, gave a reassuring but concerned smile as he continued. "As soon as she's out of surgery, I'll come out and let you know. Are you her husband?"

Carig stood there ready to answer. "No... just a friend."

Wil spoke up. "I'm Wil Crawford, Beni's only living relative, but I give Carig here permission to speak on her behalf. After all, they've known each other their entire lives; he's absolutely part of our family."

"Okay, great. Well, Mr. Crawford, if you don't mind going over to the nurses' station and filling out some paperwork for her, we would really appreciate it."

Observing the troubled look on Carig's face, he called him over to the hallway where he grabbed a blanket from the shelf, and motioned for Carig to follow him.

"Are you alright son?"

Carig shook his head back and forth, unable to say a word.

With sympathy-filled eyes, the doctor wrapped the white cotton throw around Carig, and held tightly to his shoulders, trying to console his aching heart.

"Son, look at me! You're feeling alone right now, but you're not alone. Listen, there's a chapel up on the second floor. Are you a praying man?"

"Aye, I pray all the time!"

"All right then, this is the perfect time to go and pray. I'm gonna take good care of your girl, ok?"

"Ok."

Carig walked away from the doctor, but instead of following his instructions, he started back towards the waiting room.

"Son, you're goin' the wrong way!"

"Aye, I was just gonna tell Wil to come and get me when Beni's out of surgery."

"You go on to the chapel, I'll tell him where you're at, and I'll make sure someone lets you know once she's all patched up."

It was difficult for Carig to leave the floor where Beni was, but at least praying would keep his mind occupied. Once entering the small candle-lit chapel, he sat down on the front pew and fell to his knees. At first, he felt an anger rise up from his heart.

"Are you not God who knows all things, and sees all things? Yet you allowed this to happen! You could have stopped it, or at least let it be me instead. I'm so sick and tired of losin' the people I love! First it was my parents, then my grandparents, Adina, and now Beni? I'm just a mere man, and I truly don't believe that I can survive losin' her too. So all I have to say is this, if you take her, take me as well! What is it you want from me?"

His anger soon turned to sorrow, and remorse for shaking his fist at God. Without holding back, he began weeping and begging God for Beni's life, pleading with everything inside of him that she would be spared.

"Merciful God, I come before ye now, filled with grief that penetrates down into the marrow of my bone. I can no longer feel my heart, it's as though it's gone missin', like it's somehow stopped beatin' within my chest. I can hardly breathe at the thought of losin' her, God. I know we were but children, but the moment I saw her, my world changed. Somehow I always believed that You had set her apart just for me, and me for her. Oh Lord, it was You who "knit her together within her mother's womb." It is You who gives life, and it is You who can save her. I come before Ye now and beg for her life; I would gladly give mine to save hers. Take me, not her. I commit to you now that I will be the man you've called me to be, and will always do what's right by her. I will do whatever You ask, please just spare her life! Please, Lord!"

He remained there for the next several hours on his knees, never ceasing in his entreaty to the Lord, going so deep into the realm of prayer and immersed deliberation that it almost seemed as if he were somewhere else, feeling as though he was touching the edge of heaven. The unfamiliar but glowing fortress surrounded by a briny deep expanse, blanketed him with peace. Within this welcomed stillness he sensed the familiar touch of his grandfather's hand on his shoulder, and like a refreshing gale, heard his voice. "There's nothin' to fear lad, all will be well in time!" Carig loved this hallowed place where all of the worries of his heart seemed to disappear, and he was surrounded by perfect peace. But he was suddenly stirred out of the celestial experience by the sound of Beni's name.

"Mr. Hammel! Mr. Hammel, wake up, Beni's out of surgery."

Without hesitation, Carig sat up from the pew where he had heedlessly fallen asleep. Standing above him was Wil along with an unfamiliar face.

"Who are you? Where's the doctor?"

"Mr. Hammel, I am Dr. Orr, the attending physician here. We spoke earlier when you first came in."

Carig looked at him completely bewildered.

"What about the older African American doctor? You remember him Wil, he spoke to both of us."

"I'm not sure what you're talking about son. Maybe you dreamed him?"

"I'm sorry Mr. Hammel, but there's no one here that meets that description....are you alright sir?

360

Obviously concerned about Carig's state of mind , Wil came and sat down next to him. Even though Carig knew that the person he spoke of was real, he chose not to say another word about him. He could tell that both Wil and Dr. Orr were questioning his right mind.

"Yeah right, maybe it was just a dream. I don't really know, it really doesn't matter though. How's Beni?"

"Well, she's alive and doing as well as can be expected at this point. The surgery went smoothly, but we did have to remove her spleen. As I said earlier, she's in a coma, and all we can do is wait. Head injuries are complex. The swelling caused by that kind of trauma.....well, is very involved, and many times unpredictable.

"I need to see her!"

"She's still in recovery, but once she's moved into ICU, you can go in and see her. But I just want to warn you ahead of time Mr. Hammel, she's terribly beat up."

"I don't care, I need to see her! I won't leave her again."

Wil looked at Carig, "Son, why don't you go home and at least get some dry clothes on, and then come back?"

"No, I cannot leave her, Wil. I'll never leave her! This is my fault. She came to my door first and I didn' answer it. If I just wouldn' have been so bloody stubborn and opened the door, she wouldn' a gone down there alone."

"Carig, this is not your fault. Beni's a grown woman, not a child. She's been on Devil's Knuckles hundreds of time; this was just an accident. I'll tell you what, I'll go to your house and get you some dry clothes, and bring em back. Also, I just got word that all of her things will be arriving tomorrow from California. So I'll need to be at the house in the morning to wait for them."

"Thank you, Wil!"

Once Wil and Angelina left, Carig sat by himself, refusing to go anywhere. Late into the evening the doctor finally gave Carig the green light to see Beni.

"Doctor, may I stay with her, please?"

"Well, it just so happens that there's a fairly comfortable chair in the room, but you really should go home. There is not one thing that you can do. She's in a deep coma, and won't be waking up for some time. Go home. We'll call you if there are any changes."

"No, I'd like to stay, thank you!"

"Alright then, follow me."

As they walked into the ICU ward where she was lying, Carig's already broken heart sunk into the pit of his stomach. Beni's head was completely bandaged, her face and arms ripped and bruised, with so many tubes, going in and out of her body. He quickly turned away from her, horribly disturbed to finally bear witness of the abuse done at the hand of the Devil's Knuckles. He leaned down and kissed her head, and then knelt by the side of her bed.

"Oh God, what have I done? I'm so terribly sorry lass, this is all my fault. I would give everything I have to be lyin' there instead of you! But I promise you this, ye won't be alone, not for even a second. Beni, God will be with you in the silence, and I lass will be here by your side and be your voice until you wake. You just rest, my lovely Beni, and worry about nothin'! If ye start feelin' afraid in the darkness, let the sound of my voice be your place of safety."

For the next three weeks Carig stayed with Beni every moment, faithfully reading her favorite books to her, and offering a continuous one-sided conversation about all of the things that she had missed throughout the years. Just as he had promised, he never left her side. As her wounds began to heal, and the swelling decreased, the coma induced sleep was no longer necessary. But as October quickly turned into November, Beni still remained unconscious.

With each passing day, the doctor grew more concerned and puzzled, as Beni showed no signs of waking. He informed Carig that if her condition didn't drastically improve by the end of the week, arrangements would need to be made to move her to a long-term care facility. Along with that devastating news, he explained that time had become their enemy. "A coma is kind of like a boat that's floated away from the shore. If too much time goes by, that boat will be pulled further and further away from land, making it impossible to ever get back."

Carig was already weary, but the doctor's discouraging diagnosis left him altogether exhausted. He fell back, allowing the chair to swallow him up. His burning eyes closed, and then he uttered a muffled cry of deliverance. "Gran, you promised me that all would be well, but nothing can be well or right without her. It's so dark, and I'm so alone. If you can, if you're there, please help me."

The next morning Carig woke up to the sight of Mr. Peevey sitting on the other side of the bed.

"Good morning, Carig. Good Lord son, you look like you've been through the ringer!"

"Mr. Peevey, how long have ye been here?"

"Well, not too long...It was time I came and checked on our girl. I'm sure sorry this happened to Beni. She and I had just chatted earlier, on the day of the accident. Listen son, in all honesty, I came to see you. Do you think you could break away for a few minutes and talk? How about I buy you a cup of coffee, and some breakfast down in the cafeteria?"

Carig looked at Beni, not wanting to leave her. "Okay, but just for a bit."

He informed the nurse that he'd be down in the cafeteria if they needed him. After filling up their plates with pancakes, scrambled eggs, and sausage, they sat down at a table in the corner of the room.

"What's this all about, Mr. Peevey?"

"At the risk of sounding apathetic about this situation, I must tell you something very important. The day Beni came and saw me, the day of the accident, when she signed all of the papers making the Bar Rousse Estate and all of Adina's assets hers, she had me do something else as well. You see, she was concerned about you, and positioned a document that would transfer everything to you if something were to happen to her. Now I know everyone is concerned about her making it through this and ..."

Before Mr. Peevey could finish, Carig frantically ran out of the cafeteria. Provoked by this new information, he stormed through the door of Beni's room. As if a fire had suddenly been lit beneath him, he was resolved to conduct a cold sobering discussion, with the clear-cut goal of shaking her back to life. As he began pacing from one side of the room to the other, furious pleas began to pour from his mouth. "Listen, Beni, you've been here long enough. It's time to go home. Enough of this nonsense lass, you need to wake up!

366

Beni, please wake up, please! I don't want that house or anything in it without you. Don't you dare think about leaving me! Wake up, Beni. You have to wake up!" Carig continued his appeals for the rest of the day, until he couldn't speak another word.

Living on that estate all of those years without Beni was torture. Everywhere he looked, he saw reminders of her. But the thought of her dying and leaving him there alone was out of the question.

By the end of the day he was not only drained, but barely holding on to the end of his rope. For the first time in his life, he had nothing left to give, no more words to say. It had been over a month since Beni's accident, and also since he had slept in a real bed. He couldn't stand the thought of sitting one more night in that "prison cell" of a side chair. He was done, and the only thing left to do, was surrender. If she wasn't going to wake up then he too would choose continuous slumber. As he laid down beside her and wrapped his arms around her soft warm body, he hoped and prayed that he would not only fall asleep, but that he could be with her wherever she was. He was beyond sleep deprived, and went into such a state

367

of dormancy that when he woke up he didn't know where he was, but only felt a light caress on his hand.

The much needed rest revived his weary soul, and he felt so warm and comfortable laying there that he closed his eyes once again, enjoying divine tenderness and warmth. As he pressed his body into her, he suddenly remembered that he was lying with Beni … it was she who was caressing his hand, she was awake! He opened his eyes, and buried his head in her hair, and held her even tighter, letting out a sigh of relief and thankfulness.

"Beni, ye didn't leave me, I knew ye would come back! Thank you, God!"

Carig hopped up out of the bed, wildly excited to tell the nurse that Beni was awake. But before he got too far, Beni whispered his name.

"Carig, come here, come here!"

"What is it, lass? I'm here!"

"Carig, I heard you - I heard you praying for me. Carig, come here, come closer!"

He went back over and drew in close to Beni so that he could hear her.

"What is it, lass?"

368

"I love you."

Carig could hardly contain his joy! Beni was not only awake, but she loved him.

"I love you too, mo chridhe!"

She was instantly moved to tears by the familiar term of love. This Scottish endearment was declared at least once a day by Carig's grandfather to his beautiful Mari. It was a tender reminder that she, and she alone, was master of his heart. Carig could tell by Beni's charmed gaze that she was pleased by his Gaelic declaration, and began patting the side of the bed.

"Come back and lay with me!" Not wasting a second, he did exactly as she asked. Once he roused from their blissful shared moment, the matter at hand came flooding back to Carig.

"Oh! Beni, I have to tell them you're awake, I'll be right back!"

The nurse came in, overjoyed. "Welcome back, honey! I'll go call the doctor."

Excitedly, the doctor rushed in, examined Beni, and told both of them that if everything checked out okay, she could hopefully go home in a few days.

That evening, after Beni happily ate, she and Carig sat together talking about what had happened to her and how long she had been asleep.

"Beni, I thought I was gonna lose ye."

"Uncle Wil said that you never left my side. Thank you, Carig, for everything you did. You saved me. Can you do me a favor though?"

"Anything! What do ye need?"

"I need for you to go home, get some rest, and for goodness sake, take a shower. You need a shower!"

He grinned from one ear to the other. "I don't know what ye mean lass, I don't smell anything."

"Well, if I were to be completely honest, it was your smell that woke me up."

They both laughed, "Okay, Beni, I'll go shower, but I'm coming back. I've actually never felt better in my life! Besides, I kind of liked sleeping with ye. I guess you gettin' in an accident and bein' unconscious is one way to get you in bed with me!" For the first time in over a month, Carig agreed to leave Beni. "Don't go anywhere lass, I'll be back soon."

Chapter 17

The Blessing

With great joy, the day finally arrived that I was released to go home. I was beyond ready to leave, but Carig even more so, feeling as though he had finally been resurrected from the dead. Having spent every waking moment for over a month fixed on mint colored walls, and a disagreeable vinyl armchair, he vowed to never again enter that place of torment. As for me, it was difficult recalling even pieces from my prolonged dream state. But what I did remember, was hearing Carig's voice in the dark, which in turn led me to an amber colored allusion of Adina's front door. When I walked inside the gleaming portal, still sitting on the table, just where I left it, was the unopened black box with a key fixed within the eyelet. Like looking into a foggy mirror, I was unable to make out the distorted and perplexing contents. Each time, my pursuit ended in the same way, confronted by a great wall of water that consumed me, pulling me into its depths with no escape. This dream or whatever it was that repeated itself, made me fearful and apprehensive to finally open the box.

During the days following my return to life, Carig remained by my side. It was during that time that we would talk for hours about everything, including my disturbing vision of the box that would lead to my demise. He reminded me that Adina would never do anything to put me in harm's way, and that it was only a dream. Understanding my fear, but also realizing that this task could no longer be put off, the moment we returned home he grabbed the messenger bag with one hand and mine with the other.

"Come on, lass. Your destiny with this black box is well overdue."

He guided me into Adina's sewing room where all of the pictures hung. For the first time I saw this place in a two-fold light; a memorial and account of Adina's accomplishments, but for me, a new beginning of uncharted journeys. I also knew that the man standing next to me was my rock, and he not only bore the key to the box, but he was also a vessel of wisdom that would help me unlock the layers of secrecy that had now become my life calling. Brimming with questions, I turned towards Carig and began my exploration.

"Well, I guess this is where it all begins...right? So no more waiting, tell me what you know. I mean, to start with, let's talk about these pictures and the Tempus Vector. I need a place to start, and I can't make sense of any of this until I understand what Adina's been doing all these years."

Carig was indeed a wealth of information, revealing in lengthy details the part he played in Adina's life of secrets and mystery, divulging information that until now, I was never privy to. He reflected on the moment in time when it all began for him. During the final days of his grandfather's illness, Killen and Adina came together and showered Carig with unbelievable details of their incredible journeys, then sanctified him as helpmate to the carrier of the Tempus Vector . It was a bittersweet moment for the pair, comforted by a season well lived, but grieved by the winter they now faced. With Killen's last breath he assured Carig that he needn't fear, that through the years he had unknowingly been fully equipped for the journeys ahead. He finished with words of pride for his grandson, well-pleased with the man he had become, and finally, reassured him that he would never be alone. Along with the legacy, he passed on his life charge to the one and only person he trusted to take care of Adina, and who would be a faithful companion for the next carrier. The idea of Adina being alone seemed to pain Killen the most, but knowing both the faithfulness and kindness of his grandson, he championed a countenance of peace until the very end. His faded green eyes fixed on the vibrant watch of his only and most precious blood relative, until finally he submitted his spirit. As it turned out, Adina was only able to make a few more trips. She tried to keep her eyes fixed on the unending tasks of her life calling, but it just wasn't the same without Killen. Her onset of health issues seemed to begin the day he died, leading to her steady decline until the evening when she too embarked on her final journey, joyfully reunited with Carson and her faithful Killen.

Recognizing that Adina's odyssey began soon after her arrival from Germany, and knowing that it had consumed her entire life made me uncertain about walking the same path. But almost as quickly as the familiar thought of running entered my mind, it departed. Sensing a warm and comforting presence in the room, possibly of departed saints who had thus far carried out this remarkable commission, my doubts melted away, instantly replaced by boldness and fortitude. It was as if they were surrounding me, nudging me forward, igniting my soul and empowering me to carry on where Adina had left off. I felt an unfamiliar confidence that everything was going to be alright.

"Carig, I know that you of all people understand how confusing and overwhelming this is, but I trust you, and I'm ready to know everything and move forward. Will you help me?"

Carig seemed relieved. Finally, the battle to convince me of my calling while also persuading me to stay was over. And what a battle it had been. I felt horrible causing him so much grief, it must have been exhausting. All of these years, he had waited for me, and unbeknownst to yours truly, I was waiting for him as well.

"Well, let me start from the beginning. The letter from Malachi, you've read it, yes?"

"Yes, I have. But I don't really understand what part Malachi plays in all of this, and what the whole thing is about."

I sat there for a moment lost in my own thoughts, envisioning Malachi's sweet face looking up at me from the chrome and vinyl waiting chair in the airport terminal.

"What is it, lass? What's wrong?"

"Malachi!"

"What about him?"

"I have something to tell you.... I met him, and talked with him. It was actually he who convinced me to stay."

"What do you mean, Beni? He's been dead many years now, that's not possible. Maybe you dreamed it? Besides, you don't even know what he looked like!"

"I do know! I mean, at the time, I didn't know who he was."

"You're not makin' any sense!"

"I know this is hard to believe, but he was at the airport, sitting in my terminal, staring at me while I was waiting to board my flight. I *felt* him looking at me, and then we spoke to one another. He knew my name, which at the time I thought was odd, but just chalked it up to the fact that he could have seen my boarding pass or driver's license. He also told me, in a German accent no less, that

376

I may feel alone, but that I would never be alone. Which now that I think about it, is exactly what Adina told me in my dream, or whatever that was.

"So, I didn't really give him another thought until the day I was set to leave and go back home. I found a picture of him in this room. Well, actually, the picture found me. Strangely, his photo fell right in front of me, or rather jumped in front of me."

Poor Carig couldn't tell if I was still suffering from lingering head trauma issues, or if I was just crazy.

"I didn't imagine it, Carig!"

"How could that be, lass?"

"I have no idea, but it was him. He was the same person as in this picture. You of all people should see sense in the randomness!" I held up the dated black and white, and showed Carig his image. "He was even wearing this suit and hat, and was carrying that same bag that's sitting by him in the picture."

Carig looked closely at the photograph with a puzzled look on his face.

"What is it? What are you looking at?"

"That suitcase. I've seen it before." He ran to the doorway of the room, "I'll be right back."

A few minutes later, he returned with a small leather suitcase that was identical to the one in the photograph.

"It can't be! I'm sure this is not the same bag, there's no way!"

Carig turned on a light, and pulled out a magnifying glass from the desk drawer so that he could take a closer look at the picture. On the top of the suitcase to the left of the handle, and barely obvious to the naked eye, he discovered the initials "MC". He mindfully looked back and forth from photo to leather case, verifying that both had the exact same initials in the identical place.

"Well, what do you know, it's the same one."

"Do you know anything about Malachi? I mean did Adina ever tell you about him?"

"Ye know Beni, after the death of my grandfather my life changed, just like yours is changing right now. But one thing I had that you don't, was the good fortune of spending many an hour with Adina. We were able to talk about several things that helped me to make sense of her complicated life…..I mean, I still don't understand everything for sure. But one of the people that she spoke of often, was Malachi Coffee." He went on to say that it never failed to grieve Adina, when she would speak of him.

"Ye see, the very hour of Adina's departure from Germany was also when she found out that Carson had been killed, which was devastatin' all by itself. But to make the pain worse, only moments after she fled the town of Friedlich, that October 4, 1941, it was invaded by the Nazis. Her close friends, Malachi, and his sister, Estee, were only a few of the many Jews that were taken from their homes and shipped off to God knows where. Carson kept tellin' Adina that war was coming, but he also told her that she couldn't say anythin' that might put his mission in jeopardy. She could hardly live with herself after that, and wished that she'd had the opportunity to do it over, knowin' then what she knew now about things. Even though it had been so many years, she would look at me with such brokenness that I could hardly stand it!"

"How sad! Poor Adina."

379

Beni moved in a little closer to Carig and held his face in her hands. "Please Carig, tell me what you know, everything you've seen, and exactly what Adina and Killen told you....I want to know everything!"

"Well, this gift and ability to take this journey can only be passed on to one who is chosen and who encompasses the skills to be successful. Along with bein' the keeper and bearer of the Tempus Vector, the skills are inherent.

I was immediately discouraged at his words, believing myself to be entirely ill-equipped.

"What skills?"

"Beni, Adina told me that the bearer must have a heart that is large and that has the ability to hear and discern. When you are blessed to complete these journeys, you will be given, like Solomon, understanding for each situation that you encounter."

Carig laughed at something Adina had predicted about how Beni would respond.

"She told me that you would think this was a mistake, but wanted me to assure you that it was not. Even though it may be hard for you to understand, this

380

calling for your life was planned far before you were born. Now, listen carefully because this was hard for me to believe as well. The one that is blessed to continue this journey, which is you, and is in possession of the Tempus Vector, will be sent back to certain times in history - times and places that are blemished with flaws that needs to be restored."

"How does it work? I mean, how will I know?"

"It's a mind-boggler to be sure, both simple and complex all at the same time. Like a divine polaroid of sorts, appearin' before ye very eyes, a picture card will develop within the Tempus Vector frame. Behind the picture, is written a name, date, and sometimes a place. It's like a bleary map, tellin' you where yer gonna go. All these pictures you see around you now, have come from the frame and are reminders of all that Adina accomplished."

I interrupted several times to ask questions, but Carig would tell me, "Just listen for now."

"Adina's exodus point is in the room upstairs on the third floor. Like clockwork, she would embrace the Tempus Vector in one hand, and her suitcase in the other, departin' through the door that leads out to the balcony.

Upon steppin' through the door, she was gone from my sight and would step into the place and time in the photo. She, like you, never felt completely equipped, but to her surprise was given the wisdom upon arrival to accomplish the task. While that particular entrance in time remained open, the task was attainable. She would inevitability know by that *all too familiar* uneasiness that would rise up within her, that the curtain of time was closin', and it was time to leave. Many times she would leave not knowin' if her journey was a success or a failure."

Carig admitted that there was a lot that he still didn't know, but Adina had reassured him that any unanswered questions would come to light when the black box was opened.

"Now, Beni.. before Adina died she insisted that I do something, something very important, somethin' that Malachi did for her. Kneel in front of me."

"Seriously?"

"Just do it, lass. Don't be so damn stubborn!"

I thought this so strange, but I trusted Carig, and his commitment to carry out all of the wishes that Adina had asked of him. At this point, the most unbelievable had become believable.

Next, he placed both of his hands on my head. "Close your eyes, Beni."

As he began to speak, it was as if I heard the voice of Malachi speaking this blessing to me, just as he had to Adina.

"I invoke upon you this blessing by the grace of God, that you will be empowered, and that you will come to realize and achieve your destiny with great wisdom. I commission you now with the heritage and tradition of those of us who have been sanctioned before you; the generations that have gone before you."

He then lifted my head and said, "Do not stay embittered in your past hurts and sorrow, what you have lost, or what you do not have. Rather, pursue with all wisdom the venture that is before you. You will never be alone. You may feel like an orphan, but those of us who have gone before you will be with you."

Carig took my hand and raised me up to stand.

"I am here for you, Beni - always, and I will never leave you."

Chapter 18

Ascent of the Monarch

Once Carig finished the commission which he was made to memorize and deliver to me, we sat there together, both in a daze, as this was a very unusual situation for the both of us. He was relieved that he had finally done what Adina asked of him, and as for me, I was just trying to take in this newfound intelligence that was going to change my life forever.

Carig could tell that I was overwhelmed, but also noticed that I looked pale and worn out. Having just been released from the hospital, he was concerned that I was overexerting myself. He sat down next to me on the floor and pulled me onto his lap, gently embracing me. The only thing I remember as I drifted off was the pleasant fragrance of his skin, and the sensation of his soft cotton sweatshirt on my cheek. Before I realized it, three hours had passed and I had slept the entire time in Carig's arms.

I woke up in a sudden panic.

"What time is it? I am so sorry! You sat here this whole time so that I could sleep? You're so sweet!"

Carig just smiled at me.

"How long have I known you, Beni?"

I thought that an odd response to what I had just asked.

"Well, I guess that would be about nineteen years now."

"Okay then, you are lookin' at a man who's waited nineteen years to hold you like that. So, as far as I'm concerned, there's nothing in the world that I would rather be doin'."

I reached up and held his face and kissed him. He then held me so tightly that I could hardly get a breath.

"I've waited almost two decades for that too, lass!"

I loved how his body felt against mine. So without hesitation, I allowed mine to completely melt into his, and then kissed him again. I had decided, especially where Carig was concerned, that I would never again build up walls or suppress the passion that I felt for him. I put my lips to his ear and gently whispered.

"I love you!"

Carig closed his eyes and took a deep breath, and in a hushed tone filled with emotion, he struggled to utter even one word.

"That makes two of us, lass! I want you so badly I can hardly think about anything else."

He too would no longer disguise his emotions, which was obvious by the dangerous fire burning in his eyes. Strongly exhaling, he contained his raging fervor, highly aware that our intimacy was leading to a place that he had vowed not to go.

"Not yet lass, you're worth waiting for."

Carig was a perfect gentleman whose rare ideas about love and sex were what some would call old fashioned. But as for me, I appreciated his character. His high moral standards made me feel valuable. I was well aware that a virtuous man of integrity was hard to come by these days. He believed that I was worth waiting for, and I felt the same about him.

"God Almighty Beni, you make me so crazy, in a good way I mean. I think I need to set my mind on something else besides you lass, or I might lose it!"

Seeing that we were both very curious about what the black box held, now seemed like the perfect time to investigate.

"Are you ready to open Adina's black box, Beni?"

"Yes, I believe I am."

"Alright then!"

Carig stood in front of me with an amorous smile, and reached down into his shirt, pulling out the sterling chain that hung around his neck. It held a single ornate key that would open the box. It looked more like a beautifully designed necklace than a key. Where the bow would normally be was a silver knot, like the one on the frame. The stem was wrapped in cords which all joined together at the rather small and delicate blade. He handed me the key, another job well done; a burden that he'd been bearing since his grandfather passed away.

"This is your time right now to spend with Adina and Malachi to find out exactly what you need to do."

I could tell that he didn't want to leave, but knew, that this was something that I needed to do alone

"Call me if you need me. I'll be close by."

Even after Carig left, I didn't open the box right away. I found myself apprehensive as to what I might find, and realized that once I unveiled the information and wisdom within the four corners of this container, I would forever be accountable for it. There were two locks on the heavy metal box. One in the front, and one in the back. I first inserted the key in the front eyelet, and turned it twice counter-clockwise. The clicking sound led to a partial release of the lid. Turning the box to unlock the other side, I noticed that the keyhole was much larger, with a completely different shape. Skimming my finger over the keyhole and taking a closer look, I detected that a fatter, slightly round key was necessary. "What in the world? Where's the other key? Come on Beni, think!" I began examining the very unique key. "The key, the key!" Carig was given *one* key, and *one...* key... only. Two locks..... *one* key. A key with one small side, and one fatter, round side. That was it! The *other* lock required the *other* end of the key. Like magic, with one push and one turn, the lid was unshackled.

Lifting the lid from the box, I found myself a little bit disappointed to discover three rather plain looking leather-bound books snugly tucked inside. I guess I half expected to find gold bars or something like it, considering the Fort Knox like exterior. Two of the books were tied together with what looked like a long cotton shoestring, and then the third one sat alone. All three were made with heavy shoe leather, each cover baring deeply engraved initials that were obviously fashioned by one who specialized in the artistry of hide. The two that were bound together revealed the initials "MC" and "AY." These had obviously belonged to Malachi and Adina, and appeared to be their well-used and most treasured journals. The other book, the one that sat alone, had one set of initials that read "BH." I had at first assumed that it was mine, but if it was meant to be, an obvious mistake had been made.

I began flipping through the book, and it was evident by the ream of blank pages that this journal was yet to be filled. Out of the blue, from within the center of the old and discolored sheets, slipped a frayed note that was veiled in cinnamon colored stains. It was obvious that the fragile piece of paper had been there for ages with its well-worn folds and tattered edges. While carefully opening the fragile parchment, I discovered that it was a handwritten recipe. At the top, it bore the name of the culinary artist who had been the original creator of my all-time favorite dessert. "Ira's Kasekuchen Rezepte"

(Ira's Cheesecake Recipe). This was obviously the authentic master recipe that Adina brought back from Germany. I had watched her make it many times, but never before had seen this ancient list of instructions. She knew how I adored her cheesecake, and must have wanted me to have it, but what a curious thing to be locked away within the confines of these journals. Perhaps it was just a reminder that even though everything in my life was changing, some things would forever remain the same.

When I opened the journal, I saw my name, Benidette, and the date of May 14, 1941 handwritten on the first page. So now I knew for sure that this journal was meant for me, but I didn't understand the flawed initials, and the seventy-five year old date by my name. All I could figure was that my middle initial was used instead. "H" being for Hope instead of "Crawford." Unsure of why my stamp was inconsistent with the other two, I chose not to dwell too long on the difference. In the whole scheme of things, I guess it really didn't matter. Moving forward, I began further analyzing my handwritten name and the date; the script was definitely not in Adina's hand. Because she was always dropping me a letter or card, I was very familiar with her penmanship. The tag was undeniably put there by someone other than Adina. On the next page was a handwritten letter that was obviously penned by my aunt.

"To My Beni,

Enveloped within these pages will be your chronicle of events as the privileged bearer of the Tempus Vector. You now become the symbol of the possession. This comes from a deeply rooted people and cause that stems from a passion of love and wisdom to make what was wrong, right. You may be feeling as if you are ill equipped to take on such a crucial post of repairing what is broken, but you are not. Remember, you are not alone. As you take ownership of, and become the protector of the Tempus Vector, you will be given wisdom far beyond what you thought that you possessed. Like Solomon, whose lost tribe this bequest ascends from, you will be given understanding that is more than the sands on the shore."

I felt I was reading a page from a novel, not something that was written for and to me ... something that was real. I looked once more at my name and the date, May 14, 1941. I was confused! This must have been a mistake. I picked up the two other journals, opening up

Malachi's first. I had to do a double take, as I noticed that the writing in his book was the same penmanship as the name and date tagged in my book. It was Malachi who wrote my name! He somehow knew in the year 1941 that I would follow after Adina. To compound my confusion, the fact that Malachi created a journal for me and wrote my name in it almost 50 years before I was born, was inconceivable. I decided to take the box and its contents up to Adina's room in hopes that, if I compared or combined items in the chest with the items in the box, somehow all of this would make more sense.

I sat the black box on the floor, and then removed the shoe box from the chest that held the navy blue pumps. Pulling the shoes out of the box, I began examining them more closely. Written on the insoles was the name "Coffee." After inspecting both the thick leather journals and the shoes, I was finally able to make the connection. The obscure Malachi Coffee was a cobbler, and the holder of the Tempus Vector in 1941 Germany. This would have been the time that Adina and Carson lived there, and the place where Carson died. Adina sadly returned alone, back to the United States in October of 1941. When it came to discussing that particular time in history, she was invariably preoccupied. Losing Carson, the attack on Pearl Harbor, and then the beginning of World War II, was a dark and difficult time for her, filled with painful memories and unimaginable loss. I wonder if Malachi knew when he met Adina that she was going to be the new carrier of the Tempus Vector. He must have known. If he knew about me, he more than likely knew about her long before she walked into his life. This whole idea of predestination was far beyond my comprehension, and quite frankly was making my head hurt. But it was apparent that the more I discovered about Adina, the more I realized that there was so much about her that I didn't know. I had learned more in the last week about the life she had lived, than in all of the years that I had spent with her. I felt as though blinders had been removed from my eyes, and I began to really know and understand my aunt for the first time.

I recognized the next couple of items. The first one was Adina's pencil ark. Actually, it was an antique pencil box with a sliding lid that contained vintage pencils, all of which were made in her great, great grandfather's pencil factory. She carried this little box everywhere she went, along with her pad of paper that she used to jot down measurements. I could tell that these heavy-leaded pencils authored every page of her diary.

The next item that caught my eye was her butterfly
brooch that was pinned onto a green velvet drawstring
bag. I had seen pictures of Adina wearing this pin, but I
had never seen it in real life. Like her, the colorful brooch
was beautiful and unique. Not only was the velvet bag a
resting place for the butterfly, but also a pocketbook
filled with gold coins, each one stamped with the same
knot emblem that was carved on the frame. Their craggy
uneven edges reminded me of coins minted in ancient
days with a Caesar-like stamp.

Not wanting to bombard me with complete
unfamiliarity, it was obvious that she intentionally tucked
these few personal items into the mix, reminding me that
she was still my Aunt Adina, and I, her Beni. The
colorful brooch reminded of spring in Bar Rousse. As
soon as the weather began to warm, Adina and I would
make a day of lying within the deep grassy fields around
her estate, waiting in anticipation for the eruption of
black and gold flutters to rise up from the meadow of
wildflowers. Adina was convinced that if we closed our
eyes and listened closely, we would hear them excitedly
chattering about their newly discovered freedom. Our
yearly ritual led to long talks about how one day, like
these monarchs, I too would fly. This pin was a symbol of

a transformed life, my transformed life. By saying goodbye to my previous existence, and accepting this task as the carrier of the Tempus Vector, I became like this winged creature. It was Adina's way of letting me know that everything was going to be okay; that this new journey here in Bar Rousse would be far greater than a life made of my own doing.

The last item that I pulled out of the box, was a black cobbler hammer. It was very similar to the other tools found in the chest. These seemingly pointless instruments that were important enough to be locked up and protected remained a mystery to me. Maybe Adina saved them for the sentimental value as they reminded her of Malachi. I still couldn't see how these items all together made any sense, but maybe that was the point. Thus far, Adina purposely separated each element of this enigma by design. I knew however, well I hoped anyway, that once I began reading her journal I would discover all of the necessary information to help me begin my journey.

Every page of Adina's journal was fill - brimming with writings, instructions, and drawings. The first picture that she drew was the Tempus Vector frame. She sketched every detail right down to each and every scratch. I'm not really sure why, but for some reason, she thought it important.

The next page was dated June 30, 1942.

"Malachi's journal has given me the vision of what I need to accomplish. I will never understand why I have been chosen for this task, but Malachi knew that I was the one, even before I arrived that day at his shop looking for a pair of children's boots. I do this in honor and remembrance of you, Malachi. I wish you were here to help me, but in a way, I believe that you are.

You have told me to write everything down in this journal so that one day, like you, I will have helpful information to pass on to the next carrier of the Tempus Vector. I feel rather alone in all of this, but that's okay. It won't stop me from completing the task you have put before me. I write this journal now to one called Benidette.

I don't know you yet, Benidette, but Malachi knew you, just as he knew me. Someday you will go forward from where I leave off. I am blessed to know your name. Not all carriers know the identity of their successor. If you don't yet know yours, I hope that you will, someday.

Writing to you makes me feel as though I have a friend in all of this.

I will try to make this as simple as possible, as I know that you probably feel very confused. The Tempus Vector is a secret to the world, a mystery, a gift, but also, a weapon. You must be very careful. Never leave it unattended when you are traveling; always keep it with you. There will come a time when a blessing will be given to you. At the moment of that blessing, your time as the carrier will begin.

The best way that I can explain the Tempus Vector is that it is a supernatural gift that is entrusted from one generation to the next. It's a tool that sometimes removes, and other times changes, flaws in time, correcting them with its endless and most perfect wisdom. Your willingness to be both carrier and vessel will allow this perpetual omnipotence to work through you.

At this point, I have only been traveling for a little more than a year, but have already learned so much. My advice to you is to follow my instructions closely, just as I have followed closely the instructions left me. Even now, I feel ill-equipped for this task, but Malachi was thorough, and I have been blessed by his insight and wisdom.

Beginning now, there is an unyielding connection between you and the frame. Believe me, you'll know what I mean the moment a picture appears and the onset of a journey calls you. It's a difficult experience to describe, other than to say that it is an uncomfortable but exciting disturbance within your soul; one that will unfortunately leave you nauseous and short of breath, but only for a moment. I feel half-crazy writing this, but as you connect with the Tempus Vector, you will see that a picture card has appeared in the center that contains an image of a person or a place, sometimes both. On the reverse side there will always be a date, informing you of the time period in which you will be traveling. Not until you arrive will you be given the wisdom needed to take the correct action. Sometimes the task will be as simple as a word given. Sometimes it will be an action of some sort. Always be prepared to stay as long as necessary, but ready to leave when you get that same uncomfortable feeling as you did when the photo appeared. If you tarry too long, allowing the door of time to close, you will be unable to return. Please know and be prepared that there will be times when you will fail, and will have to walk away with your task undone. Because there's a human element involved, failure will happen.

398

To make preparations easier, I have decided to line my third story room with wardrobe closets. I have been sewing non-stop, trying to fill them with suits and dresses. I have chosen timeless styles and colors which are appropriate to wear for traveling. It seems that black and navy blue are good choices, along with simple and comfortable shoes. As you travel, don't wear anything that will bring attention to yourself. Keep your focus on the task. There will be times when one or more of the details will not be revealed to you. You must focus on what information is given, not on what you do not have.

In the chest that Malachi sent me there was an old leather suitcase. This is the one you must use. It is suitable for all times; pack only what is needed. One change of clothes, and personal items that you will need, that's it! Always take your journal and a pencil. Do not take any kind of identification, or anything that will reveal your true time. Take two gold coins with you; never carry regular currency. There will be times your stay is very short, and others that are much longer. If you need money, sell a piece of gold, and use the currency from that period. It is highly unlikely that you will return to the same place twice, dealing with the same situation again. This is not your choice; it's just the way it is.

Now, the next part may seem unimportant, but even the smallest things are significant and can make the difference between success and failure. Once you are ready to leave, hold your suitcase in one hand, and the Tempus Vector in the other. Step out of the third story door onto the balcony. This will always be your departure and entrance point. I don't really know how to tell you to ready yourself for the passage from one time in history into another. It is a very strange reality, but you'll get used to it.

You will go through the same motions when returning. Wherever you are, hold your suitcase in one hand, and the Tempus Vector in the other. You will find yourself home, stepping in through the third story door.

Without fail, when you return, you'll be exhausted for days. It would be good if you can find a trustworthy soul to be there to help you when you come back. I am blessed to have found someone to assist me. I have hired a very respectable Scottish man and his wife who are helping to repair this old place. Only Killen knows, however, what I do, and he has been willing to help me. His friendship is invaluable.

In the following pages, Benidette, I have made some notes of my travels so far to help you. By the time you actually read this though, I'm sure there will be much more to go off of. One thing I have already discovered, is that there will be many things which you will learn only through your own experiences, just as I have.

I look forward to meeting you someday.

Your friend,

Adina"

It was a very curious experience reading a letter from Adina written to me when she didn't know me, and realizing that she was even younger than I am now was hard to believe. I began thumbing through latter parts of her journal, and found an entry written at the still young age of 32 years old.

The Tempus Vector took her back to New York City, December 24, 1907. Her notes didn't explain the details of her task, but what she did say is that while there she fell deeply in love with a man named Bryant who crossed her path. This was the first time that she had felt love for anyone since Carson. She and Bryant watched the first ball drop on January 1, 1908, and like many other couples present that evening, they stood in the center of Times Square celebrating the new year with endless passion-filled kisses and intimate embraces that continued even until the streets began to clear. As a cold rain began to fall, Bryant grabbed Adina's hand, and together they ran into a small wood-sided corner cafe. While waiting in line to be seated, he asked Adina to marry him. Lost in the moment, forgetting who she was and why she was there, she seriously considered his proposition, but like a sharp dagger thrust into her heart, she suddenly felt the call to return home. Even though she wanted nothing more than to stay and marry him, she returned because of me. Somehow she knew that I would need her, and quite honestly, she was right. Whether she realized it or not, every good thing inside of me came from her. I felt awful recalling the many times that I would all but hound her for an explanation of why she never married after Carson. All the while, she was probably aching for Bryant. Unselfishly, she gave up the only other love of her life for me. I thought about the huge impact Adina had on my life; without her, I don't know where I would be today. Until the very end, she was faithful to her calling and sacrificed everything so that it could continue.

"Beni ...", I heard Carig come into the house. I went downstairs and I must have looked a little sad. "Are you okay?"

"Yeah, I'm okay. I was just reading one of Adina's journal entries and discovered that she fell in love with a man from 1908, and wanted to stay and marry him, and not return back to her own time. She said that she came back because of me. I guess I never considered the idea of her, or myself, falling in love with someone from another time. She gave up love for me."

Carig walked up to me and lifted my chin.

"She just exchanged it for a different love, which was you. Adina and I had many long talks, mostly about you. She had no regrets. She loved her life and she loved you. Don't you worry yourself another minute about that. Now, let's talk about the 'falling in love with someone from another time' when you go and travel. You will remember that you have a handsome Scot at home waiting for you, right?"

Even though I didn't really feel like it, Carig made me smile, and I chuckled at his adorable and very true statement. He was definitely very good looking.

"Yes, yes I do. I know exactly what I have right here. You don't need to worry about me, my very handsome Scot!" I wrapped my arms around his neck and kissed him. "I only want you, Carig."

"An I you!"

It had been a long day for the both of us, and we were each ready to stop thinking anymore tonight about the Tempus Vector. Carig and I sat on the porch swing together, watching the sunset on the ocean.

"Beni, when you had that accident, and I thought I was goin' to lose ye, I told the good Lord above that if He would save you, I would do what was right by you. I want you! I can't imagine being so close to you now, and goin' to a different place every night….I mean, you here and me there. I don't wish to ever be separated from you. I … Beni, I want to make love to you, my body burns for you! But I want to do what's right. I made a promise. All I know is, there's no one else for me but you. I have known that my whole life. If you feel the same way lass, if there's no one else for you but me, marry me?"

Carig could tell by the look on my face that I was surprised by his proposal. I think he was unsure as to what my answer would be. I scooted closer towards him, and began caressing his face with my hand, and then pulling his mouth towards me, I kissed him.

"There's only you. Yes, my answer is yes!"

Chapter 19

Enigma Revelation

Carig and I parted for the night, but before I went
to bed I wanted to go up to the third floor and look
through the wardrobes. I was very curious about glancing
through the traveling clothes that Adina had been sewing
for years, so that I could possibly better understand what
it would really be like to delve into different times. As I
began to sort through them, I found that they were stuffed
full of dresses and suits, pants, and blouses that were put
in chronological order, by years and eras beginning with
1892. If I understood correctly, I would really only be
going to eras that took place from her birth all the way up
to her death, but honestly I wasn't really sure. The clothes
she made for me were not only tagged with a year, but
also with a number that matched a hat, or shoes, or any
accessory that I should wear with that outfit. As usual,
Adina didn't miss a detail, and she tried to make
everything as simple as possible.

I was amazed as I began looking into the
wardrobes that lined the walls. I realized that in all of the
times I had visited her, I had no idea what Adina had

been up to. All of my life, I believed that she had spent her days and years just being a Bar Rousse citizen, helping to plan the 4th of July Parade and the Catwalk Ball. She was involved in everything, and yet had time to prepare all of this for me, travel through time, and in her spare time of course, raise me. The thing is, I never felt last. I never felt as though anything was more important to her than me. The more I discovered about my Aunt Adina, the more remarkable she became.

The wardrobe that had always belonged to me, the one now holding the emerald gown, was a "confirmation of my life here and now." Those words, spoken often by Adina never made any sense to me, until this moment. She continually portrayed my wardrobe as a symbol representing my real home. At the time I believed that she was simply talking about Bar Rousse, but now I see the that she was trying to prompt the idea of remaining true to my real life. I discovered the reason for her constant reminders through one of her journal entries that was written after months of journeying.

"Just recently, I find myself unable to distinguish what's real and what's not. I get so caught up in the lives of people who no longer exist, and forget who I am.

Sometimes I wake up and I don't know if I'm in my own time or another. If I don't figure out a way to separate each side of my two-fold life, I will never survive this calling."

Adina's next entry was written specifically to me.

"Benidette, my greatest struggle thus far has been figuring out a way to not lose myself in all of this. Keep who you are, your life, your true identity very close like a best friend, while at the same time keeping your journeys at arm's length. By all means, keep the two separate! There must be a notable division between your real life here and now and your life as the bearer of the Tempus Vector. You will find that the many cares and concerns plaguing history will battle for your attention. If you let them, they'll take over your life. Of course they will always be part of who you are, but you must not let them consume you. Malachi's journal reminded me of the importance of displaying my journeys once I return. What I mean is, hanging the photo on your wall as a kind of Ebenezer Stone signifying where you've been, but also bringing closure. Don't allow yourself to live in the past, but keep moving forward. Failures will be the hardest, but they will happen. Mark them with an empty frame

among your accomplishments. I hope this information helps you not to fall into the same hollow that I did."

I appreciated Adina's warning, and now the purpose for the hundreds of pictures hanging up in her sewing room made sense.

The one thing that I was still unsure of, was exactly how far back in time the Tempus Vector would actually take me. After observing the photos, I came to the conclusion that Adina never went back further than Malachi's past, so maybe that meant that I would only go as far back as Adina's past.

On my way to bed I went up to Adina's room to get the Tempus Vector and Malachi's suitcase. To better prepare myself, I placed my journal, the pencil case, and two gold coins on my nightstand along with the Tempus Vector. Sitting right by the nightstand was the leather suitcase, all ready to go. Adina said that I would get an uneasy feeling when a picture was revealed. For right now, there was nothing, but I wanted to be as prepared as possible. While lying in bed, I found myself feeling nervous. This waiting period, not knowing when a picture would appear, was more bothersome that I had imagined. It was hard to focus on anything else. I suddenly remembered a very important piece of wisdom in Adina's journal that she knew I would need which calmed my apprehension.

"Don't let the frame consume you. Be ready when that time comes, but don't stop living...live your life!"

I heeded her words by turning my thoughts to Carig, and wondered if he was thinking about me. His marriage proposal seemed unreal, and even more staggering was my reply. The entire event was both awesome and unbelievable, kind of like everything else as of late. I then began contemplating our life together, and how unordinary and difficult it would be. I would be the absent wife that was constantly gone on business trips. It now made sense why Adina never married, as it would have surely caused this unwelcome complicating element. Thinking about how difficult it would be, dimmed my enthusiasm of marriage. I realized that Carig had been a part of Adina's extraordinary world for some time now, and was fully aware of some of the obstacles we would face. For right now anyway, he would probably say that he didn't care. But how would he feel after five years, ten years? I honestly couldn't imagine putting him through a life of playing second fiddle to my calling. I was afraid that over time our unconventional relationship would be too demanding. It simply seemed unfair and grieved my heart. By the time I was done trying to make sense of it all, I was exhausted and couldn't think about it anymore. I just needed sleep.

Unaware of how tired I was, I practically slept the day away. By the time I woke up, it was already twelve-thirty in the afternoon. I looked over to the empty side of the bed, and sitting there was a small piece of driftwood carved into a lighthouse. Tied to the carving was a note that said, "Carig Hammel requests your presence at dinner tonight, Bar Rousse Beach, 5:00 p.m. sharp! P.S. You don't need to dress warm - I will keep you warm...." His creativity and thoughtfulness touched my heart, but because of the frigid winds, I absolutely planned on bundling up. We both knew that I was a California girl and couldn't stand to be cold. Through his sweet efforts, Carig was attempting to calm my nerves and take my mind off the moment when a picture would finally appear in the Tempus Vector. I glanced at the frame sitting on my nightstand half hoping there would be an image waiting for me, and half hoping there would not. All I knew is that I couldn't live my life worrying about it, I just needed to relax and let it do what it was gonna do.

After rolling out of bed I decided to take a long soak in the bathtub and get myself ready to dine with Carig. I always loved baths more than showers, as did Adina. I drew a steamy tub of water, stirring in white and red rose petals along with a few drops of rose oil and a scoop of bath salts which all sat on a silver tray next to the tub. To make a "complete bath experience," I lit every candle in the room. We Crawford girls have always taken bath time very seriously, and those taken in Adina's freestanding cast iron were the most pleasant memories and experiences, which were brought back to life as I submerged myself into the rose-fragranced water. Adina swore that her baths with rose oil were what kept her looking so young over the years. Just as I was feeling that I would never want to leave this complete bliss, I was unexpectedly disturbed by the sound of Carig frantically calling my name.

"Beni, are you here?" In a panic, he stormed into the bathroom, scaring me to death.

"Carig, what in the world is wrong with you?" He stood in the bathroom looking down at me in the tub, just staring.

"Carig, um what is it?"

His eyes scanned up and down the length of my body. At first, I was surprised that he would be so forward. But then I realized by the look on his face that he was horrified by my scarlet blemishes. Jagged marks resembling a mosaic would now be an eternal reminder of my encounter with Devil's Knuckles.

"My God, lass! I'm so sorry...I'm sorry for staring, I hadn't seen, I didn't know!"

"It's ok, I was a little frightened the first time I saw them. They told me they would fade in time."

Immediately, I felt uncomfortable, and my bath experience had now been ruined.

"So why are you here?"

"I, I came to check and see if you were awake, but when I found that you weren't there, I thought maybe you ... the Tempus Vector ... I thought you had left."

I looked at him and I could tell that he was deeply bothered at the idea of me leaving.

413

"Carig, you know this is what I've been called, blessed to do. Why would you be so upset if I had left?"

"I know….I know that this is what you're meant to do, Beni, but I want to be there when you go … and when you come back. And…?"

"What?"

"Beni, there are some things you don't know yet; things that Adina wanted me to tell you."

I sat there looking at him, and I could tell whatever it was that he needed to tell me was troubling him deeply. He was clearly bothered. He continued glaring down at the floor, shaking, and trying to collect himself. Whatever this was about, really shook him up. I grabbed a towel, stood up and wrapped it around me, and stepped out of the bathtub.

I lifted up his head to look at me. "Carig, what is it that is making you so upset?"

He breathed out heavily and seemed to look right through me with his beautiful green eyes. "Beni, just promise me you won't ever leave without telling me. I need to be there when you leave and when you return."

I looked at him with a confused expression. "Why? I don't really understand!"

Carig moved towards me not saying anything, but only pushing his body towards mine until I was pinned against the wall. Our fingers entwined, and he kissed me with an intensity that came from the deepest part of his soul. His lips left mine and began kissing my neck with fervor.

"You smell so good, I'm intoxicated by you!" With great restraint, he sat his head on my shoulder and breathed deeply, "I can't even sleep for thinking about you, lass."

Peering into his eyes, I saw a man who was genuinely dedicated to me and who became devastated when he thought I'd left.

"Carig, what is it that you need to tell me?" I could tell there was something of great urgency, waiting to be said.

"Beni, we do need to talk. Tonight at dinner though, okay?" He walked out of the bathroom and turned around repeating sternly, "Just don't leave until we talk."

"Okay, I'll be out there at five."

I sat on my bed and began looking out the window and wondering what it was that Carig was so concerned about. Watching the winter winds rustle the trees, I was puzzled as to why he was so dead set about eating outside. It was clearly freezing, and he was fully aware of how much I hated to be cold. But, he did say that he would keep me warm.

Refusing to take any chances, I bundled up in the heaviest, warmest parka that I could find in the coat closet, along with fur-lined snow boots. The instant I opened the front door I was met by a gust of frigid wind, and was instantly thankful for my bulky down layers. When I arrived at the dirt path to walk down to the beach, I was pleasantly surprised at the candlelit lanterns that illuminated each side of the trail. The enchanting show of light continued in a circular pattern that guided me to a small wooden structure which was located next to The Flats. The towering walls of rock, known as The Flats, located within the cove, were a backdrop to the inlet that served as our favorite picnic area and Fourth of July celebration locale; this wonderful place was the setting to my best memories. Unbeknown to me, Carig had been spending every spare moment building this hideaway out of old beach wood. The front entry of this simple but quaint shelter was a large four-paneled metal and glass door that was rounded at the top, and distressed with age.

He came towards me smiling, almost laughing, most certainly at the outfit I was wearing. "You think you're at the North Pole, Beni?"

"Very funny. All I know is that it's freezing out here!"

"I know it is, and I told you that I would keep you warm, now didn't I? You stubborn lass! Come on, let's go inside."

Flooded with the burnished flames of both candles and fireside, Carig's breathtaking handiwork left me speechless. The wall of stone at the rear of the cottage was covered with moss, but incorporated within the twisting greenery was a painting of the beach at night. The moon was shining bright in the sky, but the reflection of the lunar crown rested on the sandy shore. To most this would appear only as a colorful display of artwork, but to me, it was a sweet labor of love. I knew exactly what it meant. It was created for me by the master artisan, and was his way of telling me that he would stop at nothing to give me the moon.... to give me the impossible. Identical to the cottage walls, the floors were also made of old beach wood that were hidden beneath a large braided rug that covered almost the entire area. The heart of the room was an opulent fireplace, designed completely of large gray stones which were obviously hand-picked from the clusters of rocks on the beach. Above the flames within the hearth, were two Cornish hens roasting, filling the room with a savory aroma.. A small wooden table and four chairs that bore the family emblem of Carig's people sat grandly in the center area, and was beautifully enhanced by his grandmother's white china and pewter candle holders. Not forgetting a detail, he had placed wildflowers in the center of the table, arranged within a delicate crystal vase. Tucked in the far corner was a beautiful hand carved bed with massive posts that practically touched the ceiling. The bed was charming and inviting, arrayed with soft white linens, and a billowing down comforter.

"Carig! When did you make all of this? This.... umm, what exactly is this called?"

"It's a bothy. Well, at least that's what we called them in Scotland. A small shelter of sorts. Do you like it?

I made it for you, Beni. I know this is your favorite little part of the beach, and I sure don't want you wanderin' down to Devil's Knuckles again!"

"This is beyond beautiful! Carig, I truly have no words! How long did this take you to build? I haven't even seen you working on it!"

"Well, I've been collecting the wood for a long time, and at night when I can't sleep, I've been going out to my shop and putting the walls together. The table and chairs and the bed, well I've been working on those for years. I have to admit to you, the whole time I was making that bed, I was hoping someday it might belong to us."

I could feel myself blushing. His words embarrassed me, while at the same time, made me love and desire him even more. Outside, I could still hear the wind blowing, and now rain hitting Carig's bothy, but this little beach haven that he'd created was warm, safe, and strong, like him, and would protect us from all of the outside elements.

"May I take your parka, miss?" Carig laughed again over the heavy coat that I chose to wear. "Have a seat Beni!" I sat down, and he knelt down on the ground before me and took my boots off. "Don't think you'll be needin' these either."

"Carig, I can't believe that you made all of this - you are truly amazing!"

"It was nothing really!"

"Nothing? You are so gifted, and I absolutely love your bothy! This whole place is utterly incredible! Thank you for sharing it with me!"

Carig, obviously pleased with my response, poured each of us a glass of wine, and then sat down across from me.

"Beni, this bothy is yours, just like my heart!"

He stared at me intently, unembarrassed with his bold and flirtatious gaze. It wasn't the first time that he had looked at me in such a manner, but I could definitely feel a different intensity, one that I had never felt before. Until now, he had held back his affections, but now that he was aware of my feelings for him, I couldn't tell if the heat I was experiencing was coming from the fireplace, or from him.

"So when will dinner be ready?"

"Ah, well I'd say in about thirty minutes or so."

I picked up my glass of wine and walked over to the fireplace. Encircling the gray stone hearth were large inviting pillows arranged around it. The fire was so warm and inviting that I made myself comfortable and sat down. He came and sat by me, reclining back onto a pillow.

"Carig, can we talk about what happened earlier? Why did you get so upset when you thought I had left?" He sat up, with a now serious look on his face.

"Okay, Beni. There are some things that I need to tell you about traveling with the Tempus Vector. Adina told me that these *things* are spoken, but not written….and quite honestly, some of the unwritten, I witnessed myself. So, here it goes."

Carig went on to tell me that traveling with the Tempus Vector is not always safe, but many times actually very dangerous. "You don't know what kind of situation you are walking into. The Tempus Vector will give you wisdom to get through any difficulties, but keeping your wits about you is another thing entirely. I remember as a lad, my Gran having to nurse Adina back to life after coming back from one of her journeys hurt very badly. At the time, I didn't know what was going on, or what had happened to her. Another time, my grandfather had me sit with her through the night, bathin' her face cause she was burnin' up with fever; she'd come back with some kind of ailment of sorts. Once I started thinkin' about it, I'm supposin' that she came back numerous times with broken bones and bruises, but the worst I can remember is when she came back with a gunshot wound. The thing is Beni, the carrier of the Tempus Vector has to do whatever it takes to accomplish their task, but also whatever is necessary to keep it safe at all times. When it comes to you, lass and your safety, I have a real hard time bein' ok with it - it unnerves me!"

I sat back on the pillow with what must have looked like complete panic.

"So let me see if I understand correctly. I most probably will get hurt, sick, shot, stabbed, or beaten up, and I'm supposed to be okay with that?"

"I felt the same way when it was told to me. I asked Adina if she ever thought about walkin' away, or if it was all worth it. She told me that she would do it all over again. What kept her goin' all these years, and I'm guessin' even those who came before her, was the positive outcomes that came about only because of their

422

sacrifice. To them, it was worth it; the good far outweighed the bad. Adina said to tell you that once you go, you'll understand how important you are. After that, going where the Tempus Vector takes you will no longer be a worry, but a drive to accomplish something bigger than yourself. Beni, do you understand, you'll be changing the world! And like my Gran, I'll be part of that as well."

Down deep inside of me I always wanted to change the world. I longed for it, and this was how I was going to do it.

"Okay, so now that you know that, here's the next part."

"Do I want to hear a next part?"

"Yes, I think you do - this is important, it's the foundation of everythin'."

Carig explained to me that this lost tribe of Solomon was really not "lost" at all. "Each of the ten tribes were sent out to complete different tasks that were, and still are, of the utmost importance. They are protected by a façade of fiction, labeled "lost" as far as the world is concerned. All of these many years, for the most part anyway, this ingenious approach has been successful, but with that, there are those who *do* know about it, and seek after it. They know it's legitimate, and greatly desire the power that the Tempus Vector holds. Durin' the Second World War, Hitler spent his entire reign seekin' after the frame that would allow him to plant twisted seeds of havoc in the pages of history. He along with the countless leagues of intelligence at his fingertips, caused dreaded concern for Malachi. Already, Hitler's acts of insanity combined with his endless desire for power created fear for the paramount destruction that he would bring about with that kind of power. His warnings about an evil force of men that would stop at nothing to gain access to the power of the Tempus Vector was unnervin'. Even today, there are those still in pursuit of this device and the carrier of it.

"Now, what I'm going to tell you next, is crucial for your safety. When you're traveling, if you find yourself in a dangerous situation, and need to get out quickly, grab both handles, one on each side of the frame at the same time. Whether your task is completed or not, it will bring you back. I know you're stubborn, but you must promise me that rather than die in another time, you'll do this. Adina had to resort to this outcome a few times. Her empty frames are proof of her failed tasks. There will come a time however, when you will be sent to that same place and time in which she failed. In the same way Adina was given the chance on Malachi's behalf to make right his failures. These echoes are by far the most difficult and dangerous to get through. Beni, I don't want anything to happen to you, lass! Right here, right now, I commit to you myself, to be here always to help you and take care of you no matter what. If I could go with you, I would. But since I can't, I will be here to make sure you get off okay, and you can know that whatever happens, wherever you go, I will be here when you get back."

I didn't know what to say! This journey and where it could and most probably would lead was by far the most frightening thing that I had ever faced. While at the same time, I was at a loss of how to respond to Carig and his love and concern for me. He sat there telling me all of these things that seemed so unbelievable. But instead of me being totally overwhelmed by the whole thing, I somehow felt comfort in knowing that I wouldn't be alone through it all. I once again began thinking about him wanting to marry me, and what a burden this would all be to him.

"Carig, I can't even begin to tell you how much I appreciate all that you are willing to sacrifice for me. This is the thing though. I spent all last night thinking about how difficult it would be spending your life with someone like me. I don't know if it's fair or a good idea."

"What are you talking about, Beni? You don't want to marry me?"

"No, I mean yes I do! Last night, even before knowing all of this new 'unwritten information,' I couldn't help but think how incredibly unfair all of this would be to you. I just feel like it would wear on you after a while. You'd get tired of it and then get tired of me. Do you fully understand that you would be waiting for me all the time, never knowing what kind of condition I'd be coming back in…..and then have to nurse me back to health? How are you going to feel about this arrangement in say, ten years? Twenty? Thirty? I mean what about kids? We can't ever have kids!"

"Beni, if you don't want to marry me, you look at me in the eyes and tell me that you don't love me."

"Carig… I … I …" I couldn't tell him that I didn't love him or didn't want to marry him, because I did. I

426

immediately became both angry and frustrated over his stubbornness (or perhaps it was my own), and at his question to me, and began shouting at him.

"You don't get it! I don't want to be a burden to you. I don't want you to look back on your life and feel like you wasted it on me. But, Carig ... hands down, I am so in love with you that I can barely see straight, okay? When I'm with you, my heart beats so fast, so hard, that I'm certain that you can see it pounding through my flesh. And when we're apart, all I do is think about you.....wondering every second what you're doing or what you're thinking about.....it's like part of me is missing, and I can't stand that feeling of being half of who I should be! That's the truth!" I stood up to leave. "My second thoughts about marrying you, Carig Hammel, came out of love and concern for you and your life and future. So don't you ever, *ever* accuse me of not loving you."

Carig was stunned. I had never spoken to him that way before. At first, I couldn't tell by the expression on his face if he was enraged or impassioned. But as he stood up, his renewed sense of resolution spoke volumes.

His eyes were like lasers, fiercely engaged on me, obviously charmed by my words of love.

Carig became lost in Beni's beautiful blue eyes, and was reminded of the first day they met, the moment he fell in love with her. Many believed him to be a ridiculous boy for thinking he was in love at the age of nine, but he was, and he had determined that he'd wait his whole life for her. He loved her spirit and tenacity. Her boldness to set him straight and pour her heart out strengthened his devotion to Beni even further.

I stood on the other side of the room by the door, holding my head as tears were running down my face. I'm not exactly sure why I was crying except that I was so frustrated, and my emotions got the best of me. This was the first time *ever*, that I had felt or declared love for another person. It was as if a wall that was surrounding my heart came crumbling down. This overpowering love for Carig had always been present in my heart, but until now, had been bottled up. As I turned to walk out the door, I looked out at the sea. Even though the waves were wild from the storm, the familiar ambience quieted my soul. The rain had stopped, and while the wind was still blowing, the clouds had begun to clear. The reflection of the moon on the water was brighter and more spectacular than I had ever seen.

Carig walked up behind me, lightly placed his chin on my shoulder, and began whispering in my ear. "Do you want me to pull the moon in for you, Beni?"

I turned and put my arms around his neck, and held him tightly. The truth was, I didn't want to lose him, but I also didn't want to do anything that would hurt him. "No, Carig. I don't want the moon or the stars. There's only one thing that I want, and that's you."

"You already have that - all of me. I'm yours."

"Carig, you have to know, you must know, I would rather die than do anything to hurt you!"

"The only thing that could ever hurt me, is not being with you, lass!"

For the first time in our lives, there was nothing standing in our way. We were free to love each other completely. A burning desire for one another had finally been unleashed. I half expected the room to go up in flames at any moment. As for me, I was bewitched by him. If he would have asked, I would have given myself to him right then and there; I wondered if his body burned

429

for me half as much as mine did for him. But I knew that because Carig loved and respected me, and was committed to follow through on his vow to God and Adina, that he would certainly not ask such a thing.

He kissed me and then with a peculiar look on his face said something that I didn't expect. "Marry me! Marry me now! I don't want to spend one more night parted from you."

"Right now? Are you serious?"

"Aye! Why not, Beni? Why wait?"

I couldn't believe it! This would by far be the most spontaneous thing, and the most right thing, that I had ever done in my life.

"Yes, absolutely, let's get married tonight!"

The next thing I knew, Carig and I were running across the sand, up to the house. It was still freezing outside, but I wasn't cold. I was filled for the first time with an indescribable excitement for what my future held.

Once we arrived at the house, Carig called Pastor Strong and inquired as to whether he could come over and marry us. For several moments the line was completely quiet. Pastor Strong first questioned Carig's sanity, and then asked him if he'd been dabbling in Killen's secret cabinet of Scotch Whisky. Carig told him that he was perfectly sober and had never been more sure about anything in his entire life. Because Strong had known us both since we were children, and knew without a doubt that Adina, if she were here, would wholeheartedly give her blessing, he happily agreed to perform the ceremony. Before hanging up the phone, he chuckled at Carig's high-spirited enthusiasm.

"This can't wait till morning, eh?"

Carig was completely silent, honestly not wanting to wait even one more hour to finally marry the love of his life.

"I'm just jokin' with you, son! Give me an hour or so to change out of my pajamas and I'll be over. Oh, and I'll give the judge a call to see if he'll draw up a marriage license. Don't you worry about a thing!"

Meanwhile, I called my Uncle Wil and Aunt Angelina. Of course they were shocked at first, but happily agreed to come over and be our best man and matron of honor. We decided that since the rain had stopped and the storm had passed, Adina's garden would be the perfect and most appropriate place for the ceremony. After all, that was her favorite spot, and she would have been honored that we chose it as the venue to take our vows. Seeing that we had about an hour before everyone would be there, we rushed to go get dressed.

I went straight up to the wardrobe room hoping that I would find a dress - something that was fit to be married in. But I was so unusually giddy, that I walked over to the mirror and began introducing myself as Benidette Hammel.

"Hello! So nice to meet you, my name is Benidette Hammel, and this is my husband, Carig.....Yes, he is very handsome. Benidette Hammel....Hi, I'm Benidette Hammel." I laughed out loud. I felt so silly talking to myself, but I was so gleeful, so excited about marrying Carig. The last few months had been awfully difficult, but this felt like a happy ending, or a happy beginning that had been perfectly orchestrated. I guess this is what it felt like when everything falls into place. I mean after all, how hard could it possibly be being married to a man like Carig? Surely the most challenging task would be changing the monogram on my suitcases from "BC" to "BH." "BH?".....Benidette Hammel. It suddenly occurred to me, the "BH" on my leather diary

432

that I thought was a mistake, were the initials of my married name. I couldn't even fathom how Malachi Coffee could have possibly known that I would marry Carig Hammel. This new discovery presented both a solution and a mystery that I refused to spend time thinking about at this moment. My priority was finding something to wear.

Among all of Adina's creations, I would hopefully find something beautiful. At first I looked through the wardrobes, but didn't really see anything wedding dress-ish, so I decided to head down to Adina's room and take a quick search through her closet. Sure enough, in the very back I spotted a satin garment bag. Upon opening the bag, I immediately recognized the lovely ivory lace dress. It was the one Adina wore as she stood next to Carson on their wedding day. I was beyond elated! It still looked brand new, and as far as I was concerned, it was perfect. As I stood there alone, my joy suddenly turned to sadness as I began thinking about Adina and how I would give anything if she were here. She would be thrilled that Carig and I were getting married, and would have been right in the center of everything, helping us celebrate.

I took the dress upstairs and hung it on my wardrobe, allowing it to air out while I showered and got myself ready. For some reason, I felt compelled to wear my makeup and hair in a similar fashion as Adina, which would of course be a bit darker and more dramatic; I always had a tendency to under-do frivolities. My Aunt Angelina called me as I was getting out of the shower, and was brimming with excitement at the news. She began telling me of how Adina was there every step of the way when she and Wil married, and she assured me that she would be there soon to help me in the same way. I pinned my hair up similar to Adina's picture, but a little messier; after all, I still had to be me. While I was waiting for Angelina, I decided to slip on the dress. I would let her button me up and help put the veil on as soon as she arrived. As I bent down to strap on my shoes, I noticed a clump of something in the hem of the dress. Trying not to cause too much damage, I pulled out a few stitches and saw that tucked within the hem was a folded piece of paper that had been purposefully placed there. I opened it up to find a handwritten note to me from Adina.

My Dearest Benidette,

Oh how I wish that I could be there to see you and Carig wed. I always knew that you would. He loves you so much, he always has. Didn't I tell you that one day he would grow out of his scrawniness and freckles? He has turned into a very handsome man, but most importantly, his kind heart far exceeds his good looks. But as for you, I am so proud of you, what you have accomplished and what you will accomplish. Since I can't be there, let this note be my voice. I am so happy that you are wearing my dress. I know that you will look beautiful. I hemmed it a bit because I didn't want it to be too long for your height.

There are a few things that I have for you that will add to this joyous occasion. Before you read any further, go up to my room, and take down my jewelry box from the closet.

I did as she instructed, and removed her mahogany jewelry box from the closet, set it on her bed, and then began to read on.

In the bottom drawer there is a small blue velvet box, open it. This aquamarine and pearl pendant was once a ring. I had it made into a necklace because I know that you're not fond of rings, and especially bulky ones. You have always loved necklaces though, and I wanted

you to have something that you would wear often. For
today, place the pendant on my string of pearls. This will
look lovely with the gown. This ring was given to me on
my wedding day to signify the "something blue." Well,
now it's not only blue, but also "something old."

I opened the box and, just as Adina had said, there
was a delicate cluster pendant made of aquamarine and
pearls in a teardrop shape which was placed on a gold
chain. It was truly magnificent! I removed the pendant
from the chain and strung it onto the pearls, and then
clasped it around my neck. I noticed her matching pearl
earrings sitting with the strand, and decided to wear those
as well. She was right, the blue and cream complemented
one another perfectly.

Finally, open the top lid and pull out the small
green box. Please give this ring to Carig that once
belonged to Carson. If Carson and I would have had a
son, I imagine that he would have been just like Carig. To
me, he was always like a son.

The gold ring was beautiful! It actually reminded
me of Carig. It consisted of two cords that intertwined; a
perfect emblem of the relationship and covenant that
Carson and Adina shared. That was the kind of

relationship that I hoped for with Carig. I would give him this as a symbol of my never ending commitment to him.

I hope you both know, that there is no place I'd rather be than right there watching you two get married....perhaps I will be!

I pray that every day of your life together will be blessed!

I love you, my precious Beni!

Aunt Adina

It was just like Adina to put her letter in the hem of my dress. Like all of the other mysteries surrounding me. As Malachi had known, Adina also knew that I would marry Carig, and how could she have known that I would wear her dress? All of it was far beyond my understanding. Somehow she knew the unknowable. At this point, these puzzles had become more ordinary, and less startling to me. I was thankful for her letter; reading it made me feel as though she were here.

Suddenly, I heard Angelina calling out from the wardrobe room.

"Beni honey, where are you?"

"I'm in Adina's room, but I'm on my way up!"

The moment I set foot in the wardrobe room, Angelina cried out, "Oh, you look so much like Adina! She would just love that you're wearing her dress. Just beautiful - you look so beautiful! Here, I made you a little bouquet from the flowers in my garden." The flowers were a delicate combination of paper daisies, baby's breath, and a few stalks of lavender, tied at the bottom with a blue satin ribbon.

"It's perfect, Angelina. I love it!"

She reached up and began messing with my hair. "Here honey, sit down and let me put a few more pins in your hair and some spray."

Once my hair was thoroughly set in place, she pinned on Adina's veil.

"Now go over and stand on the step in front of the mirror and let me button you up!"

As she began to fasten my dress, the length fell perfectly to the floor. The dress, the veil, the necklace.....they were all stunning! I felt very fortunate that this extremely impromptu ceremony would include such a beautiful white gown. Adina wasn't here, but still she made it into an occasion that I would cherish forever.

For a moment while Carig was getting dressed, he wondered if this was all a dream. If it was, he never wanted to wake up. After putting on his tuxedo, he went up to the Catwalk to have a chat with Adina.

"Remember when I was a lad? I had just come over from Scotland, and Beni came home from school to stay here for the summer. She was a wee little thing with dark hair and blue eyes. Just as I get lost staring out over the sea, I get lost in her eyes just the same. From the get-go she ordered me around, but it was okay with me though, cause the moment I saw her she possessed my heart. I told you then that someday I would marry that lass, and do you remember what ye told me? Ye said, 'Carig, I believe you will. Beni's a free spirit, but someday she'll realize that part of her is missing, and that part is you.' Adina, she told me that very thing tonight. Even when I got older, and I'd be so mad at her for not comin' home, you'd remind me that someday she would. You were right. I so wish ye were here to see us wed."

Carig pulled a ring out of his pocket and held it between his fingers. Before Adina died, she placed it in his hand and told him that someday *when he married Beni*, that he was to give her this ring. It was the one that

Carson had given to her, and she cherished it all of her days.

While Angelina was up with Beni, Wil began preparing the garden area, turning on the strings of white lights that hung from the gazebo, all the while whistling the tune, *Love You Truly.*

Pastor Strong walked into the garden and gave Wil a firm pat on the back. "Well, this is quite the surprise, hey Wil?"

"Sure is ... who'd have thought?"

Just then Carig came out sporting his black tuxedo. The two congratulated him and could tell by his expression that he was both overjoyed and a little nervous.

"Carig! Congratulations boy, you're gonna be just fine! Judge Bates was happy to sign the marriage license. I just need to have you two sign it after the ceremony and then I'll make it official. My word, you and Beni! I remember when you two were running around this place like a couple of wild turkeys, and now look at ya!"

"Much appreciation to ya Pastor Strong! Sorry it was so last minute - we really didn't know that it would all happen so fast."

Angelina excitedly ran out to the gazebo and announced that the bride was ready. She booted up Adina's old gramophone and set the needle down on top of the ballad that Carig had chosen especially for this occasion. It was the song that always made him think of Beni. As it played, Beni appeared at the door of the house and slowly walked into the garden. Carig stood in awe as she approached. For a split second, he thought she was an angel, an absolute picture of perfection. Like clockwork, the moment she appeared his world began to spin, followed by a familiar and rather pleasant shortness of breath. Beni's presence in a room would always lead to such agreeable symptoms, but seeing her in that gown magnified his physical reactions tenfold. As she continued closer towards him, he had to remind himself to breathe. In addition to the dizziness and erratic gasps for air, he could scarcely feel his legs beneath him as she drew closer.

Standing at the edge of the garden, I felt frozen where I stood. It seemed impossible to take another step forward. Carig's eyes were intently focused on me, but for some reason I was afraid and I felt alone. But out of nowhere, like a cool breeze on a hot day, I sensed a familiar aroma that immediately put me at ease. Realizing that this scent was that of Adina's perfume, I quickly turned around, half expecting to see her standing there, but was met only by the wind rustling through her most cherished rose bush, the one she planted the day she moved here. My eyes filled with tears because of this extraordinary feeling that she was near...I realized at that moment, that she *was* near, and I wasn't alone.

Turning back around, Carig was still looking at me, but now with concern in his eyes. I gave him a reassuring smile, and began once again, walking forward escorted by Adina's scent and the flawless harmony of the piano and violin playing *Moonlit Shore.* Except for the music, the night was completely silent. It was almost as though the sea had stopped crashing against the rocks, making no sound at all. Perhaps the wind and the wave were our guests. As I drew closer to Carig, he took my hands, lacing his fingers together with mine. My heart began beating so hard just being close to him; he was so amazingly handsome, and I was so in love with him.

With hands remaining clasped, we turned towards one another.

Pastor Strong began by saying, "Carig and Beni, I know this seems as though it all happened very suddenly, but I have to say, not really. It began like a rosebud when you were children and friends, that has now opened and revealed itself to be something quite unique and beautiful. The best relationships begin as friends. Through the years you have seen the best and worst of one another, and yet here you stand ready to declare a lifelong commitment before me, these two witnesses, and God. We all love you both and rejoice with you, for the friendship that has become a deep-seeded love. Carig, Beni, would either of you like to say anything to the other before I continue?"

Carig was quick to speak up. "I'll start, if it's okay?"

Pastor strong nodded. "Go right ahead, son."

"Beni, I stand here before God and these people to tell you that I have loved you from the first day I laid eyes on you. I heard a saying once 'she was a storm, not the kind you run from, but the kind you chase.' Beni, you are the love of my life, and I would follow you, I would chase you, to the ends of the earth and back."

We both stood gazing at one another with tear-filled eyes, and as if Carig had not already said the perfect thing, he smiled at me and then fervently continued. "Woman is sacred; the woman one loves is holy."

It was all I could do to keep my jaw from dropping to the floor, as I recognized this quote from my favorite novel *The Count of Monte Cristo*. When I used to read it out loud to Adina, I would stop at this verse every time and say, "I hope that someday the man I'm in love with says those words to me on my wedding day." Carig, who was always listening from a close but hidden corner, never forgot my wish from so long ago.

Eyes wet with tears, I continued this *Monte Cristo* narrative to Carig.

"'There are two ways of seeing: with the body and with the soul. The body's sight can sometimes forget, but the soul remembers forever.' Carig, I love you! I commit my life, my heart, and my soul to you. From this moment forward until the end of my life I vow to be yours, and yours alone."

I smiled at him and then turned towards Pastor Strong.

444

"Well then, Carig do you take Beni as your wife, to take care of always in good times and in bad times, from this moment forward?"

"I do!"

"Beni, do you take Carig as your husband, to take care of him always in good times and in bad times, from this moment forward?"

"I do!"

"I know this was very spontaneous, but do you two have rings?"

We both said yes, but each of us were surprised that the other had one to give. When Carig placed the ring on my finger, I wept out loud, knowing whose finger this once adorned; this was Adina's ring.

"She gave me this to give to my bride, Beni. She always knew my bride would be you!" Adina cherished this ring, and would not have given it to anyone else.

When I placed the ring on Carig's hand, he too was pleasantly surprised

"Beni, where did you get this, lass?....I mean, thank you!"

"Adina wanted me to tell you that she thought of you as her son. This is Carson's ring. She saved it for this night, the night in her garden when I would marry you."

As I was teetering on both ends of the emotional spectrum - total joy and happiness on one end, and grief over Adina at the other - I could tell that Carig too was struggling. I could tell, just as I was teetering on both ends of the emotional spectrum, total joy and happiness on one end, and grief over Adina at the other- I could tell that Carig too was struggling.

"By the power vested in me by the state of Maine, I now pronounce you husband and wife. Carig, you may kiss your bride!"

Carig didn't hold back; he grabbed me, and kissed me. As we came together, we eagerly tasted one another's tear-stained lips.

"Beni, I've waited my entire life for this. Beginning right now Madame, I belong to you, and you to me."

The guests could tell that Carig and I were lost in one another and hardly even noticed that they were still there, so they sweetly congratulated us and then left.

446

The two of us stood in the garden together just holding one another, but I could tell that there was something weighing heavy on his mind.

"Carig, are you okay?"

"Yes! I'm grand, perfect to be exact! But I guess I was wonderin' if you're okay that we had just this small ceremony - are you disappointed? I never even asked if you wanted a big wedding, I'm sorry."

"Absolutely not. It was flawless; exactly what I've always dreamed of! If I would have had ten years to plan a wedding, it would have been this, exactly this. It was in the most beautiful place, with the most beautiful man I've ever laid eyes on. What more could I want?"

Carig looked at me with an almost embarrassed look.

"I've never been called a beautiful man, but I like hearing you say it."

He wrapped his arms around my waist, and gently pulling me close to him, we began dancing right where we stood in the garden.

"So my Beni, what now?"

Slipping my arms around his neck, I reached up and lightly bit his earlobe and whispered, "I think I would like to finish what we started out on the beach earlier."

"As you wish, Madame."

He swept me up in his arms effortlessly, and carried me down to the bothy on the beach, just as I had requested. As we neared the doorway, I told him that he could put me down.

"Na, got to get my bride over the threshold so as not to be bothered by any demons that might be lurking about...we don't want to bring any bad luck down on our union."

As we stood beneath the entrance, he kissed me.

"Well, if that kiss is any indication of what our marriage will be, it will be hot....and sexy!"

Carig smiled from ear to ear at me calling him sexy. When we went inside, he put me down, and then went to place more logs on the fire.

"Just makin' sure you're nice and warm. Wouldn't want ya puttin that parka back on any time soon!"

He walked up behind me, and began kissing my neck and unbuttoning my dress. When the last button was undone, I stepped away from him and pulled one shoulder down at a time until my dress dropped to the floor. Carig irrepressibly came towards me, and I began unbuttoning his shirt, slipping my hands across his chest and pulling it off letting it fall next to my dress. His body made me crazy! I buried my face in his chest and breathed in his mouth-watering fragrance, and then found myself kissing and savoring every measure as he abandoned himself to my endeavors.

"Do you know how delicious you are?"

Not waiting another moment, he lifted me up and held my body on his, grabbing my thighs, and prompting me to wrap my legs around him. He carried me over to the bed, and slowly began removing my camisole. For a moment he sat silently simply admiring my body as if it were a fine piece of art.

"Oh God, you are so beautiful, I could eat you up!"

"I'm yours, Carig. My body belongs to you now!"

He laid his perfect physique next to me, and pulled my body to his. I couldn't really say how long we laid there only gazing into one another's eyes, but it was euphoric with only the shadows from the fire dancing on the walls. As our skin came together making contact, a lustful heat ignited that led into hours of caressing and becoming entirely familiar with one another's body. With every inch he covered, he continued speaking words that were brimming with pleasure.

"I love your body - I love *you*, Beni!"

We continued to envelop one another with romance and passion, making our first time together far more than one single act of love. With amazing tenderness and uninhibited mastery, Carig made love to me, taking me to a place I'd never been before. He was an extraordinary lover in every way, even his Gaelic words of passion that he continuously whispered in my ear, became a trigger of arousal. He discovered this very quickly, and continued to bewitch me with his native tongue, using it to his advantage. I have no idea what the words meant, but I didn't care. Our fervent desire for one another seemed as though it would never end, and just before morning broke, we fell asleep still holding one another.

Chapter 19

The Passage

I was the first one up that morning. I held my left hand at a distance, admiring my beautiful ring, and then began admiring my even more beautiful husband. Carig was completely unconscious as our first night together did not include very much rest. I got up and looked out at the view from the metal and glass door. Obviously this particular view was something that Carig strategically chose, as it was an ideal viewpoint. I turned around and looked at him lying there. He was an even more handsome specimen in the morning. I only hoped that I looked even half as good as he did.

The sea was calling to me, and I wanted to go stand on the shore, but the only clothes I had down in the Flats cottage was the dress I had worn last night. I did however have my heavy jacket, which I put on, and then walked barefoot down to the beach. I always loved the damp ocean spray on my face and sand between my toes. It was the best way to wake up in the morning.

Carig woke up feeling happy and completely fulfilled. The agony of waking up apart from Beni was over. She was even better than anything that he ever imagined, and even though the entire evening was full with love, he could hardly wait to make love once again to his beautiful bride. Sensing her absence, he began patting the other side of the bed and sat up quickly as he realized that she wasn't there.

"Beni?"

Looking around the room, he didn't see her. He got up looking out the window and saw her standing down on the shore. He wondered to himself how many hundreds of times he had observed her standing in that exact place, wondering if she would ever be his. He smiled as he reminisced about their incredible night together, and was overcome with emotion as he admired his new wife from a distance. He wrapped himself in a blanket and began to walk out to where she was standing. He couldn't help but marvel at her beautiful long legs, bare beneath her parka. He came up behind her, opened his arms, and pulled her under his blanket.

"Good morning, Mrs. Hammel. Did you sleep well?"

"I did, just not quite long enough."

"Aye, and you may not ever get another good night's sleep again as long as I'm around."

"Good, I've slept long enough in my life."

I turned around took off my jacket and joined him in his blanket. To say the least, Carig was quite pleased with my display of freedom, and that I was finally ridding myself of the parka.

"Well then, Beni, you'd better move in a bit closer or the blanket may not cover your backside."

I moved my body into his and he adjusted the blanket, making sure that no part of me would be cold. Just being near one another set ablaze an uncontrollable fire that could only be quenched in one way. We stood there on the beach with our bare bodies together until we couldn't contain ourselves for another moment. I reached up to kiss him, but instead, grabbed the blanket, and began running as fast as I could up to the bothy, leaving Carig standing there naked. As I was running up the sand, I began shouting out a playful jeer.

"I hear Scots don't run very fast!"

Even before finishing my cheeky statement, he had already begun running, and caught me prior to reaching the front door. With no effort at all, he slung me over his shoulder like a sack of potatoes.

"Well, look what I caught...I believe it's someone who's all talk, and no action!"

He threw me on the bed, and then began tickling me, just like he used to when we were kids.

"I'm sorry, what was it you said about Scots?"

As some things never change, I was reminded of how unbearably ticklish I was!

"Stop, stop, stop, Carig!"

"What? You want me to stop?"

"Yes, please, no more!"

"Ok then, but first tell me that I'm fast, and that Scots are far superior to silly Americans!"

"Ok, Ok, Scots far exceed silly Americans!" Please Carig, stop!"

He laid his body on mine and began kissing me.

"So, you want me to stop?"

"No, never! Make love to me!"

For the rest of the morning, we held one another, making the most of our new and most sensual romance. Neither of us wanted our incredible time together to come to an end.

Before leaving the bothy that morning, Carig handed me a large rusty key.

"What is this?"

"This bothy, my wedding gift to you, I built it, and everything in it, for you."

"Carig, I don't know what to say. I love it! But you know, I only want it if you're in it with me. I feel terrible, I have nothing to give you."

"Beni, you have given me everything I have ever wanted, *You* are my gift!"

By the time we got up to the house it was almost noon, and we were both starving. Carig being the better cook, whipped up blueberry muffins and scrambled eggs, which for some reason, were the best I had ever tasted. Even our simple breakfast together was perfect, filled with laughing and flirting. I loved every moment with him. We talked about anything and everything, and were both excited about our future together. He was, and had always been, my best friend.

Without warning, the pleasantness of our breakfast was suddenly interrupted. Carig noticed a peculiar look on my face, and then I abruptly doubled over with an excruciating pain and feeling of uneasiness within me. My fork dropped to the floor, as did I, at the sudden sensation of air being knocked out of me. Carig touched my back, trying to comfort me in my pain.

"Beni, are you ok?"

"No, don't touch me!"

"What is it, Beni? What's wrong?"

"I don't know! I can't breathe - I can't breathe!"

"Are you choking?"

My strength was gone, and I couldn't utter another word, it was all I could do just to stare down at the floor, and simply focus on filling my lungs with just one breath. Moreover, an intense heat rose up inside of me like a furnace raging, causing me to break out in a furious sweat. I felt incredibly strange, and neither Carig nor myself, knew what to do.

"Beni, tell me how I can help!"

"I can't catch my breath - my lungs won't expand!"

Carig noticed how instantly pale I had become.

"Do you want me to call the doctor?"

"No, no! Wait, I need to get to the Tempus Vector!"

I hobbled up the stairs to my room to see if this sudden onset was at the hand of the Tempus Vector. The frame was calmly and quietly sitting on my nightstand, while I on the other hand, was a complete mess. I wondered..... I hoped that this uneasy feeling was the one that Adina spoke of. If not, I had no idea what was wrong with me. I felt both excited and scared at the same time. Even though I had spent endless hours reading Adina's notes about her journeys, trying to be as ready as possible when that day would finally come, I felt completely ill-prepared.

The moment I laid hands on the Tempus Vector, the heat within me suddenly turned ice-cold. When Carig entered the room, he saw me standing altogether still, as if I were frozen, my eyes glued on the frame.

"Are you ok? Is it....?"

I looked over at him. "It's begun."

I could barely get the words out of my mouth, before a swell of disappointment crashed over us. Neither Carig nor myself were ready to be parted.

Somehow I half expected that the frame would be empty. I'm not sure if I really believed that it was all true until I saw the old picture card sitting within the walls of the scratched borders. The evidence before my eyes was not of a person, but a place, a building to be exact that was nestled between two large trees on a cobblestone-lined street. Above the door hung a large white sign that read "Backerei." The only information revealed on the back of the card, was the date of October 4, 1940.

Before I did anything else, I went up to the chest and pulled out Adina's journal. I wanted to look again at her first journey and make sure that there wasn't anything more that I needed to do, nothing that I was missing or forgetting. Part of the wisdom that I knew I needed to utilize and apply from this point forward would be tucked within the pages of Adina's and Malachi's journals. Her first entry was October 29, 1941.

Here I am in Bar Rousse. I couldn't stay in Long Beach without Carson. I hated it there without him. I feel

lost and bitter, and so alone. Only days ago, I received a
crate from Malachi. Within the crate was a chest filled
with many things that belonged to him, leaving me
confused. He told me in the letter that was hidden in the
shoulder pad of his coat, that I wouldn't understand at
first, but eventually everything would make sense. Even
though there is so much that I don't understand, I do
know now that a calling has been assigned to my life;
things will never be the same again.... I will never be the
same again. This frame, this Tempus Vector holds a
power that has been in existence longer than I can even
fathom. This force that was fathered and encompassed
within the Lost Tribe of Solomon will use me to change
flawed pieces of history; how can it be? Among the things
he sent was this journal. This is my first entry. I'm not
really sure about anything right now except that Malachi
is gone, probably dead, and I could have saved him. I
could have warned him. The town of Friedlich is rubble
now. I am here and safe in a country not at war. But poor
Malachi and Estee, Lavi, and Ira.....I'm sorry, so sorry! I
don't know how this Tempus Vector works, or even if it's
real, but if I ever can, I will go back and warn them. I
would tell them to leave and get out of Friedlich before
the invasion by the Nazis on October 5, 1941."

Her next entry was written right before she left for her first journey.

I got my call, or maybe I should say "summoning", this morning. For a moment I thought I was dying. I felt like I couldn't breathe. But when I looked at the frame, just like Malachi said, there was a picture waiting for me. Until this very moment, I don't think I really believed it to be true. I'm afraid!

I felt terrible for her. She was so alone, and had to learn everything by herself, with no real help from anyone. At least I have Carig who was able to pass on information first hand that he learned from Adina.

As I continued on, I noticed that she had left a very detailed checklist of everything that she needed to remember to bring: *a journal, pencil box with pencils, two gold coins, a bag of toiletries, a bed gown, one change of clothes, flat black shoes, and measuring tape.* I guess it was true that Adina never went anywhere, even back in time, without her measuring tape. The last thing she put on her list was the Tempus Vector. After reviewing her list, it appeared that I was ready and prepared with all of the items I would need. As I continued reading, Adina even included in her journal the clothing she chose to wear. I was thankful for her insight, and considered it a great advantage. Her talent for wearing the right thing at the right time was truly genius.

My navy blue suit is classic. I feel that it will cross the barriers of time most effectively, helping me to dwell unnoticed. With it, I will use my navy blue handbag, the larger one so that I can keep the Tempus Vector with me at all times. I sewed a hidden compartment in the side of the bag where the frame would slip in under the satin lining. If someone does check my purse, it will surely go unseen. In my handbag, I will carry the gold coins, journal, pencil, and my measuring tape." I pondered for a moment. With such a great task at hand, why would she insist on bringing her measuring tape? I came to the conclusion that not only was it her tool of trade, but a way of appearing more common, more every day to the strangers that she would encounter. After all, who would find a woman carrying a measuring tape a threat? So, like her, I decided to also include her measuring tape. That simple piece of wisdom along with a handbag that contained a secret compartment, was quite clever.

I picked up the Tempus Vector and the suitcase, and made my way up to the third story wardrobe room.

Once there, I opened the second cabinet as I would be going back to the year 1940. Sorting through all of the suits and the dresses from that era, like my predecessor, I chose a handsome blue suit. Both the jacket and skirt were fitted and tapered. With that ensemble, Adina set aside a matching felt side hat with a short skirt of tulle in the front. I laughed as I saw that she had included stockings, that apparently were necessary. Stockings were very foreign to me, and I only hoped that I could get them on without any rips. I decided to wear the blue "Coffee" pumps from Adina's chest. All I needed now, was the handbag, and maybe even an overcoat. How would I know if I would be walking into cold or hot weather? I guess I would just have to go as prepared as possible. I didn't know how long I would be gone, or what my situation would be, so I took a quick bath before I got dressed.

When I walked out of the steamy bathroom, there waiting for me was Carig. He had a look on his face that said he didn't want me to go. I grabbed his hand, and sat him on the bed, then sat down beside him with a sensual smile on my face.

"I don't feel much like smilin, Beni!"

"I know, neither do I!"

"So why ya smilin?"

I climbed up in his lap and let my towel fall to the ground.

"Well, I was smiling because I was thinking about you." I began gently kissing his face and neck. "I'm not exactly sure if this will make you feel better or worse, but I'm thinkin' it might help a little bit!" Carig enthusiastically began slurping the water droplets from my skin.

"Aye! God Beni, could ye be any more sexy?"

For the next hour, both he and I thought of nothing except one another. I was convinced that in this vast confusing puzzle that encompassed us, there was one thing we both knew, he and I fit together perfectly, and felt that we could weather any storm. He continued holding me so tightly, not wanting to let go.

"Carig, I probably better get going!"

With a long heavy sigh, he unclasped his arms.

"Don't let this make you upset."

"I'm not. I knew it was comin', but we just got married, and I guess I thought we might have a few more days anyway."

"I won't be gone forever, just a little while, right?"

"Yea, just a little while. And I'll be here when ye get back."

I told him that I didn't want him waiting in this room all day and all night for me to come back.

He looked at me strangely.

"Wait, Beni, maybe there's something that ye don't understand."

"What do you mean?"

After being there for Adina, Carig found out that the past and the events within it are real and can be altered, but a day in the past is only a moment in existing time.

"You see, being here when Adina would come back was strange for both of us. To her she had lived in another time, another place, and had experienced days or weeks, but in reality only a few moments had really passed."

"Oh, okay. So in all truth, I will be the one away from *you* for long periods of time, not the other way around. To me, it will seem like weeks that we'll be apart, right? That doesn't really seem fair!"

As I gave Carig a pouty but flirty smile, he walked over and began kissing me.

"Are you trying to distract me, Mr. Hammel?"

With his eyes closed, savoring the moment, he simply responded, "Aye."

"Carig, you have to stop, or I'll never leave!"

"I don't want ye to go, Beni!"

"I won't be long, I promise. You be here waiting when I get back, ok? The sooner I get this done, the sooner I'll return to my extremely handsome and sexy Scot, you know?"

It was difficult to make light of this sudden turn of events that was forcing us to not only cut our honeymoon short, but also face the cruel reality that this was now our life, and nothing about it would ever be normal.

Nonetheless, Carig reluctantly released me to the clutches of the wardrobe room, the starting gate of my surreal journey. I would leave from here and step into the unknown.

A simple bun would do, then affixed at an angle the blue felt hat with a vintage hat pin, one that Adina and I purchased in New York. Who would have thought that I would make use of such an item! To my dismay, stockings came next... a dreadful requirement of my outfit. Carig seemed to enjoy watching me wrestle with this torture device made of nylon, and went on to say that if this were a contest, the stockings had won by a landslide. I do remember wearing ballet tights when I was a little girl, but I don't remember them being quite so difficult to deal with. The next step in my 1940's garb was a full slip. I was not fond of the necessary undergarments, as they all seemed so bulky. Along with the suit, I wore a white button up shirt, and donning the lapel was Adina's butterfly pin. Two things entered my mind as I looked in the mirror at the finished product. I seemed way overdressed, and I was certain that I had over packed the small suitcase, exactly what Adina said not to do. I went looking in the cupboards for the large blue handbag that she had mentioned. I found it, and it was just as Adina had described. Sewn in the side was a secret compartment where I would place the Tempus Vector for safe keeping.

Finally, I was dressed like a woman from 1940, I had my suitcase packed, and I was holding in my hand an object that would either become friend or foe; I wasn't yet sure.

Carig gave me one last embrace, and I couldn't help but put everything down and melt into his arms.

"Beni, please be careful lass! I'll be waitin' right here for ye."

"Okay, I will, I promise! I love you too! I'll be back in a few minutes, right?"

I placed the strap of my handbag over my shoulder, and stood directly in front of the French door. With the familiar view of the lighthouse and the Bar Rousse shore, I half believed that one step over this transparent threshold would take me anywhere except onto the balcony. Holding my suitcase in one hand, and the frame in the other, I lightly juggled to turn the knob. With a deep exhale and eyes wide open, I moved forward. I looked back at Carig one last time, "I love you!", and then walked out the door.

Carig would never quite get used to watching someone vanish before his very eyes. When he watched Adina, he was amazed at the whole process, but not frightened for her. He had great confidence in her abilities and wisdom to handle whatever obstacle she would encounter. But it was different with Beni, she did not yet have experience and wisdom as her guided company. His greatest fear was that she had now been positioned in a time, place, and situation where he couldn't help her, even if she needed it. He prayed that this first journey would be successful, and she would come back quickly.

All that I knew in regards to the process of walking from one time into another was that "each linking passage varies." Those four words were the extent of Adina's explanation. When I first stepped through the door, I could hear the waves breaking on the shore, but the brightness of the day quickly dimmed. Set before me was what looked like a bridge. In the far distance of this passageway, I could see a tiny slit of light that I cautiously began to follow. Moving forward across the overpass, I could still hear the crashing waves which swiftly transformed into the roar of traffic and distorted chatter. Darkness evolved upon every step I took, until it fully consumed me. The sudden eclipse and deafening noise was made trio by the onslaught of a cold gust of wind. All of it together was overwhelming, and I was afraid. The thought of going back occurred to me, but as I reached one foot behind, I found that the bridge was gone. "Stay focused Beni, you can do this!" I closed my eyes and took a deep breath, and was unexpectedly comforted by the echoed promise that I would never be alone. I had faith in this power, that it would see me through to my destination. When I opened my eyes, the fraction of light on the other side became brighter, and the loud noises were soon replaced with far-off tones of stringed instruments. I began moving very quickly towards the source of light, and then all at once found myself standing directly in front of a heavy wooden threshold. The door didn't have a knob, but only a thick metal ring used to pull it closed. With the weight of my body, I pushed open the entryway that led to October 4, 1940.

The town was quaint and timeworn, like a well fabricated set in an old movie. At the far corner, I discovered the origin of the music. Two men had made their stage at a bleak intersection, playing a lovely but haunting harmony. They played as if they were performing in the finest hall, with fervent emotion that would leave their audience overwrought with passion. Curiously, they seemed unaware that their once immaculate silk overcoats were now filthy and tattered. The cello player sat upon an old barstool that was missing a leg, braced only by his impressive balance. The violinist never once opened his eyes. He was fully entranced in the world that he used to know, and had no intention of returning to that corner ghetto. Every note of their concert was flawless. It was their rapturous melody that called me to the door. As I drew closer, I noticed the damage left behind by the infliction of tears that had now engraved permanent stains upon their heavily soiled faces. I felt an all-consuming darkness in this place. Who would throw a talent such as this away? With everything inside of me, I wanted to help, but I was here for a different purpose, and although my heart ached for them, I had to cling to the belief that right here and now, a higher calling was waiting for me.

Not only did their music bring me to the door of this city, but directly to the building on the photo card. As I looked up, I saw the sign that read, "Backerei." I could smell the aroma of butter pastries and freshly baked bread. Of course, the Backerei was a bakery. I stopped and took a few moments to fully inspect my surroundings - of the unique architecture along with obscure signs and labels of the city. It was evident that I was in a small community in Europe, most probably somewhere in Germany as I also noticed black and red swastika banners crowning the rafters of various store fronts. It occurred to me that I might possibly be in a location close to where Adina lived during this same time period. I felt a bit awkward standing in the center of this simple little village, overdressed, and probably bringing attention to myself. Again, doing the opposite of what Adina instructed me to do.

The weather was very chilly and I was cold, even while wearing my overcoat . Before I did anything, I began looking for a place to sell one of my gold coins. In Adina's journal, she reiterated time and again, to first acquire money. This made absolute sense, and like any other place and time, money was a must. As I was searching, I came upon a store with a sign that said "Juwelier", which translated, meant Jewelry Store. Where there was jewelry, there would be gold, and hopefully they would buy mine. Even though I took German as a second language in high school, it was many years ago, and I hoped that I would at least remember the basics. At least enough to communicate with the jeweler.

I walked into the store, and standing at the counter, was an old gentleman with gray hair and cloudy spectacles, who was repairing a gold pocket watch. Initially, he was annoyed at the disturbance, and brazenly set the timepiece down. In an elevated tone, he asked how he could help me, "We kann ich dir ehlfen?"

Pulling the coin from my purse and then holding it in front of his enhanced vision, I let him know, to the best of my ability, that I had gold to sell. "Gold verkaufen?"

His demeanor changed when he saw the unique symbol. He first began examining it under a magnifying glass, and then firmly bit down on the curious piece of treasure.

"Hmmm" he exclaimed. "Ja, funfzig?"

"Funfzig?" At first I'm certain that response left me looking like a deer in the headlights, but then I began counting to myself in German and figured out that he was offering me around fifty dollars for the gold piece. I told him yes, and then happily left there with what I believed was a decent amount of Reich marks, that would hopefully be enough. I was quite proud of myself for making my first money transaction in the past, in a country where I hardly spoke the same language.

The weather was frigid and I was freezing, so I decided to head to the bakery for some hot coffee and maybe a butter Danish. Because this was the building in the photo, I figured sticking around here was my best bet in determining my next move. When I walked in, standing behind the counter was a large man covered in speckles of flour that just happened to match his white hair and cotton apron.

He had a jolly manner about him and was quick to welcome me. "Hallo die Dame."

"Hallo", I said back. "Uhhh, Coffee?"

"Are you American?" he asked in broken English.

"Yes, I am. You speak English?"

"Just da little. Do you speak Deutsche?"

"Uhh, just a little!"

"How about some nice peppermint tea? It will warm you."

"Thank you, that would be wonderful."

"Okay, sit, sit," he said.

His shelves were full of pastries and breads of all sorts, but what stood out among the bakery items was the square pan of Kasekuchen or cheesecake. I was suddenly reminded of the age-old recipe that Adina had slipped into my diary. I recalled how peculiar it seemed for her to choose such a trivial part of history as the spotlight of my attention, but what if it was strategically planted, a clue maybe? What if…? No, it couldn't be! I knew it wasn't possible, but wouldn't it be a curious turn of events if the man standing before me happened to be Ira? I knew it couldn't be - it wasn't possible. For the time being, I put the completely insane notion out of my mind! I pointed to the kasekuchen, and held up one finger, "Eine, please."

"Okay, okay, sit!"

His modest sized bakery was lined with small cafe tables for two. I made myself comfortable at the one closest to the corner window. Along with the aromatic tea, and his warm and cheery disposition, my host proudly set a square of cheesecake in front of me. It was cut in the same manner in which Adina served hers, squares rather than pie shaped, and it was still warm, fresh out of the oven. He stood close by, and watched me take my first bite, which was perfect, but left me with a peculiar déjà vu-type experience. It was almost as if I was sitting on Adina's porch eating cheesecake and drinking iced tea. This was her recipe, flavored with vanilla and almond. The peculiar look on my face disrupted the gentle nature of the master baker. As I took another bite, he asked me if I was alright, and most importantly, if I was unhappy with his kasekuchen.

I stood up, in a panic, trying not to choke.

"Excuse me, what town is this?"

He looked at me like I was crazy. "This is Friedlich, Fräulein. You don't know where you are?"

Friedlich, I thought to myself. The date on the back of the photo in the Tempus Vector was October 4, 1940. This is the town and the year that Adina lived in - wait, *lives* in. She must be here now! I knew that she must be here.

I could scarcely believe it! I had just met Ira, the Ira on the folded piece of paper in my journal. This Ira is the one who taught Adina to make cheesecake, and passed on his recipe to her for safekeeping. I was slowly piecing together all of what seemed like trivial bits of information, but what was I doing here? What was I supposed to do next? I began thinking about the conversations that Adina and I would have about her life while living in Friedlich. Unfortunately, she never said very much. All of it was too painful to recall.

After alarming Ira with my half-crazed behavior, he returned to his workspace behind the counter, simply watching me out of the corner of his eye. To his dismay, I remained in his shop trying to make sense of everything, hoping that I would be given the wisdom to know what to do next. Would the wisdom just appear before me or fall on me like rain from the sky? I just didn't know. Suddenly, as I gazed out the window, I noticed a small shop with an even more familiar name. On the wooden sign that was swinging from the overhang of the quaint store front, was the name "Schuh Coffee." Its intricate colors and design were identical to that of the shoebox in Adina's chest.

Within moments, I saw Adina walk by the bakery, cross the street, and go into the town market! In complete shock of what I had just witnessed, I thanked Ira, and then I too headed to the market. This was very weird, and I found myself nervous to see her. It was the kind of thing you read about in a great novel, but certainly not something that happens in real life. I walked across the street and passed by Malachi's store, touching the glass with my fingers just to make sure it was real. Once I arrived at the market, I turned the knob, opened up the door, and cautiously walked inside.

The majority of the patrons turned around and looked at me. Not only was I overdressed, but I was a stranger in a time filled with rumors of war, and I could tell that my presence made them very uncomfortable. This was a town of people who lived simple lives and dressed modestly, most in work clothes. And here I was in a nice suit, standing out like a sore thumb. But I was here for one reason and one reason alone. I was meant to be inside of Ira's Bakery so that I would see Adina walk by, which more than likely had something to do with why the Tempus Vector sent me here. I didn't mean to stand there staring, but I couldn't help it. There was my Aunt Adina holding a box of what looked like clothes, and struggling to communicate with the store owners.

Adina was even more beautiful than her pictures, stunning to be exact! The next few moments seemed like an eternity as Adina turned around and her eyes met mine. At that moment, I knew exactly what I was supposed to say, and why I was there. The words I would utter next would change her life forever!

The End

Coming Soon, *SJ2* of the Sentimental Journey Series…

||*The Monarch*||

Made in the USA
San Bernardino, CA
07 September 2017